A PRINCESS OF ROUMANIA

ALSO BY PAUL PARK

A PRINCESS OF ROUMANIA

Paul Park

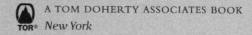

A TOM DOHERTY ASSOCIATES BOOK
New York

A PRINCESS OF ROUMANIA

Copyright © 2005 by Paul Park

This book is printed on acid-free paper.

Edited by David G. Hartwell

A Tor Book
Published by Tom Doherty Associates, LLC
175 Fifth Avenue
New York, NY 10010

www.tor.com

Tor® is a registered trademark of Tom Doherty Associates, LLC.

Library of Congress Cataloging-in-Publication Data

Park, Paul, 1954–
    A princess of Roumania / Paul Park.—1st ed.
      p. cm.
    "A Tom Doherty Associates book."
    ISBN 0-765-31096-1 (acid-free paper)
    EAN 978-0765-31096-5
    1. Teenage girls—Fiction. 2. Mothers and daughters—Fiction. 3. Massachu-
setts—Fiction. 4. Princesses—Fiction. 5. Adoptees—Fiction. I. Title.

    PS3566.A6745P75 2005
    83'.54—dc22

                                      2004065946

First Edition: August 2005

Printed in the United States of America

0   9   8   7   6   5   4   3   2   1

THIS BOOK IS FOR MY FRIEND JIM CHARBONNET,

WHO WAS GOING TO HELP ME WITH THE ENDING.

Comment

Oh life is a glorious cycle of song,
A medley of extemporanea;
And love is a thing that can never go wrong:
And I am Marie of Roumania.

—Dorothy Parker

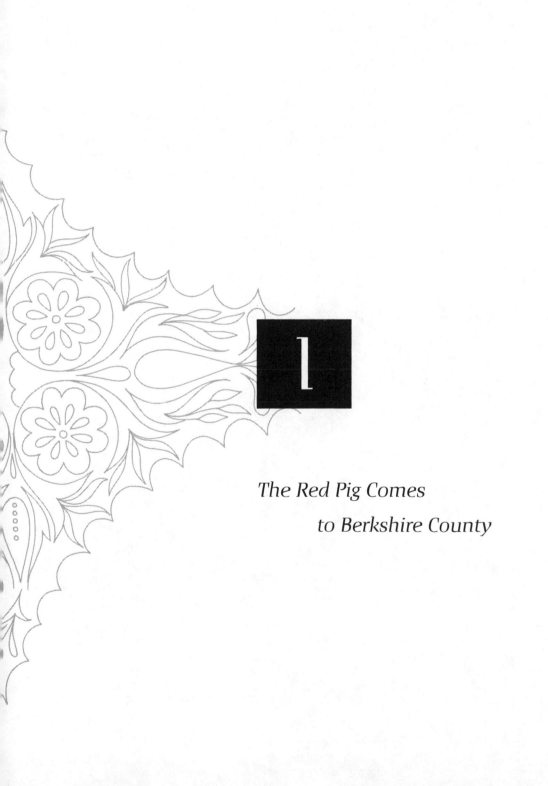

1

The Red Pig Comes
to Berkshire County

1 *Peter*

IN EARLY AUGUST, after her best friend, Andromeda, had gone to Europe, Miranda met a boy in the woods. She knew who he was. His name was Peter Gross. They had no friends in common, though their high school was a small one. Miranda was a good student, popular and well liked. Peter Gross was none of those things.

He had curly brown hair, crooked teeth, tanned skin. Because of a birth defect, he was missing his right hand, most of his right forearm. Miranda had been aware of him for years. But she spoke to him for the first time at the ice house, which was a ruined cottage next to a little stone dam in a few wooded acres between the college and the golf course.

It was a place she visited occasionally, a small stone building half hidden in the oleander bushes. It had a wooden roof that had fallen in. She used to go there to read books, to be alone, and at first she was irritated when she saw him in her secret place. Almost she crept back to her bike and rode away. Then she thought she'd wait for him to leave. Then she got interested in watching him; he had built a weir under the dam with a piece of plywood to make a larger pool. He had made a sluice gate for the water to escape, and he squatted on the dam to catch minnows and frogs. His hand was quick in the water.

She stood under the willow trees while he caught a frog and let it go. After a few minutes she could tell by a kind of stiffness in his shoulders that he was aware she was watching him. Then she was too embarrassed not to go and sit beside him and scratch her sunburned legs. She thought he might be grateful for some companionship. He probably didn't know many people. But he was intent on the water and he scarcely looked up.

"Hey," she said.

"Hey."

What did they talk about that first time? Later she couldn't remember. Miranda had read in the newspaper about his mother's death maybe a year before. Andromeda had mentioned something about it, too—Peter's mother had been a secretary in the English department at the college, where everyone's parents worked, and where Stanley taught astronomy.

Knowing about her death made Peter easier to talk to for some reason, although Miranda felt she had to tread lightly when she mentioned her own family. That summer she was having some problems at home. One afternoon in the middle of the month, she showed up at the ice house a little late. Everything she ever did was wrong, she said, and there was no part of her life that Rachel didn't want to supervise. She had no privacy. She'd got home and her shoes were lined up under the bed, even though she'd asked Rachel not to go into her room. Worse than that, the computer was on, though she was almost sure she hadn't touched it. Maybe she had. It didn't matter. She'd have to change her passwords.

Sitting on the dam, pulling at a loose piece of rubber on her sneaker, she said, "I feel as though my life isn't my life. My house isn't my house, and my parents aren't my parents. Which they're not, of course."

Peter was chewing on a long piece of grass, a habit of his. "What do you mean?"

She sat cross-legged and examined a scratch on her knee. "I guess when Rachel and I fight, sometimes I look at her and think, 'You're not my real mother. My real mother is somewhere in Romania.' "

"Why Romania?"

"Because that's where she is." And then she told him about having been adopted from the orphanage in Constanta. She kicked her foot over the edge of the dam. "It's on the Black Sea. Have you heard of it?"

Peter shrugged. The stream under the dam was almost dry. Not much wider than a snake, it slipped back and forth over a bed of dry mud.

"I know a poem about Romania."

His mind was full of scraps of poetry that his mother had taught him. Already he had given her some recitations. " 'Oh, life is a marvelous cycle of song,' " he now quoted, and then a few lines more.

This was very annoying, even though she found herself smiling. "Hey, shut up," she said, because he wasn't taking her seriously. "Sometimes I feel like crying the whole time," she said, which was an exaggeration.

Peter was looking up the slope on the other side of the stream, squinting, not paying attention, it seemed like. Now he turned toward her. He was interested in things like tears or anger, she thought.

"Why?" he asked.

"Sometimes it's just that word. Romania. It makes my stomach turn."

She was deeper into the conversation than she wanted. She had only planned to tell him about some of these things. But now she felt she had to continue, because of the stupid poem. "I was three years old. I have these pictures in my mind, but I can't tell what's real, what's made up. There's a woman I call my aunt. There's a journey on a train. There's a man and he's talking to me, trying to make me do something I don't want. There's a cottage with a tin roof, and he's talking to me from the terrace above the beach. There's a stone castle with a steeple—it's like a postcard in my mind. There's a little room overlooking the sea."

Rachel and Stanley had found her in Constanta. They'd told her how her family had disappeared during the uprising against Nicolae Ceausescu, the dictator who had destroyed her country. But then who was the woman in the picture? She had coarse skin, gray hair, dark eyes. Her hair was pinned up on the top of her head, and she was dressed with great elegance in furs. It was wintertime and she looked cold. But the smile on her frosted lips was full of love.

"God damn it," Miranda said.

Peter had wedged the stem of grass between his two front teeth, and he was smiling. "Go on," he said.

"God damn you." Miranda blushed. To her surprise, her face was hot, and some tears were moving down her cheeks. Was this a real emotion? She couldn't tell.

Peter looked away. "I'm not sure I believe you," he said. "I think you're trying to make a fool of me."

"What do you mean?"

"Everyone feels as if they're from some foreign place. Or another planet. That doesn't mean they are."

She scratched her nose. "Yeah," she said. "I guess you're right."

A few minutes before, she had pretended to be angrier than she was. But now she was furious and she didn't show it. Who was Peter Gross to condescend to her? Though he was older, he'd never acted like it before.

She looked down the stream, where it disappeared in a tangle of broken willows. She didn't look at him, though she could tell he was watching her. Then she stood up. "I've got to go," she said. "Rachel wants to take me shopping before school starts."

He had a piece of grass stuck through his teeth. "I'm sorry if I offended you," he said.

"Hey, no problem. You're right."

"Will you be here tomorrow?"

She shrugged. "I've got some things to do."

Though she stood for a while scuffing her feet, she was anxious to go. And when she bicycled away, up the dirt road behind the grounds department shed, she wondered why she should ever come back, which made her sad. She didn't need to prove anything to Peter Gross.

But maybe she did, because the next day she snuck into her parents' room and found the box of her Romanian things on the top shelf of the closet. In the afternoon she loaded them into her leather backpack and rode out to the ice house.

For a minute or so, she and Peter sat listening to a bunch of birds. Then: "Let's see," he said. She took her time. The house had a wide stone step, and the first thing she did was brush it clean with the edge of her palm. Then she opened her backpack and took out a fringed, gray velvet shawl, which she unfolded and laid over the stone step. Next she took out a manila envelope and a beaded black purse. The envelope contained a leather-bound book with gilt-edged pages, very thin, almost transparent.

"Onionskin," she told him.

There'd been a time in her life when she'd looked at this stuff almost every day. But it was years now since she'd touched it. Still, she found she remembered everything as she opened the book, the mysterious foreign words, the penciled inscription opposite the frontispiece—a hand-colored, photographic portrait of Carol I, king of Romania. His hawk-faced, bearded profile was extremely clear. You could see the grizzled hair along his neck.

"It's called *The Essential History,*" she said. "But I can't read Romanian. Stanley says that when they found me in the orphanage, I could barely speak. I was still in a crib. When I go to college, I'll learn it all again."

She placed the book carefully on the gray velvet. She allowed it to open to where the marker was, a ribbon maybe halfway through. Then she was drawing her things one by one out of the beaded purse. Most were wrapped in Kleenex, and she was uncovering them and laying them out according to her remembered ritual. First, a silver cigarette lighter, decorated and engraved with the initials FS under a small crown. Second, a silver locket on a silver chain. Opened, it revealed two sepia faces, a woman's and a child's.

Third, fourth, fifth, and sixth were all coins—big, solid, heavy, ancient, gold. And then a smaller silver one, which Stanley once had managed to identify in a book from the library. It was a Greek drachma, they'd decided, two thousand years old, and stamped with the head of Alexander the Great.

Romania had been conquered by the Romans in the second century. But even before that, Constanta had been a Greek town. As Miranda unwrapped the last of her things, she caught a remnant of a fantasy from long ago when she was small, an image of herself as a princess standing on the shore of the Black Sea, the warm water lapping the toes of her riding boots. From the terrace of the castle she had walked down to the beach. Someone was above her on the parapet—was it that man de Graz? What was he afraid of? Why was he always watching her?

As always, she had saved the best for last. Inside the nest of Kleenex was a bracelet of eleven gold beads, each in the shape of a tiger's head. And on the flat clasp was a circle of tiny letters, indecipherable even under the strongest magnifying glass, which Stanley had brought back for her from the lab.

She ran the beads through her fingers. Each one was different. She imagined they were even older than the silver coin. Once on a trip to

Washington, D.C., Rachel had taken her to a museum where they had seen an exhibition of Scythian ornaments from the Black Sea. There was a pair of gold earrings that had reminded them of her bracelet, though they were not as fine.

Miranda looked up. Through the open door of the ice house she could see the pit in the middle of the stone floor. Saplings grew from it. There were no bugs, no mosquitoes. There was no wind. The light fell down in spears through the still leaves. Miranda held the bracelet around her wrist. It glistened in the light.

Peter smiled. He pulled the grass out of his teeth. "Oh, life is a marvelous cycle of song," he said,

"Of wonderful extemporanea.
  And love is a thing that can never go wrong,
  And I am the Queen of Romania."

He'd recited this the day before to tease her with the last line. But she realized now he wasn't making fun. And she knew the definition of "extemporanea" because she'd looked it up the night before: "unprepared, unrehearsed," which didn't sound so wonderful to her. She was the kind of person who had nightmares about missed assignments and arriving at school in her underwear. The poem was by a woman named Dorothy Parker, he now claimed, when she accused him of having made it up.

She knew how much his poems meant to him. He had learned them from his mother, which made them like the things in Miranda's pack, gifts from a vanished past. So in that way they were similar, she thought. Now he sat on the stone lip of the dam, squinting into the shafts of light. With his left hand he scratched the stump of his right forearm. It often seemed to itch.

Though he was only a grade ahead, he was almost two years older than she. He'd never been friendly with her, even in elementary school. Rachel disliked him because he wasn't "college material," as she said, a phrase that implied a lot without actually meaning anything.

Now he got up. "Come on," he said.

"Where?"

"I want to show you something."

He waited while she wrapped up her things and put them away. Then he turned and jumped onto the stone dam over the stream. He knew all the little paths through the woods and across people's properties. Those two weeks he'd shown her some of them. Some were "deer paths," as he described them, and some, Miranda suspected, were maintained by him alone. Always they provided the fastest, most direct, most secret routes to anywhere. But when she got home from following him, she had to pick the burrs out of her clothes and hair.

They climbed uphill through the woods and then over the golf course. They crossed the road in front of the art museum, but then immediately took to the trees, circling around until they reached the parking lot. They climbed over the split-rail fence and down the hill into the deeper, scratchier woods. Most years there'd been a swamp back here. Now it was dry.

"Look at this," said Peter.

Under a bush, next to the rotted trunk of a tree, were the droppings of some animal. "Look here," said Peter, showing her where the bark of the tree had been rubbed away. "What do you think this is?"

That summer there had been sightings of strange creatures in Berkshire County. People said it was because of the dry weather, because there was no water in the hills. Sometimes in the paper Miranda had seen grainy photographs of lynxes and bears.

"Let's wait," said Peter, sitting down on the rotten log.

He fished his harmonica out of his back pocket and rubbed it on his jeans. This was another habit of his. It looked so grown-up and professional, the way he rubbed the battered metal till it shone. The first time she had watched him, she had hoped to be impressed. She would have been impressed by anything, even one song she recognized, no matter how lamely played. But always he just fooled around, and that was what he was doing now. He held the harmonica in his left hand, then cupped it in his right forearm where the stump ended in some strange, small knobs—vestigial fingers, she supposed. He breathed lightly into the aperture and made soft, papery noises.

Miranda would be late for supper. The sun was going down. She stood with her backpack over her shoulder, and she was going to tell Peter that she really had to go, when he lifted his mouth from the harmonica and said,

"This was my mother's favorite place on this hill. She used to come up here to gather cow flops for her garden. It's not much now, but you should see it in springtime. This whole place is carpeted in blue flowers."

She looked around. Now, as if his mother had touched it, she could see it was a pretty place, a little dell in the middle of the bushes where some big trees grew up straight. Though she wasn't even angry anymore, she could tell he was trying to make amends and give her something. "I'm sorry about yesterday," he said.

"What?"

"Pretending not to believe you. Romania—it sounded so odd."

"That's okay."

He made a few more silly sounds from his harmonica. Then, "I want to know," he said. "Can you describe it?"

"What?"

"The postcard. The castle on the beach."

She closed her eyes. "It's not really a castle," she said after a little while. "It's small. But the walls are made of stone, and the windows are narrow. The roofs are steep and a green color like old copper. There's a tower with a spire, and a wide terrace along the sea. The water comes to the edge of the parapet at high tide. The terrace is made of red tiles, and there are chairs and tables with newspapers and magazines. That old woman sits there in the afternoons, drinking tea and writing letters. I used to play there with Juliana when my aunt wasn't home. We used to throw bricks into the ocean."

She opened her eyes. "And the cottage?" he asked, but she shook her head. One picture was enough. Besides, he wasn't listening. He'd heard a noise, and now she heard it too, a rustling of leaves, then nothing. Peter held up the stump of his hand, gesturing for silence while he replaced his harmonica in his back pocket.

Then he turned back toward her. "Are we still going to be friends," he asked, "after school starts?"

She didn't know, didn't say anything. After a minute, he pointed with his forefinger to a spherical white stone about as big as a human skull. It was half submerged in moss.

"My mother showed me that, years ago. What do you think?"

Miranda knelt down to take a look. It was sort of a strange thing, and it did look very much like a skull carved out of stone. Even when she examined it closely, she wasn't sure whether she was looking at an artifact or just a piece of rock.

Either way it was a little creepy. She felt as if someone had touched her softly on the back. "Probably not," Miranda thought suddenly in answer to his question. Already she'd been asking herself the same thing.

That night she and Rachel had an argument. Rachel was a good cook, and she had made Miranda's favorite summer food, fried chicken and a fruit salad. It had been ready at six-thirty, but Miranda didn't get home until after eight.

When Rachel was angry, her voice got soft. She was a thin, light, small-boned woman. "First," she said, "I don't want you to go out without sun block on your skin. Second, I already showed you that article. I want you home by six o'clock every evening and six-thirty on weekends. Were you with that boy?"

Rachel had planned to eat outside at the picnic table in the backyard. But when it got dark, she and Stanley had moved the food indoors onto the kitchen table, without tasting any of it, apparently. That made Miranda angry, too, because it seemed like a reproach. "You don't have to like him," she said.

During periods of calm, Miranda and Rachel led separate lives. But when things were tense between them, Miranda sometimes found herself confiding in her adoptive mother, telling her secrets in an angry rush. Now she ardently regretted having mentioned Peter Gross. She and Rachel stood on opposite sides of the kitchen table. Stanley was in the living room drinking a beer. "I just want to know what his intentions are," Rachel said. "Do you know? You're a pretty girl, and he's older than you. I know he's been in trouble with the police. I don't want to forbid you from going where you want. I just want you to think about it—is that so terrible? I just want you to use some common sense. Those things of yours are valuable. I had them in my closet for a reason. You can't just carry them around."

"I can do what I like with them," Miranda said. "And I can choose my own friends. You might be too much of a snob to see it, but he's a nice guy."

Rachel stood watching with her arms crossed over her chest. Then she turned away and stared out the window over the sink into the dark backyard. Miranda could see the reflection of her mother's lips. Furious, she stamped upstairs into her room. And she was furious with herself. It seemed hollow and hypocritical to be defending Peter now, because she had almost decided to stop seeing him.

SHE WAS ON HER BED, lying on her stomach, leafing through the small, translucent pages of *The Essential History,* when Stanley knocked at the door and came in. The room was dark, but she had lit some candles. One burned on her headboard, one on the bedside table.

They lived in the middle of town, in an old house Rachel had filled with antique furniture and art. Miranda's room was on the third floor, set into a gable overlooking the backyard. The casement window was hooked back, and the candlelight trembled in the small current of air. Miranda's rocking chair, oak armoire, and dresser all loomed with shadows. Every time his in-laws visited from Colorado, they took Rachel out shopping for some new, big, dusty piece of furniture.

The light flickered on the varnished floor and wainscoting. Stanley sat down beside the high oak bedpost, and watched his daughter turn the pages of the book she couldn't read. He watched her move her lips, sounding out the strange Romanian words.

When she was little he had asked a friend to look at it, a bookseller and linguist who had been intrigued by the elegance of the binding, the beautiful small maps and portraits, the absence of any publisher's or author's name, any date or printer's information. His friend imagined the book to have been handmade by some Romanian monarchist in exile or in hiding. The descriptions of Ceausescu's government were full of bitterness. But otherwise the text was dry and full of facts. There was a good deal of rather basic natural history. There was a single section for every country in the world.

He watched her for a moment. If she knew he was there, she gave no indication even when he reached out and laid his hand on the small of her back.

As always when he looked at her—the straight, dark hair down her shoulders, kept out of her face by delicate, slightly protruding ears, his heart seemed stuffed with feelings that he couldn't identify. Happiness, he thought, although it didn't feel like happiness. Miranda lay on her stomach. One of her legs was bent at the knee, and one of her dirty, calloused, scratched, bare feet was poised near his shoulder. The other kicked at the summer quilt. Most of her toenail polish, an odd turquoise color, had scratched off.

She closed the book on her pillow. Stanley followed her eyes, staring now at the carved headboard, the candle on its little shelf. "Tell me about Romania," she said, which surprised him. It had been a long time since she'd shown any curiosity about that. Her voice was not unfriendly, he thought. But there was a softness in it that he couldn't make out.

"Your mother loves you very much," he said, but then he stopped, corrected by the slap of his daughter's foot against the quilt. He waited, and when the foot was quiet, he cleared his throat and told a version of the same story he had told her many times when she was little. Then he had tried to make it into a fairy story. But even then he'd ended up trying to describe truthfully what he'd felt when he'd seen her for the first time, standing in her metal crib, staring at him calmly out of her blue eyes in that ward of silent, disinfected children. She'd smiled and pointed at him with her tiny finger. He'd tried to describe the feelings and not the place, which had been horrifying. His little girl was gaunt, malnourished, and her head was shaved because of the lice.

"You were my princess," he'd said when she was young, and she'd put her arms around his neck and her cheek against his chest, curled up contentedly to listen. But as she got older she lost interest in Romania, except as an expression of discontent. Which was why, he supposed, she was bringing it up now.

Now he told the literal truth as he remembered. He had no gift or power to invent. "We flew to Bucharest and thought we'd come right home, but then we had to spend a few weeks. The laws were changing, and here were people in the new government who didn't like to see children adopted by foreigners, even from the orphanages, which at that time were very full. And Rachel thought it was important to see something of the country, though it was difficult. This was after the revolution against

Ceausescu and his wife. They had been killed on Christmas day. But nothing changed, really, afterward. The people who came in were all Ceausescu's men—the new president. There were demonstrations every day, people in the streets. Your mother and I had signed a contract to adopt a child in Bucharest, but that fell through at the last minute, we never found out why. But we were lucky, because then we flew to Constanta and found you."

"What was it like?"

"We went during the fall, and it rained almost every day. The hotels were terrible and there wasn't much to eat—just canned food, really. The countryside was beautiful, but in Bucharest, Ceausescu had knocked down most of the old neighborhoods. There were these terrible, gigantic, concrete buildings. But people said it was like Paris at one time."

None of this was what she wanted to hear, he thought. He waited for the sound of her whisper. He knew it would come. "What did they say about me?"

He shrugged. "Not much. They called you Miranda, which was odd because it's not really a Romanian name, as we found out. We asked about your family, but they couldn't tell us. Your family name was Popescu, but you know, that's like Smith or Jones. They said it wasn't necessarily your real name. We heard your parents had been involved in the Timisoara riots that December. But that's the other side of the country, and no one said how you'd ended up where we found you."

"Did you see a castle in Romania?" And Miranda described it to him, the long parapet along the beach.

"I think I saw a picture of something like that," he said.

"Where?"

Stanley shrugged. "I think it's famous. Queen Marie lived there before World War Two."

Still she hadn't looked at him. She lay on her stomach, staring at the candle flame. "Your mother loves you," he began, and stopped. Then, "I think things are better now in Romania. There's a different government. We could go back if you wanted. We could take a trip maybe next summer. Would you like that?"

She curled around on the bed and stared at him. She drew her hair out of her face and back behind her ear. He imagined she was trying to see if he was serious. Then she grabbed hold of his hand, so hard it almost hurt him.

"Expedite the inevitable," she said, which puzzled him, although he recognized the phrase with joy. It had been one of his father's maxims, and he had passed it on to her.

"Expedite the inevitable."

"No," she said. "I'm happy here."

He felt something sharp inside his heart. "Your mother was worried, that's all. She wasn't trying to punish you. But she knows that boy has been suspected of breaking into college buildings."

Miranda held her hand up, spread her fingers. "What about my things?" she asked.

Deflected for a moment, Stanley paused. Then: "Well, that's a little peculiar. They were all things that were left with you by whoever it was, inside the pockets of a child's coat. One of the nurses gave it to us after we signed the papers, wadded up inside some paper bags. No, it was the next day—she came running up when we were standing on the steps of the hotel. Either she was extremely honest, or else she'd never really looked at what was there. Most of it we didn't even discover until we were back home. I'm sure they never would have let them out of the country if they'd known. The bracelet and the coins were sewn into the lining. The crucifix was wrapped in newspaper in an inside pocket. Besides the book, that was the only thing she actually showed us. She said it had belonged to your mother."

In a moment Miranda had twisted off the bed and gone to the armoire next to the open window. It was full of clothes she never wore, presents from Rachel's parents, "girl clothes," as she disdainfully called them. But the coat was there, made of a dark green wool that Stanley associated with Austria. Its black velvet collar was threadbare and worn. Miranda sat cross-legged on her bed, smelling the old cloth and then searching the torn lining, as if there might be something else they'd never found, a letter or a key. The coat was for a child perhaps eight years old.

She ran her thumb along the inside of the lapel and found the pocket hidden underneath a flap of cloth. The cross was there, a tiny piece of ancient-looking steel, hanging from a steel chain.

Miranda slipped the chain over her neck. "You never asked her anything about my mother?'

"We were too surprised. To tell the truth, we didn't really recognize her from the orphanage. She spoke pretty good English, and I remember her green eyes. We didn't get her name."

Now Miranda sat holding the cloth up to her nose again, as if trying to inhale whatever small trace of Romania still was there. "A mystery," she whispered.

Stanley smiled. "A mystery. Later we wrote a letter to the orphanage but we didn't get an answer."

To tell the truth, he thought but didn't say, Rachel hadn't wanted to know too much. Maybe that had been a mistake. "Next summer we could go," he now repeated, though he imagined Rachel might forbid it.

Miranda sat for a while with the coat in her lap, then picked up the book again. "I don't remember any of the rest," she said. "But I remember this. A woman gave this book to me. She pressed it into my hands. She was dressed in red furs, fox furs or something. I could see one of the heads hanging down. She had dark red lipstick and jeweled earrings. She stood on the platform, and I was on the carriage steps. It was after dark, and I could see the lines of evergreens along the track. There was a lamppost, and the light was shining on a circle of snow. Snow fell on my face. The man on the platform blew a whistle, and my aunt pressed this book into my hands as the train started to move. She told me to keep it safe until I heard from her. She'd send a messenger."

"Darling, you were three years old," said Stanley. In fact, they hadn't known how old she was. It had been the doctors and the dentists here who'd told them that.

"You were three years old," he repeated. "Darling, don't you see how the mind plays tricks?"

Once when she was ten, before she lost interest, she'd marched up to Weston Hall and asked Marc Pedraza to translate not the book itself, but a penciled inscription on the title page. She'd come back very excited. The old man had printed it out for her on the back of a file card, which was still stuck in the book.

He reached for the card and she allowed him to turn over the pages till it showed. And he read over her shoulder the old professor's patient, trembling letters, so different from the minuscule original:

Dearest M. A hurried note to tell you once again to carry this with you and keep it safe. You know when the time will come to give it up. I'm sorry for so much. I promised your mother to provide you with a mother's love, but it's a pale version. A house on the seashore. A room in a stone tower for the white tyger! Maybe some day you will understand my difficulties, and maybe when you learn to read these words, it will be a sign you have prepared yourself. Now my enemies can hurt me, and not just the pig but many others. I must break and run or they will find you. It bruises my heart to leave you with this book and nothing else, just a third class ticket to Constanta as if you were a servant. De Graz and Prochenko will be with you, and you will trust them because they were your father's men. Rodica the Gypsy will meet you at the station. If I've been too worried and oppressed to show the love I have for you, still God knows that everything I've done has been for you and Great Roumania. God knows also I will miss you every day. And if God never grants me the sight of your face again, know your happiness and safety are the last concerns of your devoted aunt.

After a moment he went on. "It's hard to think that message is not for you, because of that stupid 'M.' It's interesting, actually, how the mind grabs at things and makes them into memories. The train, the aunt, the fancy clothes—it's all there, and then you've made a picture of the rest. Believe me, when you go back, you'll find Romania is not like this."

Her face was tear-stained when she looked up. "But if it's not for me, what does it mean?"

He shrugged, hating for a moment the sound of his own reasonable voice. "I guess it's just a mystery. Your mother and I had an argument about whether to show you any of this, or just to sell it and pay for college. In a way I wish we had. If nothing had remained it would be easier. Just this meaningless treasure, it's a little cruel."

THIS WAS A RATIONAL EXPLANATION. But it was not true. In all time and space there were only two copies of *The Essential History*. One was in Miranda's hands that night, and the other was in the attic of a house on Saltpetre Street in Bucharest. These two copies were not identical. In Miranda's book the frontispiece portrait was of King Carol I, reproduced from an official photograph of that monarch taken in 1881, the year of his coronation.

But in Saltpetre Street that name and date meant nothing. On the title page there was no scribbled note. The engraved portrait showed the malleable and sour features of Valeria IX, empress of Roumania, which in those days stretched from the Black Sea to the Adriatic, from Hungary to Macedonia. Under the engraving was a line of text, missing from Miranda's book: *The author hopes this squalid and pedantic fantasy will slip beneath your notice.* But there was no author's name.

Saltpetre Street was in the southwest quadrant near the Elysian Fields and the Field of Mars. In those days Bucharest was called the sapphire city, because of the distinctive blue-tiled onion domes of its thousand temples to the old gods. It bore no resemblance to the place Stanley remembered, Nicolae Ceausescu's gray and mediocre capital, which was also described in many sections of *The Essential History*. These sections were of particular interest to the baroness when, standing in a Gypsy's pawnshop, rummaging through a painted leather footlocker, she'd first discovered the strange book.

Later she'd had Jean-Baptiste go fetch the entire trunk and drag it home. Inside there were other interesting papers, but this book was the most interesting, she decided as she sat perusing it in an armchair in her husband's attic laboratory. There were no windows, but the lamplight caught at her husband's signet ring, engraved with the symbol of his family, the red pig of Cluj. It looked out of place on her bitten and stained forefinger, which she ran rapidly over the onionskin. Fascinated, she read about the modern history of Romania: the alliance with Nazi Germany, Antonescu's dictatorship. Fascinated, she followed the invasion of the Soviet Army, the Communist victory, and finally Ceausescu's despotic reign.

Such a tangle of inventions, she thought, and for what? She glanced at other sections too, especially the descriptions of North America. Then she was leafing back and forth until she found on the rear flyleaf of the book a penciled notation in impossibly small handwriting, which she recognized.

In Miranda's copy the page was blank. What would she have felt had she been able to read these words, in a language she didn't know, under the baroness's impatient forefinger?

You will deliver her to the Constanta orphanage. Follow the directions I have already given you. Americans will find her, will take her from that place. They will bring her to a town in Massachusetts, which is far from here. They will protect her from violence and give her everything they can. It will not be enough. The book she has cannot be taken from her. She must give it up. By herself she will discover sadness and it will not break her heart, I swear.

2 Andromeda

BUT THAT TOWN IN MASSACHUSETTS was already changing, as if from the pressure of the baroness's finger and the smell of her cigarette-perfumed breath as she bent over the page. Miranda was busy with other things, other people, and she didn't go to the ice house for a few days. Only once before school started, she biked out to see if Peter was there. But he wasn't, so she didn't wait, even though she'd arrived earlier than the usual time.

Peter's father was a nurse's aide in one of the local hospitals. His mother had been the one with the real job. Peter had stories about her, but he was vague about his father because they didn't always get along. Miranda had never seen their house, although she knew where it was—at the end of White Oak Road, three miles from town. Sometimes Miranda saw Peter's father driving down Water Street in a pickup truck. He was a fat man with a red face. His gray hair was tied back in a ponytail. Once Peter had mentioned that he used to smoke a lot of pot.

It was news to Miranda that Peter had ever been arrested. And she wanted to ask him about it. But now that she'd shown him her Romanian things, she was embarrassed. She felt she'd shared too much, particularly if what Stanley said was true and she'd invented all those memories. Besides,

Rachel was right. If she spent any more time alone with Peter, he probably would start trying to kiss her or something, although he hadn't shown any signs of that so far. But it would be awkward. Part of her liked to spend time in the woods, following the secret paths, but there was another part.

She found it hard to imagine him with the other people she knew. During the summer it had been easy to keep him separate from them. He wasn't likely to show up at the pool or the tennis courts. He didn't ride a bike.

With Andromeda in Europe, it had been good to indulge the part of her that felt misplaced and solitary. Even before she'd met Peter, she had spent time at the ice house reading the fantasy and science fiction books that otherwise made her feel a bit ashamed. Peter himself, at first, had seemed like a character from one of those imaginary worlds.

But when school started, it was different. Those first few days when she saw him at lunch or in the halls, usually sitting or walking by himself, it seemed to her that he must feel as awkward as she did. But he didn't approach her or try to speak to her, so why should she make the first move? He looked at her without smiling, which made her unhappy and a little angry. So then she took the further step of passing him in the hall without saying "hi." She knew she was handling things badly, but this was the kind of thing that happened all the time, didn't it? People spent some time together and then they stopped. If they didn't fit into each other's lives, then it was just too bad.

And she stopped thinking about it when Andromeda came back, fashionably late for the beginning of school. Her father had taken her to Greece and Turkey, where they obviously had a lot of sunshine. She looked amazing, her nose freckled and peeled, her blond hair almost white, pulled back so you could see the four new silver rings on the ridge of her left ear. When she knocked at the screen door, when she burst into the kitchen, as they hugged, Miranda was aware of physical sensations, the smell of Andromeda's sweat, the strength of her arms and shoulders, all that.

Then and later she realized how much she had missed being Andromeda's friend, the attention paid to both of them at school or as they walked together down the street. She'd missed the way Andromeda so effortlessly divided what was cool from what was stupid. Always you had to find a way to share her self-assurance, or else you'd find yourself left behind.

There was something about her that made Miranda eager to fit in, to accept what she was, an ordinary American girl. When she was with Andromeda she tended not to give a damn about any of the things she'd talked about with Peter. All that—her foreignness, her adoption—she now resented having talked about. She told herself that Peter had dragged it out of her so she could share his sense of isolation. One night, though, at volleyball practice, when they were waiting for the court to clear, she told Andromeda about Stanley's offer to take her to Constanta the next summer. This was part of the longer story about her fight with her mother about privacy. At first she thought she could tell the entire thing without mentioning Peter's name, but it turned out she couldn't. To tell the truth, it felt like a relief to talk about him, even though Andromeda wasn't exactly impressed. "You're kidding me," she said. "Wasn't he suspended twice last year?"

"I don't know."

Then later: "I met some Romanians in Bodrum," Andromeda said. "I tried to talk to them a couple of times—you know, because of you. But I've got to say they were completely sleazy."

They sat on the bleachers making fun of an old woman in a moth-eaten coat, taking Polaroid photographs of people playing basketball, of the roof of the gym, even of them.

Andromeda waved and posed. The woman smiled. Andromeda wasn't such a great student, but people loved her. Later, when the game had started, Miranda was happy to see her on the volleyball court, yelling and cursing, spiking the ball down people's throats.

Afterward the girls took showers and walked home. Miranda was carrying the backpack with her Romanian things inside. Andromeda said, "You took that to the gym?"

"I don't like to leave it home. I don't want Rachel to go through it."

"So it's safe in a locker?"

Miranda shrugged.

"You are so bizarre," Andromeda said. "What do you care?"

The high school teams were holding tryouts in the town gym. Rachel had told Miranda to be home by nine o'clock, but all rules tended to be forgotten or relaxed as long as she was with Andromeda. Adults were crazy about her, although it wasn't as if she never got in trouble. "I know she'll look out for you," Rachel had once said, and Miranda wasn't about to argue.

So they turned left across the campus and headed for Water Street to get some ice-cream cones. "I'm not surprised about Peter Gross," Andromeda said. "He's had a crush on you for years."

This wasn't what Miranda wanted to hear, so she said nothing. "Don't you remember when we were kids?" Andromeda went on. "It was like in third grade, when that kid Ricky Sheldon was harassing you. We didn't even go out on the playground for a few weeks until Peter Gross got in a fight with him. You probably didn't even notice."

It was a humid night, and the streetlights were surrounded by swarms of gnats. Andromeda was carrying the volleyball. She was sweating, and her T-shirt was sticking to her freckled skin.

"What's with these lights?" she said. "Are they new?"

"They put them up this summer. It's a security system."

The college had installed a number of call boxes, too. One of them was up ahead at the bottom of Holden Court, a black cylinder with a red globe at the top. It stood in an open place between the science center and the chemistry lab under one of the new lamps.

On an upper floor of the center, one light burned. Otherwise the buildings were dark. As Miranda and Andromeda passed the call box, their footsteps clattered on the new surface, which was smoother and harder than the sidewalk. They paused under the lamp, because there was something on the new tiles within the circle of the light, a picture of an animal six feet across, drawn in many colors of chalk.

It had the eyes of a person and the snout of a pig, and its face and body were covered with red hair. But its body was more catlike than anything else, its flanks both striped and spotted.

The animal sat on its haunches against a background of red and purple clouds. Its tail was curled around its hooves. "Cool," said Andromeda as she stepped over it. "That's better than a stupid cow"—the college mascot.

They were looking toward the lights of Water Street across the empty quad. Sounds came from there, a shouted conversation too far away to understand. Miranda heard some laughter and the sound of a breaking bottle, and then some people were walking toward them out of the distant lights.

For a moment they disappeared among the black, massed college buildings, though the noises still remained—more shouting, clearer now. Then they moved into one of the cones of light that surrounded the new security posts. Too young for college students, Miranda thought. "Come," she said, and climbed the wide stone steps to the porch of the chemistry building, an alcove of dark brick. Andromeda followed her more slowly, the volleyball still in her hand.

There were five boys. Miranda studied their faces as they shuffled into another cone of light. She had never seen any of them before, which was odd in that small town. One of them was tall and angular—much taller than the others, with long, thin arms and legs, and he was dressed in a gray suit. The other four, as they came closer, she imagined to be wearing some kind of uniform: sleeveless T-shirts, baggy shorts. They wore green baseball caps.

They moved into the dark. And as they approached another lamp, Miranda thought she heard among their soft, slow voices a different laughter. When they came into the light again, she was surprised to see there were now six of them. A girl had joined them out of the dark, wearing the same short haircut, the same earrings, her bicep encircled by the same tattoos.

Now they were coming down the sidewalk toward the call box and the red light outside the chemistry lab. Miranda imagined she and Andromeda were safe in the alcove as long as they didn't move. She glanced at her friend, worried suddenly that Andromeda might do something stupid, call out some kind of greeting, step out into the light. Whatever sense of menace Miranda felt, she didn't seem to share. She stood picking her nose with her big fingers, rolling the volleyball back and forth against her stomach. When the kids came out of the darkness onto the chalk-covered tiles surrounding the call box, Andromeda seemed ready to join them. But Miranda reached to put her hand around her friend's sweating, freckled forearm. She squeezed it, and Andromeda paused, and she and Miranda watched the strange kids moving around the box. One of them pressed the alarm button on the box, but nothing happened. One bent low to talk into the grille, but no sound came out. The boy in the suit found a long pole in the grass beside the wall of the chemistry lab, and he used it to poke at the red globe of the lamp above it. There was a spray of shattered glass, a pop that was like a small explosion, and the light went out.

After a minute, when the kids had left and everything was quiet, Andromeda stepped down onto the empty tiles and walked over to the call box. "Come on," she said, "don't be a scaredy-cat." But it took a while for Miranda to join her, because in fact she was afraid of what she'd seen in the instant before the light went out—six faces looking up. One face in particular she had singled out, the girl's. In the flash of the breaking light there had been a transformation, or else Miranda had imagined a new face, changed in subtle ways, staring up into the reddish light. The eyes were a little wider, the cheeks a little flatter, the nose a little bigger and more piglike. But then in the darkness Miranda had heard the same ordinary laughter as the kids moved around the corner of the building, up Holden Court, out of the quad.

"What language was that?" Miranda asked. In the mixture of voices she had not been able to make a single phrase come clear.

"What do you mean?"

"I mean what was that girl saying?"

"What girl?"

Miranda didn't push it. Andromeda was always hard to challenge. And then naturally a police car stopped and waited for them at the far side of the quad, where the lights went down the hill toward Water Street. An officer got out, an older man. He asked them some questions, then walked them lazily back to the alcove, where he shined his flashlight at the chalk drawing and broken glass.

As they stood in silence, the grille below the call box gave out some scratchy static. "What a mess," said the policeman. He peered up toward the bottom of Holden Court. Everything was quiet now, and he couldn't see where the six of them, five boys and a girl, had crossed under the trees and then turned left on South Street toward the art museum.

AVOIDING THE STREETLIGHTS, they walked in the shadows underneath the trees. They crossed the field behind Leake's Pond until they reached the back side of the museum. They skirted the parking lot and walked along the white marble wall. While the others went on toward the dark line of the woods, one paused. From the pocket of his gray suit jacket he produced a can of brown spray paint. He shook it, uncovered the nozzle, and then painted PORC ROSU PIG RED PORC ROSU in letters high as he could reach. For a moment he stood still under the light, a tall boy with a pale scar over each of his temples. He turned away, then hurried to catch up.

They walked in single file. They didn't speak. Security lights were mounted on the wall above their heads, and they walked underneath them. But by the time they reached the path that led away from the parking lot up through the woods, the darkness was complete. Climbing in the middle of the line, Markasev could see nothing of the others. All of them had their instructions. Sometimes he could hear the shuffling of leaves, the crack of a stick, but even so it was as if he climbed alone. Soon even those small noises disappeared, and he imagined the others had spread out along the steep path or else moved off through the trees, on errands he knew nothing of—except for one. The girl came running back with an animal she'd caught in one of her traps. She waved its fat, hairy body like a flag. "Look," she said, the only English word she knew.

Then she was gone, and he climbed through the big oaks at the meadow's edge until the path moved up a gully and then met the old logging road. Three paths came together here, and in an open place among the trees he saw the stone bench and the woman already waiting. He saw the glow of her cigarette from far away, and in its light, intermittently, the lower part of her face. She was curled against the stone arm of the bench, her back against the vertical stone slab. She was huddled in her ragged old coat, though it was a hot night.

Moonlight drifted down through the clearing in the canopy of leaves. When he got close, Markasev could read the letters above the woman's head. In Memory of Gregor Splaa (1882–1951).

The old woman inhaled once more, and then ground out her cigarette on the bench's arm. But in the red glow, before it was extinguished, Markasev could see her clearly. Her yellow hair was braided and tied behind her head in an old-fashioned bun. Her face was bloodless, the lines sharp as a bird's.

"Where have you been?" she said.

"I'm very tired," she complained as he sat down. "I still feel the flight from last week. My plane had a layover in Stuttgart, and we didn't get into New York till 2 A.M. Then I must wait for six hours at the Port Authority bus station. You were there?"

He shook his head.

"Of course not. You came the next day. It is disgusting. Nothing but drunks and perverts. I don't like this country." She turned to face him. "Do you understand me?"

He shrugged.

"We could change to Romanian if you prefer."

"Nu este necesar."

There was air here, away from the closeness of the woods. A breeze cooled his face. They sat for a while in the dark, then she spoke. "We are moving from the motel. Today I took a house for all of us at Woodlawn Drive. In the morning you will go to school. But tonight I want you to carry a letter to the beautiful lady. When you wake up you won't remember. So let me give it to you."

She handed him a sheet of paper and two photographs. The first showed some people playing volleyball. The second showed two girls sitting together on the bleachers. The one on the left, the dark-haired one, was circled in red ink.

He glanced at the photographs for a moment, but when he started to slide them into the inside pocket of his suit, the old woman touched his hand. "No," she said. "Fold them into quarters."

He shrugged.

"Hold them in your mouth," she said. "Under your tongue." She was crumpling the piece of paper in her hand.

But when he shook his head, she grabbed him underneath the jaw, her hand cold and strong. And maybe he could have shaken her off, but there was something in her touch that made him weak, and he felt his mouth pried open, the crumpled letter and the hard, slick squares of pasteboard forced inside. He was stricken with a kind of helplessness that seemed familiar. The old woman held his mouth, and with her other hand she touched his lips, his face, his eyes, his forehead, his neck, and he imagined he was drowning, suffocating, and he fell back against the stone arm of the bench. A flush of warmth overcame him, tingled on his skin. Even before he fell asleep he thought that he was dreaming, and his dreams were taking him straight up into the air through the brown leaves of the oak trees, up into the dark sky.

IN BUCHAREST, IN A DIFFERENT time, the Baroness Ceausescu unlocked the spare bedroom of her tall house in Saltpetre Street. She had come upstairs from a dinner party, which she had given for some old friends from the Ambassadors Theatre. As often, she was dressed in men's clothing, the uniform of a colonel of the Wallachian hussars. Ribbons hung from her chest. Pale and boylike, she glanced at herself in the gilt mirror by the door. The room, lit only by a candle on the bedside table, was almost dark after she closed the door behind her. Her face in the mirror was indistinct, hard to recognize, almost. She smiled at it, pouted, took a few steps across the carpet, and then went down on one knee beside the bed.

She touched her gloved fingertips together, then pulled down the coverlet and the silk sheet, revealing the sleeping boy. His hair was matted, his face dirty, and his body, also, streaked with dirt. She pulled the coverlet down to his hollow waist, then checked to see if the soft ropes around his wrists, around the brass spindles of the bed frame were secure.

She was keeping him here until his task was finished, and she could wake him entirely and reward him as he deserved. Her fingers hovered over the strange, pale scars above his temples. What had caused them? He had stumbled into the courtyard of her house in Cluj. Nor could he say where he was from or who his parents were. She would have sent him to the orphanage, only he had touched her heart. And he had a terrible gift for hypnotic suggestion, which she found useful when she began to read the papers in the painted footlocker. Now he was here.

It is a myth that evil people feel pleasure at the pain of others. Often the sympathy they feel is hard to bear. The baroness moved her gloved fingers around the boy's body, almost touching him. Then she picked up the candle on its iron spike and drew it back and forth in front of his face. His eyelids were closed, but she could imagine his pupils moving underneath them, following the flame. With her left hand she pulled his head up by his hair, then bent down to whisper in his ear.

She didn't even need him to speak. As he came awake, she could feel there was something choking him, hurting the inside of his mouth, some hard-edged thing. He spat it out, some slippery thing that seemed as if it had grown out of his mouth under his tongue. She had put the candle down onto the table; she released the boy's hair, too. Now she was wiping the old woman's letter on the bedclothes, smoothing it out, unfolding the Polaroid photographs. She touched them gingerly and spread them out on the boy's naked chest; he was shivering now. And yes, there she was in the photograph, a girl no older than he, dressed in short pants and a short-sleeved shirt, laughing at her yellow-haired friend who was posing for the camera with a ball in her hands. Yes, it was she, obviously: the broad fore-head, the straight nose of her mother's family, the dark hair and protruding ears of her father's. Even in this ridiculous and inappropriate disguise, the proud lines of her face were visible, yes. And was it a blemish on the print? No—she was wearing her mother's crucifix around her neck.

Triumphant, the baroness ran her finger over the image of the girl. Though she was younger than expected, surely there was an explanation for that. And her aunt had not even bothered to change her name, which was how the old woman in Massachusetts had found her. She was sitting with her legs spread on a long, high, wooden bench. Her black, short pants were tight around her thighs. With one hand she touched the back of her long neck where the hair was gathered and pulled tight—an unbecoming style in the baroness's opinion. How insignificant she looked, how thin and frail, her wrists and shoulders, her long fingers. Awkward, scarcely grown, with-out much of a chest under her yellow shirt—all that would come later, if she lived so long. Perhaps she might be beautiful some day. The baroness had seen girls as maladroit and gangling as she come rapidly to flower.

Inside her heart the baroness felt the first small trembling of the pain she was about to cause. Who could be sure? A war was coming, and this girl would be part of it. Clutching the photograph, she blew out the candle and stood for a moment in the remaining glow, the faraway street light diffused through gauze curtains. The window, triple-glazed, was opposite the bed. She looked down over the peaceful street. The boy was opening his eyes now, but she would leave him. She would send Jean-Baptiste to bring him water and wine.

Outside in the hallway she paused to read the old woman's letter, a cramped scrawl on the back of an advertisement, in English, for the Taconic Motel, whatever that was.

Beautiful Lady, I have followed the instructions you gave me in my crystal in Bucharest, getting a room for this boy and the others as you said. I have found clothes for him and a place to live. I have given him a name from America, which is Kevin, and I have used Markasev, which is my own surname because my father was from Odessa as I told you. No one here speaks Romanian. No one knows about Romania. In just one week I teach this child English which he learns with horrible rapidity, and I will send him to school.

I tremble with the thought of what I've done. You have given them to me but I am still afraid. Are they human creatures with human hearts? I have given them American names to comfort me, Henry, Dylan, Chuck, Brenda, etc. Now I bully them, tell them what to do as you have told me, but not much longer. They steal and break into shops. Soon I tell you the police will come. Please tell me what we do here, what I am to do. I want to help you but I am afraid.

THE BARONESS CRUMPLED UP THE letter again and put her hand to her narrow chest. And at that moment, as it happened, Miranda was making much the same gesture. She stood with her leather backpack clutched against her heart, in the middle of her mother's bright kitchen. She could feel against her body the outline of the book. She had brooded for a few hours in her room alone, then before dinner she confronted Rachel. "You didn't believe me."

Rachel wouldn't meet her eyes. "It's not that. It's just the way it sounded. A bunch of kids, none of whom you recognized. You say there were six of them, Andromeda says five. You say they were dressed one way, she says another. You say they were speaking a language that sounded like Romanian. Was that a joke? I mean, what were we supposed to think? I'm just happy Andromeda was with you."

That afternoon, when Miranda found out that her parents had agreed to split the cost of the broken lamp with Andromeda's mother, she'd felt betrayed. But now she had to admit the whole thing sounded peculiar. And it was true—the Romanian part had been a joke. But she wanted to be angry, and so she cursed under her breath at the hypocrisy of mothers, who yell at you when you do badly on a math test, but can't even raise their voices if they suspect you of vandalism and bald-faced lies. They won't even look you in the face.

If she'd cared to, Miranda could have pointed out the obvious. Some bad things had begun to happen in Berkshire County. There was an outbreak of viral meningitis in Great Barrington. Then someone set a car on fire in the Price Chopper parking lot. Stanley had wanted to go look. It was just a car, but people were really upset—more than they had been about the sick kids, Miranda thought. Great Barrington was miles away. There was a fire in an old warehouse in Greenfield, but this was close to home. This was property. And when someone broke out all the windows of the shops on Water Street, there was another huge fuss, and letters to the paper about the breakdown of society.

Also if she'd cared to, Miranda could have pointed out to Rachel that a lot of new people had moved to town, and it wasn't so incredible for her to have failed to recognize the kids in the quad. In fact she did recognize some of them as early as the next day. There were unfamiliar faces in her class— all these arguments were on the tip of her tongue. But she didn't want to rat anybody out for a little broken glass, and besides, it was too hard to explain. "You never believe me, never trust me," she said, all the more bitterly because she wasn't feeling particularly trustworthy about this matter. And it was painful to watch her mother flinch. She went for a ride on her bike and came home late for dinner.

One of the new faces in her class belonged to the tall boy she had seen crossing the campus that night. She'd noticed him the following morning. Like a lot of the new kids he had missed the first weeks of school—his name was Kevin. He was from Russia or someplace, and he didn't speak much English, and either he liked her or hated her. He sat two seats in front of her in homeroom, and in the next few weeks she'd look and see him staring back at her, his face expressionless. In the halls she felt as if he was always in her path, so that she had to walk around him. He said nothing in the classes they shared, but leaned back in his seat with his hands behind his head.

Considering the fuss Rachel had made about Peter, this behavior was another reason not to tell her about Kevin Markasev. Andromeda identified his clothes as being both stylish and expensive, from Abercrombie & Fitch, mostly. She was amused by the whole thing. "I swear he's stalking you," she said. "Pretty soon he'll be camping out outside your house."

Things had been awkward with Andromeda for a day or so. Miranda had been irritated with her for no good reason. Just because of what Rachel had said—"Thank God Andromeda was with you"—which seemed so hypocritical and unfair. Just because she'd been part of that thing with the police, who had driven them to Stanley's house and then asked questions. Miranda hated to be in any kind of official trouble. But Andromeda didn't care, didn't notice her bad mood. Besides, she was the only person who was able to see that Kevin Markasev really did have some kind of thing for her, or else really did seem to be following her around.

Peter noticed too, she guessed, though he had taken to ignoring her whenever he saw her in school. This hurt her, though she knew it was her fault. It was because she hadn't called him, hadn't looked for him, hadn't spoken to him, hadn't introduced him to any of her friends. Andromeda always knew everything about everybody, and it was she who first told her that Peter and Kevin Markasev had gotten into a fight. Peter had been suspended, Andromeda said. She never got tired of teasing: "Your admirers. I go to Europe for five weeks, and already you're hanging around with some one-armed delinquent."

Sometimes that September as the weather turned cool and the leaves started to change, Miranda got up early and walked to school. The way led over an abandoned logging road on Christmas Hill. You climbed up behind the art museum, either through the woods or else the high meadow, which in the early morning was always full of cows. The meadow rose up to the ridge where, looking back over the valley, you could see the spires of the churches and some of the larger college buildings poking up through the trees. You could see the gold dome of Schneider Hall.

Sometimes she would walk home in the afternoons with Andromeda, or alone. The logging road led for a couple of miles through the woods, and then you came out suddenly onto the ridge. Then, especially, it was beautiful, the sun sinking westward down the valley, the long light shining on the yellow and red leaves of the sugar maples.

One day in late September she was walking home along the logging road. Closer to town sometimes she saw cross-country runners from the college, but there was never anybody up at the end where the road came down toward Route 6 about a half a mile from the school. You reached it through some people's driveway where it was blocked off with enormous boulders, and was in any case so rutted and uneven that no one could drive over it without special equipment.

She climbed with her green book satchel over her shoulder. She had taken to leaving her backpack in her locker at school. The road followed the deep woods over the back of Christmas Hill.

Sometimes she imagined there were dangers here. But the odd thing was how silent the woods were now that the weather had changed. She rarely saw a squirrel or a bird. It hadn't rained all summer, and it still didn't look as if it ever would. There was no wind. The sky was empty. All the streams and ponds were dry. No one could remember a more beautiful fall. The leaves had turned early, and as she climbed out of the pines, she found herself surrounded by beeches, and aspens, and maples, and birch trees, all in their gaudiest colors. Even the oak leaves, which often were quite dingy in the fall, this year shone like polished brass.

There wasn't a sound except for her own breath, the beat of her heart, the shuffle of her boots through the dead leaves. What was more, all the smells of the forest seemed to have gone away. Once at the ice house Peter had told her to close her eyes and then told her the colors of various smells—the green leaves and ferns, the dusty white stones, the black brown mold, the yellow sand. Afterward as she followed him through the woods, those colors seemed to wash over her in waves.

Now she smelled nothing. There was something about the beauty of the trees that seemed artificial now, and sometimes she imagined that if there had been a wind, it would have stirred the leaves to clink against each other like shards of colored glass.

She came out on the ridge above the town. She stood looking down the meadow at the white marble bulk of the art museum. She could see people standing among the marble columns. The closest way to home was down that way.

The chance thought of Peter made her unhappy. But she often thought of him when she was walking in these woods—how could she not? She wanted to ask him about the fight with the new boy, because she thought she had to be involved somehow. She hated the thought of him getting into trouble.

Halfway down the hill, she moved into the trees at the broken birch that Peter had once showed her. She followed Peter's deer path through the undergrowth. Bent almost double, she climbed down the hill into the deeper woods until she found the place, the wildflower dell and the rotted tree trunk where he'd played the harmonica. She was looking for the skull-shaped rock when she heard the buzzing of a fly.

She found the rock, sat down on the log beside it. She tried to imagine what it would be like to have a mother whose favorite place was a little dell in the woods, and not, for example, FAO Schwartz or Saks Fifth Avenue. But of course Rachel wasn't her real mother. And despite what she'd told Peter, it was hard for Miranda to conjure up any coherent fantasy of her mother in Romania. Any image in her mind was always superseded by the lady dressed in furs.

A fly lit on her arm. She shook it off. Again she was aware of the buzzing sound, and she looked for the source of it—a furry, purselike body was nailed to the trunk of a birch tree six feet above the ground.

Curious, Miranda got to her feet. It was a woodchuck, she thought. And now she could see how the small belly had been cut open and a piece of metal jutted out.

She had a stick in her hand, and as she reached out, the animal dropped to the ground, the flies scattered away. In the copper-colored leaves, Miranda saw some plastic beads, some nails tied together with grass, and a coin, a five leu piece from Romania.

She knelt down for a moment over this small, headless, hairy, desecrated thing. She poked it with a stick. Disgusted, she looked around, but there was no one. Maggots were in the carcass, and a Romanian coin—she felt a sudden surge of fright, and she was hurrying through the birch trees down the slope. She crossed the golf course by the seventeenth tee. In fifteen minutes she stood out of breath on the stone dam beside the ice house, looking at the dried-up stream.

As she was running, she had thought that Peter Gross was the only person who would properly appreciate the disgusting thing, nailed up in his mother's favorite place. If he didn't know about it, she would tell him, would show him the body of the woodchuck and the Romanian coin. He would tell her what he thought. Stupidly, she imagined he'd be waiting for her.

But now, as she stood alone on the dam, she was glad Peter wasn't there. The silence of the place was a relief to her, and as she stood on the bridge, it occurred to her for the first time to be frightened of Peter Gross. She knew what Andromeda would say, what Rachel would say. Why had he picked a fight with that boy? What did he want? And wasn't it most likely that he had nailed up that thing? Who else went to that little dell in the woods?

IF SHE HAD SAID HIS name he would have heard her. He was sitting cross-legged under some oleander bushes not far away. With the fingernails of his left hand, he scratched at the stump of his right forearm.

He was dressed in a plaid shirt and dirty jeans. He had been sitting a long time. His harmonica lay in his lap. For a while he had been making what he called whisper music, but he had stopped before Miranda came. Now he waited for her to leave. Without making a sound, he moved his mouth in the shape of certain words, part of one of the last poems his mother taught him:

. . . let us be true
To one another, for the world which seems
To lie before us like a land of dreams,
So various, so beautiful, so new,
Has really neither joy nor love nor light . . .

He couldn't remember the last lines, though he had learned them from his mother's lips and knew them perfectly well. "Ignorant armies," he thought. He watched Miranda standing on the parapet beside the ice house, then watched her take the path over the dry brook. He waited for a few minutes before he went the other way, behind the grounds department shed to the fieldstone gate at the bottom of Water Street.

His father was waiting in the alley, leaning against the white clapboard wall. He wore a stained red T-shirt, tight over his big stomach, and was drinking a cup of water. When he saw Peter, he fished some wadded money from the pocket of his jeans and held it up. Three dollars—enough for two chocolate ice-cream cones that Peter went in to buy.

The store was crowded and he had to stand in line. When he came out again into the alley, his father was already moving down the brick path. His way was blocked by college students. He pushed past them, then waited for Peter on the sidewalk of the larger street. "I hate this place," he said.

He hated every place the students tended to cluster. Water Street was full of them. Expensive cars with out-of-state plates lined the curb. Peter held the two cones against the crook of his right elbow. His father plucked one out, and together they walked down to the lot at the bottom of the street.

Peter's father had parked in the shade. Ordinarily it was pleasant to sit in the front seat of the truck and eat ice-cream while the breeze blew through the open windows. Anything you might want in the way of books, tapes, tools, maps, or magazines was underfoot. Ralph, his father's red-haired, dirty, gaunt old cat was waiting for them, too. He arched his knobby spine.

"I just got back from talking to the guidance counselor," said Peter's father as they got in. "He had a lot to say. But I remember that guy, and he's no smarter than he was when I was in tenth grade. Everybody's had a couple of days to think about this and get their story straight. Fighting is a thing that's either stupid or bad. So now I'm asking you."

They stared out the windshield at the trees. They ate their ice-cream cones and stared straight ahead. Peter felt a surge of gratitude and uneasiness—his father shone in situations like this. His loyalties were clear. Outside the truck, the world was full of crooks and fools. Inside, there was no room for lies. So Peter wished this particular story didn't sound so dumb.

For a long time the bench seat in the cab had been wide enough for him to sleep with his head on his mother's lap when they'd gone on family trips—up to Maine, or every summer down to North Carolina. Later his father had bolted a roof over the bed of the truck and made a nest for him back there. The sliding window between the bed and the cab was always open, and often he had lain awake listening to his parents' slow talk. Sometimes late at night the gap between a question and an answer had been miles wide.

Now he laid the stump of his arm outside the passenger's side window. "I was trying to remember that part of 'Dover Beach,'" he said. "About the ignorant armies."

His father raised his eyebrows. "This is relevant?"

"Not really."

A drip of ice-cream had fallen onto his father's shirt, onto the bulge of his belly. He picked it off with his broad thumbnail and then held his hand out to Ralph the cat, who licked at it enthusiastically.

"Your mother used to teach you more on a Saturday afternoon than those clowns did all week," he said.

They finished their ice-cream cones sitting side by side. There was no rush. The truck was in the back of the lot, pointed into the woods, and for a moment Peter imagined they were driving someplace through the trees, the bushes reaching for the windshield. "Here's what happened," he said finally, "and I can't explain it very well. I had a dream on Monday night. After I woke up, I could remember almost every part of it. There weren't any of the crazy things that usually happen in dreams."

He paused, then went on. "It was winter, and I was standing in the snow next to the soccer field. And there was this new kid, Kevin, standing next to me. He's from the Ukraine, and he's living in a house on Woodlawn Drive. There's a bunch of kids up there, and his mother, I guess. Anyway, I could feel the cold and see his breath when he talked. He was clapping his gloves together, stamping a circle in the snow with his boots. The snow was deep and smooth as if we'd been dropped there by a bird. He was telling me I had to do something for him. We argued for a while. Then he said something about my arm, and I woke up."

There wasn't much room between Peter's father's belly and the steering wheel, but Ralph the cat had climbed up in there and was licking his fingers, held out for the purpose.

Peter said, "The next day when I saw him in line, he came over to talk to me, which he never does. I tried to walk away and he grabbed hold of me. Then he said the same thing he had in the dream, the same thing about my arm. He's got a foreign accent, and it's a weird phrase, so I couldn't be wrong. So then I—"

"Yes, I know the rest," said his father. "You punched him in the stomach and ripped a hole in his shirt, and when he was down you kicked him in the ribs, which I don't like to hear. But let me ask you this. What did he say to you?"

"You mean in the dream?"

"I don't care about the dream."

Peter shrugged, because he didn't want to repeat what Markasev had said. The whole thing sounded stupid to him now. But his father would not be put off, would wait forever if he had to.

"He called me a hurdy-gurdy boy."

Peter's father pushed Ralph off his lap, then wiped his fingers on his red pocket handkerchief. For the first time he turned to look at his son. "Well, that's not the worst I've ever heard," he said.

"No, sir."

Peter was looking out the windshield at the trees. "Here's what I did," his father said after a little while. "I paid for that kid's shirt. We'll figure out a schedule, and you can pay me back. You'll go to school tomorrow. I'll drive you in. We have a meeting in the office—no big deal."

"Yes, sir."

He reached out to touch Peter's hair, a brief and clumsy gesture he reserved for special occasions. "Don't be too hard on yourself," he said after a moment. "You've had a lot to overcome. Your mother and I . . ."

He still talked about her as if she were alive. He rubbed his nose, then started up the truck and backed it out into the lot. Peter knew what he was referring to, and it wasn't just his arm. It wasn't even his mother's illness. But when he was about five, he'd stopped talking for some reason for about eight months. Obviously it had made a big impression. "The longest year of my life," his mother had once said, though he wondered now if she would have included her last year, when she'd had to get all those transfusions, and those smelly sores were beginning to break out on her neck and shoulders.

His father glanced at him as they turned onto Water Street. His eyes were fierce, though he was smiling. "That's the end of it," he said.

But it wasn't quite the end, Peter thought. It was fine to say you didn't care about a dream, but there it was, as clear as something that had really happened. Kevin Markasev, standing in the snow, had asked him what Miranda kept in her leather pack. He had asked about the book, all kinds of specific details, and Peter had told him.

There was another strange thing. Kevin Markasev was bigger than Peter, and he had two hands. But he had lain there and let Peter kick him in the side.

3 | *Miranda*

"YOU WON'T GUESS WHERE I found it," said the baroness. "It was in the back of a jewelry shop in the Old Court. I was having some rings reset. I came early to pick them up, and I'm glad I did. I was poking around the back when I saw your painted locker and I recognized the seal. Your book was in a leather case inside. When I touched the binding, I could feel an ache in my teeth and my fingertips. It was like an electric shock."

"Really."

They spoke in French. "It must be hard for you to imagine your private documents for sale in a Gypsy's shop. Particularly something as important as this. I condescended to bargain with the old woman, and was able to purchase it for almost nothing."

The baroness wasn't doing herself justice. In the Gypsy's shop she had pawned a platinum bracelet and a ruby ring, and would have pawned her husband's signet ring as well, if the old woman had shown any interest, if she had not, in fact, spat in the corner and made the sign of the evil eye. The footlocker of papers had been on a rubbish heap to be discarded, and the baroness was lucky to have noticed it. She had cowed the old woman into giving it away, and when she thought how slim a chance that had been, she shuddered, a feeling again like an electric shock.

Now she ran her gloved fingers along the cover of the book. "The essential history of the world. You know it's quite remarkable how this was done. It's like a magic box where the inside is larger than the outside. Or one of those decorated eggs, and when you peer in you can see a whole town."

"I don't understand."

"Please don't make a game. No one but you could have created such a thing."

The book lay between them on the rough, pine table. The Baroness Ceausescu sat shivering on a wooden stool while the princess served tea. She stood above the table in the single, cold room, pouring tea into white porcelain cups that she must have inherited from her mother, for they carried the mark of the Brancoveanu family, the same mark that the baroness had noticed on the leather trunk, half obscured under layers of dirt—a ring of gold letters, so small they could not be deciphered. But the porcelain cups were true imperial ware. How was it that they had not been sold? How had they survived the wreck?

Nicola Ceausescu had every reason to hate this old woman, she told herself. Over the years, she told herself, her hate had turned to pity, because the woman had lost so much. But because what she called pity still had so much hate in it, she found she had forgotten about the woman's self-possession, her dignity, or indeed any of her other qualities. Now she remembered. Even now, when she must have known the game was finished, Princess Aegypta was entirely calm.

The baroness wore her greatcoat over her riding clothes, and she was still cold. But Aegypta Schenck von Schenck had only a white linen shirt tucked into leather hunting trousers. She had been walking along the snow-dusted path with her shotgun broken over her arm, and the baroness had had to turn her horse to pass her again before she recognized her. She'd last seen her at one of the empress's receptions years before, dressed in a purple Chinese jacket, surrounded by her court.

Of all the Brancoveanu land she had inherited from her mother, there remained only these few acres of worthless forest. Only this thatched, one-room house in which the baroness sat shivering. Impatient, she had ordered her own men to bring in wood and build up the fire, now that the kettle had been taken off.

It was a sign of the old woman's condescension that she did not sit, that she poured the tea out like a servant. Angry and ashamed, the baroness pointed to the book again. "How dare you?" she said. "How dare you use my name? This foul animal, this pig," she said, meaning Nicolae Ceausescu, the character in the book, the son of peasants, the leader of the Communist Party of Romania, who had murdered so many, destroyed so much out of his capricious vanity.

At other times, reading, she had been flattered and amused. Now she was angry. She put her gloved hand on the cover of the book and flipped it open to where the ribbon lay—a description of the party conference of 1977, a drawing of the dictator's disgusting face in which nevertheless she could see her own, though she was only thirty-four years old and a beautiful woman, as everybody said.

Now she was angry, especially when she thought she saw in the woman's eyes a hint of mockery. For a moment she imagined crushing the teacup in her hand or throwing it against the wall. Then she sat back, put it down. "This tea—do you have something stronger?"

Aegypta Schenck turned to the shelf above the basin and pulled down a jug. Then from beside it she produced another beautiful object, a cut crystal goblet, decorated also with the ring of tiny letters.

"It is raki," she said, pouring out the colorless liquid.

The fire was roaring in the cast-iron stove, and the baroness could feel its small warmth. She didn't touch the glass. Instead she stood up, stripped off her glove, then carried the book to the middle of the cottage. She stepped over the rough-sawn, muddy planks. How astonishing to imagine the woman's life here in this single room! There was the straw mattress where she slept under those blankets, those rolled-up sheepskins. Along the far wall were the bins of turnips and potatoes, and above them stood shelf after shelf of jars and cans. There on an overturned crate was an altar to her obscure Jewish god. Bunches of onions and garlic hung from hooks in the rafters—all the work, the baroness imagined, of Aegypta Schenck's own hands. But there'd been a time when her brother had commanded armies. And on her mother's side she was descended from Miranda Brancoveanu and the golden kings.

"Well," she said. "I thank you for returning it to me, though I fear it's not as important as you think. If you were hoping for a reward . . ." She shrugged, then gestured around the room. "But if you've come to make amends, I'm glad of it, because what's past is past. There were some other papers, too. . . ."

The baroness suppressed a bark of irritated laughter. "Yes," she said. "Forgive and forget. But tell me this—why is your world so much more terrifying than the real one? Why isn't it a place of peace and understanding? Was all this necessary, just to make a place of refuge for your niece? These wars, these names and dates. These fantastical theories—Copernicus, Darwin, Freud. Look at this section on the United States." Her fingers moved over a summary of the NASA space program, a description of the achievements of Apollo XI. "As if anything like this could come out of that wilderness."

The woman shrugged. The ugliness of her face, the coarseness of her skin gave her a kind of distinction, the baroness thought. Especially when contrasted with the beauty of her voice: "I had ninety scholars working for a decade. Those references to Ceausescu were not in the initial drafts."

She hesitated, then went on. "The project was not finished when the empress turned against me. At the end I was working by myself. Originally, of course, I had hoped to transform the world."

How smug she was! The baroness felt her hatred seeping back, her desire to wound. She opened the book to the last page and revealed the flyleaf, inscribed with the woman's own handwriting. She held up the book, then read out loud. " 'By herself she will discover sadness . . . ' "

Carefully, she tore out the page, then crumpled it up. The stove had a small plate on top, which she pried off to reveal the fire. She dropped the sprig of paper and watched it burn. Suddenly she felt her heart was breaking as she imagined the woman's pain. Or no—when she looked up, there was again the flicker of a smile.

"You'll never find her," said the woman, a piece of bravado. The orphanage in Constanta had kept records, and the town in Massachusetts was a small one.

"Alas," the baroness murmured, and from elsewhere in the book she produced the battered photograph of Miranda Popescu.

"You cannot hide an entire world," she said.

Then after a pause, "You must think I'm a fool. But you are the stupid one. Maybe I don't have the resources you once had. Ninety scholars, but I can follow simple instructions. Yes, there were other papers in your trunk. Yes, I was able to decipher your pathetic code. There was a woman who told fortunes in your Bucharest. She gave lessons in the English language, and she had a shop. I spoke to her through my ouijah board. She answered through her ball of quartz. I gave her directions, sent her on a trip to Massachusetts—is that right? What an absurd name! She posted me this photograph; you see? It's called a Polaroid. Color. The process doesn't exist here."

She'd been examining the fire. Now she looked up, confident that the grief in Princess Aegypta's eyes would be as much as she could bear. But there was nothing like that, only a false look of puzzlement. "You're lying. Nothing can cross . . ."

The woman caught herself, was silent. But the baroness finished the sentence: ". . . unless what? Unless the book is destroyed? You are wrong. I found a way."

She was torn now between her desire to boast, to pretend she was as great an alchemist as her dead husband, and her desire to hurt. As always, boasting was a pallid sensation, second best—"You led me by the hand. I couldn't have done it without you."

It wouldn't matter if she told her. The two soldiers she'd brought with her knew no French; they spoke nothing but Roumanian. Besides, they'd been her husband's men when he was with the army. Now they stood in the doorway, bored by what they did not understand.

"I sent five spirit children from the prison at Cluj," the baroness went on. "They were my—what's the word? I read it in your book. They were my archetypes, and very crude. Then when I had read some more, I sent another one, a boy from my own house, whom I control more easily. The woman from Bucharest has kept them safe, though I haven't told her what I plan to do. It would be cruel to ask her to conspire against her own existence. I've sent the five to hunt Prochenko and de Graz, though it's been scarcely worth the trouble. They have not been—what shall I say?—effective guardians. Certainly they can't protect her from the boy, who will accomplish what I want. He'll get her book from her. Already he has put my mark on what you've made."

Placid and calm, the princess looked at her. She was standing by the cistern pump, one big hand on the enamel trough, supported in an iron frame. Nicola Ceausescu was by the little stove, leafing through the pages of the book—"I don't understand," the princess said. "If you're not here to return my papers or sell them back, why are you here? I saw you looking at my teacups. Perhaps we can arrange a trade."

The baroness disliked questions that began with the word "why." She was here because of a great impulse, a tingling in her body and her hands, a sadness marred only by a wisp of anger as she caught a glimpse, again, of Nicolae Ceausescu's pudgy face, this time in a chapter about détente. The dictator was shaking hands with Richard Nixon; momentarily she closed her eyes, because she did not want to feel her sadness overwhelmed. Tears were on her cheeks. She lived in the heart's chaotic realm, and this was not the moment to explain the obvious. Why should she trade these papers for a few pieces of china, when the girl in the Polaroid was worth millions of francs? Why should she deny herself a sensation of victory over an old enemy, who had never given her an instant's consideration or politeness, even when the princess's brother had been alive?

She shut the book and held it up. "The world is in two places. One false and one real," she said, dropping the book into the fire where it began to smoke. She picked up a pair of tongs. But before she could step back, Princess Aegypta had grabbed her shirt between the lapels of her coat, ripped it open with her coarse hands, thrown her to the floor.

The baroness had chosen an awkward moment for her triumph. Her men were outside the door, bringing in more sticks from the woodpile, leaving her defenseless. Now they dropped their logs with a clatter and seized hold of the woman, dragged her back. *"Neciopliti!"*—idiots, the baroness snarled, then scrambled to her feet because the woman was loose again. She had twisted loose and now had put her hand into the flames and snatched out the burning book, which was spitting fire, blazing like a torch. She held it up, and the baroness scanned her ugly face, searching for a glimpse of real emotion, some real grief, and not this pretense of tranquility. She held her big nose high, and her lip was lifted in an expression of aristocratic disdain. Then when she couldn't keep the book from burning her fingers, she let it drop to the raw wooden boards.

"Take her outside!" the baroness commanded. "Please," she continued as the soldiers looked at each other—she knew what they were thinking. This gray-haired lady had once been a champion of the poor, a patron of charity hospitals, and this was her own cottage, after all. Surely . . .

"I don't have to remind you," she continued, "of her brother's treachery."

This wasn't much, was old news after all. Uncertain and ashamed, the soldiers wouldn't meet her eyes. "Please," she said again.

She had recruited them in Cluj, where they'd retired from active service. Since then she'd paid them badly and infrequently, and she now wondered if the princess opened her mouth, if she gave a command, whether the men would turn to her, help her extinguish the burning book, throw the baroness out into the gathering snowy darkness, as she deserved. But Aegypta Schenck did nothing, merely stood with her hands clasped together, and then after a moment strode across the smoky room and out the door.

And when the soldiers followed her, and the baroness was alone, she breathed in the smoke as if it were incense on the altar of Cleopatra's temple. It was the smell of the narrow triumph she liked best, and without thinking, and because she had pictured for a moment the statue of Cleopatra in her mind, she started to move. Even in riding boots, her feet remembered the old paces of Cleopatra's dance, which she had performed on the boards of the Ambassadors Theatre when she was still a girl. The dance comes at the end of the opera's second act, and in it the goddess-queen destroys the synagogue of her enemies—lithe and graceful, now the baroness was stirring around the room, and with her flat, open hands was swatting at the strings of onions and garlic overhead, knocking away the crystal goblet and the teacups. They shattered on the floor. Then after a minute, her movements still passionless and stylized, Nicola Ceausescu was pulling down the plain curtains and overturning the chairs. The book was smoking, and she smashed a kerosene lantern over it and upset the jug of liquor so it spilled into the rag carpet and flared up. In the opera the dance had lasted several minutes, and had been always greeted not with applause but with bewildered silence—she had been barefoot and half-clothed, her lips red and her eyes black with kohl. The applause had come later and the howls of delight, and by the time she finished now the room was on fire. She stood on the threshold. It was starting to snow.

Princess Aegypta was on the walk, hands on her hips. The baroness stepped down onto the slates and stood beside her, watching her and not the fire. She could hear the soldiers farther back, muttering to each other, and the baroness could feel their confusion and disapproval, as if a smaller fire burned behind her. They were wondering what they should do—should they bring buckets from the cistern? And if the princess had begged them, if she had cried or cursed they would have done what she wanted. They were soft-hearted men, not like the baroness, who was already feeling the tickling of remorse—they would not have burned a defenseless woman out of her house, a princess of Roumania, whose brother was von Schenck the traitor, but a hero before that.

If she had shown any expression, doubtless they would have helped her. But it was Nicola Ceausescu who was buffeted with emotion. The princess's face was quiet as she watched the glow behind the dirty windows.

After fifteen minutes they had to stand back from the heat. Snow fell on their heads. Aegypta Schenck von Schenck reached out to warm her hands. She needed nothing, the baroness decided. There were many who would take her in near here. Her family had been well loved.

Still, it was a cold night. And the baroness always had to press a little farther. "Give her your coat," she said to the soldier who stood behind her, who was beckoning to them now to go.

IN 1966, THREE LOCAL DISTRICTS had combined to build a new junior and senior high school in northern Berkshire County, on a hill above a dairy farm several miles from town. The building was made of glass, steel, cinder blocks, bricks, and consisted of four single-story corridors around a central courtyard—not the kind of building that would easily burn. But the fire set that night got into the walls and ceilings. Several classrooms were damaged on the west side of the building. Until it started to rain, eighteen hours after the first alarm, the roof over the library was still smoking.

Andromeda didn't hear about the fire before she went to bed, because

she was talking to Miranda on the phone. On Tuesday morning, Andromeda's mother let her sleep late. After breakfast there were a lot of phone
calls to make, so she didn't hear from Miranda again until past one o'clock.
Andromeda assumed she was calling about volleyball practice, but then it
turned out there was something else, something hard to understand, because
she was gulping and swallowing her words. Then she calmed down.

Miranda had left her backpack in her locker at school. The bracelet, the
old coins, the bag of strange items she had inexplicably lugged around for
the past few weeks, now she was afraid she'd lost them in the fire. That
morning she'd made Stanley drive her out, but the police hadn't let them in
the parking lot. She said she'd gotten out of the car and run over to the
soccer field where there were some other people standing around. "The
whole west corridor was hidden in the smoke," she said.

She didn't cry, but she sounded numb and stupid. "I would have stayed,
but Stanley had to go to class," she said. "I promised Mom I wouldn't go
out by myself. Now I'm here alone."

She never called Rachel "Mom." It was a bad sign. "So what are you
doing?"

"Watching TV."

She never watched TV. Andromeda canceled some things and rode over
Miranda's house, which was on the green in the center of town. She parked
her mountain bike in the yard next to the fence. She went up the steps to
the screen door and, sure enough, there was the sound of canned laughter
inside the house. So she pounded on the open door until Miranda came
out, and together they went bike riding in Petersburg Forest. It was a beautiful October day, the sky full of clouds, the trees orange and red and gold.

"I can't think what would burn," Andromeda said once when they'd
stopped beside the stream. "I mean the doors are wood, I guess."

Then they rode out to the firehouse and watched the trucks come back.
"They'll wait until it's safe and then go through," Andromeda said. "In the
meantime you should call the principal's office. There's probably a lot of
valuable stuff left inside. Probably a lot of people lost something."

But it couldn't be that simple. Something was obviously on Miranda's
mind, but she wouldn't talk about it. At six o'clock they went back to her
house for supper. Rachel had prepared Mexican food, and Stanley was

telling them about what he thought were some amazing developments in the Horse Head Nebula, seen through the Hubble telescope. He was a professor of astronomy and a sweet man, though very thin. When he got excited, as now, Andromeda thought he was kind of cute—at least for a dad.

After supper, upstairs, Miranda pulled back her windows to watch the rain falling in the backyard, the first rain for months and a welcome sight. She'd hardly said a word all day, but now she was full of news, mostly about current events in Eastern Europe. This had never before been a subject of conversation. She turned on the computer and showed Andromeda some Web pages from Romania.

"What's this about? What is wrong with you?"

"I had a dream last night. After we talked on the phone."

"Great," said Andromeda, who was easily bored. Miranda often told her about her dreams, which tended to be complicated. Even so, they always managed to retain that special boring quality. Andromeda herself had never dreamt of anything that made sense, or that she remembered thirty seconds after she woke up.

But now she found herself sitting cross-legged on the bed while Miranda spoke. "It was night time. I was in the woods. I was lost. I came into a ring of birch trees. There was a woman, and she talked to me. It was in a foreign language, but I could understand. She was an old woman with a big nose. She said someone was trying to hurt me, and when I woke up, the first thing I heard was someone lit the school on fire."

"And the connection would be . . . ?"

Miranda rolled her eyes. She was sitting on the side of the bed, a candle in her hands. Outside it was getting dark.

"Life is not just about you," said Andromeda.

But Miranda interrupted. "She said she couldn't have spoken to me before, because then people would know. But now people knew anyway, and they would try to hurt me. They were sent by enemies of hers and mine. Do you remember the kids in the quad? She said I would know who my friends were. She told me not to turn away from my friends. She told me I had two friends I could trust and who'd do anything for me. She said one of them would show me some kind of sign and talk to me about my own country. He'd show me something from my own country. He'd offer me something, and that's how I'd know to trust him. I can't believe it. I've been so unfair."

"I don't know about 'anything,' " said Andromeda. "I don't know if I'd do anything for you. It was just a dream."

Which turned out not to be the right thing to say. Miranda was staring at the candle flame, trembling in her trembling hands. "It wasn't just a dream. It was more real than you. I saw the light on the birch trees. Frost on the yellow leaves. I smelled the smoke. This woman grabbed hold of me, and I could feel her hands. She said she was my father's sister. Then she told me that my mother was in a place called Ratisbon, and she touched me on the forehead with her fingers."

Andromeda sat watching the candle flame until Miranda blew it out. "I spoke to Peter Gross," she said. "He's going to meet me in the yard. We're going over Christmas Hill."

Andromeda stared at her. "I'm missing something. You told me—"

Miranda interrupted, shook her head. "Maybe I wanted to believe it, because I hadn't called him. Maybe I wanted not to trust him. But he's got to be my other friend who's trying to protect me. That's why he got into that fight."

"Well, come on. I don't think you should change your mind because of some dream. You said that animal was in the place where you'd last seen him. That dead woodchuck or whatever. You said you'd been talking to him about Romania. You said he probably stole one of your Romanian coins. That he was angry at you for dumping him."

"I didn't dump him. There was nothing to dump. This was a modern coin. Rachel kept a few from when they went."

"So maybe he broke into your house. Besides, how do you know your dream was about him? Maybe it was about that guy Kevin. He's the new kid. He's from Romania or someplace. He's the pretty one. Maybe Peter Gross is the bad guy. The one-armed bandit in the night."

She wasn't serious, but Miranda was. "Don't you get it? Maybe he did nail that thing up, but that's the sign. The thing from my own country. It's not as if he hurt me. And besides—you're wrong. You don't even know him. He's a nice guy. How did he know I'd go back there?"

"Yeah, well, suit yourself."

After a moment, Miranda spoke. "I tried calling you this morning. But your phone was always busy, so I called him. He knew immediately why I had to go. I didn't have to explain it."

To Andromeda, this felt like a rebuke. She decided to stop teasing. "You're walking to the school?"

Miranda nodded. "Someone would see us on the road. Peter doesn't ride a bike."

Because he was missing his hand, Andromeda thought. His right forearm ended a few inches past his elbow, and then there was an odd stump covered with scaly skin and what looked like warts. His clothes looked like his father shopped at Wal-Mart. He wore sneakers to school even in winter, and his teeth suggested bad nutrition. He lived in what was basically an old farmhouse out on White Oak Road, with a lot of garbage and broken-down trucks in the front yard. Andromeda had seen him mowing the lawn once, when she was going on a run.

Actually, she had seen him more than once, as she often ran out that way. But once she'd stopped to watch him. Actually, she'd been impressed to see him work the power mower with his one hand.

Miranda emptied the books out of her green satchel. Now she filled it with two hammers, two flashlights, and a coil of rope, which she took out from underneath her bed. She put on running shoes, black jeans, and a black sweatshirt—a ridiculous ensemble, Andromeda thought. "How about a gas mask and rubber gloves?" she said. "You're probably not even going to be able to get inside."

"Probably not."

"I don't understand why we can't go by ourselves. It's nothing we can't do alone."

Miranda shrugged.

"Hey, I can drive you out there," Andromeda continued. "What can he do for you?"

Later she rode her bike home in the rain. She slipped in through the side door and stood in the dark kitchen, running her fingers through her wet hair. She was watching the light through the closed glass doors that led into the living room. She could hear her mother talking on the phone, and she supplied in her mind the words of another drunken call to California, her mother talking on and on when there was nothing to talk about. Her father was a patient man.

She took the keys to the Volvo from her mother's purse. After midnight when the rain had stopped, she drove back into town. The brake and clutch felt good under her wet, bare feet. The risk made her happy, which was nice, because she'd been depressed before. The fact was, she was curious about Peter Gross. She wanted to see him and Miranda together. Maybe she was jealous. She didn't have boys fighting over her, especially not older boys.

They were waiting for her at the corner, as they'd prearranged. They slipped into the back without a word. They sat together in the darkness, and Andromeda had to drive them like a chauffeur. The gearshift was a little rough. "Do you have a license?" Peter asked when they reached Field Park—a stupid question. How old did he think she was? She had learned to drive that summer, though, in Greece.

In her mind the car ride was the bribe she'd offered them to be included. She pulled onto Route 6 out of town, and in five minutes they saw the sign at the top of the hill. They drove into the school parking lot, which had a new white trailer in the middle of it. Lights were on in the trailer. Cars were parked outside.

"Shhh," Miranda said, and that was stupid, too. Andromeda pulled into a space, turned off the lights, then killed the engine and they sat for a while. No one came out of the trailer to yell at them. So they got out of the car, just to see if they could take a look.

Miranda hurried on ahead. Andromeda could see the beam of her flashlight when she and Peter passed the corner of the wall. Almost invisible in her black clothes, Miranda was waiting at the history department offices, and she shined her light across the field, then back at the narrow panel of safety glass in one of the steel doors. It was starred and crumbled, kept in place by wire mesh. The door itself hung ajar, fastened to the other by a padlocked chain that ran through both doors' handles.

"Let's be quick," Miranda said. She thrust the flashlight into Peter's hand, and knelt to remove a hammer and a cold chisel from her bag. Then she was smashing at the padlock, obviously not caring about the noise, which was like the clanking of a bell.

"Stop," whispered Andromeda. She'd rummaged for a piece of cloth in Miranda's bag and had come up with the second flashlight and a blue bandana, which now she wrapped around the lock. Peter put the light down in the wet grass and picked up a hammer. Andromeda held the chisel for him. In six strokes the mechanism broke apart.

"Wait here," Miranda said. But that was idiotic, so Andromeda followed her into the building, into the warren of small department offices. Some of the teachers' desks in the common room had been pushed against the wall. Books and papers were scattered on the floor. The carpeting was soggy, covered with black footprints. There was a wet, charred, rotten smell.

THAT DAY AT HOME, after Miranda's telephone call, Peter had imagined himself climbing through pits of charred rubble. He had imagined precarious ceilings and falling walls. Now, when they had passed the inner doors, he could see the line of blue lockers, which continued out of reach into the darkness. Things seemed disappointingly intact. Again there was a mess of sooty footprints down the center of the floor.

He was wandering around, shining his light through some of the open classroom doors when Andromeda and Miranda returned, the leather backpack in Miranda's hand. Without a word she led them back the way they'd come.

Now it was almost an anticlimax how easy and uneventful this had been. There was no reason to be panicked or feel brave. The double doors stood open, but on the other side, of course, were two men waiting. Peter could scarcely see them in the bright, sudden light of their torches. He stood with Miranda on one side, Andromeda on the other, while the light played on their faces.

And even that probably wouldn't have been so bad. They hadn't done anything terrible. The pack was Miranda's property. This wasn't the kind of thing that would have made his father angry. They hadn't stolen anything, and he was helping a friend.

The best thing would have been to try to explain. But there was no time. The two men had barely opened their mouth before Miranda bolted away into the darkness, running as fast as she could for the shelter of the trees. Then there was nothing to do but run after her, while Andromeda scattered in another direction.

Of course Miranda had left her green satchel outside by the door. Of course it had her name and address printed on the inside flap in black magic marker. And of course he himself was highly recognizable, because of his arm. So that was that.

He crossed through the woods behind the soccer field, then across Route 6 and up the Pollocks' driveway on the way to Christmas Hill. When he came up the slope—shivering and soaked—he was surprised to see Andromeda waiting for him, ghostlike, perched on one of the pale boulders. He was surprised she'd gotten there before him. But now here she was, hugging her long, wet legs. She wore no shoes. Had she always been barefoot? Now her feet were covered with white mud and bits of grass.

"This is stupid," she said. "I can't believe this. My mother hates to be woken up."

"Where's Miranda?" he asked after a pause. She cocked her head past him up the logging road, which led under a row of sugar maples.

"Shit," Andromeda said. "She's got what she wanted. It's the two of us who are really screwed." She climbed down from the boulder and followed him onto the road.

"Should we go back for the car?" he asked.

She shrugged. "It's too late now."

For years he'd known Andromeda's name, known where she lived—a big, square, modern house off Syndicate Road. But he'd never spoken to her before tonight. Now she walked beside him, breathing easily as they came up the steep part of the hill. She wore black bicycle pants and a gray T-shirt. She did not complain about the cold.

He found himself catching sidelong glances of her when he thought she wasn't looking. The sky was clear now, and it was remarkable how much you could see by moonlight. Andromeda's skin was pale, dusted with liver-colored freckles. Her arms and legs were covered with fine white hair—he'd never been this close to her before. She reached up to push away a branch, releasing a spatter of wet drops. On the underside of her right wrist she had a long, white, hook-shaped scar.

He'd always found her intimidating. She was an inch or so taller than he was. Her eyes were a cold color, almost silver when she turned toward him. Her voice was hoarse and soft. "I'm so pissed off—I'm sorry. But it's good to get a chance to finally meet you."

What did she mean by this? She could have met him any time. Though he was a grade ahead of her, it wasn't as if she'd never seen him. The town was too small for that. Once she'd stopped to watch him mow the lawn. She hadn't said a word, or even waved.

"Miranda told me about you," she continued. "How you looked out for her when I was gone away."

Looked out for her? Is that what he'd done? She'd barely spoken to him for a month. Of course he hadn't really expected that she would, after school started up. He'd learned not to expect much from girls, because of his arm. Sometimes just with one other person he could forget about it, and so could she. But that was always harder in a group.

Peter hesitated. "Why do you think she called me today? She said she wanted to thank me for something I had done."

"You should ask her."

He had asked her. Then he'd asked again after he'd walked down to her house that night. But she'd been anxious, nervous about Andromeda's car. And he'd had some hurt feelings that still had to be pushed out of the way. He wouldn't have come at all except she'd sounded so upset.

"Maybe she likes you," murmured Andromeda.

Above them masses of black leaves broke up the moonlight. Was she teasing him? He couldn't tell. He knew better than to think she'd recognize him tomorrow, but just at that moment she seemed easy to get to know, and not just because they could talk about Miranda. Soon Andromeda had left that topic behind, and she was telling him about her plans to circumvent her mother's anger about the car, about how she would appeal directly to her father, a philosophy professor who was living in Berkeley, California, with a woman half his age. She had a brother whom she rarely saw.

"Why did your parents split up?" he found himself asking, a question that related, obscurely, to his own mother. And her answer related, obscurely, to himself. "I think I was a problem child," Andromeda said. "Hell, I didn't even talk till I was five."

There seemed nothing to say to this. Was she just boasting? At first Peter thought Miranda would wait for them at the gate in the wire fence. But when they got there she was gone. They stopped for a moment, then moved on through the deeper forest. He could smell the oak trees, and the black night was all around. Andromeda was walking close to him, sometimes letting her right arm brush against his left arm. It wasn't his imagination. He could feel the soft white hair on her forearm, and sometimes their shoulders touched.

They climbed along the spine of the hill. What was he doing here? What was he doing with these girls? He was going to read a book and go to bed—he hadn't asked for this. It wasn't just Andromeda—after tonight, he told himself, neither of them would speak to him again.

He felt Andromeda's shoulder against his shoulder, her hand against his hand. He knew enough not to respond. He pictured his mother lying back against her pillows, sick from lung cancer, though she hadn't smoked for years. "Let us be true to one another," she had murmured not even a year before.

MIRANDA WENT ON AHEAD. She knew she was behaving like an idiot. Not wanting to face Andromeda or hear her accusations, she hurried over the muddy, rutted road. The leather pack had a weight and a solidity she knew by heart, but at that moment she was embarrassed to be carrying it. The panic she had felt on losing it, she couldn't reconstruct. The dream she'd had the night before had lost its urgency—what was it that the old woman said? That she'd recognize someone from her own country?

When she got to the stone bench, she sat down to wait under the carved name of Gregor Splaa, who had taught Romance languages at the college before the Second World War. Once Stanley had mentioned that when they were walking up this way, and she'd remarked on the strange name.

Expedite the inevitable, Stanley had told her more than once, which was why she was waiting here now. She didn't worry about Peter, because it wasn't as if she and Peter had done anything really wrong. Maybe they'd get detention or something, but Peter at least was used to that. Andromeda must be furious, though. She'd known the whole idea was stupid from the beginning. And she was right, thought Miranda miserably, and Stanley was right, and the stuff in her backpack was just stuff. All the rest was dreams and wish-fulfillment, and the scribbled note of someone's aunt.

When she saw the two dark figures coming up behind her, squeezed together as they tried to negotiate a pair of mud puddles, she sat forward on the stone bench. "I'm really sorry," she said to Andromeda as she came up.

And for a moment she thought Andromeda would stalk by without a word. In front of them, at right angles to the road, lay the path down through the woods toward the upper meadow and the art museum. There was a wooden gate through the barbed wire, and Andromeda had her hand on the gatepost before she turned back. "I'm glad you're sorry," she said, "because this is a fucking disaster. You know I'm supposed to be starting driver's ed. Now I'll have to wait till I'm sixteen, even if my mother ever lends me the car again, which I totally doubt."

She went on for a while more. Miranda had often heard this kind of rage turned on other people, and in a way that had felt good, as if Andromeda were protecting her by abusing others. Now it was as if she'd lost her special status. But she also knew that Andromeda sometimes said more than she meant, and it was good to let her blow off steam. Maybe she'd be over it by tomorrow, and she'd be able to admit that none of this was entirely Miranda's fault.

"I'm sorry," she said again. "Let's . . ."

But Andromeda was gone, striding away through the tall trees, and then she disappeared beneath them in the dark. Peter Gross came to sit beside her and put his hand on her wrist.

"We did it," he said—words which filled her with a sudden gratitude.

"It's a beautiful night," he said. She looked up above their heads to where the canopy of trees gave out. Above her she could see the open sky, the clouds rushing past.

"There'll be some yelling," he said. "There's always a little bit of yelling."

She sat beside him with her backpack in her lap. She dug her hand down through the circle of leather laces that held it closed. She fumbled around until she found what she was looking for, an old pasteboard box from I. Manin's jewelry store in Bucharest.

She could recognize the box just by the feel of it. She opened it without looking, without taking it out of the pack. Inside were eleven very small gold coins, thin as paper, the faces and numbers on them almost worn away. She pinched one of the coins between her fingers.

It had been her intention to bring it out into the open air, to press it into Peter's palm, to reward him for his loyalty, especially after how she'd treated him for the past month. But what had her aunt said to her? Protect the book, protect these memories, which always could be stolen or given away. So after a while she closed the box and pushed it down again under the gray shawl into the bottom of the pack. Then she asked him about the dead animal she had found in the birch trees. "That's why I didn't call," she said, which was only partly true. "I was a little afraid. But now I want to know, did you leave that there for me? Were you trying to say something?"

He was close to her on the stone bench, and she turned toward him. "Were you giving me something from my country?"

But she could tell he had no idea what she was talking about. If only she could remember her aunt's words. But she couldn't make them clear, because they had been spoken in Romanian.

"I don't go there very often," Peter said. "It was my mother's favorite place. So I wanted to show it to you, to see . . ."

"What?"

"Well, if you liked it too."

That was very sweet. Later when they walked down through the woods, she could feel he was walking too close to her. He kept on brushing up against her, bumping her with his shoulder. She believed him when he said he had nothing to do with the dead woodchuck, but instead of being relieved, now suddenly she resented him. And if he touched her with the stub of his arm, then she was sure she'd have to throw up. She moved away, walked faster, then slowed up again, because she didn't want to go home. When they came out into the meadow, the moon was down behind the mountains and the gray clouds were drawing in.

"What's that?" she said.

He touched her on the shoulder when she stopped, but she pulled away. "What is that?"

There was something in front of them in the path. She found her flashlight and flicked it on, revealing something in the beam. A small animal, a monkey—it sat on its haunches in the middle of the path, hugging itself with long, naked arms.

"Look," she whispered.

They stood without moving. The animal seemed to have no face until it twisted its head around. Then it opened two enormous lidless eyes. And maybe she would have been frightened except it was so small, so plainly terrified as soon as it saw them. It unwrapped itself and scuttled away out of the light, dragging its bottom along the grass.

"A monkey," Peter said. But its arms and back and shoulders were as hairless as a child's. It couldn't move very fast over the hummocks of the meadow. She could see it was wounded. There was a long red cut on its pale belly.

"Let it alone," Peter said. They stood and watched as it reached the shelter of the trees. "It's somebody's pet," Peter said. "Or maybe it escaped out of some lab."

"We can't just leave it."

But they did. They watched until it disappeared and they could no longer hear the rustle of dry leaves. She promised herself that she'd tell Stanley as soon as she got home. She was looking for something to think about, and so she pondered the animal until they reached the next small ridge. She held the picture of its small, scared face inside her mind until it disappeared again, driven out by what she saw down at the crest of the hill overlooking the art museum—a bonfire. Shadows moved around it.

Several paths crisscrossed over the open field, which had been stirred into uneven hummocks by the hooves of cows. Now they climbed down through the pale rocks and solitary birch trees of the meadow. And they could see Andromeda below them, waiting among the milkweed and goldenrod, where the fire threw back long shadows of the trees. Miranda was relieved to see her, even if Andromeda had stopped to yell at her some more. She deserved it, so it was best to get it over with. Besides, Peter was beginning to make her uncomfortable, or else not Peter exactly, but the intimacy of walking together in the dark. Already she'd glanced forward to the time when he'd be saying good-bye to her in the yard of Stanley and Rachel's house—surely he'd earned something from her, and she was grateful. What was she supposed to do, kiss him? But it would be nice to have Andromeda there, nicer still to be alone with her. Even now, if she wanted to go back and try to retrieve the car, Miranda would go with her. And it would be too much to ask Peter or allow him to come. He already had a long walk home from town.

These thoughts moved quickly, and they kept her from seeing much beyond Andromeda's pale shape, and the shifting ragged line where the light gave out among the goldenrod. Andromeda faced away from them, perched between a boulder and a birch tree, her long legs crossed. She was looking down the pasture, and it wasn't until they had crept over to her and squatted down with her that Miranda recognized Kevin Markasev standing by a bonfire, fifty feet away.

"There," whispered Andromeda. "I told you he was cute."

He had his expensive clothes on, a soft shirt open at the neck, showing a silver chain. He hadn't shaved. He wore baggy, pleated pants and leather boots. He was opening a bottle he had taken from a paper bag. Several empty bottles lay on the ground. A girl was with him. Miranda recognized her T-shirt, her baseball cap, her tattoos, but not her face, which was covered with pimples and red spots.

"I could use a beer," Andromeda said.

She wasn't looking at Miranda, and she didn't seem so angry anymore. Or maybe, Miranda thought, it was just that her anger had gone cold. She couldn't really be thinking of going down into the firelight. It would be easy to pass by without being seen.

"No," Miranda whispered. And of course Peter was standing back beyond the light's reaching edge. But then Kevin Markasev raised his head, and looked up toward where they were squatting near the birch tree in the dark. He had a concentrated expression on his face, as if he were smiling and frowning at the same time. It was obvious he knew someone was watching. For all Miranda knew, he could see them clearly. He gave a friendly waggle to the bottle in his hand.

"What's the big deal?" Andromeda said. "It could be fun. Besides, my feet are freezing."

"It's not a big deal. Only . . ."

Only what? She didn't really know. Only a sense of menace, left over from the night in the quad. And the way he behaved toward her in school, which could be a misunderstanding or could even be her problem. Miranda often felt her own anxieties dissolved or at least diluted in Andromeda's self-confidence—that was part of why they were friends. Don't be such a worrywart, Miranda told herself.

But what about Peter? He wasn't about to go down with them. And as if to emphasize that, Andromeda now leaned to her and said—loud enough for Peter to hear, loud enough maybe even for Kevin Markasev to hear, "Look at him. Which of these two guys would you rather spend your time with?"

And before Miranda could respond, she stood up and walked downhill into the light. As she approached the fire, Miranda and Peter could hear the sound of her voice, but they couldn't understand what she was saying. The girl in the baseball cap took a pack of cigarettes out of the pocket of her jeans, shook one out, and gave it to Andromeda. But Kevin Markasev wasn't looking at her. He hadn't stopped looking uphill.

"Is that you, Peter?" he said in his soft accent. "Please join us. I am sorry. The shirt was . . ." He made an odd, dismissive sound, accompanied by a gesture of his left hand, as if he were throwing something away into the darkness.

Peter was squatting behind Miranda and a little to one side. Now he stood up and stepped back behind the birch tree. But Kevin Markasev didn't stop smiling. He turned his head, and Miranda could tell he'd shifted his attention to her. *"Buna,"* he said. *"Ce faci?"*

It took a while for this to sink in. When it did, Miranda got up. She rubbed the wet knees of her jeans. The girl in the cap had put some more sticks on the fire and it had blazed up so the light was at Miranda's feet.

Markasev smiled and shook his head, as if to answer a question she had not yet asked. "Not far," he said. "From Ukraine. But close. So, of course . . ."

He repeated the gesture with his left hand, as if he were throwing something away. "Here, you see," he continued. "Raki. Roumanian homemade beverage—not the best quality. Would you like?"

"Oh," she murmured to herself.

For a moment she remembered her dream. What was it that her aunt had said? But then she put that aside and didn't answer, cheered to see Andromeda by the fire, sitting now and talking with the girl in the cap, smoking a cigarette, holding her hand out.

Kevin came a few steps toward her up the slope. *"Te rog, esti invitatul meu,"* he said—"No, you don't speak? Forgive me. . . . My grandmother was from Constanta. Ah, you know?"

"Come on," she said to Peter, but he made a face. And that was too bad, because Kevin obviously wanted to be friends, and not just with her. Besides, what did she know about the fight? For all she knew, it had been Peter's fault.

When Markasev held a bottle out to her, she climbed down over the uneven grass. She examined the red Budweiser label as if it might contain some clue. She sniffed the top of the bottle and then took a sip of a bitter, fiery liquor that brought tears to her eyes.

"Come, sit," he said. She looked behind her and saw Peter beside the birch tree. He came a few steps down the hill so that the firelight touched his face.

"Please, my friend," said Kevin Markasev, gesturing with his left hand up the hill. "No, I am sorry. I apologize. These things are an understanding," he said, smiling.

But was he drunk? Miranda remembered the way he had spoken once in class, and it was not like this. "There, now, you see. Listen . . ." Now everything was expressed in single words and broken phrases. "Listen," he repeated. "You know Constanta. Black Sea. Every summer. Train from Odessa."

These words were accompanied with many small sounds, grimaces, shrugs, and gestures. As long as she was looking at him, he was easy to understand. "We go fish," he said. "Marsh, swamp, I think. Houseboats, painted colors, you know—red, green. Herons, storks, anchovies, all kinds, so many."

Andromeda sat cross-legged, smiling up at her. "This is Brenda," she said, indicating the girl in the cap, who didn't seem exactly friendly. When she smiled, the firelight glinted off the gold in her teeth. Miranda inspected the tattooed ring above her elbow as she squatted down beside Andromeda. She now identified it as a ring of numbers and unfamiliar letters. When the girl spoke, her accent was so thick that Miranda couldn't understand, though she inferred some kind of greeting. Maybe that's what the problem had been with Kevin Markasev, some kind of language barrier or cultural misunderstanding, none of which made any difference to Andromeda. Miranda felt a comfort to be near her, a warmth that was greater than the warmth of the fire, and which had dispelled all sense of danger as she watched Kevin Markasev. Or maybe there was still a little thrill of risk, but that was part of anything fun, as Andromeda had often reminded her. Certainly there was no real danger—they were three against two, and Peter had already beaten Markasev in a fight. But why was she even thinking about that? He seemed really nice. And she could see what Andromeda meant about his looks, his heavy eyebrows and dark eyes, his pale skin and the hint of a beard. And he'd been to Romania.

Now Miranda listened to his story, which flowed easily as long as she supplied most of it, filling in the gaps between the words with mental pictures—an opossum, she thought. It must have been an opossum she saw. But the memory of that small creature on the hill was now supplanted by a multitude of other more exotic animals and birds, native to the Danube River delta in Romania. There as it approaches the Black Sea, the stream of the great river breaks apart into a skein of tiny channels through the reeds, a marsh which covers hundreds of square miles. She had seen photographs. All the waterbirds of Europe stopped there on their annual migrations.

She knew about this from the Web, and books she'd taken out from the library. "Train from Odessa," repeated Kevin Markasev. "Beautiful city," and in her mind Miranda saw the domes and spires of the town beyond the railway yard, the great black locomotive bellowing gusts of steam—a photograph she remembered, doubtless, from an old book. She shook her head. "What is wrong with me?" she thought, taking another drink of raki. Is this the enemy her aunt had warned her about? Is this the friend? She sat and listened while Markasev told her how one summer when he was thirteen he had gone to Izmail with his cousin. They had borrowed a flat-bottomed boat and gone out fishing with a murderer named Ion Farting Breath. His teeth were full of gold. He had showed them a place where the stream came into a tidal estuary and the water was clean and cold. In the boat they had drifted over a sunken wall, part of an old castle that had belonged to the emperor. They had found a place where the water was twelve meters deep over a glass mosaic of a woman's face, the goddess of the sea inside the old temple of Neptune. There were no fish, no weeds, nothing except small flickers of light in the black water when the sun went down, which Ion Farting Breath had told them were the sunken ghosts of dead animals, part of the emperor's menagerie, destroyed in a great storm. Now they preyed on the bodies of dead sailors. The emperor's mistress had preferred animals with stripes: tigers, zebras, kudus, and okapis, all of which had drowned. And it was true. As Kevin Markasev looked down, he had seen cages, manacles, chains.

What emperor? Miranda thought. There hadn't been an emperor in that part of the world for a thousand years. She took another sip of raki. Beside her, Andromeda had finished her cigarette. She was laughing at something Brenda said. Now she turned to Miranda. "Show him your backpack," she said, as if it was the most natural and normal thing in the world. And then to Markasev: "What's this—Romanian old-home week?"

"You have . . . ?"

This was going a little too fast, too far. Miranda shook her head. She tucked her backpack under her feet. Andromeda went on. "She has a book. That's where we were tonight. We went back to the school to get her book."

"Ah," said Brenda. "We also, we were there. We like the fire."

She was easier to understand now. The light gleamed from her gold teeth. Miranda made a gesture with her hand, and then she turned around toward Peter, who looked uncomfortable and awkward sitting by the birch tree. Miranda beckoned to him, but he didn't move.

Andromeda smiled. "I told you he might come in handy," she said. She was talking about Kevin. "Maybe he can help you with the translation. You know that note from your aunt."

Miranda didn't even remember telling her about that. Glancing back toward Peter, she shook her head. But why did she have to worry so much? Surely it wasn't such a big deal to take out her book and show it to Kevin Markasev, who understood about Romania.

He stood above them, a smile on his handsome face, but he was frowning, too. He reached out his white, long hand. When he spoke, it was to Andromeda. "I know about . . . these things. This book . . . these things are famous in my country. Your friend is from a famous . . . family."

Miranda was conscious of her heartbeat. "You know about my family?"

The boy made an elaborate shrug, raising his delicate, thin shoulders. "Who . . . does not know? Miranda Popescu from Constanta on the sea. When I was . . . small, my grandmother told me stories. How she . . . disappeared."

Was it her imagination, or was he speaking more coherently than even a few minutes before? This is all baloney, she thought, like the baloney about the emperor.

When she'd decided that, she felt both happy and relaxed. The boy seemed suddenly unthreatening. She had been squatting in an uncomfortable position, but now she stretched her feet toward the fire with the backpack on her lap. She turned to look at Peter, made another gesture for him to join them, but he did not come.

The grass was wet under her seat. Brenda threw on some more gray sticks from a pile beside the rock, first snapping them with her big hands. Andromeda took a drink from another bottle of Budweiser. "Sure," she said. "It's not such a big mystery."

Markasev stood above them, and Miranda could see the movement of his shoulders and thin arms. His green silk shirt was unbuttoned halfway down, and she could see the bones of his chest. "Of course I would like to see the Brancoveanu bracelet," he said in his sibilant harsh accent. "The white tyger . . ."

Miranda didn't hear the rest of what he was saying. It was a phrase from the penciled note at the beginning of the book. "And I see you wear your mother's cross," the boy. "Made from the nails."

She clutched at the crucifix around her neck. Markasev laughed—"Is not such a mystery, I say. Your mother is in Ratisbon—not so far. Your aunt is in Mogosoaia. North of Bucharest. A little village about fourteen kilometers. You can take a railway from the Gara de Nord."

"You know them?"

"Not at all. I know a lady who takes you to these places. I go for Thanksgiving holiday. I take a letter."

This is bullshit, thought Miranda. Almost to reassure herself, she put down her bottle and then started unlacing the leather strings of her pack. Glancing backward, she saw Peter Gross had gotten to his feet, but then she was fumbling with the envelope and the folded shawl. She had to see the sentence about the white tyger, and something about surrendering the book and knowing when to do it. Was Kevin Markasev the person from her own country, the person who would give her something? Maybe that's what the raki was—she put the bottle down. Where was the card from that old professor? The book fell open to the frontispiece, the picture of the king.

Markasev squatted down behind her, so he could read over her shoulder. "A small history of the world," he said. "Ah, this is very interesting. This is the note to you? Yes—'Dearest M.'"

First his long hand was over her shoulder, and he was running his finger over the words. Then the book was in his hands as he squatted above her.

"Look at the inscription," said Miranda. She recited from memory—"'A hurried note to tell you . . .'"

"But it doesn't say this."

He'd stood up. Twisting around so she could see him behind her, Miranda could also see Peter Gross coming hesitantly down the hill. She shook her head. "No—where it says about the time will come . . ."

"But it doesn't . . ."

Markasev was leafing through the book. He was caressing the leather binding, smelling the pages. "Small history. Romans . . . Turks . . . kings, queens. Fascists. War. Communists. Ceausescu. Revolution. You, in Constanta orphanage." He shrugged, then made a little squirting sound between his lips. "Future must come. Everything is here." He made a gesture that included the book, the hill, the sky, the fire, and all of them.

"No, where it says, 'Dearest M.'"

Markasev squinted, shrugged. Now he was looking at some photographs she had placed inside the book: she and Stanley and her grandparents at Disneyland when she was ten years old. Rachel holding a bouquet of flowers. "World is here," he said. "And note from father's sister. 'When you read this, you will know this book will be . . .'"

His index finger moved along the penciled words. How could he have known about the Constanta orphanage? "What did you say?" she asked, sick to her stomach from the raki and then suddenly remembering dreams or visions or actual past times, when the woman with the fur hat on the frozen train platform had told her to protect the book, protect it with her life, or else surrender it to a man from her own country—was that it?

The woman had clapped her woolen gloves together. When she spoke, Miranda had been able to see her breath. "Something precious will be given, something stripped away," she'd said—the same woman Miranda had dreamed about the night before.

"Give it back," she said, reaching for the book. Markasev was standing before the fire. He was holding up a picture of her that he had found in the back pages, a posed portrait, taken when she finally had her braces off. "How beautiful," he said. "Beautiful face, beautiful eyes, beautiful hair," he said, laughing. She knew he was making fun of her.

Brenda threw some dry pine branches onto the fire, which spat and crackled and flared up. Then Markasev was squatting down again. He had his finger in the last chapter—"You have not read? But here you are, your father, mother. Everything. Every day. Here we are," he said, running his finger along the lines of the last page. "Here on this hillside, here." He was shrugging and grimacing, holding the book out toward her.

"So," he said. "Would you like to come to Bucharest?"

She felt tears in her eyes. And suddenly it was as if part of her were rising up into the sky, looking down at the hillside, at the fire and the people grouped around it. From the shelter of the trees, a white-faced opossum looked toward her. Then Miranda moved up even farther into the cold air, and she could see spread out below her the town where she'd grown up, the art museum and the lights of Water Street, the old house on the green where Rachel and Stanley lay asleep, the flat roof of Andromeda's house on Syndicate Road. She saw the college buildings poking up below her through the trees. Cars drove slowly down Route 6, peering around corners as if looking for something. She watched a yellow dog run across the museum parking lot and then into the tangle of underbrush.

After a moment she forced herself to smile. "Yes," she said, "I would like that," and with a casual, small gesture, Markasev let the book drop into the flames.

Peter came down the hill. Shouting, he grabbed hold of Markasev's arm. Miranda was on her knees, snatching at the book with her bare hands, but it was horrible how quickly it erupted with fire, how quickly and completely it was consumed. There must have been something in the onion-skin, the scented leather, that allowed it to explode before her eyes.

RIGHT BEFORE MARKASEV dropped the book, Andromeda realized something. She'd been talking with Brenda while Miranda was taking her stuff out of her backpack. She'd been trying to figure out what Brenda and Kevin Markasev were doing up here in the middle of the night. As Markasev told Miranda about Romania, Brenda was muttering in her thick, slow accent, and as she listened, Andromeda felt a shiver of alarm, a "frisson," as her mother might have said, that started at her tailbone and climbed the length of her back: "So. Finally you are here. I am bored from waiting. Many nights this week we wait for you, light fires, drink raki. Kevin says this time we have to smoke you out. He is clever. Here you are!"

A line of gold caps shone along the left side of her jaw. Andromeda smiled, too. "I don't get it."

"Don't you? At school. Kevin says we have two chances. But we can't get into the west corridor. Doors too strong. Kevin says, 'No problem.' We do what we can."

"You were there tonight?"

"No, stupid. Last night."

Andromeda had made a big mistake. Kevin Markasev was squatting behind Miranda, leafing through her book. Miranda was staring up at him with an adoring expression—no, not that, but it was close to that.

Sure, Andromeda had been pissed off about the car. Of course she was still irritated, so when she saw Kevin and Brenda at the bonfire, she had thought it was a good idea to bring them and Miranda together, partly because of the Romanian thing—if Miranda was going to obsess about it, she might as well have her nose pressed into it.

Partly also, she couldn't stand the idea of Peter Gross and Miranda walking home together by themselves. Now she looked up toward Peter; he was running down the hill, alert as she was to the problem. Too late: Markasev dropped the book just as Andromeda lunged forward and stretched out her hand. And maybe she might have even caught in on the fly, except Brenda held her back, grabbed hold of her shirt and held on even after Andromeda had given her a backhand slap across her ugly face—too late. It was all too late. Miranda was poking at the embers with a stick, but the book was gone.

Whimpering, she staggered up away from the circle of the bonfire. Andromeda got up to follow. She followed her toward where the woods began a hundred yards away. But then she turned back when she heard Peter shout; he was having a harder time with Markasev this time, and Brenda was there, too. It was difficult for Peter with his one hand. But he was quick and turned away, and then Markasev was sprawling backward on the ground. He stopped to let him up, which was stupid because Brenda was behind him. And there was something in her hand that she'd pulled out of her shirt, and Markasev was getting up. Andromeda paused to pull a stick up from the fire, and she was thinking Peter Gross and she could take care of these putzes, these *neciopliti*. Nothing was more sure than that. She was happy to do it, happier than she'd been all night. The stick was charred along its length except for where she held it. Its point was a mass of sparks that made a pattern in the air. A line of red followed the tip, and as she pulled back her hand the line seemed to thicken and hold its shape as the air changed around her.

MIRANDA STAGGERED ACROSS the field into the shelter of the woods. She crawled into the shelter of the trees and pushed herself into the protruding roots of a big hickory tree. Shuddering and crying, she tried to vomit, tasting again the raki's bitter taste. She rubbed her forehead into the ragged bark, pressed it into the unyielding wood.

At the moment when Andromeda's stick described a long gash of red, she fell asleep in the shelter of the hickory tree. Later she would be surprised how in a moment like that, she would be able to lose consciousness. But then she would imagine that it wasn't ordinary sleep, but rather a dazed trance in which the hickory tree was gone, and she saw standing in front of her a shadowy, enormous figure. Nor was there anything comforting about the embrace of those hard arms, and she was bruising her forehead against the front of the woman's rough coat; it was in wintertime, that's all she understood, a cold, dark wintertime. And the woman was speaking to her in a language she didn't know: "What's done cannot be changed. You must find Rodica and Gregor Splaa. Rodica the Gypsy will tell you what to do. Go to the house by the dam. She is in the house by the dam. I've left you a letter, and a letter from your mother. De Graz and Prochenko will protect you now as they always have, so there is nothing to fear, nothing . . . ," and then something else which she was unable to grasp, because already she could feel herself waking up, could feel the dream receding just as it was taking shape.

Just as she imagined she could see the woman's face, she found herself awake. The words that seemed so urgent hovered around her and then disappeared, because now she was awakened by the sound of screaming, a hoarse, constant, desperate screaming, and she recognized Peter's voice.

Time had gone by, she knew. Gray shadows hung around her, and it was very cold. Morning was coming, and as she stood up, she saw the thin white trunks of the birch trees glowing in the mist. Her head hurt. Peter screamed, and she didn't know where he was. The sound was all around her. But then she stumbled out into the frozen meadow and saw him crouching underneath a barberry bush. She saw the bright red berries. He was holding out his arms, and she could see he had two hands.

At first she could not take this in, because it made no sense. In her dazed state she noticed it but didn't understand it. Nor could she tell, when she got close, whether he was screaming in terror or in pain. She herself felt light-headed, dizzy, stupid. "De Graz and Prochencko," she thought, names from her dream, names that had haunted her throughout her life—Peter's hand had a mark on it, a raspberry-colored birthmark. She knelt in front of him on the white, frozen ground and watched as he stretched out his hands, the left one small and familiar, the right one pale and huge, a man's hand on a boy's arm. Its fingernails were chipped and dirty, its knuckles thick and gnarled. The back of it was covered with black hair. The birthmark was below his thumb, in the shape of a bull's head.

She thought she'd seen that mark before. "Does it hurt?" she asked stupidly, looking into his panicked face, his open mouth. For a moment she was surprised to see him look so young and vulnerable. His face was gray with terror, as if his skin had turned pale under his tan. His curly hair hung limp and damp. His eyes were dark and wide and big, and they were staring at her, and there was something about them that was both familiar and un-familiar. It occurred to her that she had rarely looked into his face. One of them had always been looking away.

His lips were thin, his teeth crooked with wide gaps between them. Why was she studying his face as if she were trying to memorize his fea-tures? She looked down at his hands again and grasped hold of his hands, clasping them in her own until his cries subsided to a kind of whimpering. Then, standing up, holding his left hand, she pulled him to his feet.

The trees had lost their leaves. Snow was on the ground, though it had blown away in patches.

Suddenly she remembered the book, the fire, Markasev. Where was An-dromeda? "Come," she said, and pulled him away from the woods, out into the meadow. Where was her backpack, her bracelet, her Roumanian things? She pulled him to the crest of the hill, and for a moment she could not bring herself to look down through the mist over the bare arms of the trees. For a moment she held and captured in her mind the view that she had seen a thousand times. Then timidly, but with a sense also of exhilaration, she stared out over the empty, wooded valley, where she could not see the mar-ble bulk of the art museum, or the brick library, or the gold dome, or the spire of the Congo Church, or any building whatever. There were no streetlights in that winter morning, no streets, no town, nor anything except the woods and mountains where they'd always been.

From Peter she heard a quick, sobbing intake of breath. She held him by the hand, dragging him back to the cold, extinguished circle of the bonfire. Bottles lay scattered about, and a crumpled paper bag. The girl and Marka-sev were gone. But Miranda's backpack was there, thank God. And in the shelter of the boulder, curled around herself, slept a yellow animal, a big yel-low dog, which at first they didn't recognize.

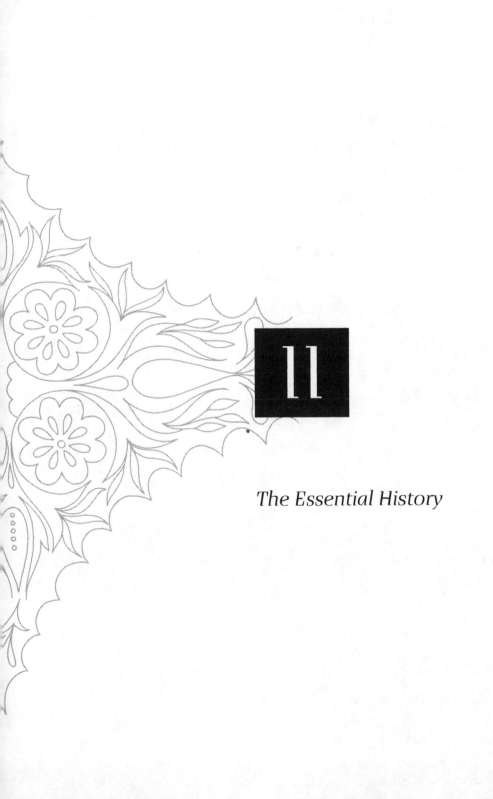

11

The Essential History

4   *Nicola Ceausescu*

THE BARONESS CEAUSESCU was not given to abstract thought. But on horseback sometimes, or to quiet her anxiety, she indulged herself. And since she'd read the papers of Aegypta Schenck, she'd had to question what she knew, what everybody knew. The universe spreads out from the center of the Earth. The planets turn around it in concentric spheres—first, the moon's sphere, drawn by the moon's watery orbit. Second, the wall of fire, the orbit of the sun. Then there are four planets, Mercury, Mars, Venus, and Jupiter. Beyond them lies the sphere of light and aether, heaven itself, the galaxies and stars.

But if this is so, how could there be another world that revolves around a star? The Earth itself sits motionless. Jupiter made it and molded it, but then stopped. Venus scratched with her thumbnail the line of the Danube river and its small tributary, the Dambovita. But she did not draw the road that follows the riverbank, along which the Baroness Ceausescu spurred her horse upstream toward Bucharest on a February afternoon.

She felt the heavy, shifting muscle of the horse, the jarring trot as she slowed to join a wider way. Always, when she was in the saddle, she tried to isolate herself, pretend she was alone with her horse on a deserted road. As she came into the environs of the city, that proved more and more difficult—flushed and sweating, she remembered her conversation with Aegypta Schenck. In these matters there was such uncertainty.

Triumphant in the burning house, the baroness had half expected the Popescu girl to appear out of the smoke, once the book that held her was destroyed. That was why she had brought the soldiers, she told herself now. It wasn't because she was afraid of the old woman.

Or perhaps the girl would just materialize in the cage in the baron's laboratory. Or, at worst, in the North American forest, which was why she'd dispatched Raevsky at such expense—none of that had happened yet.

No, the girl's book was the important one, and the book the baroness had burned was just a decoy, a fishing lure that the old woman had not lifted a finger to protect—she was a powerful conjurer after all.

And that was why she was so smug. She did not think the baroness had yet discovered the book inside the book—no, the girl's book was the one to burn. Markasev would do it, or might do it with a little luck. It was frustrating to rely on others, when everything was so unsure.

Of course it was unsure. How could anything be imaginary and also real? The baroness pondered this. Then, irritated, she suppressed her thoughts, because she loved this part of her journey on this bright, unseasonably warm day—the wide wind, the thud of her mare's hooves on the rough road, the smell of sweat and leather, and the great city up ahead. In those days nothing in Europe could rival the richness of the sultan's court, or the palace in Alexandria where the Pharaohs (brother and sister, husband and wife) sat on alabaster thrones side by side. Since the burning of Rome, nothing could rival the splendor of Meroe and Timbuctu. But of all northern cities, Bucharest was the proudest and most beautiful. That winter day as the baroness rode toward it through the outlying farms, it seemed to gather and rise around her out of the mist of the plain. She rode under the Vacaresti Arch and up the Boulevard of Martyrs, past white cliffs of public buildings, light-struck hills of palaces and apartment blocks. Ahead of her was the blue dome of the temple and the long machicolated wall.

Formerly the Ceausescu family had kept a stable at the city wall. That was in the days before the baron had died, and there was still money. Now the baroness rented horses as she needed them, from a public stable on the Tineretului road. There she hung up her mud-stained riding coat, revealing underneath the gray jacket and tight trousers of an imperial cadet. She stood in the stone arch of the door for a moment, smoking a cigarette, which was not a constant habit. Then she slipped into the stream of people moving through the gate. Most, if they didn't look too closely at her face, took her as she appeared: an eighteen-year-old boy, narrow shoulders hunched, hands in his jacket pockets, whistling impudently as he sauntered through the crowd. And even those who looked carefully might have been fooled, so smooth her skin, so glossy her short, chestnut hair.

Others of her rank took cabs or private carriages. But for many years she had strolled like this through the cobblestone streets, even sometimes when her husband was alive. Sometimes she had left the old baron in bed to walk alone through the small ways.

Now abruptly she came into the town on the other side of the Curtea Veche, the Old Court. She was near the Gypsy pawnbroker where she had found the book. Her way meandered through the wooden houses and led gradually uphill. After a few minutes she passed through the iron fence and into the park that surrounded the Cleopatra Temple.

The weather was mild and she had come early to her rendezvous, so she spent a quarter of an hour walking up and down the gravel paths, admiring the polled, naked branches of the pear trees under the red sky. But when the tower bell rang six o'clock, she walked up the steps of the church into the alcove. There was a stoup set into the wall. The baroness moistened the tip of her gloved finger and drew the mark of the goddess onto her forehead.

When an additional five minutes had passed and no one had joined her, she pushed through the swinging doors into the church itself. The lamps in the nave were lit, but instead she passed through the stone screen into the aisle on the right-hand side. Up ahead, candles decorated the shrine of the goddess, but it was dark where she was walking until the sun came from behind a cloud, and the last sunlight of the evening pressed through the long windows. It reddened the floor under her boots. Then suddenly both walls were lined with images from the life of Cleopatra, the stained glass on one side showing the painted statues on the other. The baroness strolled from the beginning of the story toward the end. Though familiar, it was always poignant to her, a narrative that had kept her company throughout her life. She glanced up at the window that showed the presentation of the young princess, surrounded by the kneeling kings of Asia. But her crown was not secure, and after her father's death she had to fight for it against fools and rebels and her own brother. She bore a child to the god Julius, but returned to Egypt after he was murdered. There she ruled alone until she was betrayed.

The baroness was halfway down the aisle when the sun disappeared again, the images faded into darkness. In front of her was Cleopatra's shrine, where a single, slender candle burned. The baroness paused, deposited a five-leu piece into the box, and lit another candle under the image of the queen offering her breast to the snake, a furious expression on her face.

The baroness could scarcely afford even this small indulgence. Her husband had owned a farm outside the city, and she had just come from arranging the sale of it—a necessary payment to her creditors, regardless of how things turned out with the Popescu girl.

When she'd arranged this meeting, she'd expected to have the girl in hand. But Markasev had been too slow. It couldn't be helped. "Sir," whispered the man behind her.

She had been aware of him for several moments, but now he spoke. She turned and saw, as she'd expected, the charming and handsome junior attaché from the German embassy, Herr Greuben, whose generosity helped pay the household bills. Once a month she met with him in some anonymous location and told him gossip from the various parties he had not been invited to. It was harmless, really, and the money was important. Things had been difficult since her husband's death eight years before.

Today was the feast of Caesarion, commemorating the birth of Cleopatra's son. Now in the belly of the temple, acolytes were preparing for a festival mass, while the baroness and Herr Greuben walked up and down the west aisle. As always, Greuben was courteous and full of jokes. He was younger than the baroness, and she was aware of a desire to please him. Aware also of her own tendency to act on impulse, to make things happen by predicting them—"And one more bit of news," she said. "There's a rumor that Miranda Popescu has been found."

Greuben turned to face her, and in the candlelight she caught a glimpse of something in his face. Then he smiled, urbane and civilized again, maybe a little embarrassed. But for a moment she had glimpsed a hidden part of him, something savage and mean, and she felt a shiver of recognition.

All human souls have at the same time an animal nature that shows itself at moments. In Herr Greuben the baroness recognized a small fierce beast, a wolverine, perhaps. Now instantly she regretted what she'd said; it was too soon, too soon. Always she acted without thinking. Her rashness would destroy her, and yet it was her strength as well. She might have known the Germans would be interested. They still held the girl's mother in the house at Ratisbon, if she wasn't dead.

Once the baroness possessed the girl, the white tyger, Miranda Popescu, once she had caught her in the cage she'd built for her in her husband's laboratory, it would be time to weigh her choices. The obvious one was also the safest—to turn her over to the empress in return for various considerations. But in this moment, with Roumania so shaken by internal struggles, so menaced by foreign enemies, maybe the empress—no, it was important to choose the winning side. The empress was no friend of hers. Since the baron's death, the empress had spared no effort to impoverish and humiliate her. And there was always her son's future to consider.

"This information would be worth a great deal," said Herr Greuben.

She shrugged. "I will enquire."

Now suddenly he seemed less congenial and less at ease, anxious, in fact, to leave her. Together they passed through the doors into the alcove, then onto the outer steps.

Outside the sky was dark. Greuben put his hand on her sleeve, a familiar gesture. She tried to pull away, but for a moment he held tight. "There are German citizens in bondage here," he said. "The time is coming when my government will not ignore them. Then we will know our friends. Do you understand me?" he said, as if he were speaking to a servant. Angrily, she shook him off and turned away down the worn stone steps into the park.

How could she have been so stupid? It had been foolish enough to boast to the girl's aunt, Aegypta, whose house had burned in that regrettable accident. But she had nowhere to go with the story, except to those who knew it already. Now the rumor would fly, and the baroness was connected to it. She strode home, kicking at the stones.

All her husband's land in Cluj had already been sold, and that autumn, finally, his ancestral home, though it had been so heavily mortgaged she had realized nothing. She had spent so much on Raevsky and his men, now she had little left for emergencies—what a waste of money that had been! Aegypta Schenck had not even mentioned it or recommended it in her instructions. She'd implied that Markasev could bring the girl straight back to Bucharest. But the baroness had thought it best to cover every last eventuality. Not that she had heard anything since she'd seen Raevsky off on the train to Bremershaven more than three months earlier. They should have had plenty of time to take the steamer to New York and to get into position. But it was all so damned uncertain—everything in that continent of darkness, that blank wilderness. Only desperate people found their way across the sea, English-speakers, trying to cut a new home out of the forest after the loss of their miserable islands. Failure was possible. Raevsky might already be dead. Time and space were not the same in the two worlds.

But it was worth the money, worth the risk. She could not continue as she had, poorer and more insignificant each year. The goddess herself—Cleopatra or Fortuna—had put Aegypta Schenck's book into her hands. The goddess had given her this chance, and she would take it.

Ordinarily she would have chosen a more circuitous route, but now she hurried home through the dark streets, down the Calea Victoriei, through Elysian Fields and down Saltpetre Street. Her house was tall and narrow in a block of tall, narrow, brick houses. A cartouche of the red pig hung above the door, high on the wall where it could not be defaced. But there were some obscenities scrawled in chalk on the sidewalk in front of the steps, under the gaslight. While her husband was alive, she had been too powerful to insult.

Jean-Baptiste, her steward, waited in the hall. She handed him her gloves. "The mail has come?"

"Of course. There is your invitation to the Winter Keep tomorrow night."

She climbed the stairs to the suite on the fourth floor. From the landing she went first into the boudoir, where the lamp was lit. Then in her dressing room she changed her clothes, kicking off the boots and throwing the jacket onto a chair. She chose a shirt from the long closet, and then went barefoot into what had once been her husband's bedroom and was now her own, a beautiful, spare space, lined with yellow wallpaper. She had to check on Markasev. Buttoning her shirt, she strode past the unmade bed and into the far corner of the room.

A small door, its knob hidden by a secret panel, led to what had been her husband's laboratory, where he had engaged in alchemical research. It was a dark, windowless room with quilted walls. Much of his equipment—the alembics, kerotakis, beakers, pipettes, and glass tubes—still gathered dust on the tables where he had labored to turn base metals into gold, a painstaking and prohibitively expensive process, as it had turned out. Purify, always purify, though he had not been successful with himself, the empress's government, or even his young son.

Light came from oil lamps set in sconces in the walls. In the middle of the floor there was an iron cage three meters square. It was intended for Miranda Popescu, but Markasev now lay in it on his cold bed, a blanket wrapped around his naked legs.

The baroness cursed under her breath. Was it too much to ask for a little luck, for something to proceed as planned? As she came into the room, she had pictured in her mind what she wished to see—the boy and girl together, naked and cold, clinging to each other to keep warm, just stirring with a rose of color on their skin.

According to von Schenck's instructions, she might expect some variant of that. But the boy lay unconscious. So he had not yet succeeded in finding the book. He had not yet succeeded in bringing the girl back. When he did, the baroness would reward him as he deserved, would take him out of this cold cage and give him a room of his own—a room with windows. She would send him to school.

Near him, five baby pigs slumbered in a wooden crate. One had a line of tattooed numbers on its foreleg. The baroness could see the blue letters and numbers under the pink hair. As she watched, the pig began to stir.

FOR HIS PART, when he'd separated from Nicola Ceausescu on the temple steps, Hans Greuben waited for a moment and then followed her, admiring even in the cadet's uniform her slim hips and waist. Those high boots, those trousers with their purple stripes, he told himself, concealed superlative long legs, superlative firm buttocks that he imagined pushing apart, marking with strong fingers—a brief fantasy. Then he turned away when they reached the Calea Victoriei, sauntering north through the evening crowds.

On the boulevard there was a chilly wind, but he did not close his long black coat. Nor did he turn off to the left when he reached the corner of the Strada Millo and the German embassy. Instead he continued straight on to the Piata Enescu and the Athenée Palace Hotel, a building that irritated him with its decadent luxury—he himself could not afford to stay there. He could scarcely have afforded a drink at the bar.

At the malachite reception counter, he gave his name. And while the clerk telephoned ahead, he entered the brass cage of the elevator and rose to the fifth floor, where he found the elector's suite—the door was open. Light spilled from it across the rose medallion of the carpet, and he could hear the elector's soft and modulated voice call out to him before the cage had scarcely closed. "Dear chap, dear fellow"—friendly words in which Greuben nevertheless detected a hint of condescension, though it was always welcome, he reminded himself, to hear German spoken in this nest of Francophonic savages. "Dear chap—please!"

Always in the elector's presence he had to steel himself to the man's ugliness. Now as he crossed the threshold he held out his hand. When the elector took it in his small, soft, effeminate fingers, could he feel how he made Greuben's skin shiver and creep?

Greuben smiled; he did not think so. What was the use of diplomatic training if you could not hide such things? Even so, for a moment he hesitated before he looked into the elector's face. He let his gaze slide from the crimson cummerbund up the elegant shirt-front and starched collar, out of which rose the elector's white neck and smallpox-ravaged face, a cratered mass of blotches and scars, out of which peered two enormous, penetrating eyes—women's eyes, Greuben thought, with long lashes and a kind of shimmering surface, as if, despite his evident good humor, the man was going at any moment to burst into tears.

"You catch me just before I'm going out—one of these tiresome dinners of the German Friendship League. But come in just for a moment; I am glad to see you! You have something for me?"

He was not about, Greuben reflected, to offer him a drink, though an array of bottles and soda water siphons lined the sideboard. He gave the impression both of being in a hurry and having nothing but time, doubtless an aristocratic trait. He was, after all, the hereditary Elector of Ratisbon, with an hereditary seat in the Reichstag. And though he held no official post here, he had the highest possible connections at the embassy, which did not keep him from making separate arrangements with a junior attaché.

Now he closed the door behind them. Though it was hard to interpret the expressions of his small, ruined face, again Greuben detected some impatience. So he said at once, "I have come from my monthly interview with the Baroness Ceausescu."

The elector smiled, revealing his perfect teeth. "That disgusting whore," he said. "What did she want?"

Then after a moment, after reconsidering, he went on—"Not that she wasn't a brilliant artist once! Fifteen years ago—I can't remember—I saw her in Milan, in a production of *Ariadne auf Naxos*—my God! She was a magician!" Here he raised his bunched fingers to his crimson lips. "What did she want, besides our money?"

"She told me Miranda Popescu had been found."

The elector's smile disappeared. He stepped across the carpet, and Greuben found himself looking down at those limpid eloquent eyes. "Where?"

Greuben could smell the elector's sweet breath, with a hint nevertheless of some astringent fragrance—was it caraway? "She didn't tell me. She said it was a rumor."

"Yes, of course. But she is able to find out?"

"She will make enquiries."

"Ah!"

As if he had only just noticed he was standing too close, the elector stepped backward to the middle of the floor. "The white tyger of Roumania!" he continued. "You understand why this is important?"

Greuben wondered if he did. Walking up from Cleopatra's Temple, he had rehearsed this conversation, because he wanted to avoid a certain subject. He wanted to dispense his information without reference to the elector's great defeat, his failure, without which he doubtless would have been prime minister of the German Republic, or at least foreign secretary, despite his ugliness.

At the time of the change of government, when Valeria Dragonesti had been pushed onto the Roumanian throne, the Elector of Ratisbon had planned an invasion, a liberation of the German-speaking sections of the country. The excuse had been the murder of Prince Frederick Schenck von Schenck, a distant cousin on his father's side. The widow had taken refuge in Germany—he still held her in his *schloss* in Ratisbon. Naturally, Greuben had thought, he'd be interested in the daughter. A regiment of German cavalry had been cut to pieces at the border, at Kaposvar.

Now Greuben didn't mention to any of that. "A symbol of Roumanian nationalism," he murmured.

The elector seemed relieved. "Yes," he said. "Hans—yes, that's very good."

He took another step backward, and brought his small hands together. "A symbol of national aspiration," he went on. "Roumania is divided now. The empress is unpopular, and General Antonescu. We must not allow them to be supplanted by a more . . . charismatic or . . . inspiring figure in the people's mind. Not at this . . . delicate moment, when our interests . . ."

His words trailed away. Halfway through this speech, he'd turned his back on Greuben. He had wandered over to the window overlooking the city and stood mumbling there, his hands clasped behind his back. Now his voice came sharply, clearly, though he didn't turn around. "You will arrange for me to meet that creature, that gaudy prostitute, on the behalf of the German government. Doubtless she will have been invited to the empress's reception. I myself cannot attend. . . ."

There was no dear fellow now, no dear chap. After a few moments, Greuben felt himself dismissed like a servant. He stood for a moment in silence before letting himself out.

WHEN THE DOOR WAS CLOSED, the Elector of Ratisbon put his hand to his forehead, feeling the first indication of a migraine headache—a small sound he could almost hear, like the cracking of an egg. He stood looking south across the piata toward the north façade of the empress's palace, the colonnade and the massed bulk of the Winter Keep. Perhaps he himself should attend her reception the next evening—no. He could already tell his headache would be incapacitating. And he was not convinced he could control his feelings—the white tyger! He had had her once!

Twenty years before, he had let the mother into his house, let her take refuge there along with her thrice-cursed sister-in-law, Aegypta Schenck von Schenck, who had disgraced and befouled a proud German name. Two women and a baby had thwarted him, and while he kept the mother on behalf of his government, he had let the aunt and the daughter slide through his fingers with the plans to his great project, two years in preparation, till it was betrayed by a superstitious and benighted woman who even now did not cease to thwart him and constrain him, and who even now could not see, half-German as she was, that the future of Roumania lay with his country, with modern science and republican government, with land reform and technological innovation, and not with magic and barbaric superstition, and empty genuflection on the altars of empty and nonexistent gods. He had failed once. This time he would not fail.

But where was the girl now? Where had Aegypta Schenck hidden her all these years? In what corner of Roumania was she hiding, or where was she abroad?

5   *The Attack at the Ford*

THE DOG LIFTED her yellow muzzle, sniffed at the cold morning air. She barked once, howled once, then pricked up her ears. Peter Gross held out his new dark hand. "You see?" he cried, pointing to the hook-shaped scar on her right foreleg. "You see?" he cried, catching at the silver rings along her ear until she growled and showed her teeth. Then he pulled back, raised his left hand, afraid of getting bitten, Miranda thought. "It's her," he said. "You know it is. Look at her eyes."

First things first. Stanley had once told her that the way you get through things is one at a time, or you'll be overwhelmed. Only morons see the big picture, he'd once said—something like that. So now Miranda rubbed her nose, then rummaged through her backpack, which she'd found on the frozen grass next to the extinguished fire. Pushing her fingers through the leather laces, she felt the shawl, the beaded purse, the empty, crumpled manila envelope where the book had been. But the bracelet was there and the rest of her Romanian things—Markasev had not robbed her, at least. But how stupid she was feeling, how dizzy and light-headed—still, first things first. There was a flashlight that might come in handy.

She slung the backpack over her shoulder, then went down on one knee.

She reached out her fingers, and the dog reached up to smell them and lick them as Miranda scratched her ears.

"Hey," Miranda said.

The dog lay curled in a nest of clothes, a gray Donna Karan T-shirt and black sports bra, red Victoria's Secret panties and black bicycle pants—that combination was so Andromeda, Miranda thought. "Are you okay?" she asked.

Almost she expected the dog to speak. Instead it whimpered, licked her wrist, then yawned. And she didn't seem injured, didn't start or yip when Miranda ran her hands down her legs, stripping the red underwear from around one of her back paws—Miranda would tease Andromeda about that, when she saw her again. And she'd pack the clothes. Andromeda would thank her later. The T-shirt was frozen stiff.

Miranda sucked in the cold air. Almost it made her weak, light-headed, sick. She dug her hands into the rich fur of the dog's chest and neck, seeing each hair that curled along her muzzle, seeing her cold, silver eyes, the surface of them dusted with some other colors, red and black and blue.

Then she stood up. She was shivering, and her teeth were chattering. "We should go back," she said.

"Yes," cried Peter, "I have to go home. My father . . ." His eyes were bleary, his nose red. "Can we call my father from your house? I have to go to the hospital."

What was he talking about? He was acting like a kid. But Miranda looked out over the familiar mountains. The meadow, the open crest of the hill was smaller here, just a bare place among the trees.

"Where do you think they are?" she asked, meaning Markasev and that girl Brenda, but Peter didn't answer. "Can you walk?" she said, and the dog got up, turned in a circle, limped a few steps and then bounded away, which was encouraging.

More than once Stanley had described the scientific process in his laboratory—small victories. Narrow focus. Step by step. "We'll go down," Miranda said. It was too cold in her sweatshirt and no gloves.

And maybe Stanley was right, because right then, as if liberated by the decision to move, the words of the old woman or her aunt or whoever it was came back to her. The ice house. Gregor Splaa. "Come on," Miranda said, turning downhill.

The dog went on down the slope, the frozen hillocks dusted with snow. Now she looked back with one paw raised.

"Where are we?" Peter cried.

He didn't understand, Miranda thought. He couldn't smell the difference in the air as they came down under trees that were ancient and immense, oak and white pine and shag hickory. And as they came off the hill he stared around, as if expecting the walls of the art museum to come together suddenly among the trunks of the trees, or else their broken ruins. "We'll go to your house," he said. "Don't worry, my father can come pick me up. I'll call him at work. It doesn't matter. He'll find his way. He'll know."

"We're not going home," she said.

The flatness, the sureness in her own voice surprised her. And it wasn't true—she'd read a lot of books like this, where the girl wakes up and she's a beautiful princess in another world. But she always goes back again. She always goes home. "We're not going home," she heard herself repeat.

Then in a little while she went on. "This is a different place, but it's connected. So we're not strangers here. A lot of what we know can help us."

They stood beneath a hawthorn tree near where the barbed wire had been. A hawthorn—Stanley had been a nut for the names of trees. The dog came prancing back, and Miranda squatted down again. She dug her hands into the fur of the dog's throat and let her lick her wrists. Already the flesh around Andromeda's earrings was swollen and inflamed, so Miranda picked at the tiny clasps until the rings fell open. She slipped the tiny silver loops into the pocket of her black jeans, rubbed the sore place with her stiffened fingers, then bent down to bury her face in the dog's fur. Something will be stripped away.

Now almost she felt the urge that Peter felt, to search among these trees for the exact place where her house had stood. But what was the use of that? That's not what her aunt had said. "Come on. We've got to find some shelter and some winter clothes. We've got to find the ice house. You know this place. See where the land slopes down. That will be Christmas Brook."

She rose to her feet, and the dog jumped away. It was true—Peter knew this country like the back of his own hand. Looking at him now, she could see the surge of recognition as he looked around. "We're not wandering around until we freeze," she said. "We've got to have a plan. My aunt told me to find Gregor Splaa."

Peter was examining his forearm, scratching at it. "That's good," he said, his voice brittle and shrill. "Only he's been dead for fifty years."

"I don't think so," Miranda said. But she was reassured by his attempt at sarcasm, reassured by the dog's evident joy as she dug her muzzle into the new snow—small victories. "She said the house on the dam, but that must be the ice house. She said we'd find instructions there, and people who would help us. Prochenko and de Graz, and someone blind."

It was good to listen to instructions, good for both of them, and Miranda could hear the calming sound of purpose in her own voice. But at the same time, a bunch of doubts came back—Peter was right. Gregor Splaa was the name on the stone bench. These other names, this sense of recognition— Stanley had told her how the mind plays tricks. Often before she'd had dreams that seemed real.

She said, as if to reassure herself, "And if Gregor Splaa is alive here, and the ice house is here, then maybe there are other people, too. People that we know."

Now she saw in her mind's eye Rachel and Stanley in their old house on the green. She saw them going down to the kitchen, making coffee, sitting at the oak table with the lion's head feet, which she had decorated with blue nail polish when she was six. She had seen them making English muffins and reading *The Berkshire Eagle*, then calling up to her.

She sucked at the cold air to clear her head. "I know it's not much," she said. "But it's a start. If we can't find them, we'll figure out something else."

Now Peter was staring at her with a puzzled expression, as if he were noticing her for the first time that morning. "What happened to you?" he said. "What's wrong with your face?"

She put her hand up to her nose as if to brush away some smut. A beautiful princess, she'd thought. No—maybe an ugly princess. What was wrong with her face? What was he talking about? Why did he say that?

"Look at yourself," he said. "You're different."

Which maybe didn't sound so bad. She didn't feel any different. "Of course I am," she said.

Something would be stripped away. Maybe Gregor Splaa would have a mirror. First things first.

In the meantime she was right about Christmas Brook. After a few more steps downhill, she could hear the sound of water. Before, the stream had been a tiny, seasonal affair, a dry rut most of the year or else a muddy bog. Only at the ice house had it been visible year-round. But now she clambered down a small ravine and there it was, rimmed at the edges by shelves of shattered ice, coiling through the trees at the bottom of the hill.

The dog walked downstream a few paces and then looked back, her forepaw raised above the snow. Which was typical—Andromeda had always had a crummy sense of direction. "Where are you going?" Miranda asked. "It's this way." She wondered if the dog could understand her, wondering also what name she should give her now—not Andromeda, surely. "Andromeda," she called out, and the dog cocked her head, then dropped her muzzle to the snow. "Come on," Miranda said. "Let's find the ice house. Then we'll figure things out." And then to Peter: "Can you take us there?" although she knew the way. They'd just have to follow the brook upstream.

But she'd gotten Peter moving. Now there was a change in him, too, a childlike curiosity. He stood above her on the bank, an expression in his face she recognized. Always he had had a sense of purpose in these woods. He stood cradling his big right arm in his left arm. But maybe now he'd be interested in finding his way, interested in this larger landscape, which nevertheless was so familiar to them both. He took a few steps along the stream bed, and reached up tentatively with his right hand to push away a drooping branch. Where had she seen that mark before, that red birthmark below his thumb?

Snow had sifted over the pine needles and dead leaves. The dog ran on ahead. Last in line, Miranda stole a glance behind them as they turned upstream. Then she hurried after Peter's retreating back; she wanted to get in front of him. But it was easy to be distracted and go slow. She felt she couldn't look at anything, because if she did, then she would stare at it forever. It was as if the ground had come to life. Even that simple landscape of black tree trunks, snow, and black dead leaves filled her with an excitement that was hard to bear. The stream sang in its bed. Above their heads the cold light seemed to glow. "Sometimes you read a story," Miranda found herself saying. "You wake up from a nightmare and you're glad. Sometimes you wake up—it doesn't matter. You can't . . . ," she said.

The dog came prancing back. She jumped up, licked at Miranda's hands. "I'm sorry," Miranda said, lamely and absurdly. But the dog pulled her head away. Andromeda had never remembered or cared about her dreams. She was awake, scratching at the soft snow.

Peter stood above them on a rock, and he'd gone back to cradling his new hand and arm as if the bones were broken and the flesh were dead. "I'm sorry," Miranda repeated, too softly for him to hear. Because there was no way she was not responsible for what had happened, one way or another.

Peter wanted to tell her something. "Look," he said. "Look there."

Miranda saw a trail of footprints following the stream. "What do you think?" she asked.

Again Miranda wondered about Kevin Markasev and the girl—where were they now? Where were they in these woods? She'd seen no footprints in the meadow up above, where the snow was blown away in patches.

But these weren't their prints. These were the large nailed boots of a man walking alone, not long before, she thought. "Come on," she said. "Let's hurry."

The dog went on ahead. Sometimes Miranda recognized a rock or a certain tree. Sometimes Peter pointed something out. "Look," he said. "That's the seventeenth green. Where the stream crosses by the water hazard. That's all gone. But look there."

He was pointing to a bare place in the trees, and a ring of strange, symmetrical hillocks where the traps had been. "My dad's a member," he said. "Every Tuesday. You didn't know that."

If trees had grown up over—what was it called—the fairway . . . ? Maybe they had gone into the future. In which case . . . She'd read books about that, too.

But how could there be no trace of anything, just these strange similarities? She pressed on, hurrying now, eager to see some kind of building or structure. "What makes you think the ice house will still be there?" Peter asked. "That's where the clubhouse was, by those big pines."

She pressed past him, and the dog ran on ahead. Dreams didn't have to mean anything. They were coming toward the dam from the opposite direction from Water Street. They sank into a ravine with the stream at the bottom and then came up suddenly through the trees. The land flattened out, and she was following the footprints and Andromeda's prints too, until they reached the ice house, and there it was. They came out of the woods and there it was, and she was relieved to see it—a small victory. The scale had changed, of course. The land was open, the hills larger and more gradual. The pool was bigger under its skin of ice. The house was bigger, too. And it wasn't staved in. On the contrary, it looked occupied, a wooden cottage trimmed with bark, with a thatched roof, diamond-paned windows, and smoke in the chimney.

"You were right," said Peter Gross.

ON THE SLOPE ABOVE THE house, under the shelter of the trees, four men stood watching. One stripped off his gauntlet to wipe his face. They'd had to run through the woods and the uneven snow, hoping to catch the girl before she reached the house.

Captain Raevsky and his men had spent the night on the hill, waiting in the bitter cold. They'd tried a different place on every night. Plans that had been vague even in Bucharest were insufficient now, and if it weren't for the presence of the house, he might not have known for sure that he was even in the right locality. His men had taken shifts and been out every day and night. It was too much to expect that they should find the right clearing, and for a week now he'd been convinced he was on a wild donkey chase, until he'd heard the boy screaming. Even then the echoes had confused him, and he wasn't expecting a boy's voice—just a girl's. Now they were paying for his stupidity.

He wiped his forehead with his sleeve. He was a bearded, grizzled, grim-faced man, worried now. He would be worried until the prize was safe, until they'd managed to cross out of this wood to Albany. It had been months since they'd left Bucharest for the steamship docks. They had come a long way through cold country just to make a mistake here at the end. If they had run a little faster, he could have taken Miranda Popescu before she reached the dam.

He could not wait to see what happened at the house. He didn't want to go inside and fetch her. No one had said anything about a boy. But the girl could not be harmed, which made things difficult.

He brought up his field glasses for a moment. A yellow dog was already on the shore of the ice pond. He could see the girl through the birch trees. She was older than he'd expected, older than the photograph the baroness had shown him: not a child at all, really—a young woman with the pale, narrow face and dark eyebrows of her father's family, and she looked older than the boy, who was holding his right arm. It was broken or swollen. But surely he recognized that boy. He tightened the focus, held him in the circle of his glasses—no, a chance resemblance to an older man.

The day before, and on several occasions since they'd made their camp, he had stood in this same place for several hours, hoping to catch a glimpse of the inhabitants of the little house. Toward evening a woman had come out, carrying a bucket to a line of cages under the eaves—rabbit hutches, he presumed. She'd opened one of the cages and took out something he couldn't see. As she did so, a man had crossed over the dam and gone inside without pausing or saying anything.

The first time he'd seen the woman and the man, he had known they were enemies. He'd kept his men away, and they'd kept to themselves— without a doubt they were Roumanians. He could tell just by the look of the place. The cottage could have stood in any mountain village between Cluj and Brasov. And they must have guns, the captain thought, to live here in the woods so far from any town. Worse, they must have some method of conjuring, for the woods here were full of savages and God knew what else. How had the boy and the girl come here after all, except through conjuring? Every night since they had left the Henry Hudson River and then paddled up the Hoosick into the deep wilderness, he'd kept watch over his men from midnight until dawn, looking out for wendigos and magic—his guide had told him. Men died in their blankets without a mark on them, claiming they'd seen wives or women who were far away.

The boy and the girl were going straight to the house as if they knew about it. Now the captain rubbed his lips, wondering if someone had gotten word to them. Without a doubt the inhabitants of this place were spies, sent on the same mission by an opposite power. Who was interested in the

white tyger? Anyone who hated Roumania, and quite a few who loved it—
were these the empress's people? Antonescu's? It was impossible to think
they might be Germans, Turks, but if not, what were they doing here? If so,
it was important to act quickly, before they were able to make plans.
Raevsky had left four men at the river camp, and the three he had here
were not a lot, not in these woods. He touched his heart, and as he did so,
he brushed with his fingers the embroidered emblem on his breast: his tal-
isman, his lady's emblem, the red pig of Cluj.

AT THE ORIGINAL ICE HOUSE, where Miranda and Peter had first met,
the spillway of the dam was made of stone, with a stone bridge across it.
Here, most of that was wood. A simple wooden bridge crossed the stream
over the mouth of the pond, and led immediately to the door of the little
house. Miranda came out of the trees and climbed the slope on the far side,
across the stream from the house, and there the bridge ended in a wall of
rough, big stones about two feet high, which soon subsided into the rocky
bank. Miranda climbed onto this wall, then walked along it to the wooden
bridge across the top of the dam. Under her feet, the water flowed into the
stream behind a broken column of ice.

The dog had run ahead of them as they'd climbed the bare bank, had
run out onto the ice over the middle of the pond. She was barking toward
a slope of evergreens on the other side, perhaps a hundred feet away. Miranda could see some men there, walking down through the trees. They
were dressed in green uniforms and green woolen caps.

One was bare-headed, and he raised his hand. "Miss Popescu," he
shouted. "Please."

Standing on the wall beside the bridge, Miranda felt another surge of relief. These people knew her, and the ice house was here, and these four men
were probably Gregor Splaa and the others her aunt had mentioned. De
Graz, maybe, or Prochenko—"Oh, thank God," she said, but when she
turned toward Peter she could see nothing in his face but confusion and
concern—"It's all right," she said. "Now it's all right." But the dog was
barking, Andromeda was barking, and the men paused on the bank. The
one who'd spoken was a gray-bearded man, and his gray hair was clipped
short. "Please," he repeated. "I have a message."

He spoke English with an accent. He put his hand inside his coat and pulled out a yellow envelope, which he held above his head. When he tried to step down off the bank, Miranda could hear Andromeda snarling, see the thick fur rise along her back.

"Oh," Miranda said. Her aunt had mentioned Gregor Splaa would have a letter. But now the stupid dog was running across the ice, and when she came to the man, she leapt at him and knocked him down. Two of the others pulled revolvers from their coats, but they hesitated when Miranda yelled, when she jumped down off the dam and came sliding toward them, following the dog's track. "Andromeda," she called, "Andromeda—it's all right!" until the dog let go of the man's arm and came back to the middle of the pond where Miranda was waiting. No cracks appeared, but there were threatening noises as the ice settled under their weight.

The man got to his feet. Miranda heard him cursing, and the others put their guns away—old-fashioned six-shooters, Miranda now noticed, with long octagonal muzzles. Rachel's father had a similar one in his collection of Civil War memorabilia.

Still, the guns weren't a good sign. She went down on her knees on the ice and put her arms around the dog's neck. The gray-haired man had circled round a bit, trying to find a place where the ice was solid. "Miss Popescu," he shouted with his gauntlet to his mouth. "I bring a letter from Roumania."

Miranda listened to the dog's low growl. She felt the vibrations of it in her arms and chest. The dog's breath was sweet, her teeth were white next to Miranda's ear.

"We come to fetch you, yes?" continued the gray-haired man. "We come to take you home."

"Gregor Splaa!" Miranda shouted. "Gregor Splaa! Is that you!"

"Please, miss," he called back. "No, I am Raevsky. Raevsky is my name." He tried to step onto the ice again, except his boot went through and he jumped back. "Please," he repeated. "Come see. I have a letter from the empress. Also chocolate."

Raevsky wasn't a name she recognized. And the letter should be from her aunt. And these men had guns. And as the gray-haired man was talking, one of his soldiers circled around the pond toward the stone wall where Peter was standing. He was a yellow-haired man in a green cap, and there was nothing friendly about him, nothing friendly about his movements, nothing friendly about any of them, Miranda decided, and Andromeda had known. She was growling with her lips pulled back.

Miranda turned and called to Peter. "Go to the house. Go knock on the door."

As she spoke, the door to the little house opened behind him on the other side of the bridge. A woman came out onto the step. Her red hair was streaked with white, and she spoke words Miranda couldn't hear.

The yellow-haired soldier was moving faster now. He had climbed the bank and jumped onto the wall that led to wooden bridge. He was only a few steps from Peter, and the old woman in back of him. "Look," she yelled, and Miranda heard her. She was pointing with her finger toward the soldier on the wall. "Red pig! Ceausescu."

The gray-haired man—Raevsky—had found a little spit of shoreline that curved into the ice, and he was closer to Miranda now. He didn't have to shout. "The empress wants to meet the daughter of such famous parents," he said.

Andromeda growled. Miranda stood up. Raevsky was smiling as he held the letter out. So maybe it was all right after all—she took one slippery step forward. But the woman on the dam was yelling, "Ceausescu, Ceausescu!" which made her stop.

THE CAPTAIN WAS STILL SMILING as he watched her expression change. He tried to appear happy as he learned the worst. The girl knew enough to be frightened of the baroness's name. She wouldn't come any closer. But maybe she was close enough, so he lurched forward off the bank and grabbed her by the wrist. The ice broke under his boots, but the water wasn't deep next to the shore. He floundered with the water around his shins, trying to drag the girl onto the bank where his man Carl was waiting with his arm outstretched, a revolver in his hand. There was no point in pretending now. The ice broke in a long crack, and the dog was coming at him, its claws scratching and slipping as it gathered itself to jump. But Carl had room. He fired, and the dog, poised in its leap, collapsed onto the ice a few meters from shore.

The captain ducked down with his arms around Miranda's waist. She was shouting at him, batting at his face, and she was stronger than he'd expected. There was blood on the ice, though the dog still moved, still dragged itself toward him.

Now there was another cry from the dam. He'd told his man Ferenc to circle round, but he hadn't meant him to go that far, especially if there was someone at the house. He should have kept to the trees, but there he was on the wall itself. The Gypsy woman hadn't budged from her own step, but there was the boy with the swollen, broken arm. He didn't look like much of a threat, but where was the other man? Someone must have a gun inside that house.

"Ferenc!" he called out. But then Miranda Popescu had shifted in his hands, was smacking him around the head again, and he had to find a way to pinion her arms. When he looked up again, he saw his man and the boy struggling together on the wall, and Ferenc had his gun out, and Raevsky listened for the shot—"Come back," he shouted. "I've got her now." But he didn't have her; she was fighting him again, and when he looked up his man had fallen on his back off of the wall, and the boy was still standing there. Carl and Alexandru circled round to help him, but now they stopped, confused by another gunshot, which was not from Ferenc's pistol. It came from a rifle, so it wasn't any of theirs. Raevsky could tell by the sound. He knew there was another man in the house, not just the old woman who was standing there. But the sound hadn't come from that direction. For a moment everything was still.

The captain's ears were ringing from Carl's first shot at the dog, which had come too close to his head. The second, from the rifle, had a flat, clapping sound, and the captain placed it somewhere on the hill behind and above them. Miranda Popescu had stopped resisting, and the captain stood with the water to his shins, his arms around her waist. He was waiting for the third shot.

They all waited. When it came, it slashed across Carl's cheek and left a wound. Another centimeter and it would have killed him. He dropped his gun and put his hand to his face, and the blood seeped through his fingers.

Miranda Popescu whispered in Raevsky's ear. "You let me go."

After that, things happened fast. Alexandru was pulling Carl into the shelter of the woods. Then he came back to help Raevsky. Not that it mattered—though she was straining against him, he had the girl's arms pinned. Her face was near his own. The letter from the empress drifted in the water. And he was safe, at least. The girl was too close to him for anyone to risk a shot.

But the dog struggled to its feet. Blood dripped from its side. And now the boy beside the dam took a step onto the ice. The red-haired woman from the house was bending over Ferenc on the shore. "Help him," Raevsky shouted to Alexandru, and at the same time Miranda Popescu took the lobe of his ear between her teeth and bit on it until the flesh parted, while she twisted suddenly away. She waded out into the water to the broken edge of the ice. She broke through twice in the shallow water. Then she was clambering up where he knew he couldn't follow, where he knew the ice would break under his weight, and besides, he was exposed now to the man on the hill. Their own rifles were back at camp.

But the man on the hill wasn't much of a shot. The fourth bullet passed close to his bleeding ear. Marksman or not, someone was trying to kill him, shoot him in the head. Carl and Alexandru were crouching on the bank, and he climbed up to join them among some rocks and bushes, out of sight of the little house.

He gave his orders. After Carl was bandaged, he'd go back to camp, so Gulka could bring up the long guns. Gulka was at the river with the pirogues and the others, twenty minutes through the woods. Raevsky cursed his own stupidity—it had been his decision to leave the rifles behind. He hadn't wanted to scare off the girl. But he could have hidden them in some closer place.

He and Alexandru would have to go after that idiot Ferenc. Alexandru was the captain's nephew, his sister's son, and Raevsky kept his hand on his shoulder as they climbed out of the shelter of the rocks. Raevsky wouldn't allow him to be hurt; keeping to the trees, they climbed over the rise until they saw the house again, in the clearing on the far side of the frozen pond. The door was open. There was no one on the wall and no sign of his man. Miranda Popescu still knelt on the ice over the fallen dog. The boy was too heavy to add his weight to theirs. He was standing by the shore.

He could hear the boy's voice, but couldn't understand what he was saying. God, what a mess. With luck the baroness would never hear about it, though that would depend on what happened now. Where was Ferenc—had the Gypsy woman brought him inside? And the original problem remained. Miranda Popescu could not be harmed.

He watched her struggle to her feet, hoisting the dog in her arms. He was surprised she could lift it. She stepped over a crack in the ice and then staggered toward shore, away from the triangle of muddy water where she'd bitten him and he had let her go. The envelope still floated there.

The red-haired woman now appeared at the side of the house. That was where he'd seen her the day before, feeding her animals. Now she stopped at the line of cages. She opened the first one and pulled out a small bird, holding it in the nest of her hands for a moment before throwing it into the air. He watched it climbing steeply toward the sun, a gyrfalcon or a kestrel. Then it was gone.

Miranda Popescu walked unsteadily over the ice, carrying the big dog. She was forty meters away, not more. Once she paused and looked toward him where he crouched in the shelter of a tree.

Another bird rose into the air, larger this time, a traveler's eagle, he thought. Disoriented for a moment, it flew in circles around the pond.

And as he watched Miranda carry the dog onto the bank, two more birds went up.

LIGHT CAME FROM THE OPEN door and from two kerosene lamps, which had been burning when they came in. The inside of the cottage was dark, smelly, wonderfully hot. There was no furniture but only piles of clothing and supplies. There was a stack of fishing traps against the wall.

The soldier lay unconscious in the middle of the floor, a boy as young as Peter, or only a little older, with thick lips and stiff yellow hair. Peter himself stood beside the woodstove, pressing his hand into his armpit, staring at the raw boards under his feet. He'd tried to help her on the bank, but when he touched Andromeda she'd snapped at him; now Miranda held the dog's chest and haunches in the circle of her arms. The burden was too heavy. "Help," she said. The woman was coming up behind her through the door—she'd brought the soldier inside and then gone out again to fool around with her birds. Together they laid the dog next to the stove.

Miranda's feet were freezing, soaked. She stripped off her socks and running shoes, then sat cross-legged and took the dog's head into her lap. She could feel the beating heart, steady and strong against her thigh. Good—and there wasn't a lot of blood. She dug her fingers into the thick fur, searching for the wound, while the woman squatted next to her.

She was older than Rachel, perhaps fifty, with a barrellike body and fleshy arms. She wore a black wool skirt to the middle of her shins, under what Miranda decided was a smock—a loose shirt that left her neck and forearms bare.

The dog was trembling and her eyes were closed. "Mustn't worry," said the old woman under her breath. "Mustn't worry, no."

Which was easy for her to say. Miranda didn't want to look. Instead she ran her hand down Andromeda's smooth flank, searching for a wound. "Please," she said. "It's all right. We can—" But she stopped when she felt the dog stiffen, felt the rumble of a growl too soft to hear.

"No," said the old woman, grasping her hand. "Don't touch. Wait now. Watch me. Dog is good."

She got up. Now she was wandering around the house gathering an assortment of objects from various boxes and piles: a hand mirror, a syringe, a comb, a drum, a hammer, a fan, a straight razor, a glass jar, a length of rubber tube—Miranda was not reassured. Nor was she pleased to see the woman squat down over the wounded soldier. She made a pile of the things she'd gathered on the floor.

"Ceausescu," she said, the name she'd spoken on the bridge outside.

"Who is that?" Miranda said. Stanley had told her that her parents had been involved in the Timisoara riots, when President Ceausescu's soldiers fired on the crowd. But that was there, and this was here.

"He is Ceausescu's man," she said, which didn't help. "The red pig," she said, pointing to a mark on his shirt." Though her voice was harsh, her hands were gentle, fat and spotted as she rubbed the soldier's neck and cheeks. He opened his eyes.

She unbuttoned his green coat, and with the razor she cut away his shirt and undershirt along the front of his body. His chest had a black mark on it. The woman made some clucking noises when she saw it, half laughter, half concern. "So," she said to Peter. "You have not lost skill. Not all." She held the mirror to the soldier's lips.

By herself she must have dragged him across the bridge and into the house. But from the water, with Raevsky's arms around her, Miranda had seen Peter knock the soldier down, as he had knocked down Kevin Markasev, and even the kid in the playground—Miranda felt a surge of gratitude. The man's pistol lay in a corner of the room, next to the green cap. But what did the woman mean by losing skill?

"Hey," she said. "Where is Gregor Splaa?" And there was another name, too. Someone blind.

Peter sat down now with the dog between them. He put his left hand into the fur above her tail, and Miranda heard her growl. "Stop that," she told him.

"One comes," said the old woman. "Must work fast. Dog must wait."

"She can't wait," Miranda said. But in spite of herself, she was fascinated to see the woman force the neck of the glass jar into the man's mouth. She forced the rubber tube so that it ran out the side of his mouth behind his teeth. He opened his eyes wider, but he seemed stunned or drugged. The woman clamped her hands around the neck of the jar, covering the man's nose until his feet and arms began to shake.

Then abruptly, she took her hands away. She dragged aside all of her equipment and let him breathe again. "Not yet," she said. She was kneeling over his head, and now she sat back on her heels. She hugged her arms over her enormous chest and, closing her eyes, began to sing a small melody, a whisper of Roumanian words.

"Come on," Miranda said. How long had they been in this new place? An hour? Two? Already everything had gone wrong. She thought about what had happened on the ice, when she'd escaped from Raevsky, the gray-haired man who'd called her by her name. He and the rest had run away. Guns had been fired. Thankfully, that phase of things seemed to be over.

"Where is Gregor Splaa?" she asked again, irritated. No one was talking to her, not the old woman or Peter either. Though she was out of her saturated socks, her legs and feet were still cold. No one was answering even her simplest questions. And Peter wouldn't even look at her. He was staring at the woman's hands.

There was a movement at the door, which opened. Miranda saw the silhouette of a man in the white light. Then he was inside, crouching down below the window frame, a rifle in his hand. The door swung closed.

The woman shook her head as her song came to an end. "Great hunter," she said. "How can you miss so much?"

"Please, mother," he said.

But she smiled at Miranda, winked. Her eyes were a bright shade of green. "I am mother when he fails, only. You see it is my way now. If de Graz and Prochenko—"

Those were the other names. Mirada was relieved to hear them from her lips. She was about to say something when the man interrupted. "We've got half an hour," he said. He was dark-haired, hook-nosed, bearded, dressed in wool and buckskin leather. His cheeks were sunken, hollow. He spoke better English than the old woman. "They will attack as soon as they can."

This was terrible news. Again Miranda wanted to say something, but this time the woman interrupted. "Is not attack. Not fight like this. Is my way now."

She turned, poised as if listening. "One comes."

The wounded soldier lay on the floor, breathing softly under her hand. His eyes were open. "It's their captain," the man said at the window. He raised his gun, reached for the door.

"No." The woman shook her head. "You miss him at ten meters. Let him talk."

Now there was no hesitating, and she took one end of the rubber tube between her lips. Again she put the neck of the jar into the man's mouth, while at the same time sucking on the tube that ran behind his teeth. As Miranda watched, his eyes glazed and hardened, and then she saw for a piece of a second a shape in the jar, as insubstantial as a hologram, a tiny, hairy beast. Then it was gone.

"Have it," muttered the old woman.

Miranda ran her hand down Andromeda's hairy flank. In the thick fur she encountered Peter's fingers—his left hand—and did not pull away. She glanced at him, but he was watching the jar.

The woman rubbed it in her hands. Now from moment to moment Miranda could see the little animal nosing around the inside of the glass, appearing and disappearing, diaphanous, multihued, alive. The woman fitted a cork into the jar's mouth. Then, limber and light-footed in spite of her bulk, she stood up and made a little skipping dance across the floor.

She had a flowered shawl tied around her waist in place of a belt, and she slid the bottle into it. Then she bent down in front of Peter and snapped her fingers under his nose. "I say you can be your own son. A boy—is looking so. Is this Prochenko here? Hah, there are big mistakes! Always this is true! In a dream I went to that place once, that terrible Romania, that terrible Constanta—yes, when she was young." And as Peter jerked back his face, the door opened and Raevsky stood there, unarmed, hands at his sides.

The woman's skin was covered with moles. Her neck was fat and short. She had some gold teeth, and she smelled of liquor as she bent down over Miranda. "Captain Raevsky," she said. "Do remember me?"

The captain blinked as he peered into the room. He said something in Roumanian, but the woman stopped him. "I was servant in the summer palace long before."

She partly blocked Miranda's view with her big body. But Miranda was comforted by her proximity—her and Andromeda, and Peter on the other side. In any case the captain was looking at the other man, whose gun was pointed at his stomach. "I've come for him," he said, meaning the soldier stretched out on the floor. When no one said anything, he went on. "I promised his father I would bury him—"

The woman laughed. "You must please yourself. Is no hurry. Is not dead."

As she was speaking, she took from inside her scarf a leather case, which contained a glass syringe. She chose a needle and screwed it on. Then she found a rubber-stoppered vial in her pocket, filled the syringe, and ran the needle into Andromeda's side. Almost immediately Miranda felt the dog's heavy head subside into her lap.

The old woman was still muttering. "Prochenko! Always some mistakes. With his yellow hair. Nose in a pretty girl. So, it does not change."

"Good," said Captain Raevsky. "You are glad to know the other one will live. Hit in the face, as you know. There is no necessity for more blood."

Miranda was relieved to hear him say so. He went down on one knee over the sleeping soldier, and put the back of his hand against his cheek. The other man followed his movements with the end of the long gun. "What can you give us?" he said.

Raevsky frowned. He turned toward Miranda. "Miss Popescu, we have gifts. Important messages. No harm will come. We are your friends. The man who hurt your dog, he is already punished."

Miranda looked at Peter, and was surprised to see him shake his head. "I'll stay here," she murmured. It didn't seem like much of a choice. She felt secure here in this warm room, despite its strangeness. And Raevsky had grabbed her, put his hands on her. He might have killed the dog.

"No, that is not right," said Captain Raevsky. "Do not force these ones to defend you. Gypsies and Jews—your place is not with them."

Gypsies and Jews—what kind of talk was that? Miranda would stay with the old woman—there was a silence in the crowded room. The man with the long gun ended it. "That's enough," he said. "She's answered. As for this piece of garbage, he's our guest." He nodded toward the sleeping soldier.

The woman ran her hands over the dog's stomach. "Listen to him—'piece of garbage.' Is good, is a brave man now. They call me Blind Rodica," she whispered. "That is Gregor Splaa."

Miranda was happy to hear these names. "I'll stay," she said again.

The captain gave her a disgusted look. "You have no right to bring a danger to these people." He stared at her, and she stared back defiantly. Why was he even talking to her? His men had shot Andromeda. And her wrists were still sore where he had grabbed her.

He had a heavy chest and powerful arms. But his legs were thin. "I have a letter," he said finally to Splaa. "May I give it?"

There was no answer, and so he reached inside his coat to produce the same soggy yellow envelope he had offered her before. He turned his back to Splaa and stepped across the room in his wet boots. Miranda looked at him as he approached. She put Andromeda's head aside. Almost she cried out to Splaa, because anyone could predict what Raevsky would do. He would grab her by the arm again. Or he would turn and knock the barrel of Splaa's gun aside. There was a red mark on his ear where she had bitten him. His face was stiff and tense.

But then Blind Rodica stepped between them and took the envelope. "I am with my lady in the summer palace," she said. "Sophie's Guest House, but you don't remember? I recognize your smell. You came with the Baron Ceausescu. Prince Frederick and the Chevalier de Graz were there."

When Raevsky heard this name, his expression changed. Miranda watched him glance at Peter and then look again. Suddenly there was no further chance he would attack them. There was no more stiffness in his shoulders and neck. In a moment he seemed panicked, almost eager to be gone.

"We will wait one hour," he said as he stepped backward. And then in a pleading voice: "Please, miss, you must do what we say. You must not keep here with these people. They are not friends to you."

He stepped backward toward the door. He was fumbling behind him for the latch, as he stared at Peter's face. "In any way you have no choice," he said. "I have men from Cluj, and better guns." Then he was gone, and Splaa closed the door behind him.

Splaa shrugged, dissatisfied, and nodded toward the soldier on the floor. "He has six men and his guide from Albany. Tell me why I let him go."

"Is better this way," said Blind Rodica. "He protects. He won't hurt the white tyger—if he is dead or so, the rest don't wait." Then she laughed. "Is frightened of the Chevalier de Graz. Is frightened, anyway. His master was the most cruel alchemist in Great Roumania, and now his lady, too. But is afraid of my small tricks."

"What is the white tyger?" Miranda murmured.

But Splaa didn't hear. Miranda had taken Andromeda's head into her lap again, and she had spoken the question almost to herself, because she didn't want it to sound as if she didn't know anything. Maybe she'd learn something just by listening.

Splaa was by the window. "They've got their guns."

"They won't risk," said Blind Rodica. "They go around the house and wait for dark. He won't lose someone, and wounded will not be convenient. Is afraid."

"He should be. I could hit three or four."

Rodica laughed, winked at Miranda. "So you say. Is also possible he will wait more time. After some days, he thinks."

They spoke as if Miranda weren't there. But they spoke in English so that she could understand. "What is the white tyger?" she repeated.

Blind Rodica had knelt down over the dog again. Her hands were hidden in the yellow fur, and they were bloody when she drew them out. She found the envelope in the pouch of her scarf, and drew out a single sheet of damp, expensive paper.

"In proper time," Rodica said. "There. A forging. Why will the empress say these things to you? She will put you in a prison if she catches you."

This was useful information. "What does it say?" Miranda asked.

She shrugged. "I cannot read." She crushed the paper between her hands and tossed it across the floor.

Frustrated, Miranda put her hand on Andromeda's sleeping head. She would have been relieved to see Rodica shave the wound, or stitch it up, or bandage it, or merely wash it. But the woman had done none of these things since she'd given the injection, just rubbed and worried the dog's side with bloodstained hands.

Now Rodica reached into the dog's mouth and seemed to produce from there a slug of lead the size of a pea. "Not trying to kill—ha, ha," she said, and then her body was quivering as she started to laugh. She snapped her fingers, and the bullet disappeared.

"Bounced from the bone. And you," she went on, snapping her fingers in front of Peter's face, "wake up."

Peter jerked his head back. And it was true—he did look a little dopey. He hadn't said anything in a long time.

Gregor Splaa was standing by the front window. Every minute or so he walked across the room to the back of the house, where he looked out another small window on the opposite wall. There was a field out there, a wide, snowy expanse before the trees began.

Miranda kept her hand on Andromeda's head. "I've got some questions," she said stubbornly.

Which made the woman laugh harder. "I think you do. I think so." She got up, and without washing her hands she filled a kettle from the first of a line of buckets against the wall, and put it on the stove.

Now Andromeda and the soldier were asleep. Peter was sitting beside the stove. He sat cradling his arm, leaning back against a pile of blankets and pillows. As Miranda watched, he ran the fingers of his left hand along his big right forearm, and was opening and closing his dark right fist.

Splaa walked back and forth between the windows, carrying his gun. Miranda cleared her throat, but Blind Rodica interrupted before she could speak. "We are your servants, miss. Your aunt Aegypta put us here to wait."

"Yes," Miranda persevered. "You've got some letters. Not that one." She nodded toward the message from the empress, unread, crumpled in a corner.

"Is not time," the woman said again. "White tyger—what are these names to you? But your aunt keeps us here to protect you from those murderers! Splaa was a stableboy, is true. Now he is a big man with his gun, but we don't think so—hah, we know him! I work in the nursery after you are born. One week after you come from Germany."

Miranda shrugged. "Where . . . ?"

"No, in Constanta, child. Roumania. Where else? Your aunt brought you from Germany when you were two days old."

"And he's your son?" Miranda motioned with her head toward Gregor Splaa. They were talking too softly for him to hear.

"No, child. But I take him. Roumania has orphans in those days and now still. Your aunt would not separate. He is just a boy when I come here."

Gregor Splaa walked back and forth. "Tell her the story."

But she was making food. She mixed the water with some meat stock from a greasy jar and put it in a pot on the stove. Then she sat beside Peter slicing vegetables into a bowl, muttering and singing to herself.

The walls were charred and stained with soot. Long, soot-covered cobwebs hung from the rafters. They trembled in the draught Splaa made as he walked underneath. The flame of one of the kerosene lamps trembled also, and cast flickering shadows. "She's blind," Splaa muttered. "She does everything by touch. Don't trust her pranks. That's all it is, make-believe.

"This boy," he went on, touching the soldier with his foot. "Maybe she drugged him. But the rest is Gypsy tricks. Not what we need now."

Rodica laughed when she heard this, winked her grass-green eyes. She was slicing pieces of smoked ham into the pot. And now she took from the pouch of her scarf what looked to Miranda like the same jar that had contained the little animal. She opened it, turned it upside down, shook out a pinch of what looked like salt. Still, how could she be blind? Later she sat and rolled a cigarette with expert, practiced movements.

"Stop that," she said to Gregor Splaa. "They will hit through the window. I tell you nothing happens before dark."

6 A Second Assault

THE INSIDE OF THE LITTLE house was full of distinct smells. Lying near the stove with her eyes closed, without moving her nose, Andromeda could separate them out. There were onions and garlic. There was deer meat and dried rabbit meat. There was a small stink of urine, and two kinds of blood. There was salt and wood and smoke, which almost overpowered all the rest. There was dirt and sweat from the Gypsy woman. There were Miranda, Peter, and there was Gregor Splaa.

She opened her eyes. In the afternoon, in the little house by the stone dam, Gregor Splaa walked back and forth.

Andromeda watched him from the floor. Her head, too heavy to lift, lay on her paws.

It had been the shock of being wounded that had felled her on the ice, more than the seriousness of the wound itself. Now Andromeda lay waiting for the drug to wear away. Moving her eyes, moving her head in tiny increments, she could see Miranda and Peter Gross on the other side of the stove. Hugging his hand into his armpit, Peter had lain back against a strapped-up bedroll. He was asleep with his mouth open. His food, a wooden bowl of soup, lay untasted on the floor.

Hands on her hips, old Rodica looked at him appraisingly. "Is good," she said. "Rest now. We will need him."

She reached into her sash and produced a glass bottle of black pills. Now she squatted down to press the bottle into Miranda's hand. "Just to sleep. Not now. One each night—no more. These next nights will be bad dreams for you."

Standing, she pried up the lid of the stove and fed it with chunks of wood. Andromeda could smell the dust and the powdered sap. Miranda was staring at the yellow-haired soldier, whose body lay in a corner of the room. She slipped the bottle of pills into the pocket of her jeans.

Gregor Splaa stood beside the diamond-paned front window, looking out. He had a long, narrow face, a high, hooked nose. His beard was long and soft, as if it never had been cut. It was tucked into his shirt. He was in his twenties, an ugly man picking his lips. He was nervous now. Andromeda could smell his sweat.

"Twelve years," he said. "We built this house, built the dam, cleared the field—oh, we had lots of projects. Princess Aegypta never told us what to do. We haven't heard from her. One letter every year, in Albany. Sometimes not even that. I didn't expect this—Ceausescu's soldiers. We were a contingency."

"But so easy to see," muttered Blind Rodica.

Splaa stepped across the room to the rear window by the stovepipe. "I thought you'd live your life in that place your aunt prepared—grow up, have children, die. I never thought you would depend on us. Great Roumania has fallen, or will fall, Turks on one side and the Germans on the other, and the Tartars, and the Muscovies, and all the rest of them like cockroaches on a cake. It's a matter of time. Who are you? Just one girl."

"No time for this," grumbled Rodica.

"No, but your father took me in, an orphan in his house. I'll lay down my heart and life. Rodica, too. Don't worry about that."

"Is not worried. Raevsky will come at dark."

"Tell me about my parents," said Miranda suddenly. Andromeda thought: What was different about her? Black hair the same, and her wide forehead, narrow cheeks.

Splaa said, "Yes! Your mother. . . . That's the truth—it's been twelve years. It doesn't matter—here, when Julius Caesar came back from his Roumanian campaign, he brought a Dacian princess who was pregnant. When Brutus stabbed him on the senate floor—chaos—the girl fled. She gave birth in the mountains, in Pietrosul—is that what you want to know? It could not be true. But how can you explain the power of your family?"

After a moment he strode back to the window by the door. "You are hope to all our people," muttered Rodica.

"Yes," agreed Splaa. "A white tyger was prophesied, and a white tyger was found in the Carpathians. Your father was already dead, and your mother chose the name 'Popescu,' the commonest name in all Roumania—this isn't hurting you?"

"Go on," Miranda said.

What was different about her? Her hair was the same length, kept in place behind her ears. Her dark eyebrows were the same, and her blue eyes. She was more solid, somehow. Had she put on weight? Was she taller? No, but something had changed in the expression of her face. Her skin looked rougher, darker, older.

"Baron Ceausescu was your father's friend, but he betrayed him," said Gregor Splaa. "He forged a letter from the German ambassador. Testified against him at the trial—it was a joke. No one believed. It didn't matter, they were looking for excuses. Your father was shot, they say, trying to escape. This was five months before you were born."

While Splaa was talking, Blind Rodica gathered a pile of gadgets and utensils on the floor below the stove, between Andromeda and the sleeping soldier. She had about her now a smell of wax and grease. She sniffed, rubbed her nose—"Is twenty years ago. Now, but tonight—no time for explanation. Must make plan—first first. Twelve years to think. Raevsky's men will come around the house. They will set the house on fire."

Miranda interrupted. "Tell me about my parents."

Splaa answered. "Frederick Schenck von Schenck—half German, see? That makes things difficult. Your mother called him Freddie. His mother was a Brancoveanu like her. They were cousins. How they met. He was at his grandparents' for the winter holidays, near Brasov. And she, of course, well, she . . ." Splaa walked back across the room.

"Tell me."

"The white tyger. Does this mean nothing to you? You take after your father, of course. But your mother held the story of the tyger in her bones. Your father couldn't use it, because he was a German. Always foreign-born. Oh, but he was a great prince! You should have seen him ride his horse through Vulcan's Gate after he'd stopped the Turks at Havsa. The whole city turned out to cheer him. He had the armistice in his hand. After his death, of course, the sultan broke the line."

"He had all but beauty," agreed Blind Rodica. "Is why they hated him, Ceausescu and the others. Why they killed him."

All this time Rodica had been preparing an altar in the middle of the floor. The centerpiece was a small brass statue, which Andromeda identified as representing the Hindu god Ganesh. Once her father had brought her a chalk drawing back from India—why did she remember that? She never could remember dreams.

"What are you doing?" Miranda said.

The statue had four arms. It was elephant-headed, sitting on a rat. Around its feet lay all kinds of loose bric-a-brac—tiny bottles, tools, pieces of wire. Rodica lit some incense from a wooden match, then sat back on her heels. "Light won't last," she said.

Turning now, she reached inside the collar of Miranda's shirt and un- covered the steel crucifix on its chain. "Many times I saw this on your mother's neck," she said. "Please let—"

Miranda put her hand up to her neck, but the cross was already gone. "Permit me," said Blind Rodica, turning it between the pads of her finger and thumb. "You see is old. Made from the nails."

"Give it back." Miranda reached out her hand, but paused when Rodica hung the crucifix from one of Ganesh's outstretched arms. "Now gold," said Blind Rodica. She looked expectantly at Miranda's backpack, beside her on the floor.

Miranda made a resigned gesture with her hand. And the old woman dug her hand into the laced-up top, then brought out a little pasteboard box. Miranda had shown it to Andromeda years before. It was from a jew- elry shop in Bucharest.

Rodica selected the eleven thin coins and arranged them in a circle around the altar. The sun was down behind the hills now, and darkness filled the middle of the room. Squinting along her nose, Andromeda could see that each coin had a letter stamped on it. Together, they spelled out a word.

" 'Sennacherib,' " muttered Blind Rodica.

"Gypsy tricks," said Gregor Splaa. "Don't pay any attention to her."

But it was impossible not to pay attention. Miranda sat on the step, staring at the Gypsy's hands. Splaa was above her in a corner of the wall, smoothing out the empress's damp letter, which was in English, apparently. He read it aloud. " 'It gives me happiness to welcome you and commend you to the care of my trusted captain. . . . ' "

"What was my mother's name?" Miranda interrupted. "Wasn't there a letter from her? What did she say we should do?"

"So poor child," said Blind Rodica. "Your mother cannot help now. We will help. We will get you out. Maybe would be different with Prochenko and de Graz—great warriors. Heroes—not so useful now—one asleep boy and one dog. And one stableman and one blind Gypsy, we will help you. Everyone tries tricks, you don't forget. Valeria Dragonesti is your enemy, and Ceausescu. Antonescu above all—do not forget these names if we are not here to help."

Shadows were gathering in the corners of the room. "They're lighting fires in the wood," murmured Gregor Splaa. "Four—no, five."

He stood at the back window. "Don't worry," said Rodica. "Not worry. Sennacherib will come. He just needs . . . what? Coaxing." Between these words, she was muttering something in a foreign language, gesturing in the incense smoke, rocking back and forth.

"There's no point to this," said Gregor Splaa. Then in a little while— "It's starting to snow."

"Yes, yes," muttered Blind Rodica. And more words in the language that was neither English nor Roumanian. From the scarf around her waist she now produced a glass jar with a beast inside, a field mouse or a shrew, and she put the jar upright next to the burning stick of incense. The little animal nosed around the cork.

Andromeda raised her head off her paws. Peter Gross was moving too, shaking his head, though he was still asleep. Andromeda had forgotten about him. But now she was looking at his black, hairy hand, and the red birthmark on the joint of his thumb—de Graz's mark. So he had de Graz's hand at least. No, more than that. Andromeda could see now in his brown curls and brown skin, his bent teeth and brooding, heavy brow, a small version of a face she recognized.

She pricked her ears. His smell, also, was a washed-out version of de Graz's acrid sweat.

He spoke, and Miranda gave a small cry of surprise. His eyes were still closed. Still he lay against the bedroll. His mouth lolled open and his voice, when the words came out, was empty and strange.

"There lay the rider distorted and pale,
  With dew on his brow, the rust on his mail:
  The tents were all silent, the banners alone,
  The lances unlifted . . ."

"A poem," Andromeda thought.

"Yes," said Blind Rodica. "Is just . . ." Then to Miranda—"Your aunt sent two soldiers with you to protect you. Friends of your fathers. Officers of the guard."

"What do you mean?"

"They are not what they are," said Blind Rodica.

Peter's eyes, open now, stared down at the little altar. His voice was low and flat and halting. Though soft, it filled the room: "WHY HAVE YOU SPOKEN?"

"Sennacherib," breathed Blind Rodica.

Seated by him, Miranda reached over to take hold of his left hand. "WHAT HAVE I TO DO?" he said. "THERE IS NO SACRIFICE."

"No, but I have one," said Blind Rodica. "In Christ's name."

"I DO NOT NAME HIM. TELL ME WHAT YOU WANT."

"I can see the men now," said Gregor Splaa. "I see them near the fire."

"Enemies have us in a ring," murmured Blind Rodica. "You are the protector of the weak."

There was a silence, and then Peter spoke again. "WHAT IS THE SAC-RIFICE?"

The voice was distorted, low. Peter was slumped forward now. "Here," said Blind Rodica. Andromeda could see the mouse was motionless at the bottom of the jar.

"RELEASE IT."

Rodica twisted the cork and put the jar on its side. After a moment the mouse came to itself. It nosed its way out of the jar, then ran across the floor in the direction of the sleeping soldier. On the way it fell into a seam of shadow and disappeared. But the soldier, who had been lying still, now rolled over onto his back. "Ah, well," said Blind Rodica. "Is too poor a gift."

"WHAT DO YOU OFFER ME?" whispered Peter. "DEATH FROM DEATH."

"Enough of this," said Gregor Splaa. He paced across the room. "They'll come in from all sides. Maybe I'll shoot three or four. You have a chance. You be ready."

"What do you mean?" Miranda asked.

"There's a coat and a pack of supplies. I dug a hiding place." Splaa put down his gun and turned over a corner of the floor, a square of planks three feet on a side. "She's right—we had twelve years to prepare. We'll go out, and in the dark they can't be sure. They follow us, and you stay here. Then you join us. Run for the woods, and then you'll meet us at the river. Upstream to the black rock. They'll go downstream if they chase you."

"What if I give myself up?" she asked.

"He'll shoot the rest of us and shoot you later, by a firing squad in Bucharest. This is a war."

Andromeda had pulled herself onto her haunches. She lay with her muzzle between her paws. The soldier was awake now. He lay on his back, saying something in Roumanian.

"There, you see?" Blind Rodica still knelt before her altar. "Do not listen to these plans. You will not do these things. My way is good. Raevsky knows."

Splaa threw down the trapdoor, leapt forward. But it was too late. The soldier had flung himself across the room to the front door, which crashed open before Splaa could get his gun up.

Miranda jumped to her feet. Lethargic and slow, Andromeda now staggered up. She stood looking at the gray, swirling snow through the open door. She heard two gunshots, both quite close. She smelled the powder. The soldier had rolled partway down the slope, then got to his feet, screaming and shouting, and disappeared into the half-light and the snow.

Splaa was cursing. "What did you do? What did you do? Miss Popescu, please . . ."

Blind Rodica was on her hands and knees. Now she got up, went to the door, and closed it. Another gunshot fired. "It does not matter."

But Splaa was in tears. "Mother, how can you say that? Did you see him? Did you see him through the door?"

Rodica grimaced, smiled. Her hand was still on the wooden latch. "Raevsky knows. That boy will tell him, and then he will know."

"He didn't know. Why would he know?"

"But he knows now. He will set the roof on fire. You see my way is best after all."

"Unless they killed him as he ran out. What way? Gypsy nonsense."

He had put his gun aside and was sobbing into his hands. For the first time Andromeda realized that Rodica had been hurt. She staggered forward into the room, then flopped down on her knees. Andromeda could smell the new blood on her hands. "Given," she said, and then Peter spoke.

"YES."

"What have you done?" Splaa said. "What have you done?" He and Miranda had their arms around the old woman now, and they supported her as she slumped onto the floor. Then she was sitting with her legs splayed out, hands on her stomach.

"You don't be stupid now," she murmured. "You tell my lady what is happened. Is a letter for my mother in her pawnshop in the Old Court, and package for my daughter in Constanta—you will see. Aegypta Schenck will pay to her my wages— that is what I want. She can't be shamed for her old mother. Is married to a good man. God bless Roumania. Jesus help me. Freely given, remember. Is freely given."

"YES."

"You stupid Gypsy fool," said Gregor Splaa. "Twelve years. Oh, God," he said. "Does it hurt? Where is it?"

Now there was a lot of blood. Andromeda could smell it as it spread out from her hands. "Oh my friend," she said. "My son, we saw the white tyger. A sacrifice—we can do not more. You tell my lady?"

Miranda had a stunned expression on her face. She had her arms around the Gypsy's shoulders.

There was a wind around the house. Andromeda could hear it in the stovepipe. Outside the window, the snow was falling thicker every minute.

"Lie down now, lie down," said Gregor Splaa. "Let me—" but there was nothing to be done. Blind Rodica grabbed Miranda's hands and held them as they laid her down.

"You have trust," she said. "Trust in Sennacherib. If no trust, then you can fail. Raevsky will be gone, men will be gone. But you will go quickly—take their boats! Find Ion Dreyfoos in Albany—that is all. Oh my son—brave boy—you can do this!"

Her voice was weak. Gregor Splaa was crying. Andromeda could smell his tears. "Talk to her. Talk to her," he sobbed, and Miranda did, telling her a story that Andromeda had heard before, which was about when Stanley took her hiking in the White Mountains in a place called New Hampshire. Early in the morning she had gotten up to pick blueberries. And she had found a field with a bear doing the same thing, and she had sat in the same field as the bear, picking blueberries as the sun came up.

OUTSIDE THE COTTAGE the wind blew. It was peculiar, Raevsky thought, because at first he could feel nothing on the ground. He stood at camp on a small promontory above the ice pond, watching the door of the house through his field glasses as the snow came and the light grew dim. But when he put down his glasses, in the trees beyond the house he could see movement in the bare, high branches and the evergreens. A current of air ran through them, making them toss their heads. Around him, the air was still. The snow fell in large flakes.

Raevsky circled the pond to the next fire, where Gulka sat among the evergreens. Gulka was afraid that in the darkness and the snow, someone might slip through the cordon. Raevsky had put his men in five protected positions around the house, each with clear sight lines and an open space in front.

The darkness would help them more than the enemy, he explained. The snow would help them, too. Gulka was the oldest of his men at twenty-one, and a bit slow. The baroness had not wanted to pay for soldiers, except for him. So he'd picked farm boys from Cluj and given them guns. He'd brought his own sister's son. They would have been enough to find Miranda Popescu in the woods and bring her home. They'd have been enough to snatch her from the Gypsy and the Jew.

Now Raevsky was less sure. "I swear to you, it must be his son," he said. "He'd be the right age. If he's like his father just a little bit, there could be a difficulty. So leave him to me. I was with the army when de Graz fought the Turkish champion."

Gulka was a thin, nervous man with a weak beard and a spot on his face. "When it is dark, we all move forward," Raevsky explained for the third time. "At six o'clock we burn the rats out of their nest. When the fire is lit, we can see everything."

He spoke gruffly and confidently, though he was concerned. The problem then would be to recognize Miranda Popescu. With any luck they wouldn't fire a shot.

The old Gypsy was a witch, that much was sure. Where had the girl come from after all, and de Graz's son? Miranda Popescu must not be left in there, he told himself, to be turned into a vampire or a ghost. Now he understood what his lady had said—that they must rescue her, save her from her enemies. But he was sure this Gypsy had some bad surprise for him.

At quarter past five, Ferenc got up from beside the fire. He was the one who'd escaped from the house. He'd come yelling across the bridge, and he was lucky no one hit him when they fired at the open door. Later he sat covered in blankets next to the fire in the birch trees, and as the snow grew thick he told the captain what he had seen. The guide had given him a cup of tea.

Raevsky had just made the circuit, and was headed back to the main camp by the promontory when he saw him. With his blanket over his head, Ferenc walked out into the open, down the slope and onto the ice surface of the pond.

"What are you doing? Get back!" Raevsky shouted, but the snow was thicker now. And then the wind came up, and his words were thrown into his face by the wind. He ran down to the edge of the pond. From where he stood he could see four of the five watch-fires. But then he couldn't, and they disappeared, and he thought it must be a trick of the snow. Certainly it wasn't possible for all of them to be extinguished in a single moment, blown out like so many candles. He couldn't see the lights. Yet it was not too dark to see the tops of the pines turn over as the wind passed through. Nor was the wind so strong that he couldn't hear noises in the trees, branches ripped down. He turned and ran back toward the camp in the birch trees. He called out for Alexandru, his sister's son.

Five minutes before, Raevsky had been with him. That camp was at the far side of the pond, guarding the house on the north side. As he ran, he expected to see the fire reappear, hidden by the trees or a trick of the snow. But when he got there, the fire was dead, the embers scattered, dead. The boy lay on his back, cold and scarcely breathing. The wind howled and tore at the trees.

Shouting a charm his mother had taught him, Raevsky dragged him up, threw him over his shoulder, and staggered back through the trees. There was a sheltered place among the rocks that he'd chosen for an emergency position, and now he headed for it—an outcropping of rocks and a deposit of dry leaves. Before he went back for the others, he stripped his mother's amulet from around his neck and wound it around the boy's unresisting fingers. He gave the boy a hug, held him in his arms, tried to warm his cold body. Then, keeping in his mind the image of the Baroness Ceausescu's beautiful face, he plunged off again into the snow.

IN BUCHAREST, IN THE HOUSE on Saltpetre Street, in her cold, upstairs room, the baroness sat waiting. Markasev had returned. He lay naked in the cage under a horsehair blanket. For several minutes his eyes had been open. He had sat up, moved his arms, given some nonsensical responses to her questions. But then he had slipped back into unconsciousness like a swimmer desperate for air, who had found his legs entangled in some wreckage and had sunk again below the surface.

Something was wrong. The pigs in the crate had sighed and squealed. Now they no longer breathed. Jean-Baptiste would dispose of them.

Something was wrong. Markasev had failed. Or something was the matter with the science. Or else Aegypta Schenck had tricked her. Or else

Markasev had made a fool of her—in any case the girl had not come with him. Jean-Baptiste had built this cage for her at some expense.

The baroness sat watching in her leather armchair. If Markasev had brought back the girl, if he'd not disappointed her, then the baroness would have helped him. She was a generous woman, and she'd been yearning to help him for many weeks. She'd imagined his gratitude—she would have found a home for him. But now this cage would be his home, at least until he explained himself: now he tossed and struggled, and threw his head from side to side. "No," he muttered, "no, what will you do? Oh, Sennacherib," a word that filled the baroness with anxiety and rage. She didn't show it. She sat in her husband's armchair, her bare feet crossed on a stool. Nothing disturbed the smoothness of her face. From time to time she ran her big-knuckled fingers through her hair. But what was happening in America? What was happening in that place?

All night and now past noon, she had sat in the leather armchair, chewing her nails. Now she kicked aside the footstool and stood up. Gathering her dressing gown around her, she stalked past the cage. Beyond it was a long, ironwood table, in the center of which rose a crystal pyramid, one meter on a side. Flanking the pyramid stood a black mirror and a hanging pendulum.

Most of her husband's laboratory equipment she had never touched. She was not interested, as he was, in chemical research, or metallurgy, or the quest for the philosopher's stone. If he had not died, he would have beggared them with his experiments, the ceaseless expiation of his guilt. But there was one area of knowledge where her interests coincided with his, one part of the room that she still used. She'd dragged this table away from the wall, and on it she had laid her husband's astrological charts, his books by Zosimus and others, and his divining instruments.

Now she ran her stained, bleeding fingers along the polished wood. An enlarger was clamped to one end of the table, and beside it stood the big box camera with the Zeiss lens, which her husband had bought in Dresden. A chance imperfection in the lens had enabled him to capture not just faces and landscapes, but spirits and souls.

Her husband had a book of black and white prints that he'd prepared himself. She leafed through it. "Sennacherib," she said. And there he was, in a series of three. The first was out of focus: a grinning, freckled child about six years old, taken at Lake Como on the beach. The second showed a bear in the snow. And the third was difficult to make out, a swirl of shadows around a glowing center.

There were notes in her husband's handwriting, which was clear and precise. Nevertheless, the words were difficult to read. Often he used a kind of code. And finally she was too impatient. She consulted the chart tacked to the wall. Her husband was in the circle of brass.

There are seven spheres of life, seven of death, and the Baron Ceausescu was in the third of these. In a year or so, as he dropped downward, he would be harder to reach. But now she glanced at her watch, glanced at his plotted trajectory on the chart and made some rapid mental calculations. He was always waiting for a transmission from his wife.

She pressed the coordinates into the ansible, an iron box fifty centimeters long, ornately painted with a pattern of exploding stars. Typewriter keys protruded from one side, and her stained fingers played on them. Then she waited. Her husband didn't sleep now, didn't eat, didn't rest, so he was always at her service.

From the back of the ansible rose a horn made of lacquered paper over a wooden frame, like the horn of a Victrola. The baroness adjusted the lever, then stood alternately gnawing and examining the cuticle of her right thumb. She was waiting for a flicker of movement in the surface of the crystal pyramid. Now she saw it.

Shortly after her husband's death, she had had carried into storage the various portraits of him that had decorated the house—all but one—because it hurt her to look at them, she'd said. It was the truth. She'd always been oppressed by his ugliness, his heavy, sagging features and bald head, his pig's eyes. Mercifully, all that was gone now, rotted to nothing inside the Ceausescu mausoleum. The image that now came to her out of the spirit world was of a young woman with a long throat, her golden hair tied up. There was no sign of the red pig.

The image flickered and burned below the crystal surface of the pyramid. The girl's face was happy. She smiled when she caught sight of the baroness and gave a small shy wave. The baroness studied her thumbnail. She was waiting for the sound of her husband's voice, unrecognizable and airy in the depths of the lacquer horn. First there was a sound of wind, the static of the spheres, and then a girlish whisper, "Nicola, oh, are you there?"

The baroness rolled her eyes. "Of course," she typed into the machine.

"I could bear a thousand years of this if I could see your face. What are you wearing?"

Death hadn't changed him. "Show me the place," she typed in.

"Nicola, don't make these mistakes. Learn from me."

The girlish voice was covered sometimes with a rushing sound, a swell of ions or of wind. But the intention was clear and the baroness ignored it. Always when he was alive he had oppressed her with his opinions, his advice, and now it was the same. If it were up to him she'd be a virgin in the temple, and she imagined he had many reasons for wishing so. What did he care now about money or her position in the world? What did he care about her son's future? She'd been twenty-six when he died, and he had left her with enormous debts and no one to rely on but herself.

"Please," she typed in. "If you love me." He had never loved her. Only he had wanted to possess her, touch her body with his old hands.

Now there was silence except for the ionic wind. The girl under the pyramid disappeared. The baroness came closer and peered into the crystal surface, which now seemed opaque. Nothing was there. She brought the lamp closer and examined the reflection of her own face in the triangular glass. As always the image of her face came as a surprise to her.

She lived her life as a beautiful woman, because that was the way people treated her. She herself couldn't see it. When she glimpsed herself in mirrors, she had the impression of an unattractive stranger. The pouting, small-featured woman who confronted her seemed as foreign as the girl inside the pyramid. She put her bitten fingers on the image of the woman's lips, then watched her face dissolve, though not before it had given her a haughty frown.

Instead a landscape seemed to form under her hand. She extinguished the lamp so that she could see more clearly into the pyramid's depths; the detail was minute. Now it was almost as if the sloping sides of the pyramid had disappeared. The tiny landscape seemed to spread across the surface of the table, and she peered into it as if she were a spirit or a god.

It was almost too small to make out. But she saw the little house next to the pond, the wall and the wooden bridge. The hills were ghostly, white—new snow had fallen. It didn't lie thick and uniform, but rather in blown drifts. Many trees, also, had blown down completely, or else the tops had snapped off. There was no sign of movement, except now she saw a dog running on the surface of the pond where the snow had blown away to show the ice beneath.

The door of the little house stood open, and three people came out, loaded with gear. The first—it enraged her to see—was Miranda Popescu, dressed in black trousers and a black coat, and carrying a bag over her shoulder. And the next boy seemed familiar, a youthful version of the Chevalier de Graz, who had lived in Constanta after Prince Frederick's murder. And the last was a tall man with a long-barrelled gun. The baroness, who had a capacious memory, fumbled for a moment and then recognized his face—Gregor Splaa, an orphan whom the prince had hired in his stable. A Gypsy had adopted him when he was on the street.

Even in spite of her frustration and disappointment, she was conscious also of a sense of triumph—she'd been right to send Raevsky after all. She had been right to spend the money, even as a last contingency. "Where's Raevsky?" she asked. "Can you see him? Was he there?" But there was no sound from the ansible except the rushing of the wind.

"I thought Sennacherib was one of yours."

She heard her husband's coughing laugh, soft now, almost swallowed up in static. "He belongs to no one. But every night Princess Aegypta prays to him on King Jesus' altar. He does not despise a broken heart."

She turned back to the tiny landscape. Almost she could feel the wind blowing out of it, see the glare of the sun on the snow.

ON THE STONE DAM, MIRANDA squinted up into the morning light. She could feel the presence of a world above this one, beyond the dazzling arc of the sky. She shuddered, then buttoned the flaps of her new coat. It had been Blind Rodica's. Her fingers were clumsy in Blind Rodica's gloves.

First things first, she told herself, because there was a lot she didn't want to think about. She had woken that morning and lain still for a moment, seeing in her mind's eye Rachel and Stanley in their old house. So, a bad dream she told herself savagely, even as she lay awake.

But in that vanished town, every morning when she'd woken up in bed, she'd been able to remember every dream in every part. How could it be different now? With part of her mind she could not but imagine Andromeda's mother looking out into the empty driveway, and Peter's father alone in his little house, and people going up to search the hill, and the whole town going on without her. It would take more than waking to consume that dream, more than burning to unwrite that book.

The night before she had not taken any of the black pills. "Bad dreams," Rodica had said, so probably they were supposed to help her forget. What was the point of remembering?

All that was finished, done, and yet she didn't quite believe it. No matter how real and true and right this new world seemed despite its terrors, still she would keep faith with Rachel and Stanley—especially Stanley. She would not stop imagining. At least, it would take more than a pill.

When Rachel's parents had visited from Colorado, on Sundays they'd all go to St. John's church. Afterward, when Miranda had come out of the church vestibule and down into the street, always she had been astonished at the brightness and clarity of her real life. Now as she came down from the little house into the morning, she felt the same astonishment, the sense of new-minted value, even in the chaos of broken trees. But she wondered if as time went on she would no longer be as sensitive to it, as close to tears.

Blinking, she looked down, and found herself staring at the corpses of four men, dusted with snow, arranged below the wall. Blank-faced, frozen, they were laid out below the dam like the trophies of a cat. Raevsky was not one of them.

Horrified, blinking again, she turned back toward the house. Through the open door she could see Blind Rodica's body, laid out with candles at her head and feet.

That morning, with Rachel and Stanley in her mind, she had sat up and watched Gregor Splaa light the candles. She'd sat in her nest of blankets, hugging her knees as Splaa talked, telling stories about the dead woman.

"She had a house in the Piata Italiana, a seamstress's shop before the baron signed the Gypsy bill," Splaa had said. "That's why she hates Ceausescu. The empress confiscated most of those businesses. Rodica didn't want to go back. Her daughter was passing as a citizen. She didn't want to damage that, you understand."

"Not really," Miranda had muttered to herself. But she did understand a little bit. Listening, she was able to piece together a story of how a boy and a middle-aged woman had crossed the ocean, had lived in the woods for twelve years, seeing almost no one but each other, just to help Miranda now. It seemed impossible.

"She took me in when I had nothing," he said. "That was when your aunt could protect us in Roumania."

Then he spoke to the dead woman, reminding her of how she'd saved his life when he was attacked by the panther. He reminded her of when he'd caught his leg in his own trap, and when he'd had the fever that wouldn't break. He told parts of jokes and stories, and sometimes whispered a song in his cracked voice. Hugging her knees, Miranda listened. She was trying to gather shreds of another story, how a proud empire had been throttled by corruption and violence.

"Hundreds of years ago, we were there before," said Gregor Splaa. "The Germans and the Turks and civil war. That was the first of the white tygers, Miranda Brancoveanu. Her son Constantin was the first of the golden kings."

Later, "Twenty years ago, the generals put Valeria Dragonesti on the throne. Your father fought against them—why they hated him. Madame Twelve Percent," Splaa called the empress, which was her share of the Transylvanian oil field.

And there was someone else, a general named Antonescu. He was seven feet tall, weighed hundreds of pounds. Miranda imagined him striding across the countryside, reaching out to grab men and machines.

Now she stood under an early-morning sun so bright it made her want to sneeze. Splaa was on the step of the house, strapping up his knapsack. He ducked into the house again and came out with a burning torch. He walked along the side of the house until he turned the corner of the wall.

"I can't leave her for the wolves," he said. When he'd finished the circuit, the thatched roof of the house had started to smoke on the far side. He'd thrown away his torch, and had a bird perched on his wrist, an eagle or a hawk. "Rodica let them go last night, but she came back. I was the one who trained her. She was in her cage, waiting for me."

Miranda saw some rabbits running down the slope, away from the far side of the house. He must have freed them—Splaa dug into his pocket and produced the little crucifix, taken from the statue of Ganesh. There was a leather pouch hanging from the thigh of the immense bird, and Splaa slipped the cross inside. Then he threw up his wrist. This time the eagle rose straight and sure into the sun.

THE BARONESS SAW IT as a scratch appearing on the surface of the crystal wall. She turned away, distracted by a noise behind her. Markasev struggled underneath his blanket. She strode over the cage and put her hands on the bars. Now she found herself overcome with pity. He lay on his back, the blanket twisted around his waist, and his skin seemed bruised and flushed. Hectic spots stood on his forehead and his cheeks.

She slipped the lock and took a step into the center of the cage. "Poor boy," she murmured. Then in a moment she had gone and returned, and she was kneeling over Markasev with a towel in her hands. Gently she took him into her lap and dried his face. She put a corner of the towel into a bowl of water and used it to moisten his blistered lips. "Tell me," she murmured, for he was coming awake now. His eyelids fluttered open. His pupils, which had rolled back in his head, now seemed to look at her. But his eyes were bloodshot.

He started to speak, but not to her. His mouth was open, but he didn't move his lips. "We were together on Walpurgis night," he said now. "That was the first time I saw him with my master. He was a child, and my master played with him. Threw him in the air until he squealed. My master had pig's eyes. That was not a wind that broke the tree. He was not a black bear on the snow. Not a cold white blanket on the narrow bed . . ." on and on till she was sick of it, disappointed by failure. Still she felt pity, but it was for herself. The boy seized hold of her arm. She had a hard time freeing herself. She had to pinch him. It wasn't his fault. None of it was his fault. She'd send Jean-Baptiste to tend to him, feed him, give him a bath. Then she'd try to decide what to do with him, whether something could be salvaged out of this.

But she needed her own bath first. She had an invitation to the palace that evening, and already she had wasted time. Now she got to her feet and dusted off her hands. She left Markasev lying in the middle of the cage, locked him in, blew out the light, opened the door to her bedroom and then closed it behind her. For a moment she leaned against it, listening. Then she walked through to the bathroom.

Jean-Baptiste had lit the water heater in the basement without being asked. He knew about the invitation, and the warm pipes were a sign that he expected her to go. She herself was not convinced she had the heart for it. Nevertheless, preparing for a visit to the palace was a complicated task, and she began it now. The first step was not to think about her husband's laboratory or what it contained. Instead she concentrated on the pain in her stomach, the racing of her pulse. She had a sudden memory of herself at fourteen, standing in the wings of some theater or opera house, waiting for her cue, her face heavy with paint. Then as now, a successful performance needed some rehearsal, and as she stood in her bathrobe waiting for the copper tub to fill, she went over possible dialogue in her mind. Behind her in her bedroom she could hear Jean-Baptiste fussing around. He didn't stand on ceremony. He'd been with her a long time.

She had a sudden memory of the instant when all this had started: the end of a performance of Klaus Israel's *Cleopatra*, in which she'd danced the title role at the Ambassadors Theatre. She'd stood in the smoking footlights as the flowers fell around her. Looking out, she'd recognized the baron, recently a widower, one of the most powerful men in Bucharest. He was deputy prime minister, which was the post the generals gave him for his testimony against Prince Frederick. Alone of all of them he was not clapping or stamping his feet, but only staring with his pig's eyes at her as she stood almost naked on the stage.

Now tonight she would see many of the same people who were in the audience at that performance. They still tolerated her, for her husband's sake. Or else, she hoped, they remembered the famous artist. Before that she had been a child of the slums, a servant like Jean-Baptiste, which was why he felt he had a right to talk to her through the half-open door as he made the bed and laid the fire. "Bring back money," he said. "Your solicitor came by today."

Later she thought he had gone. She was in her bath, soaping the blood out of her bitten fingernails, when she heard his high, soft, insolent voice. "I've seen the guest list. You're still young."

He was always hoping she would marry again.

She lay shivering in her bath, although she'd run it hot. Sometimes when she was young she had been unable to step out on stage, she'd been so frightened. Now she remembered that fear, and as she scrubbed her arms she decided she would not be able to tolerate walking up the steps of the Winter Keep, friendless and alone between the rows of guards. If Miranda Popescu had been a prisoner in her husband's laboratory, or if Raevsky had caught her in the snowy woods, then it would have been easy to go. The knowledge would have been like money in her pocket. But Markasev had failed, Raevsky had failed, and the baroness had failed with them.

At the same time it was essential to be seen, to go out into the world so that she would not be forgotten.

Maybe it was not fear that disabled her so much as anger. Princess Aegypta had done this, had summoned the death angel and stopped Raevsky and his men. The baroness couldn't imagine making herself beautiful, making small talk with the women, flirting with the men, while that old woman laughed at her in Mogosoaia. She couldn't bear it. She stepped out of the bath and seized a towel.

In her mind there was a way opening up to her, though it was dangerous. Never had she used it in a public place, but only in secret. Only in private. Conjuring was a dangerous art, because it was illegal. But sometimes a woman had nothing else, if there was no one in the hard world she could depend on.

Sometimes a single woman had no recourse. There was a charm her mother had given her, passed down among prostitutes from the beginning of time. She herself had taken and improved it, and she spoke it now. She stood on the mat, wrapped in a towel, looking at the stranger in the long mirror on the back of her bedroom door. She spoke the separation charm again and was rewarded by a change in the surface of the mirror, which grew dark.

She put on her robe. Then she was motionless for another moment, sitting on the rim of the tub, looking at her small feet, humming a song. She was waiting for a knock on the door to her dressing room. Sometimes it was brisk and forceful, sometimes a small, whispering sound. This time she simply felt a presence, and she couldn't wait. She turned, flung open the door. There was the image from the mirror, a simulacrum of herself made into flesh, its hand outstretched.

"Here, you'll catch cold," she murmured. The simulacrum didn't move. Flushed from the bath, it stood with a quizzical expression on its face.

Another robe hung from a hook inside the door, a Japanese kimono of blue silk. Mystified and appalled, the baroness took it down and slid it over the woman's shoulders, while at the same time she was admiring her beauty—her dark lips and shining chestnut hair, the tinge of color on her flawless cheeks.

The woman couldn't speak, not yet. She stood with her legs apart, her arms raised. "You'll catch cold," murmured the baroness again, and then she was singing again in her hoarse, breathless voice while she began the work of preparing the woman for her evening at the Winter Keep. As always when the decision was made, it was important to act quickly and ignore your doubts—she sat the woman in the chair and then turned to open the lacquered boxes of cosmetics and colored shadows. She chose a palette first, chose some pencils and brushes, smiling because again she was reminded of her mother, this time fussing over her when she was young, maybe singing part of this same song. She laughed for a moment and then hushed herself, frowning into the mirror above her dressing room table, afraid that she might by some noise or word bring Jean-Baptiste from wherever he was toiling in the quiet house.

Now that she had swallowed down her misgivings, the work was fun. She took no pleasure in preparing her own body for these ceremonial events. But this woman was so calm, so accepting. She never flinched while the baroness lined her eyes with kohl and purple dust, shaded the holes of her ears and nostrils with black pigment mixed with gold dust, painted a gold line around her lips. She sat quietly while the baroness rubbed and dusted her body with a perfumed powder, slipped on her stockings and undergarments, and put aside the Japanese kimono. Then she stood while the baroness arranged on her body the layers of silk brocade; she was famous for the simplicity of her attire. Almost alone among the ladies of the court, she wore no wig. Now she brushed her hair until it gleamed. When she was finished, the woman was indeed a stranger, beautiful beyond a doubt.

The baroness brought a hand mirror and held it up in front of the woman's face. When she saw herself in the reflection, the woman came alive in a different way. She took the mirror and held it up, and smiled. The baroness waited with her velvet shoes, and the woman appeared to notice her for the first time.

"You will go in the rented carriage."

". . . rented carriage," said the simulacrum.

"HEY!" MIRANDA SHOUTED. "That's mine!"

She hadn't noticed the cross in Splaa's hand. She'd thought she would leave it for the old woman who had died for her. She thought she would leave it with the eleven coins, but this was different. She jumped onto the dam again. "What are you doing? Stop!" But then the bird was gone.

Peter stood on the shore, staring down at the dead bodies. "It is a message for the princess," said Gregor Splaa. "In Roumania."

"That's ridiculous. How could it fly so far?"

Splaa shrugged his shoulders—condescendingly, she thought. He shifted his big pack, took up his gun. "It's my bird," he said. "When I was ten, my falcon made the flight to Budapest in just two days. Your aunt gave me a box of Turkish candy and a leather glove."

Which was all very well. "Wait a minute," Miranda said. "Peter, come. Let's talk about this. I guess we're not coming back here."

The cottage was smoking under its wet thatch. Miranda wondered if it would even burn. Probably it was difficult to set fire to a house you'd built yourself.

Last night, the wind had howled and shaken the roof. After midnight it had died away, and Splaa had gone out with his rifle, leaving them alone with Blind Rodica's body—Peter had woken up, though he wouldn't say much, wasn't much comfort, was still groggy. But when Splaa came back, even before he'd kicked the snow off his boots he was talking as if there was no danger anywhere, and it had all blown away with the wind. The old woman was dead on the floor, and he was saying everything was all right.

They could make plans about what they were going to do. They could talk about Roumania and home.

Now, standing on the stone wall above the line of pale bodies, Miranda wanted to talk again—"This isn't right," she said.

Four men in a row on the bank of the pond. All were wrapped up like little packages with their arms hidden, their feet laid close together. Now that she looked closely, she could see how young they were—just boys, really.

"We go down to the river," said Gregor Splaa. "There's a path downstream on the south bank. Or mother says we'll find the boats. There's a hunting camp. I know we can find friends. . . ."

He'd said this the night before. In the light of day, it seemed a pretty feeble idea after twelve years of preparation. And Miranda could hear the uncertainty in his voice as he continued, "There is a village called Albany on the big river. We are one knot in a web, Rodica and me—in Albany there is a man who will forge papers. Ion Dreyfoos—we had thought we'd take you south to New York Island. Now I think it will be better to turn north into the French territory—come now, please. Captain Raevsky will have—"

Behind them the wet thatch smoked, and through the door she could see the body of Blind Rodica. Splaa and Peter had both stepped down to the bank beside the stream, but she stayed on the wall, looking down at the dead bodies. "What about him?" Miranda interrupted. "What about these guys? Aren't these their footprints? Didn't they come up here from the river?"

"We don't worry about him. Please, come."

Miranda could tell he wanted to get her away from the house. But she wouldn't step down. No matter how distressing, she didn't want to lose her view of the four boys, and Blind Rodica through the open door. "Why not? Yesterday they were trying to kill us."

Splaa shrugged. "We don't have to worry."

"Sure." She felt an anger that surprised her.

Splaa wiped his nose with his wool sleeve. "Didn't you listen? You must have faith—it's true. And in the morning he is gone. They are gone. Sennacherib . . ."

His words fumbled away. He held the barrel of the long gun in his mit-tened hand. Once again he seemed eager to move on, but she wouldn't budge. "I don't see Captain Raevsky here," she said, meaning where the corpses lay behind her.

Splaa turned away. He looked down the path beside the stream, flowing noisily under its shield of ice. "Rodica made us safe," he murmured. "If you knew her, you would not doubt. Sennacherib . . ."

But she interrupted. "Last night you didn't believe any of it. Gypsy nonsense."

Where did her anger come from? she asked herself. Everything was mixed together in her head. Ever since she'd stepped outside that morning she'd felt close to tears, and maybe anger was a way of covering that up, keeping that down. She'd felt tears in her nose in the bright sun. She could see five corpses from where she stood, an old woman and five boys her own age. All of them dead for her, fighting over her. And she couldn't help thinking that if she'd done things differently, if Splaa had done things dif-ferently . . . How dare he say the danger was all gone? How bad could it have been? If it had all blown away in the night like a bad dream, surely she could have . . .

Besides, she felt so alone. All morning since she'd woken up, she had been missing Rachel and Stanley. And Andromeda—the yellow dog ran back and forth along the surface of the ice near where they had fought with Raevsky the day before. On top of that, Peter still wasn't saying anything. He just stood there in the snow, his head a couple of feet below her. He'd scarcely said a word since they'd got up. When she'd asked him, he'd said he didn't remember much about the night before. But he remembered the poem. Now he spoke up. "It's called 'The Destruction of Sennacherib,' " he announced. "He was an Assyrian king."

It had been cold in the early morning. But now they could no longer see their breath, and the snow fell in clumps from the trees. The ice had melted on the small slope below the dam. In front of them the trail broke away, and ran north along the stream through a stand of evergreens. They'd come that way the day before from Christmas Hill.

" 'The Assyrian came down like the wolf of the fold,' " said Peter. " 'And his cohorts were gleaming in purple and gold. . . . ' "

She felt a surge of gratitude and relief just to hear him talk. Just to hear him quote his poetry, as he had when she'd first known him at the other ice house. "Thank you," she said, her eyes suddenly wet. "How are you feeling?" she asked.

Peter smiled. And Splaa smiled, too. "We go to the river now," he said, as if everything had been decided. Peter and Miranda watched him as he started down the path. A thin man in buckskins, he was swaying under the weight of his enormous pack. He was holding his rifle by the barrel, using it as a kind of walking stick, which made Miranda think it wasn't even loaded.

What was it that Rodica had said? We don't depend on him—something like that, and now Miranda was beginning to suspect why. She took a last look inside the door of the house, a last look at the bodies under the dam. That morning they had been dusted with snow. But now their blankets were covered with little drops of water.

She couldn't just stay here. And they had to keep together. If that captain wasn't on the bank, then he must be somewhere, and maybe even Kevin Markasev was somewhere, too. On the wall, suddenly she felt exposed, and so she jumped down and put her hand out to touch Peter's sleeve. They followed Splaa a few steps into the woods before Peter answered her question.

"I keep telling myself my name is Peter Gross and I live at 351 White Oak Road," he said. "But it's not doing much good."

Andromeda had come running back across the ice. Now she pranced around them in a circle. She seemed eager to go down the path, and after a moment, she ran on after Gregor Splaa.

"I know what you mean," Miranda said.

"My father told me he once took some drugs in high school. He woke up in the hospital. So I'm thinking about that."

"But you didn't take any drugs."

He walked in front of her, and they made slow progress. Through the dark tree trunks, the yellow dog ran back and forth.

It was a comfort to watch the dog and talk with Peter. "That was pretty good," she said, "the way you knocked out that soldier."

She felt she could say this because the man with thick lips and yellow hair had not been among the bodies on the bank. The man who'd shot Andromeda, however, was.

Peter shook his head. "I just pushed him and he fell over. I was always pretty good at fighting, considering."

"And now you have two hands."

"I guess."

They were hidden in a pair of Splaa's gloves. The right glove looked swollen and stretched. Now Peter reached up to push a low bough out of the way. "'Sennacherib' is a mediocre poem," he continued. "My mother told me. She wasn't crazy about Byron, but she wanted me to learn the second-rate stuff. She said you couldn't spend your whole life in the tops of trees."

And yet the treetops were so bright in the morning sun. The woods were so fresh. Andromeda ran around them in a circle, her nose low to the ground.

"What do you think?" Miranda asked. "Are we crazy?" She gestured down the path toward Gregor Splaa.

It was warm for gloves, and Peter took his off. He flexed his big new fingers. There was the red mark on the joint of his thumb, the birthmark in the shape of a bull's head, and Peter rubbed at it. "I wasn't adopted," he said. "I live with my dad on White Oak Road. I don't know anything about Roumania."

Which wasn't an answer to her question. "I mean," she said, but he interrupted.

"I'm not sure we have a choice."

And that was probably true. So expedite the inevitable, as Stanley might have said—their small path had left the stream. It met a larger trail now, which had been used recently by many people. It wound through some granite boulders strung out in a line, and Miranda realized she recognized them. But they had always stood in a clump outside the astronomy laboratory at the college, and she had often played on them. Now they were scattered down the slope. One was pressed into the trunk of a big tree. Turtle Rock, she'd called it. There was the place she used to sit with Stanley, a protuberance like a turtle's head.

She stopped, put her hand on it, and Peter turned around to face her. "Are you coming with me?" she said.

He smiled again, timidly, she thought. "Sure. My father had a job in Albany." He looked around. "This will take us to the bottom of Cole Avenue. That's where we'll meet the river."

It was like something he might have said a couple of days before. She felt another rush of gratitude. "I'm sorry to get you into this," she said. "You and Andromeda. My aunt told me there were two people I could trust, and I know you're one of them."

" 'Oh, life is a marvelous cycle of song,' " muttered Peter, and she smiled.

"Anyway," he said. "Andromeda looks like she's having a good time. Wouldn't she know?" And it was true. The dog was running back and forth along the path.

"What about you?" Miranda asked.

He shrugged. "I'm worried about my dad."

Gregor Splaa was coming back for them. "Miss Popescu, come!" he said. "This way. There are the pirogues. She was right! Sennacherib—"

EVERY TIME HE HEARD THIS name, Peter thought about the poem. "For the Angel of Death spread his wings on the blast," he thought. "And breathed in the face of the foe as he passed. And the eyes of the sleepers waxed deadly and chill, and their hearts but once heaved and for ever grew still."

These lines came automatically, which did not make them welcome. They reminded him of what he'd seen that morning—four men in a row, some wrapped in blankets with only their white faces showing. Snow had blown over them during the night.

He closed his eyes to get away from them. And then immediately he found himself with another mental image, just as unwelcome—his mother sitting up with him after supper when he was supposed to be doing homework, and his father watched TV in another room. She'd taught him the Byron poem, the Dorothy Parker poem; now as he looked at her soft face in the middle of his head, he felt a kind of panic. To distract himself, he opened his eyes again and studied Gregor Splaa's hooked, narrow nose, his chapped lips, his beard tucked into the collar of his shirt.

The stream had turned away from them and Peter could no longer hear it. It would reach the river upstream of where they were. They'd cut off a big circle coming down this way. Gregor Splaa already must have found the riverbank. "Sennacherib has given us their boats!" he said.

"What do you mean?" asked Miranda.

"This trail leads to Raevsky's camp. We will take his boats. Rodica said so—I know all about his camp. He was here some weeks."

"To his camp? What are you talking about? Why—?"

"I tell you he is gone. Gone, disappeared. There is no reason to be afraid. Rodica died for that. You must have trust."

He pointed down the path. The dog came back, and she was excited, too. She barked and hesitated, as if eager to show them the way.

But Miranda was furious and unsure, Peter thought. A flush came to her cheeks. "You said you had some letters from my mother. Can I see them now?"

Splaa shook his head. "They are in my pack—no time. I will show you tonight when we are in the tent."

"I thought you said there was no danger."

"No. But still we have lost time."

Now Peter was studying Miranda's face. Her expression first: doubtful, suspicious. And then the rest of it, because she'd changed.

He'd been wondering about it off and on. The summer before, when they'd first been friends, he'd spent a lot of time watching her face and her body, too, when he thought she wasn't looking. Now he knew she was different from that girl. But because the difference wasn't obvious, wasn't like, say, a new arm or a new taxonomy, now he found the older image steadily supplanted. Black hair, square jaw, pale skin, dark eyebrows, dark blue eyes, which he'd loved to look at and still loved to look at—all that was the same. Maybe, like everything here, she was just more solid, denser, and more real.

"I'm not going to his camp," she said. Maybe the difference was in her voice. Or in her gestures. Before, Peter had always been conscious he was older than she. Now she was the one who seemed older, like a grown-up.

She turned to him. "What do you think?"

"I don't know," he said. He'd barely paid attention to the argument. Andromeda seemed eager, though. She stood with one paw raised, whining.

———

"IT SHOULD BE ALL RIGHT," said Peter after a pause.

Suddenly Miranda felt like a coward. And it wasn't as if she had another plan. It was true—she must have trust. Faith in Andromeda, in Peter, and in everyone who was trying to help her. Everyone who had looked after her all these years. Twelve years Gregor Splaa had had to plan for this. Only it was hard to ignore a whining voice of doubt.

"Well, okay," she said. But even so she let the others go on ahead. The path ran through some oak trees along the length of where Cole Avenue had been. And then the river was there, flowing broad and flat through the trees. Miranda could see below her the steep bank, and a wide, gravel strand set about with boulders.

Splaa was climbing down, and Peter followed him. Miranda hung back to pee.

Andromeda was at the water, but now she turned back suddenly, spooked and frantic. Miranda had stepped off the path, had slipped off her backpack and was squatting in an awkward and vulnerable position when she felt between her shoulder blades the pressure of a small, steel circle. She would have known what it was, even if she hadn't heard Raevsky's voice telling her what to do.

7   *Princess Aegypta*

IN BUCHAREST, IN THE HOUSE on Saltpetre Street, Nicola Ceausescu was alone. She had stood at the bedroom window and watched her coach drive out of sight. She had watched Jean-Baptiste climb the icy steps of the house, a smile on his thin face—she had fooled him, she was sure. Now by a pressure of the mind she could put herself into the cold, jolting carriage, could feel the paint on her face, the bench under her hand. At intervals that night she planned to enter part of the simulacrum's small mind, so she could observe at intervals the palace decorations, the dresses of the ladies at the empress's supper. Observe also how people treated her, how they responded to her words and gestures—that would be painful, she knew. But there is power in the world if you can seize it.

Now she looked to herself. She flung open the door of her long cabinet and ran her hand along the clothes and costumes. She'd heard Princess Aegypta was now living at a chapel in the woods, a hermit's cottage at the shrine of Venus not far from where her house had been. Monkey-people lived in those woods. Peasants brought food in return for the water of the fountain, which took away their sins.

Standing at her cabinet, Nicola Ceausescu began to understand what she would do. Always her understanding lagged behind her instinct. It was not to punish her that she would seek out Aegypta Schenck. It was not anger that would drive her, but self-interest, as was prudent, as was right.

After Prince Frederick's death, his widow, Princess Clara, had escaped to Germany. The German government imagined they could use her, use the outrage at the prince's murder. Invasion plans were complete. Roumanians of German blood were to be liberated. Schenck von Schenck would be avenged. But his widow told what she knew to his sister Aegypta, who had come Ratisbon to help her with the pregnancy. Aegypta Schenck had smuggled the baby out. She brought it with her on the train when she crossed into Roumania. She warned Ion Antonescu, an ordinary battalion commander at that time. The German cavalry was cut to pieces in the woods near Kaposvar, as they reached the Roumanian frontier.

That was why the Elector of Ratisbon had put Princess Clara into prison. And that was why the Germans were interested in her daughter, who had slipped once through their fingers. Maybe they imagined if they held the white tyger, then Roumania would fall. Whoever gave them the white tyger, the baroness now guessed, they would make rich.

How wonderful it would be to leave the city, live luxuriously abroad, in Venice maybe, or Alexandria! Now the baroness imagined the beginning of a plan. If Raevsky had failed, then Miranda Popescu was in the hands of Gregor Splaa, who was Aegypta's man. Would it be possible for her to convince the princess, even after what had happened, that they were on the same side? Or at least that they wanted the same thing, a country freed from Antonescu's tyranny?

Now she regretted her impetuousness on the night the princess's house had burned. But even so, all might not be lost. Maybe she could convince her that she might be useful, even if she couldn't be forgiven. And if that was impossible, maybe she could find out how Aegypta Schenck could communicate with Gregor Splaa, what her plans were, what she might do next. The important thing was to stay close to these events as they transpired.

The Baroness Ceausescu hesitated for a moment, then chose from among her clothes the gray woolen robe of a pilgrim, a traveling friar, complete with a hood and long, open sleeves. It would attract attention in the city, and so she rolled it up and packed it in her bag, along with a rope, a stiletto, and a flask of brandy. Then she dressed in her ordinary clothes—riding boots and pants, a silk camisole and a wool shirt. She pulled on leather gloves, and then her leather coat and black cap.

Jean-Baptiste was in the kitchen, so she slipped down the back stairs. From the cellar there was a passage under the street. It led into the house opposite, which she rented out. From there it was a simple matter to slip unobserved into the garden, then into the street beyond.

It was five in the afternoon when she left her house. A light snow was falling. She took the train from the Gara de Nord and sat in the smoking car. Sometimes she read from a newspaper, but sometimes also she slipped into the palace for ten or twenty minutes at a time. She was there when Herr Greuben approached her in an upper gallery. She dropped her glove, and he bent to pick it up. "The Elector of Ratisbon is interested in what you told me," he whispered over her hand. "Meet me tomorrow at the Cathedral Walk. Two o'clock?"

". . . two o'clock."

Aegypta Schenck had ruined everything. The Elector of Ratisbon was a powerful man. He would want to bargain for Miranda Popescu, when it was no longer in the baroness's power to deliver her.

The simulacrum felt no anger, but the baroness felt it. In the railway car, she watched them light the lamps in the suburban stations. She felt the ties go by under her feet. The conductor asked if she wanted tea. Irritated, she shook her head, and in an instant she was standing by the balustrade again, looking down at the dancers from the mezzanine gallery. Servants had lit the gaslight chandeliers, and under them the men and women spun and twirled. The band was loud. She found herself in conversation with a Monsieur Spitz, who owned a number of jewelry stores here and abroad. He was speaking French, as was the custom. Roumanian was what you used to talk to servants, which Monsieur Spitz was not. He was an elegant man of fifty-five, with a good stomach and good legs; he leaned over the stone balustrade, making rude remarks. "There's the general's wife," he said, pointing out a small, pretty woman on the floor below them. "Tell me, how do you think it's possible? A dachshund married to a Great Dane." As if to emphasize his words, General Antonescu now appeared in a corner of the room, towering above his aides. The empress was with him. The top of her elaborate headdress reached the middle of his chest.

Or Monsieur Spitz was talking about precious stones. Words that might have been vulgar and stupid in someone else's mouth did not seem so in his, because of his passion. His eyes glittered when he spoke of rubies and diamonds, as if instead of pieces of crystallized carbon he was describing religious relics or pure ideas.

"Look," he said, "that one was stolen from an African temple," or else, "I sold her that for one hundred thousand francs." Standing in the gallery, he and the simulacrum were well situated for this kind of conversation, because the fashion of the moment was for women to wear their stones in their hair, either as part of a headdress or else in a simple net. "There's Mademoiselle Corelli—does she have it? Yes! I'd give all the rest for that one," said Monsieur Spitz with true emotion. A horse-faced girl waltzed underneath them.

"Kepler's Eye," said Monsieur Spitz. "Oh, it is astonishing. Do you know the history?"

The simulacrum nodded, shook her head.

"Johannes Kepler was the richest man in Germany. After his death, the doctors had his body broken apart. The story is, that stone was found inside his skull, a tourmaline. Who knows? People say that it will show you secrets of the universe, although that doesn't seem to have affected its present owner."

". . . present owner," the baroness heard herself say.

"Oh, it is priceless, because of its pedigree. But it can't be sold. I would say two million francs. See how it burns!"

It was a clear, green stone. ". . . can't be sold . . ."

"It is too famous. I'll tell the truth, I am amazed she wears it openly like that. Of course here, not everyone will understand what it is. But her father keeps it at the bank, because there have been five attempts to break into his house . . ."

Later Monsieur Spitz talked of other things, of German politics. "Do you think there'll be a war?" he asked.

". . . a war?"

"We are too weak. We are just waiting for a provocation. . . ."

He didn't seem concerned. He shrugged. Her hand was on the balustrade, and he put his hand over it. He almost touched it. "Please," he said, "I'd feel a fool if I didn't at least ask you for a dance. You'll humor me?"

North of the city, the baroness heard the squeal of the pneumatic brake. Her train stopped on the curve, then limped into the station at Mogosoaia, where she left Monsieur Spitz to lead the simulacrum down the stair. The baroness was the best dancer in Bucharest, but she felt the simulacrum would not disgrace her. She imagined the other dancers might pull back to leave room.

She put her bag over her shoulder and got out on the dark platform. No one was there. She walked through the turnstile and down the road toward the village. On the other side of the lake was the centuries-old palace of Constantin Brancoveanu, and from where she stood, she could see the lights of the park. Around her the houses were wooden and poor. She strode to the end of the dirt street and set out across the snowy fields. But after a few miles she came into the canopy of the oak forest, so she turned aside through the trees and followed a dirt road past the ruins of the princess's house. It was a cold night, and the stars shone like diamonds, sapphires, rhinestones, tourmalines.

There in the dark beside the collapsed timbers, she changed clothes. She hung her leather coat on a protruding nail and unrolled from her bag the pilgrim's robe.

Venus was the goddess of beauty. Her shrine in the woods was a holy place to many soldiers especially. As she put on her robe, the baroness put on the part of one of them, as if preparing for the stage. She arranged the hood over her face. She said a few things out loud, roughening her voice until it sounded true. She took a mouthful of brandy, gargled it, and spat it out.

Now her bag was almost empty—just her cap in it, the flask, the stiletto, and a length of silken rope. She put it over her shoulder and strode whistling down the path, kicking at the stiff, frozen mud. After a few steps she had found a walk—flat-footed, pigeon-toed—that suited her, that matched the soft whistling.

This was her special skill. During her years on the stage, she had become famous for the way she could transform herself, not with masks and makeup, but with these small details. Pieces had been written which required her to play half a dozen parts—a sailor, for example, a pig farmer, a clock maker, a prostitute, a waitress, a king. During her performance, not once did she once change her costume, contort her face, or adopt an artificial voice. Yet people were astonished when they saw her name at six places in the programme. Even when they were looking for the trick, they were astonished. Watching her now, it would have been hard to imagine she was a small, weak woman with small feet. The pilgrim's cloak was a disguise; it was meant to appear so. Yet it seemed to cloak something different from what she was. Almost you could see under it the features and qualities she had assumed: the heavy face, the four-day beard, the menacing, strong arms.

After ten minutes or so she found a smaller path into the woods. She followed it for about an hour through the pines until she found herself in a small clearing. There ahead was the shrine of the goddess, the cottage, the low cliff, and the cave that led into the rock.

A light burned in the stone house. The baroness stood for a moment on the mossy path and smoked a cigarette. Though she had brooded about it in the train, still she would not have been able to explain how she would accomplish what she intended. Always she tried to act first, then decipher what she planned by what she did. What was the rope for? She didn't know. Yet her hands had selected it and tested its strength, a soft, white length of cord. It would not chafe or bite. But why was it necessary? Would it help her to convince the princess of her good intentions? Would it help her find out how she'd conjured up the demon who'd destroyed Raevsky and his men?

Why even was she wearing a disguise? She'd have to see. It must be because if Aegypta saw her, she wouldn't even let her in, wouldn't listen to her. She ground out the cigarette under her boot heel. Then, frightened suddenly, she let herself slip back into the simulacrum. She wanted to postpone the moment when she knocked upon the door, to see also what was happening at the Winter Keep, and if she might be lucky enough to taste at second hand some of the empress's collation. Maybe it would give her strength. She had eaten nothing all evening. But still it must have been too early: She found herself in line for the second seating. Leaning her shoulder against the wallpaper, she watched the general and his wife, the empress, and the first rank of aristocracy eat at a central table in the dining room. In fact she had chosen the worst time to return, because she could see and smell the food without tasting it. The general was a big eater, and his manners were disgusting; he took a spoonful of cold soup and wiped his lips with the back of his hand. The empress picked at a small plate of unappetizing herbs. She was self-conscious about her weight, and made a show of eating nothing, though doubtless she would gorge herself in private.

The baroness was glad she wasn't sitting at that table. So she admired the cut flowers in the vases, and listened for a moment to the person who was talking to her. She turned her head and saw with surprise that it was Mlle. Corelli—the steward must have called their names in alphabetical order. She found herself staring at Kepler's Eye, which appeared now green, now purple as the light touched it. But just a piece of rock after all, and she might not even have glanced at it, had it not been for her earlier conversation. It was set into a band of wide, flat, carved, silver links, which Mlle. Corelli had strapped around her forehead below her widow's peak. Now the baroness remembered what Monsieur Spitz had said. There was a fire in the stone, and indeed Mlle. Corelli's eyes also burned with an unusual ferocity, though she was not a beautiful girl. But it seemed she was eager to talk to the baroness. It seemed—yes—that she'd been at some of the last performances at the Ambassadors Theatre. If so, she must have been very young.

"I waited backstage with my programme—do you remember? You were so kind to me. Papa was furious. The next day I told him that I wanted to be an actress—no, I wanted to be you. Then I wrote you some letters, but you must have been too busy; that was the same time you were married. You see I kept the photographs from your performances and pinned them up over my walls—Papa was in a rage. He'd rip them down, and in the morning there'd be new ones. I was heartbroken when you left."

". . . heart-broken," murmured the simulacrum, while she watched the dish now being served: ciorba de burta and some kind of Turkish pilaf. But Mlle. Corelli went on. "I just had to tell you the effect you had on a young girl, and not just me. My friends at school, we all vowed we'd never marry, and you see? I've kept my word."

For a moment, the baroness wondered how she could shut her up. She imagined what the effect would be if she could reach out with the simulacrum's hand and put it over the girl's mouth. But then she remembered she could slip away, and in a moment she was standing in the cold night outside the shrine of Venus, a goddess who had often come to men and women like a thief in the night.

The baroness watched the plume of her breath. Above her the stars burned. She looked up at the constellation of the crown and orb. There is a power that must be grasped, the baroness thought. She pulled her hood over her face and knocked on the cottage door.

"Come in," said a voice, as if she were expected. The door was wooden, studded with nails; she pushed it open and stepped inside. She felt no change in the temperature of the air, and she remembered the day when the princess had served her tea in her cold house. Now as then, the woman was not dressed for the weather. There was no fire on the hearth.

"Come in," she said again. She stood in the middle of the house, a raw-boned woman with coarse features and coarse skin. Her gray hair fell to her shoulders. She wore black trousers and a white shirt, and she was cleaning a revolver. It lay in pieces on a low table, and she was rubbing part of the interior mechanism with a dirty rag.

The Baroness Ceausescu saw the room at a glance, the elegant furniture and comfortable chairs. Light came from kerosene lanterns. At the back, a curtain was pulled aside to show the doorway to the bedroom.

There was a Turkish carpet on the rough, stone flags. The baroness let her bag dangle from her hand. "I was told I could receive your blessing, but . . ."

"Please," said Aegypta Schenck. She gestured toward a bench along the wall near her right hand. "You will excuse me," she said. "I was making some tea. Would you like some?"

She spoke in the Roumanian language. It sounded beautiful in her coarse mouth, the melting vowels and liquid consonants. She put down the piece of metal she'd been polishing. "*Domnul*—sir, will you not show your face? No? But there's a chill in here. Allow me."

A stone fireplace occupied the whole of one wall. Wood was stacked under the raised hearth. The princess selected several pieces, and soon a fire was burning while she fussed over a primus stove. The kettle whistled. "What is your name?"

The baroness had prepared one, but she didn't use it. She sat on the bench, her head abjectly bowed. "I was told you were the keeper of my lady's fountain."

"If you are thirsty," said the princess, "this house is open to you, for we are all guilty of mistakes."

The Baroness Ceausescu stared at her boots. She remembered how the woman had grabbed her by the lapels of her coat the last time she had seen her. She remembered how easily the woman had thrown her to the floor. Suddenly she felt threatened and afraid.

"People who come here bring an offering," Aegypta said. But she shook her head when the baroness dug her hand into her pocket—she hadn't yet removed her gloves. "I mean of themselves. Why are you here? You must understand that there are many kinds of thirst."

She put the cups on the table beside the pieces of the gun. Then from hampers and wooden boxes she was producing food. The baroness watched her rough, big-knuckled hands as she sliced bread and meat and laid them out on a trencher along with pots of horseradish, mustard, and mayonnaise. To the baroness, fresh from the scent of the empress's supper, it smelled oddly delicious, though of course she was a vegetarian.

She let the bag slip between her heels and took a slice of bread with meat on it, a glass of tea. The tea, especially, was unlike anything she'd ever tasted. She wondered if it was drugged.

"Let me see your face," Aegypta said.

But there is power in the world, if you can seize it. There it is, there where your hand is. The baroness had a story prepared, but she didn't use it. Instead she opened her mouth and told a version of the truth, how she had run away from a muddy mountain village and come barefoot to the streets of Cluj when she was ten years old. How she had found work with many different men.

"There is no shame in that," murmured Aegypta.

Her kindness gave permission to invent. Suddenly the baroness remembered her false name. She remembered her false confession, how she had been a soldier in the war against the Turks. How she had served with Frederick Schenck von Schenck during the siege of Adrianople. How she had deserted with two other men, and when the police came they had run away into the woods. They had robbed a man on the road, beaten his head in, left him to die, etc., etc.

When the baroness told the truth, she felt the weakness of the starving girl that she had been. When she lied, she felt the strength of the false soldier. She went on and on: year after year of violence since that time.

"When I remember my life when Prince Frederick was alive, it is a forgotten paradise," she said. "I know all Roumania thinks that, though he was a German." This was the biggest lie of all. When von Schenck was alive she was still homeless, sleeping in boxcars and stables. Since then she had made a name for herself, a place in a difficult world.

But the princess had tears in her eyes. "He was my brother," she said. "Perhaps God led you to my door."

It was the soldier who went down on his knees before the princess, who was sitting on the arm of her chair. But it was Nicola Ceausescu who had secreted, while he was talking, the stiletto in her hollow sleeve. What for? The baroness felt the woman's hand fumbling at the edge of her hood. Holding her breath, she released the catch on the stiletto. For one last lingering moment she took the soldier's face into her face, as she felt her hood peeled back. Then she looked up and smiled, though there were tears in her eyes.

"You," murmured Aegypta Schenck.

"Please forgive me," cried the baroness. "Please forgive all this, and hear me out. I was afraid you wouldn't talk to me. But I must . . ."

This was the moment. It all depended on this. The tears were wet on her cheeks. "I need forgiveness for my sins, and in return . . ." She tried to grab hold of the princess's hand again, while at the same time she was studying her face, looking for a sign of weakness or of strength. But then Aegypta pushed her away, and the baroness felt a shudder of hatred pass through both of their bodies. It was enough. She seized the old woman by the waist and flung her down on the stone floor. She knelt above her with the stiletto in her hand. Its long, blue blade was pressed into her throat.

Now what? Well, of course. This was what the rope was for.

THE EMPRESS WAS THE FIRST of her family to rule in Bucharest. "Valeria" wasn't her real name. She had adopted it two decades before, after the generals put her on the throne. Eight other queens had used it, and she imagined her subjects might find it comforting.

She was a soft, large woman of forty-five, and she loved money. The government paid her a monthly fee in return for the legitimacy she seemed to offer. The prime minister was required to meet with her every six months, but she had no influence with him. Since she had no husband or children and was not loved by her people, she found herself much blessed with time. This she spent on various projects. She was a patron of music and musicians. But her greatest enthusiasm was for gathering money.

Or rather, not money itself, since her allergies made her unable to touch coins or bank notes. But she had a powerful mind, and she was aware of all the fluctuating balances in her various accounts. Her bookkeepers reported to her twice a day. She was no miser, and enjoyed spending large sums— that night, by the time Aegypta Schenck von Schenck had found herself fully bound, gagged, curled up on the floor, the empress had already wasted half a million francs on food, flowers, fireworks, frivolity, during her patriot's-day celebration at the Winter Keep in Bucharest.

Outside the palace, the fountains were illuminated by gaslight flares, which shone in a spectrum of colors in the mistlike spray among delicate towers of ice. The rose-colored, neoclassical façade of the building was lit by thirteen bonfires placed around the perimeter of the Piata Revolutiei. The crowd was kept back by a regiment of her majesty's own dragoons, who also stood in a double row on the wide steps of the palace. Each soldier had his right fist clenched against his chest; each stood as motionless as a statue, and the guests walked up between them. All the candles were lit in the hall of mirrors, in the banquet hall, and indeed in every room where people might find themselves, at a cost of fourteen thousand francs in beeswax alone. Then there were new gold curtains and quilted wallpaper in the reception chambers (fifty-seven thousand), a hundred cases of French champagne at twelve hundred and twenty francs a case, food for three hundred and fifty guests at four hundred and seven francs a place, including vegetable aspic and foie gras, stuffed partridges, and sherbet. Then there were the absurdly extravagant displays of irises, tulips, and columbine, brought up from Turkey on a special boxcar at a cost of ninety-eight thousand francs.

The empress kept all these numbers in her head, and she made mental calculations, small subtractions with every popped cork and exploding rocket. Against this mounting debit she had chosen to set one single credit. At seven o'clock she had sent her chamberlain to inform the Baroness Ceausescu that the pension she'd received since her husband's death would not be renewed. Eight years was a long time, too long.

At seven forty-five she waited for the chamberlain in the peacock room, which, since it was rumored to contain real peacocks, was always empty of guests. "How did she take it?" she asked.

"Ma'am, I found her in the billiard hall, where a crowd of men was watching her play. I believe she was under the influence of liquor or else some narcotic, because she said nothing to me, even after I took her aside and gave her your majesty's letter—she was with the Corelli girl. She looked at me with glassy eyes as if she didn't understand. She said not one word as I described to her the respect your majesty retains for her husband's memory. Then I heard some laughter as I left."

This, was unsatisfactory. The empress would have preferred violence or tears. She knew the baroness was close to bankruptcy. She was a conjurer and a whore's daughter. What would it take to drive her from the city?

"Ma'am, you remember she was on the stage for many years. Perhaps she was able to hide her feelings. . . ."

PERHAPS, BUT PERHAPS NOT. It was the simulacrum whose eyes were glassy and bloodshot, whose breath smelled, whose heart was equable and dull. But in the shrine of Venus, the baroness felt her fingers thrill with rage, barely suppressed, barely understood. She felt it as she pulled the soft rope around the wrists of Aegypta Schenck, as she cut the rope and pulled it tight again. Then she tied her ankles together. Then she made a slip knot of the last of the rope, and put it around the woman's neck.

She stripped off her gloves, slid the flask of brandy out of her bag, and took a drink. "I don't mean to hurt you," she said. "I want you to listen to what I say. Are you comfortable?"

She had gagged the woman with a silk handkerchief, which she now removed to offer her the flask. But the old woman said nothing. She just lay there on her side, watching the baroness's face. Her eyes were dark with an odd tint of yellow, the same as in her gray hair, though it might have been a trick of the firelight.

The Baroness Ceausescu sat on the ledge of the fireplace. Sweating, she pulled off her robe. Then she unbuttoned her wool shirt. "Tell me how you did it," she said.

The woman stared at her. She lay curled on her side. She didn't complain. Her breath went in and out. "What?" she said after a moment, as softly and comfortably as if she'd been sitting in her chair.

"You killed the men I sent."

When Aegypta said nothing, she went on: "Yes, and weren't you surprised to see them there? It was nothing you wrote about. It was my idea to send them. Guard the back door, I thought, though you think I'm a fool."

Nothing: "No—you were the foolish one. You told me it was possible to bring her straight to Bucharest. I read it in your papers, but you were wrong."

Again, nothing. The baroness sat with her knees apart. "My men. You murdered them. You don't have to deny it. I saw it in the glass. It was Sennacherib. Do you have an altar here?"

Still there was something peculiar about the woman's eyes. Now the baroness understood—she had no eyebrows. No, but their color made them invisible. "Don't lie to me," said the baroness. "There's no reason to lie. I'm not angry. I want to know how it is done."

She got up and stood over the woman. After a moment she stretched out her booted foot and pressed her in the side. "Why won't you talk to me? It doesn't have to be like this. We could be friends."

The words came out of her almost against her will. Immediately she was ashamed of them, especially when the woman closed her eyes. "Not friends," the baroness amended. "We've hurt each other too deeply for that. For my part, I'm sorry for what I've done. Are you sorry?"

She was referring to the death of her husband eight years before. The princess had been accused of killing him with witchcraft, poisoning him with sickness and remorse until he took his own life. There'd been no proof. The court case had collapsed, though the scandal had ruined Aegypta Schenck von Schenck. She'd been stripped of her title and the last of her inheritance. Already four years previously, the baron had chased her from her brother's house near Constanta on the beach.

The baroness herself had not believed the charge. But now she could imagine convincing herself that it was true. "Look at me," she said. "Listen to me. If I've hurt you, I am sorry. But you've hurt me also."

Still no response. In the corner of her mind that she shared with the simulacrum, she could picture the black stationery, the first words of the empress's letter: "Madam, after much internal consideration, we have decided that the sum of . . ." But how dare they? Not one of these aristocratic snobs was fit to lick the soles of her shoes. Not one of them had suffered what she'd suffered, overcome what she'd overcome.

"You will talk to me," she said. She knelt over the princess with the stiletto in her hand. She pressed the point into her spotted neck under the knot of the white cord, but didn't prick her. Then, suddenly disgusted with herself, she got to her feet and put the dagger down on the ledge of the hearth. She had a headache from the brandy and whatever was in the tea, and she was breathing hard. "I won't let you," she said. Then to calm herself, she threw some more wood on the fire and started to explore the house.

This was the larger room with the fireplace and the armchairs, the table and benches. The princess cooked on a primus stove. There was a food cupboard set into the wall. Opened, it revealed a plethora of delicacies: marmalade, cornichons, olives, pickled cherries, sardines, smoked oysters, teas. Many of the bottles and cans had foreign labels.

"You know it's true, what I told you," the baroness said. "I came from a village near Pietrosul. Seven of us in a room. Not like this—we had nothing. Just a wooden shack in the mountains. Water from the stream. Cold in the winter, I remember. Oh, I remember . . ."

She stood on the threshold of the inner room and pushed the curtain back. Maybe she had imagined something different, some saint or hermit's alcove of bare rock, maybe a pallet or a narrow bed. Or else something to suggest the simple, peasant cottage that had burned. But she was not prepared for the richness of this room, the soft gray carpet with a pattern of snow lions, a carpet that was not even from Turkey, but from some more exotic country farther east. She was not prepared for the carved four-poster bed, the embroidered coverlets, the brass lamp stands and gilt-framed water-colors. One thing only was rough and plain, a wooden cross over the bed.

In the corner was a mahogany armoire, which she pulled open. It contained some gowns and dresses. And inside an inner drawer there was money, a great deal of money, a bag of currency in small denominations.

The baroness bit her lips, drew blood. "You understand?" she called out. "A dirt floor shack, chickens with us in the room. When I ran away I had to eat from the garbage heaps, sleep in the train cars—do you know anything about that?"

There was a nightstand with a basin, a pitcher of water. Beside it on a shelf, several pots of unguents, skin cream, and perfume, which obviously had no effect. The old woman's skin was like leather. But there was no altar, no statue of the goddess. Only the cross of King Jesus on the wall over the bed.

The baroness returned to the front room. She sat down again on the ledge of the hearth. Now suddenly she was filled with sadness. "I understand what you must feel," she said. "I understand how you must want to protect your niece. But there's no reason to be afraid. I myself would never hurt a child. I am a mother, after all—did you know that? My son lives in an institution in the city. It is very expensive. And I don't understand how in the book you wrote, the shelter you made for Miranda Popescu, you still made it possible for doctors to blame a woman for her son's illness and keep her from him, chase her away. How is it possible that anyone could love him more than I?"

The princess had said nothing, but now she spoke. "The book is longer than we wrote."

"Talk to me—yes. Thank you for talking to me. And you must explain to me this uncertainty, because—yes, I admit it, you are wiser than I am. And you must explain to me why though I follow your instructions, I do not get your results. My husband also made a mess of his alchemical experiments. You alone make no mistake—is it because you pray to God? Sennacherib—where is the altar? Where is Venus's fountain? I feel I must drink from it, just a little drink. You wouldn't deny some water to a woman like me?"

"This place is free to all."

"No, but it's not free. What's the money for?" And when she didn't answer, the baroness explained: "The money in your room. What's it for?"

The woman lay on the floor, staring at her with her intolerable eyes. When she didn't answer, the baroness went on. "It was a condition that was his since birth. He didn't learn to speak. Normal and affectionate, I mean in his bones and body. He was my boy, only they took him away. What can they do for him that I can't do? They said it was my fault."

She felt the pressure of the rage inside of her. "What's left for me to do but pay and pay? Oh, you," she said, as she sat down on the hearth. She put her face into her hands. Then she looked down into the princess's narrow, unblinking eyes, and remembered why she'd come. "Like you I hate what has happened to my country. I hate what General Antonescu has done to us. The rich live in palaces while the poor cannot afford a crust of bread. Do you understand how someone like myself could yearn for the white tyger, could imagine how Miranda Popescu might be the one to help us? Is it such a crime to have brought her back? Now will you promise not to struggle or cry out, so that I can untie you, and we can sit together and discuss this, and discuss what must be done?"

The princess stared at her. "I did not kill your husband," she said. A pause, then: "Though I did not mourn his death. The laws he wrote, they have destroyed us. I think he was driven mad by guilt. As for these men of yours, not all of them are dead, I think. You're wrong—I make my full share of mistakes. All of us are fumbling in the dark. I pray my niece is safe, that's all."

Again the baroness felt her heart swell with rage. Was it possible the old woman told the truth? No, she was a liar, like all of them. The baroness stood up, stood over her, and brought back her boot to kick her in the side. Then, overcome with self-disgust, with hatred for those yellow, dark, unblinking eyes, she pulled herself away, pulled open the door to let in the night air.

She staggered out the door and stood with the back of her head pressed against the stone wall of the house. She stood there a long time, waiting for her nausea to subside. And as she stood, a new suspicion occurred to her.

It had been from the princess's papers that she'd learned about the girl and how to bring her home. But the text had been mistaken in one single detail. The baroness had thought she could bring back the white tyger straight to Bucharest, to her husband's laboratory. No, she had been led to think that, and if she'd sent Raevsky and his men to North America, that had been her decision, her insight, her stab of brilliance.

But that Jew Gregor Splaa had lived there long enough to build a house. So Aegypta Schenck had known the girl would come that way. And if she'd suggested something else in her papers, she'd been lying. And if she was lying, then she'd meant them to be read by someone else, used by someone else. And if that were so, maybe those descriptions of the absurd dictator had been meant to goad her. What is it the old woman had said—that the name Ceausescu had not even been mentioned in the early drafts? So was it she who had been meant to find the papers and follow the instructions that now seemed so carefully laid out?

A suspicion took hold of her, that she had been manipulated and duped. When she heard a noise, she peered around the edge of the door frame. She saw the Princess Schenck von Schenck sitting upright by the hearth.

She had managed to seize hold of the stiletto; she was holding it between her wrists while she was cutting at the ropes around her feet; now her feet were free. But the knot was still hanging from her neck. The baroness leapt on her and pulled it tight, and then watched herself keep pulling and pulling with all the force and strength of a soldier or a criminal or a murderer—how was it possible? How could she be capable of such violence? Surely this was not part of her plan—until the woman's eyes bulged and the cord cut into her throat and she was still.

"Traitor," said the baroness. "You traitor. Hypocrite." Suddenly horrified, she stepped backward, stepped through the curtain into the inner room. Without thinking, she found herself ransacking the armoire, searching among the dresses for some clue, while at the same time she looked for refuge in the Winter Keep, away from this place, far away. She found herself sitting in one of the smoking rooms, sprawled in a leather armchair while Mlle. Corelli sat on the footstool, peering up at her and talking, talking. Kepler's Eye shone on her forehead, a stone that seemed now like an eye indeed, a third, unblinking eye that burned with many colors, though the core of it was dark.

"That year I ran away from boarding school," said Mlle. Corelli. "I slept out in the woods for two nights until the policemen brought me back. I don't know what I was thinking. Now, it seems strange. But I think you can't just accept the life that people give you, that people just assume . . ."

No help there. When the baroness came back, she was knocking her head against the door of the armoire. Clutched in her hand was the old woman's store of money, a canvas bag filled with banknotes and coins. The baroness forced herself to get up, forced herself into the main room again, where she found her own leather bag and pushed the smaller bag into it. She looked for anything she might have dropped. She decided to leave the stiletto. She didn't want to touch it.

She didn't want to look at the princess's body. She didn't want to look at the mouth of the corpse where now a shape was gathering. The mouth was open and the image of an animal was there on the gray tongue. And it wasn't some worm or duplicitous snake, some violent monster. But instead there was a bundle of translucent feathers made of air and breath and spit, and then a tiny bird flew straight and sure out the open door and up into the night, a brandywine bird, pretty and innocent.

She followed the bird out. Then she was leaning in the same place she had stood a few minutes earlier, except all had changed. And now she could see the entrance to the grotto, a hole in the cliff. The night was cold and still.

"I've thought about marriage," said Mlle. Corelli in the smoking room. "My father has some officers in his regiment. But you give up so much freedom, and for what? No—to tell the truth, I've been so miserable. I hate my father; he would beat me if he knew I had taken his precious jewel. He'll know tomorrow. I swear he cares more for it than he does for me. If I had money of my own, I'd run away to Paris. In some ways I couldn't forgive you for marrying that old man, especially since it meant you gave up working—and for what? You must understand I have an artist's heart."

No respite there. Coming back to herself almost at once, the baroness found she was standing inside the cave. There was a short tunnel in the rock, a flicker of light, and the sound of rushing water. There was steam in the air, a smell of sulphur, and when she turned the corner into the shrine itself, she saw the source, a brimming basin in the rock floor of the chamber. Kerosene lanterns stood in niches. The air was hot because the water was hot, a pool of water heated by some volcanic vent.

Wreathed in coils of steam, the shrine rose from the center of the pool, a gold statue of the goddess. She had left her clothes on a heap on the rocks, had let her hair down and strode naked across the pool, which was as still as a mirror of glass. This was an image from the life of Venus. Once she had appeared in this place to an ancient king of Dacia who had wept for shame.

Now the baroness found herself stripping off her clothes. Now she stood up to her knees in the scalding water, scrubbing her shoulders and her back until they burned. Sobs choked her, tears ran down her face, because she was mourning Aegypta Schenck von Schenck, a princess of the old blood who had not deserved to die like this, strangled by a worthless murderer. In the days when she was rich, she had used her money to help those in need. The baroness herself, one night when she was eleven years old, had come into the Children's Hospital in Bucharest with blood poisoning and a broken, abscessed foot, and the women had taken her in for more than a week. They had fed her and washed her and let her sleep in a real bed— why had she held back the memory until now? But she remembered the cross above her bed. She'd had no money. "Thank the princess," they had said, and this was how she'd thanked her. "Oh," she murmured, imagining the white silk cord pressing into the soft neck.

When her brother was murdered, and her friends left her, and she was dispossessed of all she owned, the princess had not stooped to robbery and conniving. The proof was in her spirit image, the brandywine bird, who sang so sweetly in the hedgerows in the early morning.

And when her brother was struck down, his men had been amazed to see a butterfly trembling on his lips. Some said it was golden, some said it was blue, but all had been astonished that such a man, the greatest general of the age, had been able to summon from his last breath so pure an image.

The baroness could already recognize her own spirit beast. She had seen it when she glanced sidelong at mirrors. Doubtless it was here in the surface of the pool, but broken up and made unrecognizable by her flailing. Maybe a pig like her husband, or else a flea-bitten, baggy-kneed, mangy old cat, though now as she stood here in the pool, she knew she was as beautiful as the goddess herself.

This was the fountain that took away sins. She had imagined the water would be sweet to drink. But she bent down and with her cupped hands she skimmed up a draught of the sulphurous, nauseating liquid. She stood with the hot water dripping from her fingers, and then she raised her head. She heard a dog barking.

Always she had hated dogs.

She leapt from the pool onto the greasy floor. For a moment she stood listening, and then she scrambled for her clothes. It was good to be quick but not careless; she pulled on her pants and boots, her undershirt, and all the rest. She pulled on her pilgrim's robe and hid the bag of money under it. Then she was out in the cold night, striding along the path the way she'd come. The barking was in the woods behind her. She thought she'd avoid it, until she saw the flicker of torches through the trees.

Should she step away from the path and try to hide among the bushes or the pine trees? Probably, but she did not. To hide would be to proclaim her guilt, and besides, the dog might find her. It was her custom to confront trouble, and so she drew her hood over her wet face and pressed on, pigeon-toed, flat-footed, whistling, until she met a dozen or so men and women. They were carrying torches, wreaths, and dried bouquets. She stood aside to let them pass, but they'd have none of that. They were in a joyful mood. One reached up to seize her by the sleeve.

"Sir," he said, "have you come from Mother Egypt's house? Is she awake? My friends are coming from their wedding feast, and they need her blessing."

He spoke in a whistling, high voice. He was drunk. There was the bride, hideous in her embroidered, country clothes, her face painted like a doll's, although no paint could change her round, flat face. There was the groom, cheeks wan as yellow apples; the baroness put her hand out. "I congratulate you," she said in her hoarse soldier's voice. "As for the keeper of the shrine, she's gone to bed."

Two small young boys were walking hand in hand. "You can see the light," chimed one, pointing down the path toward the little stone house. "And the dog is barking."

They took off at a run. The baroness cursed under her breath. "Please," she said. "I have to make my train." It didn't matter. None of them were paying attention. Instead they were singing songs and making jokes; she slipped away. But since she'd mentioned the train, she couldn't take it, and it was a long night's walk into the town from Mogosoaia. Again she cursed herself, hurrying along the path, waiting at each moment for the sound of shouting. How could she be so stupid? When she reached the burned ruins of the house, she paused, fumbling among the timbers for the coat that she had left hanging there. But it was gone.

8 The Wild Men

"MIND THE DOG," said Captain Raevsky. "I will shoot."

Miranda stood up, yanked up her pants. Then without thinking she turned and took hold of the long barrel of Raevsky's pistol as it moved past her toward Andromeda. The dog had bared her teeth, was bounding toward them with a look of great ferocity, which changed.

Another man came out of the bushes. He wore a green woolen jacket with the insignia of the red pig. He carried a rifle, and as he raised it, the dog hurtled past Miranda, hurtled past Raevsky into the undergrowth and disappeared.

Miranda saw this. She heard the crashing in the bushes while she wrestled for the gun. Raevsky wanted to capture her, not shoot her, which gave her an advantage. His finger wasn't even on the trigger as she twisted the gun down.

But he had hold of her now. Miranda stomped on his foot, and though he grimaced, licked his lips, he didn't budge. Her face was near his face, his grizzled beard. She could see the scab on his ear where she had bitten him.

Then Peter came scrambling up the riverbank. "Get away!" he said. "Get back!" A man was chasing him and tried to grab him by the waist and pull him down. But Peter slipped through his arms somehow, and the man went sprawling in the weeds.

She kneed Raevsky in what she hoped were his testicles, but he didn't move. He yanked the gun away from her and pointed it toward Peter as another soldier clubbed at him with his rifle. Peter clutched the stock as it came around, but the man behind him had gotten to his feet. He hit Peter with a paddle on the back of his head and knocked him to his knees.

"Stop!" she cried. She'd gotten hold of Raevsky's gun again. But where was Gregor Splaa? There he was, standing on the gravel bank. His pack was gone, but he did nothing.

Had he led them into a trap? Had all that crying over Blind Rodica been just bullshit? His face was white with fear, and there was a man behind him with a gun, and he was just a stupid idiot after all.

Miranda turned to Peter, and she had the strange impression he was happy. Unarmed, he was fighting the two soldiers, but he took the time to glance at her and give her a fierce smile. Raevsky was yelling something in Roumanian while the man with the rifle swung it round again. He was the man Blind Rodica had dragged into the house, which meant this was his second try at Peter. But he wasn't having much more luck, because Peter caught his rifle stock again and was twisting it away when the man with the paddle swatted him across the back of the head.

Raevsky pulled the gun away from her. Try as she might, she could not budge his arm. He was too strong. He was behind her now with his arm crushing her chest and his beard scratching her ear. "Please stop," she said. The man with the paddle raised it up again above Peter's head. Then it came down, and for a moment no one moved. The air was warm. The snow was soft in the undergrowth. In places it had melted to reveal the starved, yellow stems.

"What will you do?" Raevsky muttered in her ear. "This is your fault."

Was that true? She was a fool to have trusted Gregor Splaa and not herself. That much was true.

Peter lay on his back in the wet weeds. His eyes were open, and there was a red welt on his forehead. And the soldier with the paddle raised it again. "Stop it!" she cried. "I give up."

And Raevsky grunted something more, and the soldier paused. He was a young man in gold-rimmed spectacles, and he stopped with the paddle above his head.

"Enough," Raevsky said in English. He let go his grasp, then pulled her forward by one arm, his pistol pointed toward the sky. "Enough of this."

He pulled her down the slope. And they weren't taking any chances with Peter. The man with the spectacles stood with his paddle raised, while the other man pointed his rifle. She tried to catch Peter's eye; she wished he could say something, but he was stunned. He was looking at the sky. Andromeda had run away, though. She had escaped, so that was something.

Now she could see the river between the trees, and the beach that undercut the bank. Gregor Splaa was there with his hands tied in front of him. And the fourth soldier, with his pistol drawn, was coming up the bank with a length of rope in his other hand—she didn't like the look of that. So in a trampled patch of undergrowth she tried a second time to pull away. But Raevsky grasped her from behind again while the other man came toward—he was not dressed like the others. He was wearing a leather shirt and had an Asiatic face. She didn't want him to touch her. But the soldier with the spectacles had his paddle raised. And she couldn't let him bring it down again. She felt Raevsky's arms across her breasts as the Asian man tied her wrists in front of her with many loops of coarse twine.

They led her down to the river bank where Splaa stood. He wouldn't look at her as Raevsky pulled her down to the gravel beach where four boats were drawn up in a line. There was the fire pit and bundles of supplies. A shelter of tarpaulins was slung on ropes between the trees. Splaa's pack lay where he'd dropped it.

Blind Rodica was dead, and he had led them straight into this camp. Was it possible he'd betrayed them deliberately, engineered all this? But if so, why did he look so unhappy and defeated now? No, it was stupidity pure and simple, hers as much as his. She hoped he was just as wrong about the firing squad.

They stood in the middle of the camp beside the flat, flowing river. The Asian man climbed onto a boulder and sat down, the barrel of his gun pointing up between his knees. Raevsky started to pack up camp. He stowed the rolled-up ground cloths and tarpaulins. He was staving in the flat bottoms of the boats—pirogues, Splaa had called them—drawn up in a line. He had an axe, but it looked as if he could have used his hand, the thin wood broke so easily.

Two he left undamaged. He rolled them over and slid them to the water. Then the man with gold spectacles brought down some canvas bags, which meant the other one had stayed with Peter. No one spoke. The soldiers were in a hurry. Splaa wouldn't catch Miranda's eyes. He muttered, "I worked in the stables. They might have sent a proper soldier. If Prochenko . . ."

Blind Rodica's death had robbed him of all strength. He spoke in a frightened squeak. "If you're going to do it, please. Don't make me wait." This to Raevsky, who turned, came toward him with his revolver in his hand.

"If you were a soldier," Raevsky said, "you would not think so I would waste such lives."

There was a gap in his teeth on the right side of his jaw. "Last night I lost four men, dead as kittens. Boys from my village. You are the murderers, I think."

Then to Miranda, "Miss Popescu, I remind you—nothing of this was necessary. You will remember how I warned you yesterday. Look what is happened. I tell you again, you have not to fear from us. I do not understand. . . ."

Now the bright day had disappeared. The soldiers were stowing their canvas bags in the two boats, including, she was surprised to see, her leather backpack, which she had dropped beside the path. In a moment it was done. Raevsky came toward her with his hand held out.

"Get away," she said.

"Miss Popescu," he said, "there is no choice for you."

"I won't go," she said.

He shrugged, and then he pulled her down the gravel strand alone to the boats. Her hands were tied together at the wrists. He was relentless, but again she struggled, tried to break away, because she could not allow herself to be tied and led like this. Andromeda was gone, and Peter—now she saw Peter on the bank above her. The yellow-haired soldier from the hut was backing down the slope. He kept his rifle pointed toward the middle of Peter's chest.

So what could she do but let herself be tied and led? Peter didn't look at her, but at the mouth of the long rifle. Miranda could see the red stripe on his forehead where they'd hit him. "Wait for me," she said, so he wouldn't do anything stupid. "I'll find you," she said, but he didn't look at her. He was staring at the rifle's mouth, and when he turned it was to look at Raevsky's long revolver, also pointed at his chest. At the same time the Asian man floated the boat in the water. The water was around his legs.

The soldier with the rifle walked backward down the beach. And the one with gold spectacles held the other boat. He laid his paddle along the gunnel and prepared to hoist himself aboard—in a moment, Miranda understood, there'd be a race. The Asian man was in the front of her boat, and now Raevsky had to put down his gun to force her aboard, scramble aboard. They splashed through the icy water, and Miranda was over the thin side. Raevsky forced her over, and then their boat was away, and it found the current of the river and headed off downstream.

But she got her head up in time to see the yellow-haired soldier throw his rifle in his boat and spring aboard. The one with the gold spectacles guided the boat out, and at the same time Peter came charging down the slope and jumped into the water. Raevsky fired his pistol as their pirogue swung round, and for a moment his body was between Miranda and the other boat—she couldn't see. But she heard a cry like a wounded animal and felt a spasm of nausea—no, it was all right. The man with gold spectacles had pushed the boat away and scrambled aboard. Peter stood roaring and shouting with the water around his waist.

"Wait for me," Miranda whispered as the boat pulled away. She found she couldn't make a louder sound. She thought that with Raevsky busy she might sink the boat, unbalance it, and so she struggled to her knees. But Raevsky dug his fingers through her hair, and as the Asian man paddled their boat, he forced her down against the thin boards. Raevsky had his gun in his right hand, and with his left he dragged her by her hair, and with his fingers tangled in her hair he pushed her ear to the varnished wood. She heard the pebbles grind along the bottom of the boat, and then the flapping of the water.

Then Raevsky let go. He needed both hands for his paddle now. She couldn't see his gun. She sat in the bottom of the boat, and she watched Peter roar and struggle in the water while Splaa stood on the shore, surrounded by abandoned bags and baggage and the wrecked boats of the soldier's camp.

Peter was still bellowing in the water. The boats had scraped across a sandbar, and now Peter waded out to it and climbed onto it, so that suddenly he seemed enormous, as if walking on the surface of the stream. She didn't think he'd been hurt. He raised his arms above his head, his boy's arm and his big man's arm. And he looked at her now, and she saw in his face an expression she had never seen before on him or anyone. His face was distorted almost beyond recognition. And he called out like a wounded beast, and raised his arms as if he meant to fight the world.

The boat swung round a bend in the stream, and she lost sight of him. Because she couldn't bear to see his terrifying face, his splayed teeth and his shouting mouth, at that last moment she looked away at the trees rushing past, the undercut bank, the stones at the bottom of the stream. She didn't want to think he'd changed from the boy she'd known. She felt conscious of every little thing. The soldiers pulled the boat into the center of the stream. Miranda sat between Raevsky and the Asian man in front. The other boat pulled past them and went on ahead.

After ten minutes of work, Raevsky took his paddle out of the water. "So, he is not the man his father was, not yet. Because his arm is hurt, maybe."

What did he mean by that? She was too dazed to ask. She sat huddled in the bottom of the boat and she said nothing. Then, after a few more minutes, "You see it makes no difference. Where are you going through the woods? Home—is it not so? We will take these boats to Albany in some days, and then New York on the paddle steamer. Then the *Carpathia* will wait for us—you have never seen such a boat. So," he said, gesturing toward shore, "Don't cry—it doesn't matter. We all go to the same place, to Roumania."

She had no intention of crying. She pressed her lips together while Raevsky looked into the tall trees and mumbled something. When he turned back, he tried to avoid her eyes. "Prayer to dead," he muttered finally. "They are on the river of the dead."

Miranda sat in the bottom of the pirogue between some canvas bags.

There were some long guns, and she wondered if they were loaded. She was looking at Raevsky, trying to read his face, trying to control her own.

"So, you will tell me. Was it the demon of this forest? That old Gypsy—where is she? My boys were cold as snow. White faces. God help me, I ran away."

Now he seemed eager to speak. "And you will tell me about Pieter de Graz?" he asked. "It is his son—is not so? Is maybe sixteen years, I think. The right age, and that is de Graz's face. He was in Constanta with Aegypta Schenck, but we heard Antonescu murdered him with all the prince's men. This boy—I could not recognize him in the Gypsy's house. Never could I shoot a boy, de Graz's son. But I was with the army when the Chevalier de Graz went down to Adrianople to fight the Turkish champion. Three falls with the sultan watching! We all drank his health that day!"

She had heard this name before in many contexts. Was it Peter's name in this new world?

Raevsky looked behind them to the riverbank and then continued. "You think I am a monster. So—listen—ground too hard to bury them, I tell myself. Shall I go back now? Spirit death—I take you to the steamship, then return. I will not go home with you. Alexandru will take you home. For me is too much shame. Stay here in this damned country. I will not see my lady Ceausescu after this. Maybe I join de Graz's son. It is my fortune."

The river was broad but not deep. Miranda could see the gravel bottom. Occasional large stones broke the surface. Peter and Splaa were long out of sight. The river cut through a forest of tall pines. Numb and sad, trussed up in the bottom of the boat, Miranda imagined a yellow dog upon the southern bank, running through the trees. She imagined Peter trudging through the underbrush. When the land changed and outcroppings of rock appeared along the shore, she imagined Peter keeping pace with them. But when he jumped onto a boulder by the shore, in her thoughts she had to turn away from his roaring face.

What would he do? she thought. Where would he go to find her? What had Splaa said—a hunting camp? No, but she would find the trail on the south bank and follow it back, and Peter and Andromeda would wait for her.

The first thing was to escape. She could not let herself be bound and tied. She raised her wrists toward Raevsky. When he shook his head she pulled her forearms apart, searching for some slack in the cord, at the same time looking in the bottom of the boat for some sharp object. The strands were a rough hemp, tight and strong.

Captain Raevsky sat in the stern. Miranda studied the man in front of her, the Asian man in the leather shirt, who was different from the other three. His long black hair was braided behind him and tied with a leather thong, to which was attached five coral beads. A necklace of shells was around his neck. And when he turned back toward her from time to time, she could see his long black goatee, his flat, heavy face. Though he took enormous cuts at the water with his paddle, he was not, like Raevsky, out of breath.

In time Raevsky stretched his paddle across the gunnels of the boat. "A wind came without noise," he said. "It broke trees, but I hear nothing. I could not breathe. I feel a crushing on my heart, but I said the prayer to Mars. Then I run away."

Up ahead the land was rising on either side of the stream, which was narrower here, deeper and faster. Miranda pictured Peter on the shore, shaking his arms, but then she turned away. She understood the captain was confessing cowardice to her.

It was no consolation. "Where are you taking me?" she asked.

"Don't you hear? This stream comes to the Henry Hudson River and then down. Ferenc and Alexandru will take you on the ship from New York to Bremerhaven, then to Bucharest. Did you read the letter I gave? My lady Ceausescu, you will see her."

Miranda said nothing. After a moment, Raevsky went on. "You must trust my lady. She will protect. The empress does not fight against a woman because her father sold us to the Germans. That was twenty years ago."

"My father . . ." Miranda said. How could she feel protective of the reputation of Prince Schenck von Schenck, whose name she'd heard for the first time the day before? That wasn't it.

But she didn't want to hear that Captain Raevsky was her father's enemy. There was no comfort in hearing that, because she was alone and in his power and close to tears.

She had an idea. There were tears on her cheeks, and her nose was running. She brought her hands up to touch her face. She turned aside and took one of the strands of twine between her teeth.

Raevsky stared at her a moment, then put his paddle down. He reached into his pocket and produced a handkerchief, which he dipped over the side. Then he was dabbing at her cheeks and nose with the cold, wet cloth. The handkerchief was clean, the linen soft and fine. A red pig was embroidered in one corner.

He sat upright again. "Miss," he said, "I know is hard. I don't know what they do. But my lady will not hurt you. Your place is your own country. You are loved there, you will see. Maybe the Baroness Ceausescu will take you to her house. If so, you will be lucky, because she is beautiful and kind. She knows what it is to be alone without friends."

This was not comforting. "She lives in a rich, tall house," Raevsky said. "She goes everywhere to all the parties and the palace. I think you are luckier than me, because I won't see her again."

This was not comforting to Miranda. Baron Ceausescu had betrayed her father—Splaa had told her that much. How could what Raevsky said be true?

She bowed her head into her aching hands, and worried at the twine with her teeth. The Asian man in the front was talking now. He said some words in a strange language, then pointed. "Look."

On either side of the stream, the rocks had risen into granite cliffs fifty feet high. Miranda was familiar with the Hoosick River, which ran west out of Williamstown toward New York State. It followed Route 346 and joined the Hudson somewhere north of Albany. But this river was three times as broad, and she had never seen this place, this forest of pines, these walls of rock. Now above them where the man was pointing, she saw a movement in the trees. A woman came and stood on the rocks over their heads.

She had long yellow hair. She went down on her hands and knees and peered over the boulders at them. Miranda could see her face was smudged with color, charcoal or black paint. There were stripes on her cheeks and neck. She opened her mouth. From fifty feet away Miranda could see her teeth, her tongue sticking out.

Now the man in the front of her boat was shouting in a mixture of languages. "Back," he shouted, "back," which Miranda understood, and Raevsky too. He put the blade of his paddle in the water to turn the boat around, while at the same time he was calling to the other boat ahead of them. But it was too late, for now from both sides of the gorge men appeared under the trees. They were dressed in skins, like old pictures of American Indians, except for the yellow hair. Some had big stones in their hands, which they raised up.

The stream was narrow in the gorge. As their boat turned, Miranda could see the other boat trying to steer into the middle, the men paddling hard. Then it flipped over in a trough between two rocks as their own boat came around in a circle. Raevsky had turned it, but when he saw the others go down, he brought it around again. Two men were floundering in water above their waists. One lost his footing and was swept downstream, while the other struggled into shallower water on the right hand side. But he was pelted with rocks from above. Miranda could see a gash over his eye.

The lead man in her own boat, who had first pointed to the wild woman and told them to go back, now flung himself over the side. The water was not deep where they were. He held his gun and his bag above his head as he stumbled toward shore. He never looked around, but climbed up through the rocks and disappeared, while Raevsky steered the boat into the gorge. The light pirogue was overbalanced by the sudden shift in weight, so Miranda crawled into the lead seat while Raevsky grunted and cursed. Still he managed to guide the boat to where his man stood bleeding and confused, the water about his waist. It was the soldier with gold spectacles, and Raevsky dragged him into the boat. Then they were off downstream through the shower of stones, which struck the water all around them, struck Raevsky too upon his shoulders and his head. Miranda was not touched.

"English! Savages!" Raevsky shouted. "No—"

Past the gorge, the land opened up again, a wide strand of gravel on the right hand side, where the river made a turn. Wild men stood there. Miranda could see they had dragged the yellow-haired soldier from the river and were beating him. One had stripped off the green jacket. He held it on the end of a stick, shouting as the pirogue swept around the turn and

Raevsky brought it ashore. He leapt onto the strand carrying three of his long guns. He shot one of the wild men who had rushed toward him brandishing a club.

The men had yellow hair knotted with feathers or pieces of bone. Now they scattered into a thicket of saplings. They dragged the soldier into the shelter of the thicket, together with some bags they had salvaged from the water. Others came from the woods on the other side of the river.

Miranda sat in the boat with the wounded man. One of the lenses in his spectacles was broken. His clothes were sopping wet. He lay without moving.

The sharp, brass gunnel of the boat had a break in it, and she was rubbing her hands along the break. There was a weak place in the rope where she had bitten it. One by one, the coarse, loose strands of hemp gave way, and then her hands were free.

Racvsky was walking slowly toward the thicket carrying his bundle of guns. But on the other side of the stream a man had jumped down into the water and had started to wade across the shallow water toward the boat. Though the air was cold and there was ice in the crevices of the rocks, he was bare-chested, a big man with painted skin, carrying a club that ended in a lump of quartz.

Miranda stepped over the side of the boat onto the wet strand. Raevsky had pulled it into a trough of fist-sized rocks. She drew it out into the water until the keel came off the stones.

All she had to do was jump aboard. Raevsky had found the soldier in the thicket and was standing over him. But when he looked up and saw what she was doing, his face took on such a naked, wide-eyed, horrified expression that she paused. He threw down his guns, then stumbled back toward her over the rough stones.

The man with the quartz-headed club was shouting from the stream, which rose around his thighs. Others were behind him. The current was tugging at the boat, and Miranda couldn't see how she could hold it steady and climb aboard. The men had almost crossed the stream now, and one was reaching for the boat—not the man with the club, but another one with feathers in his hair. But then there was a shot and he staggered backward, and Raevsky was running with his long pistol in his hand. Then he was beside her holding the boat into the current, forcing her over the side.

The men in the stream had splashed backward a few paces. The men on the shore were squatting over the guns. Raevsky scrambled into the boat and took his seat. For a few minutes he and Miranda paddled like mad, but then he paused to put his fingers on the neck of the wounded man, still lying in the bottom of the boat. The river was quiet here, broad and shallow. They went on a little farther. Then, sooner than Miranda thought was safe, Ravesky brought the boat to shore.

"We camped here on the other way," Raevsky said. Enormous pines grew near the shore, and they pulled the boat up the bank onto a carpet of black needles. Miranda was shivering because her pants and feet were wet, and the wounded man was unresponsive, cold and stiff under his blankets. The gash on his head was dry. Raevsky stripped off his clothes and wrapped him, naked, in a feather sleeping bag, then Miranda sat with him while Raevsky gathered firewood. There was plenty of dead wood among the trees. He tore it down, then built a fire in a hearth set among the boulders. He lit the kindling with matches from a silver canister, and piled on more wood than was prudent, Miranda thought. Later, gathering branches as the sun went down, she saw the fire burning from far away.

She imagined throwing the branches down and striking out to find the hunters' camp, the path along the south side of the stream. She imagined Peter and Andromeda waiting for her, and for a moment she saw in her mind's eye Peter's face as she'd last seen it from the boat. So—she would find him the next day. Night was falling and Raevsky's fire burned bright between the trees. She had no blankets or gear. Besides, there were the wild men, the Indians. What had Raevsky called them—English? It seemed ridiculous.

"Tomorrow I will go," she thought. "Probably he will let me go, after all this."

Despite herself she was impressed by what Raevsky had done, how he'd fought for his men and cared for them. And in the meantime he had made a comfortable camp. In the gathering dark he'd boiled water and made potato soup out of a powder. He gave her crackers and sliced sausage and German chocolate, all without speaking. He pitched a tent for her, a military pup tent made of thick, bleached canvas. Then he fussed with the wounded man—Alexandru, he called him, his sister's son. He whispered to him, chafed his arms, checked his heartbeat and his pulse.

She saw him bending over Alexandru as she returned with her load of wood. He scarcely looked at her. So then she crawled into her tent and watched the shadows of the fire on the canvas walls. She listened to Raevsky muttering and chanting in Roumanian, before she fell asleep.

In the morning when she woke, it took a moment for her to realize she was not in her own bed in her own room. Gray light came in through the canvas wall. Miranda lay in the blankets that Raevsky had given her, imagining Rachel and Stanley and the old house. What day was it— Thursday? She wondered if school was open again, and if not, where her classes were being held. She supposed they could find room in their old elementary school in town. Then she imagined the police searching the woods on Christmas Hill, and Stanley, and Peter's father too, while Rachel sat with Andromeda's mother in the kitchen. What must they be thinking now?

In her warm tent, Miranda lay still until she started to cry. Then she got up, unbuttoned her tent, and went down to the stream to wash. But it was too cold. Her breasts ached, and the rocks were slimy with ice. She cupped some water in her hands to drink, patted her cheeks with her cold hands, then sat brushing her hair with Blind Rodica's brush.

Since she was a child, Miranda had told herself she wasn't comfortable in her own parents' house, that her real home was elsewhere, in another country. Now this morning and the one before, she had thought of Berkshire County when she woke. As she brushed out her hair, Miranda found herself remembering another dream from earlier in the night, torn and covered by these thoughts of Stanley and Rachel and the house on the green. Now again the dream came back to her in rags—it was her aunt once more. The gray-haired lady with the fierce, hard face was bending over her as she lay in her blankets. "You must find them. Follow the path. In the dream life I will send a messenger. . . ."

The rest drifted away. The harder she though about the words, the slipperier they seemed. Why couldn't the woman say what she meant, give her something real, tell her what was going on? Was that too much for the white tyger to ask? Dream life messenger—what crap was that? Frustrated, she got to her feet and walked up to the camp.

Alexandru had died during the night. Captain Raevsky had laid him out on a flat boulder. The fire still burned in the circle of rocks. Miranda stood holding her hairbrush, watching Raevsky fussing with the body—how many corpses had she seen in just two days? Making up for lost time. She'd been to Stanley's father's funeral when she was eight, but the casket had been closed.

Was it possible she was hardened to this already? Or was she just numb from the cold. Certainly she felt no special horror at the sight of the dead man. He looked asleep. She sat down by the fire to warm her hands. Water was boiling in a handleless tin pot, and even though she pulled the cuff of Blind Rodica's shirt over her fingers, still she burned herself when she drew it out. But Raevsky had showed her the enameled cups the night before, the tea in its silver foil. She sprinkled tea into the bottom and poured water over it, doing a better job with the pot this time. Perched on a rock, wrapped in a blanket, she held her cup in both hands and stared into the fire.

Where was Peter now? She would get away from here and go back up the trail on the south bank. That's all that she could do. When she came to where the wild men were, she'd go in a circle through the woods.

Or should she cross the river? What would Peter do? She didn't want to miss him in the woods. But Andromeda would find her, if she'd figured out how to use her nose.

The night before, she'd thought she'd wait for daylight. But now she wondered if the darkness was better. Or else, if he'd been up all night, maybe Raevsky would fall asleep—to her annoyance, she could not keep her thoughts to these important questions. Always they were escaping backward. When Kevin Markasev had held her book above the fire on Christmas Hill, before he let it drop, for a moment she had guessed at what was happening. When he had asked her if she wanted to go to Bucharest, he was asking her permission—she could see that now. Perhaps the change could not have taken place without her welcoming it. So why now did she feel she'd give up everything just to be home? She had no right to feel that way. All these men were fighting because of her.

Not far from where she sat, Raevsky was digging a hole in the bank near a collapsed tree. With gloved hands and a piece of wood he was pulling out stones, shoveling out black masses of pine needles until he had dug a sort of cave. He was muttering to himself, and Miranda watched as he walked past her without a word, then returned carrying Alexandru's body. He curled it into the small space as best he could, then covered it with needles and stones and dirt, more and more until he'd made a pile and the body was hidden from sight. He made a tower of stones and against it he laid a rifle. In a crevice he placed Alexandru's spectacles and a book. Then he stood chanting, a bottle of colorless liquid in his hand, which he was alternately drinking and pouring on the rocks. When finally he came and sat next to the fire, he smelled of alcohol.

"Raki?" Miranda asked.

"Turkish ouzo." Raevsky shrugged, pulled his gloves off. "So, we have a legend that a river leads into the *tara mortilor*—the country of the dead. No one can cross unless their body—see? Now there are many ghosts haunting me. These young men, I could not do what I must do. Killed by a demon. Skin so white. I was afraid to touch. All these witches must be hunted. Germans have the good ideas in this. German laws. That boy Ferenc, he will haunt me."

"Who were those men?" asked Miranda.

The liquor in Raevsky's bottle was a quarter gone. He shrugged. "Many tribes here. Cannibals. Ishu told me before he ran like an *iepur*—a rabbit."

Ishu must have been the man with coral in his hair. "Indians," Miranda said.

"They are English, so I tell you. After the earth moves they are coming across the sea. Big wave—a big wave. Floods in the Black Sea—this was more than one hundred years. Some go to France and Spain, Roumania, even. Some here."

He stared into the fire. Miranda was full of questions. Finally, "What are you going to do now?"

Raevsky spat into the fire. "I promise to bring you to Bremerhaven, so maybe now I have to go with you. Maybe I send telegraph. But I will not return to my own place. How can I see my people there? This was my sister's son."

His stubbornness was terrible, Miranda thought. But if he was awake all night, he could not stay awake forever. She would wait till he was drunk and then escape.

So she sat with him that day as he was talking. He told Miranda how he had fought with her father and the Baron Ceausescu against the Turks. He was the baron's man from the baron's town of Cluj, and after the war he had returned there. He had a farm, no wife, no children. Then in the autumn he had hired the men for this journey—boys from the countryside or students.

"I was tired of looking at the *curu magarului*—the back of my mule," he said. "Madame Ceausescu remembered me. She saw me just some times, but she knew my name. Oh, you will see that she is beautiful and wise." He brought a locket out from underneath his shirt. He split it open to reveal a portrait of a woman.

Miranda had her backpack between her knees. It still contained her Roumanian things as well as some supplies that Splaa had given her from his house—a toothbrush, a towel, socks and gloves, a bar of soap. These Miranda felt with her hand as she fished for her own locket, opened it. "Who is that?"

Raevsky studied it, surprised. "You never saw your mother's face?"

"No."

"So, that is Clara Brancoveanu. Her husband was von Schenck the traitor, but she paid for it. She told us the date and time of the invasion when the Germans came to Kaposvar, so we are grateful. She paid with her freedom—that was twenty years before. When Aegypta Schenck must close her Constanta house, what did you do? You were—tell me—eight years or so. I never saw. The story is that you were dead or else in Germany. Tell me the truth. Where did you come from? That Jew and that Gypsy did not raise you in that house. My lady did not tell me that. Every night we were waiting on that hill, she said. For what? But some trick! You and de Graz's son."

It was too complicated to explain. Miranda said nothing, and soon Raevsky started to talk again. He sipped his bottle and told her stories of Roumania. He spoke good English, learned in the baron's service. He told her about a cabin in the mountains where he had hunted bears and wild boar. He told her about a lake where he'd gone fishing.

"Your father was a great man," he said. "That is why he is so shamed—or so. Twenty years before, he died. Is long enough . . . ," he said, but how could it be twenty years ago? Miranda herself was only just fifteen. She'd had her fifteenth birthday in the summer.

Her hands were cold. She put her hand into her pocket and felt the bottle of Blind Rodica's pills.

Miranda thought she'd give him one more chance. Enough time had gone by. Maybe now he might be able to think of her as more than just a duty or a task. So she thought about her predicament until she had a lump in her throat. "Please let me go," she interrupted him.

Raevsky stared at her. After a pause, he went back to talking about things he'd done.

"Please let me go back to my friends," she said.

He looked at her as if he didn't understand.

"Now you're alone," she said. "You can't do this by yourself. I could have left you last night. I could have left you on the riverbank. Please, will you take me to my friends? Peter and . . . I promise we'll go with you. We won't fight you any more."

He looked at her, then spat into the fire. "It will not be bad," he said. "All Roumania will love you. The Baroness Ceausescu . . ."

Miranda did not want to hear that name again. "What do you think?" she said. "You think she sent you here to bring me back, just so she could take me to parties and send me to school? You had to shoot an old woman and take me from my friends? You had to give me a forged letter and see your men killed by maniacs, just so all Roumania could love me? I was going there anyway—you know that. Those people were going to take me to my family!"

After a moment, he cleared his throat. "The letter is a forgery, is true."

Then in a little while, "But it will not be like that, so you see. Bucharest with its blue domes like turnips. The Baroness Ceausescu will protect you from the Germans, that is true. And from Valeria Dragonesti—so, I think. She does not tell me everything."

He was obsessed. After a little while she asked him, "May I have a drink?"

He reached for a tin cup but she shook her head. He was drunk enough to hand her the entire bottle. She had hidden some of her black sleeping pills in her palm, and when she wiped her mouth after a sweet, burning sip, she dropped them one by one into the bottle's neck. Raevsky wasn't looking. He stared into the fire.

But for a long time the pills had no effect. Captain Raevsky told her stories through the afternoon until the light fled away. Miranda ate potato soup and sausage, but he didn't do anything but drink. Inch by inch, he slouched deeper in his blanket roll. And it took a long time, but finally he was asleep, and the full moon rose. Miranda watched it though the trees, then walked along the riverbank in the cold, clear air, so she could see it in the open sky.

She came back to the fire and Raevsky hadn't budged. She covered him with blankets. He lay snoring on his back.

Under the moon, as she picked through the camp, more than ever in her life she felt she was Rachel and Stanley's daughter, alone and far from home. This fire, this snoring soldier, the dead man in his cave covered up with rocks—maybe she could believe in what she saw and heard and touched. The moon and the cold night. All the rest was just a story, a family in Roumania named Brancoveanu. A woman named Miranda Brancoveanu, who freed her country long ago.

She took down her tent and packed it into its roll. She took warm clothes, dried food, and slung them into a canvas pack. She wouldn't take too much because she had to travel fast. She'd follow the river upstream again, and she wouldn't think about the wild men. And she'd meet Peter and Andromeda along the path on the south bank. Maybe they had come for her, and they were close.

Again she felt a stab of terrible regret. What had she done for Peter, that he would chase after her now? It was her fault he was in this mess with her. When she'd surrendered to Kevin Markasev on the hill, she'd dragged him out of his whole life. And even before that, she'd not deserved to be his friend. When Andromeda came back from Europe, she had ditched him.

Around her neck she hung the locket that contained the sepia face of Clara Brancoveanu. On the cold riverbank, Miranda found it hard to think about her. Instead she imagined there were times in the past year when she'd been cruel to her own mother, had hurt Rachel deliberately in little ways. And even though, now standing by the fire, she couldn't think of any specific incidents, still if she ever . . .

When she was small, Stanley had often put her to bed, had read books and sung songs to her. Her favorite one he made different every night, though there were verses that came around again and again:

Hush, little baby, don't say a word,
Papa's going to buy you a mocking bird,
And if that mocking bird don't fly,
Papa's going to buy you a pizza pie,
And if that pizza pie's too cold,
Papa's going to buy you a crown of gold,
And if that crown of gold gets lost,
Papa's going to buy you the holy ghost,
And if that holy ghost flies away,
Papa's going to buy you a sunny day,
And if that sunny day clouds over,
Papa's going to buy you a dog named Rover . . .

Etc., etc., and she was always sleeping by the end. Now she picked up a stick, poked at the fire. Raevsky was snoring, and there were shadows among the trees. Miranda straightened up, then felt suddenly light-headed and crouched down again. She had a pain in the pit of her stomach, and an odd, burning sensation lower down. She unzipped her jeans, and found that her underwear was streaked with blood. At first she imagined she'd been hurt.

A secret source of shame for her was this: Long past the age when her friends—Andromeda, for instance—first started menstruating, she had not yet crossed this bridge, as she imagined, into womanhood. "This is just great," she said now. Then she walked down to the water to wash herself, thinking at the same time about the pirogue. She had to hide or destroy it. If Raevsky woke, he must think she had taken it downstream.

Once outside the fire's circle of warmth and light, she had a momentary image of the wild men coming quietly along the path, raising their quartz-headed clubs. Furious at herself, she stepped over the wet stones, peered across to the far bank. There was a flat rock sticking out into the stream.

Miranda stripped off her boots, her pants. Naked from the waist, she squatted down next to the freezing water. She examined herself as well as she could, then looked away.

She looked up at the river of the sky as it flowed through the treetops, following the curve of the river at her feet. Stanley at various times had taught her all of the constellations, and now she looked for some hint of the familiar winter patterns: Orion fighting Taurus, his dog at his heels. But the stars were dim, unrecognizable, washed out by the moon.

She had thought and worried about her period over the years. But it hadn't occurred to her she'd feel so light-headed, so intoxicated. Either that, or one sip of ouzo had affected her. Looking up at the sky, she felt nauseated, dizzy, and her heart was beating hard. When she looked down again, Andromeda was there.

She had lost her dog's shape. She was her own self again, on her hands and knees on the flat rock across the stream, drinking from the water. The moonlight shone on her bare skin, her big shoulders, her long arms and legs. Why was she naked on this bitter night?

Miranda closed her eyes, then opened them. Andromeda stepped into the shallow stream, and though the water was fast, she made scarcely a ripple as she waded across. She climbed onto the bank, and Miranda could see that the glow on her skin was not moonlight at all. But her skin was covered with yellow hair. The hair was thicker on her head, and it ran in two thick ridges down her neck.

Miranda stepped back. Her friend came toward her with her arms out, but Miranda shied away. What she was seeing was not real, she thought. It was a ghost, something out of *tara mortilor*. If she tried to touch her friend, then she would fail. But she could hear Andromeda's voice. "I thought you were gone for good, I swear to Christ. Who were those guys up on the rocks? Those cavemen with the spears? That was completely nuts."

Miranda put her hands up, palms out. She said nothing, but Andromeda answered her: "What do you mean? Oh yeah—Miss Canine of Berkshire County. I'll tell you later. Let's get you away from here. Are they asleep?"

Miranda shrugged. Her body was full of a sensation that was like drunkenness or the effects of marijuana. More specifically, she had once taken Ecstasy during a concert in Saratoga Springs—just a quarter of a dose, enough to be a good sport and to keep Andromeda company. And maybe it was just a sympathetic reaction, but that night she had felt some of the same distance from herself, the same lack of faith in her perceptions. Now she was conscious of a sweet, peculiar smell like perfume or cologne. "Something is happening," she thought stupidly.

"So put your pants on. Get your stuff."

Miranda had brought some rags as a towel, and as her friend watched, she tore off a strip of cloth to lay into her underpants. Then she got dressed.

She pulled the pirogue fifty yards upstream, and Andromeda didn't help her. The farther away she walked, the better and more normal she felt. The splash of cold water as she pulled the boat ashore, the smell of the balsam branches she used to cover it—all that seemed to revive her, clear her head. As she came back toward the firelight, she thought she wouldn't see her friend again, that what she'd seen was an illusion conjured up from longing and cold fear. But then Andromeda stepped out from the well of shadow beside one of the enormous pines. "We're just a few hours through the woods," she said, and when she spoke, Miranda felt a tingling in her body. Her stupidity and light-headedness came back.

Raevsky had rolled over onto his side. His snoring had changed into a weak, snuffling noise. His dirty hand clutched his bottle as if it were a doll. Miranda gathered up her backpack. "I've got your clothes," she said.

Andromeda scratched her side, and under the yellow hair Miranda could see a scab.

His face painted with firelight, his cheeks glowing red and orange, Raevsky suddenly looked vulnerable, old. His forehead and the corners of his eyes were creased with dirty lines. His nose seemed brittle, sharp. His neck was covered with a red rash where his grizzled beard had pricked his skin.

Suddenly it seemed cruel to leave him alone with the ghosts of his dead men. She wondered if she had given him too many of Rodica's pills.

She looked into Andromeda's face, trying to see if she could catch some kind of human expression. "Come on," Andromeda told her. She was like a dead ghost of herself, a yellow shadow fading through the trees. Miranda's aunt would send someone—was this the messenger? Was this the dream time? Miranda had a sudden fear of being left behind, and so she stumbled after the yellow shadow, up the bank and through the trees.

They left the river and struck south. The way was easy under the pine trees. But then they were in another, different wood, and the land was rising. Miranda stumbled through the thickening undergrowth. The trees were smaller here and the light better. But there was more snow, too. Sometimes she sank over the tops of Blind Rodica's boots. Sometimes she lost sight of Andromeda, and then she stumbled on, looking vainly for footprints.

When Andromeda wasn't with her and had disappeared behind the trees, then Miranda would notice a small wind in the cold air. For a moment her dry wits would return to her. She would struggle to a stop. Startled, she would look around. Then Andromeda would come to sit beside her on a rock or a fallen tree. The air was motionless again, and Miranda would smell that hint of perfume or cologne, and imagine how the drug that caused these feelings, these illusions, was in the air she breathed. What was it her aunt had said?

"Once I went out in a place where there were open fields," Andromeda murmured. "A town in the distance in the valley. I could see the lights. I was cold, and I went down to see if I could find a warm place and some food. I had an idea that I wanted a slice of pizza, but there was nothing like that. The streets were full of snow. The houses were locked, and everywhere I went, the dogs were barking. I looked through the windows at the people sitting by the fire, kids doing homework, reading books. The only place that was open was this white, wooden building, and there were people inside singing songs. A man came to the door with a gun, so I ran away."

Or, "I saw a way lit with fire along the hills. It was midnight, and as I was climbing I saw others in the trees, dogs and creatures, giants and dwarves. One man with two heads and a hammer in his hands. And I'm thinking, he looks really friendly. This looks really good. I found an open place. There was a crowd of people and animals. But the next fire burned by itself in the clearing. Then there was the entrance to a cave, and the animals were coming in and out, where the shadows were dark. I was afraid to go into that cave."

Or, "I was in the tall grass and the sun was going down. It was so hot, I just lay on the ground. All around me were the mice and other kinds of rodents weaving in and out through the grass. They were talking to each other, whispering, but I could hear it. I could understand their voices. 'Look for the white tyger. Oh, the white tyger will come.' The sun was setting in a purple glow and I was lying with my tongue stretched out, too hot to move. But I could see the tops of the grasses pushed aside, as if there was some heavy body coming through. The little mice were dodging past my feet saying, 'Here she is. Here is the white tyger.'"

These strange monologues could only feed Miranda's sense of unreality, sitting on a broken tree, moonlight shining on the snow of a strange world. She had a groaning in her stomach and her crotch. For a long time she sat without listening, as the light around her grew and spread. The dawn was coming, and the sky was paler toward the east.

But she was comforted by the mention of pizza. "Is Peter with you?" she asked, the first time she had spoken. Andromeda sat picking her long nails. "What do you think is happening at home?" Miranda asked.

"Home?"

"You know. Do you think your mother had to have her car towed?"

Miranda watched a spasm of anger pass over her friend's face. Then something else that was like fear. "Look," she whispered. Bending down, she thrust her hand down through the snow. She brought it up full of loam and dead leaves and held it for Miranda to smell. And the dirt itself seemed to have a perfume like chocolate and cinnamon, and it was shot through with gleaming ice crystals. Or that's what she thought until they started to move, and she saw that they were bugs, golden and silver beetles, the moonlight reflecting on their backs.

"It's your choice if you live with ghosts," she said. "I cannot help you."

Miranda had been staring at the handful of dirt. Now she was alerted by a sudden strangeness in Andromeda's voice, the hint of a foreign accent. She looked up, open-mouthed, light-headed, and saw a new face in front of her, a young man who was like Andromeda in every detail, who smelled of tobacco and cologne. And abruptly it was as if whatever spirit had sustained her during that long night was gone, and whatever narcotic had dulled her—its effects were gone, and left her terrified. She put her hands to her face and yelled, and yelled again, and kept on yelling till they must have heard her in the hunters' camp over the hill. Later, Splaa came running with the yellow dog and found her on her knees in the wet snow, alone.

IN BUCHAREST, THE BARONESS CEAUSESCU came to her own high house on Saltpetre Street in the early morning. She had walked most of the night from Mogosoaia except for the last few kilometers, when a milk cart had stopped for her and brought her to the city. They had come in through the Gate of Mars, headed toward the Piata Romana where the driver expected a crowd. Five women—thieves and fortune-tellers—were to be publicly denounced, which was something the baroness had no wish to see. Once inside the walls she left the old man with her thanks and a coin, walked the last way through the cobbled streets. Without her coat, and having buried her pilgrim's cloak in the woods, she was grateful for the warmth of the sun when it finally rose. Still she felt vulnerable and exposed, afraid of being recognized, and she slouched along with her cold hands in her pockets, keeping to the shadows until she reached her own neighborhood. There she forced herself to walk more openly. Here in the streets around her house, it was not unnatural for her to be out on an early stroll. But she entered her house through the tunnel from the cellar across the road. She had no desire to meet Jean-Baptiste at the door.

She was both anxious and tired. Earlier she had tried one last time to slip into her simulacrum, but had failed. And she thought this was because of either of two reasons: The simulacrum was asleep, or else she herself was too exhausted and discouraged to find her way across that mental bridge. She imagined she'd recovered from her remorse over the princess's death. There was no use crying over spilt water. The future was always more important than the past. Still it was worrisome, her lack of self-control.

She slipped first into her bathroom and turned on the water in the tub. It ran cold for a moment and then hot; Jean-Baptiste had stoked the heater for her morning bath. Relieved, she dropped her bag off of her shoulder. It was full of money, mostly, now, which she had taken from the princess's cabinet. While she was waiting for the tub to fill, she went down on her hands and knees to open up a secret compartment behind the baseboard. Her husband had been fond of such architectural details. She found the catch, the baseboard opened up, and she was stuffing the bag down into it behind the singing copper pipes.

She opened the door to her bedroom and peered inside. The curtains were closed, but she could see the bulge under the coverlet where the simulacrum lay. Relieved, she turned again into the bathroom and began to take off her clothes. She unbuttoned the wool shirt, then walked over to the washbasin to rinse her face. There was a mirror above the basin and she didn't look into it. She caught a glimpse of matted, chestnut-colored hair as she peered down at her hands, her close-chewed fingernails.

She was surprised the basin was so dirty. There was a brown ring halfway up the bowl, brown smudges on the countertop. She rubbed at them with her thumb, while at the same time she was muttering the prayer of dissolution. When she went to bed, she wanted to be alone. She wanted the simulacrum to be gone.

But halfway through the prayer, she paused. She looked into the mirror now, looked at her wet face, her puzzled expression. Then suddenly she turned, stepped through into her bedroom. As she approached the bed, the bulge in the coverlet subsided and flattened with a tiny sigh. She stripped away the sheets where the simulacrum had lain, and was shocked to see brown smudges there. She saw the print of a hand on the pillowcase. Her own fingers often bled where she had bitten them, but not like this. The gown on the floor stunk of sweat and cigar smoke. The gloves were stiff with blood.

She wrapped the clothes and the bedclothes together into a ball and locked them in her closet. She washed out the basin, washed away all of the brown marks, then stripped off the rest of her clothes and got into the bath. She had run it hot, yet it failed to relax her. She had a greasy feeling in her stomach.

Still she felt better when she was warm and clean and sitting in her bathrobe in her dressing room, clipping her toenails and toweling her hair. Jean-Baptiste knocked on the door, a signal that he'd left her breakfast on the threshold. Sometimes he stayed to share a word with her when she opened the door, but this morning he was gone. The landing was empty. She picked up the tray and brought it inside. She poured herself a cup of

tea, inspected the pumpernickel toast. Then she unfolded the morning paper, glanced at the headline, which was about the burning of several shops
among the German minority in Transylvania. Under that story, at the bottom of the front page, was another in the form of an editorial: TWO VIO-
LENT AND FELONIOUS MURDERS.

Readers who have allowed themselves to feel complacent because of a
reduction of the number of violent crimes here in the capital will find
themselves shocked to learn about the brutal murders of two prominent
citizens during the same night in two separate locations in the city and
its environs. Though the metropolitan police have been successful in
breaking up many of the most dangerous Gypsy gangs, still it is obvious
that stronger measures are needed. Domnul Claude Spitz, the jeweler,
was apparently beset by thieves while driving home from an imperial
celebration late last night.

The other victim was Miss (formerly Princess) Aegypta Schenck,
who had been living in seclusion near the shrine of Venus in the
Mogosoaia woods. A sum of money, donated from local villages, is also
missing, and we can assume that robbery was the motive for this outrage. . . .

After a while came Jean-Baptiste's knock again, too loud to be entirely
respectful. He spoke at the half-opened door: "Ma'am, I've made up the
bed. The sheets were missing, as you saw."

"Thank you."

"Did you have a pleasant time at the reception?"

She didn't answer. She was reading the newspaper article. Later she went
into her bedroom and saw where he had laid out on the table beside the bed
some personal items, which she imagined Jean-Baptiste had picked up from
the carpet. There were her house keys, her change purse, her pocketknife.
Beside them in a clean ashtray was a large green stone—Mademoiselle
Corelli's tourmaline, Kepler's Eye.

She lit the bedside lamp. At that moment the stone looked like an eye to
her, staring mournfully. No matter how it was oriented, you could always

see a place on its surface where the surrounding light would gather and re-fract. At the same time, by some optical trick, there appeared to be a source of light inside the tourmaline itself, a glow that varied in intensity and hue.

What had happened the night before? Her last memories had been of leather armchairs, of talking with Mlle. Corelli in one of the upper smoking rooms. But what had happened after that?

She'd been so discouraged by the princess's death, it never occurred to her that she would come home to find something worse. All night as she'd walked home she had worried about her lost overcoat and tried to remember if there was anything in the pockets to connect it to her. But now there was blood on her clothes and a stolen jewel in her bedside ashtray—could it be possible, she wondered, that Mlle. Corelli had given her the stone? At least the girl had not been murdered, so far as she knew.

These thoughts occupied her as she dressed. She put on riding boots and pants, a man's shirt and a sleeveless, cashmere vest. She picked up the stone, wrapped it in a handkerchief, and slid it into her front pocket where it made a bulge.

There was a knock at the door into the dressing room. "A gentleman from the police to see you, ma'am," said Jean-Baptiste. His tone was formal and correct, which was unusual. When she went onto the landing, he was there. "Shall I tell him you are sick?"

She shook her head, said nothing as she preceded him down the stairs. Once again she was aware of the necessity of a performance. She tried to quiet her misgivings and dismiss all thoughts. Only she concentrated on the squeak of her palm against the polished bannister.

The policeman waited in the drawing room on the first floor. He was an elderly man in a tweed suit. He had a lot of gray hair that he combed straight back, and it contrasted oddly with his small, black moustache. His eyes were blue. When the baroness entered the room, he was standing with his hat in his hands, examining a portrait of her husband above the mantel-piece. Over his arm, she saw with horror, was a long, leather coat.

He was carefully, even elegantly dressed. He cocked his head to one side as he looked at her. His name was Luckacz, he said, which was a Hungarian name. He spoke with an accent: "I beg your pardon, ma'am. I served under your husband in the foreign ministry, then at the central bank. He was a great gentleman. If it hadn't been for him, we would be speaking German now."

The baroness allowed herself to smile. "Please, did Jean-Baptiste offer you something? Would you care for a cup of coffee? Perhaps something stronger?"

Luckacz held up his hand. "No, ma'am. I won't be lasting long. I asked my superiors for this opportunity to be of service. For the sake of your late husband. I had heard that he had married an actress, but I was not prepared . . ." His voice, dry and precise, trailed away. The baroness suspected he had intended to flatter her, but had changed his mind at the last minute. Frowning slightly, she stared at him. His moustache must be dyed, she decided.

"I see you found my overcoat," she said. "Please, it has a sentimental value. But I can't think where . . ."

The policeman shrugged. "There were ticket stubs to the Commedia for last Friday night. That's how we knew."

"Yes, of course. I went to the eight o'clock performance. Is that where you found it, at the theater?"

"No." A momentary crease to appeared between the policeman's brows. "Not there. Was it stolen?"

"Nothing so sinister. I lost it, I'm not sure where. If you knew me, you would know how absentminded . . ."

"I refuse to believe that. An artist such as yourself . . ."

Again it was obvious he was uncomfortable. More than ever, the baroness was aware of the bulge in her pocket where Mlle. Corelli's tourmaline lay. She prepared herself for the inevitable question, which came after a slight pause: "Are you acquainted, ma'am, with Aegypta Schenck von Schenck?"

"I was reading about her in the paper."

"Yes," said the policeman. "It was a crime. One doesn't sympathize with her, perhaps—the sister of a proven traitor. She herself spoke better German than Roumanian. She was accused of complicity in your husband's death."

"I never believed that."

"No? Then let me tell you it was true. Because she was not convicted, it does not mean there was no evidence. I am relieved to hear you felt no animosity. That is the correct attitude under the circumstances."

The baroness rarely used her drawing room. It was small, uncomfortable. The walls were pink. The furniture was not designed for comfort. "I'm trying to discover what you're asking me," said the baroness. "You must have heard about an argument I had with the princess several months ago."

"Yes. You took with you a soldier from the baron's former regiment in Cluj. But he did not speak French, and was unable to inform us—"

"You've been busy."

"Yes, ma'am. I'm sorry. These choices are not mine. I was an admirer of your husband's. And I'm not as generous as you, at least as it concerns Miss Schenck. But I must ask you to explain. The soldier mentioned a book."

The baroness shrugged. "That was it. I had a book that belonged to her. The rest, it was an accident."

Luckacz stared at her, his head cocked to one side. Doubtless he expected more from her. After a moment he went on: "That's what the soldier told us. I'm sorry to ask. But your overcoat was found in the cottage that burned. After Miss Schenck's death, it was turned in to the police. I would have thought you left it there that night, except for the tickets."

Now came the moment for the baroness's performance to begin. First she was stupid: "My overcoat was found. . . ?" She put her hand to her mouth, and allowed a procession of emotions to pass over her face.

"Yes. Not far from the shrine of Venus where Miss Schenck was killed."

"Oh, no." There was a wing-backed chair next to the piano, and she allowed herself to sit in it. Nothing exaggerated—she was not overcome with horror or fear. She sat primly on the edge of the seat. She was concerned, that's all. And her mind was racing forward, or so it appeared.

"Someone must have put it there."

"Yes, ma'am. You understand you have some enemies. After all . . ."

"I was at the empress's reception last night. Many can vouch for that."

"That's what I meant. But the conductor claimed to have seen you on the train yesterday evening. Wearing this overcoat."

Puzzled, she knotted her brows. "Someone dressed like me!"

"That is our theory, ma'am. Someone who knows you and Miss

Schenck had a discussion. Witnesses saw a man walking away from Miss Schenck's house, shortly after she was killed. A soldier in a pilgrim's cape. There were different reports, but it is possible to think he could impersonate you on the train."

The baroness pursed her lips. She was puzzling it out. "I don't understand. The coat was found . . ."

"Not at the shrine. One of our witnesses took it from the burned house. She brought it to us after Miss Schenck was discovered."

"I don't understand. If the idea was to involve me, why not leave it . . . ?"

"Perhaps he thought it was too obvious, ma'am. Perhaps he wanted to suggest that it was you who were disguised like the pilgrim. If so, you would not have left your overcoat at the scene."

"But this is terrible!"

"Yes, ma'am. It is lucky you spent the evening in such a public place."

"I can't believe it. I decided to go to the reception at the last minute. My idea was to stay home."

"Perhaps you can think who might have been aware of that."

The baroness's drawing room was decorated with pink wallpaper with a recurring pattern of gold birds. There was a clock on the mantelpiece, and she listened to the tick, tick. She decided she'd say nothing until the policeman spoke again.

"You must understand. Your husband's death was a great loss. We were grateful not only because of von Schenck's plot. When the baron was in government, he brought a sense of honor and honesty that is lacking now. I resigned after his death, as did others. We thought there was a reason von Schenck's sister was not successfully charged. Corruption hates what is not corrupt, and there were many in his own department who were happy to see him dead. That is when I resigned, because of course our policy is not to tolerate the smallest violation of the conjuring laws. So this morning— three days a week there are hangings in the market, and it is always a miserable business. Scapegoats of all sorts. As far as I'm concerned, Miss Schenck got what she deserved."

"It was not proved," the baroness said again.

"That is the correct attitude, ma'am, if someone comes to question you.

But you are wrong. When her house in Bucharest was broken into, they found a secret room under the rafters. On a table in the middle was a clay statue of your husband, the breast split open to reveal the internal organs, baked in clay. The skull was opened to reveal the brain. Tell me, how could a man like that, a soldier and a statesman, married and a father, have been driven to such despair?"

The baroness sat on the edge of her seat. She looked up at the portrait of her husband, a small, ugly man with a head too big for his body, and pig's eyes. He looked ill at ease in his dress uniform with the gold braid. Even in his official portrait, the clothes didn't seem to fit.

The portrait was painted in the last year of his life. It was the only one still in the house, and the baroness hadn't looked at it for a long time. Now she saw among the medals on his chest, the star of Roumania, awarded by the empress's own hand after his testimony against Prince Frederick. It must have been a heavy weight to him. Would Luckacz have been as sure he had been murdered if he knew what she knew, that the documents convicting Schenck von Schenck were forged? Would he have been so convinced of the baron's honor if he had heard him mumbling and praying in the middle of night, weeping on his knees after a nightmare? She had given him laudanum to make him sleep. No wonder he had been so scrupulous in his public life. Perhaps he thought by good works he could sponge away his crime. No ghost or spirit from Aegypta Schenck's laboratory, the baroness now thought, could have added or subtracted anything from the burden he carried: his betrayal of his only friend, the coldness of his wife, the sickness of his infant son, which he was convinced was a punishment from the gods.

No, Luckacz's hatred of the Germans had blinded him. Perhaps he or his family had been refugees when the Germans invaded Hungary. The baroness looked away from the portrait, wondering as she did so what had become of the silver candlestick on the mantelpiece, one of a matched set. The other was in its place beside the clock. Domnul Luckacz stood as before, her leather coat over his arm. His expression was unfriendly, his blue eyes shrewd and piercing, and suddenly she wondered whether to believe him. Perhaps all of this—these protestations of respect for her husband, of hatred for the princess—was a trick.

Fortune loves the brave, she thought, a lesson which her husband's cowardly death had taught her. "The newspaper mentioned another murder last night," she said.

"That is another strange thing," said the policeman. That was a Domnul Spitz, who—"

"Yes, I know," interrupted the baroness. "I saw him at the reception."

"You spoke to him?" Luckacz phrased these words midway between a question and a statement.

"I spoke to him. He asked me to dance. The newspaper suggests he was attacked by Gypsies."

He shrugged. "It is possible."

Which meant he didn't think so. Perhaps "attacked by Gypsies" was the explanation that was always given out during an investigation. Either way, perhaps it was unwise to seem too curious. After a moment: "Please, you say you were a friend of my husband's, but I've never seen you here. Can I show this house to you? I've tried to keep it as it was."

"Ma'am, there is no need . . ."

"No, but it would give me pleasure." She wanted to make him understand she had nothing to hide. And she imagined he would scarcely ask to see her bedroom and her private bath.

So she took him up and down the stairs, pointing out her husband's study, his library, the daybed on which he'd died, etc., etc. . . . Luckacz followed with his hat in his hands, her coat over his arm—he showed no signs of surrendering it. He was polite and deferential as if touring a museum.

Fortune loves the bold, she thought. She would show him everything, and he would leave the coat and go away. "Let me show you my husband's bedroom," she said, as she led him up the stair to the fourth floor, through the bathroom into her beautiful yellow bedchamber with the heavy curtains and the big four-poster bed. "This is where I sleep now," she said, and he had the politeness to blush. Of her husband's presence in that room, no trace remained. She walked past the bed, whose heavy silk coverlet, she now noticed, showed a mark of dried blood.

The baroness touched her fingers to her mouth. The policeman stood blinking in the middle of the room. She went to her closet and turned toward him, leaning her back against the door, imagining the dark knot of bloody sheets and clothes inside. In the bathroom he had walked straight through, his foot passing a few centimeters from the baseboard hiding place. There she had felt a secret thrill. But now her heart beat wildly and her throat was closed. On the yellow coverlet was one tiny bloodstain. The room contained too many secrets, chief among which, she now realized, was not even the stone in her pocket or the bloody bundle of clothes. But in the corner of the room stood the hidden, quilted door. Behind it the boy Markasev lay in the dark.

And at that moment from the landing she could hear the sound of the high, trilling bell that Markasev rang when he was hungry. She closed her eyes, savoring the sound. Surely she was lost, she thought. Surely this was the end. But Luckacz didn't seem to hear. He stood with his hat in his hand, peering at her with his pale blue eyes. "The front door," she managed to choke out—an absurd lie. He had entered that way. Doubtless he had noticed the brass knocker and no bell. What would he think when they descended and there was no one?

The bell on the landing rang for a long time, then stopped. "Shall we go down?" she asked. Sometimes Markasev would shout, and she could hear him from this room. Sometimes he would ring the bell and then cry out while she put her fingers to her ears. "Shall we go down?" she pleaded, but the policeman stared at her, his face drained of any cunning or shrewdness. He gave a weak, embarrassed smile, and she realized that his dyed moustache was suddenly ridiculous. She realized further what his smile meant. He found her beautiful just then, and her beauty was confusing him. She imagined that all he was able to think about in that room of secrets was her long neck and delicate jaw, the light on her cheek and hair. The way her nose looked now and in profile.

No, she thought, relieved, he was not the one. He was not the one who could destroy her. Calmer now, she put her hand out for the coat, and he gave it to her. The closet had three doors, and the one behind her was locked. She turned toward one of the others, opened it, and slipped the coat onto a hanger, all the time waiting for Markasev's cry. It did not come. Instead she heard a knocking at the door and Jean-Baptiste's uncharacteristically polite cough. Sent by the gods: "There's a Mademoiselle Corelli on the front steps," he said. "Shall I turn her away?"

9 | *Prisoners*

FOR TWO YEARS after her husband's death, the baroness did not disturb the laboratory where he'd spent so much of his time. She did not move the bookcase he had drawn over the little door. She associated that room with the collapse of her husband's fortune, her son's sickness, and the bad luck that seemed to follow her. But in time, as her social schedule was gradually curtailed, then she had the leisure to wonder about the hidden room. She opened it up, lit the lanterns. She pored over her husband's books and notes. Little by little, knowledge seduced her. As she grew more skilled, she took greater risks.

She had acquired Markasev in this way: She had spent the summer at Cluj in her country cottage, now sold. Late at night she had been reading about imaginary travel in her husband's books. Past midnight she'd been seated on the leather divan. And when she heard the boy scratching at her kitchen window, she had let him in. She had nothing to fear. He was wet, bedraggled, and she gave him some warm milk like a kitten. He was wet from the night rain, dressed in a few rags. She could not even tell whether he was Roumanian, because he would not talk. This was the detail that touched her heart, because it had reminded her of her own son.

Now as the baroness went downstairs to show the policeman out, she imagined him lying in the half-light of the kerosene lamp, his long fingers holding the string of the distant bell. She stood in the vestibule while Jean-Baptiste fetched Luckacz's coat, wondering now for the first time why he had kept his hat with him in the house. Something to occupy his hands, she thought, watching him wrap himself in his heavy, woolen cloak, all the time finding a way to hold his hat under his arm, even in his teeth—anything to avoid putting it on in her presence. It was not until she stood outside with him in the cold, bright day, that he placed it on his head. He was muttering various things, but now she was convinced he couldn't harm her, she wasn't listening. She watched to see he wasn't looking for the nonexistent bell-pull on the outside door, the source, she had told him, of the ringing inside the house. He walked down the steps into the street, then turned and squinted briefly up the narrow façade to the windows on the fourth floor. She wasn't worried. She stood watching her breath and letting her mind move ahead to what she'd say to Mlle. Corelli, now waiting for her in the front sitting room. She had seen her peeking out as she came down the stairs, but had ignored her. She had not wanted to introduce her to Luckacz.

The baroness came inside again and stood for a moment in the small square vestibule at the bottom of the stairs, behind the double doors that led into the street. She could feel her heart beating with nervousness and fright. What was she to say to this woman? Without a doubt she was connected to the mystery.

She stood on the threshold of the sitting room. Mlle. Corelli had her back to her, and was huddled over the porcelain stove. "How cold it is!" she said. "Why do you keep it so cold?"

It was not because the baroness didn't feel the chill. She imagined she was more susceptible than most. It was true. She kept the house very cold, and Jean-Baptiste often complained. Fuel was expensive in these times.

This room, like all the rooms on the lower floors, was small, high-ceilinged, square. Like all of them it was rarely used. The blue wallpaper had roses on it, and the curtains were made of blue velvet. There was some horsehair furniture. The stove was scarcely warm.

"I'll ring for Jean-Baptiste," she said.

"Please don't. I don't want him to see me. Oh, Nicola, what are we doing? What have we done?"

This was a question the baroness couldn't answer. She hoped if she said nothing, then Mlle. Corelli would answer it herself. The young woman stood rubbing her arms. Her hair was tied up on top of her head, and she wore a high-necked woolen dress.

"Let me offer you a shawl," murmured the baroness. She stripped one from the back of the settee, a piece of embroidered Chinese silk. But instead of holding it out, she wrapped it instead around her own shoulders. As was her habit, she found herself infected with sympathetic feelings. The way out of it, as always, was through anger. How could this tiresome, plain young woman have involved her in this nonsense, whatever it was? How dare she address her by her given name?

"My dear," she said, and put her arms around Mlle. Corelli's shoulders. It was a small, superficial gesture, so she was surprised how the girl clung to her. Mlle. Corelli was solid and strong, qualities that went with her big-featured face, and the baroness found it difficult to pull away. More than ever she was aware of the stone in her trousers' pocket. "Jean-Baptiste will bring us coffee."

"No, I don't want to see him. Please. I want you to tell me what to do."

"What do you mean?"

"I can't cash the cheque now, can I? My God, today I thought I would be far away."

The baroness said nothing.

"He gave me the cheque and told me I could cash it in the morning," said Mlle. Corelli. "Nicola, you said I could trust him. Then in the morning I was packing my clothes. I was ready to come here or else go out to Monsieur Spitz's hotel. To tell the truth, I hadn't slept all night. I'd changed my mind. I couldn't do this. I must have had too much to drink. How could I steal from my father and hurt my family in this way? I wanted to find Monsieur Spitz and return the money when I saw the newspaper."

The baroness was relieved. The mystery was not hard to understand. Hadn't the girl confided to the simulacrum that she felt stifled in her father's house? Hadn't she said she wanted to go live in Paris among artists? Maybe the simulacrum had convinced her to sell Kepler's Eye to Monsieur Spitz.

"What am I to say to my papa? The stone is gone. The cheque is worthless now."

"Maybe not."

"How can you say that? If I take it to the bank, that would involve me in what came afterwards."

"Not at all. The jewel was not found last night."

"How do you know?"

"That was the police inspector who just left. He said Monsieur Spitz was robbed. You have the cheque, that's all. Believe me, you've done nothing wrong."

The girl began to cry. "I'm so ashamed," she said, and the tears ran down her long nose. The baroness imagined taking out the tourmaline right then, wrapped as it was in her handkerchief, pressing it into the girl's hands. The stone could not easily have been sold even before Spitz's death. It was useless to her. But what story could she give?

Instead she led the girl to the settee and pushed her onto it. She rang the bell. When Jean-Baptiste put his head in the door, she asked him for coffee and to build up the fire. Sobbing now, the girl didn't see him. After a few moments he came in with a brass pannier full of charcoal and birchwood chunks. He looked more frail, more gaunt, more emaciated than usual, and the baroness noticed he hadn't shaved. Hair bristled on his long chin, his long neck. She watched his Adam's apple knot and relax, knot and relax. Some anxiety was making him swallow over and over again.

Later he put coffee and chocolate toast on the small table. "What did happen?" the girl asked. "He was going to take you home in his cabriolet. You should have come with me."

Sitting beside her, the baroness stared at the back of Jean-Baptiste's old-fashioned, light blue coat. She stared at the threadbare space between his shoulder blades and imagined he was listening. So she spoke evenly and calmly. "That was all. I don't know. I got out at the corner of Elysian Fields. He continued to his hotel. When I saw the story this morning, I was as terrified as you."

Mlle. Corelli shivered. "You should have come with me in my carriage. Why did you go off with that man?"

"My dear, it was out of your way."

She herself was curious why her own carriage hadn't come. It was supposed to wait in the piata with the others. Maybe the driver had stayed away in protest, because she hadn't paid her livery account in six months.

The simulacrum had accepted a ride in Monsieur Spitz's cabriolet. You couldn't have expected it to be discreet. She felt no responsibility for its actions. But Monsieur Spitz was cruelly murdered, after all.

She waited until Jean-Baptiste had left the room before she turned back to the girl. "Here's what you must do. I know a jeweler in the Strada Stavropoleos. I myself have had to sell my jewels one by one, and he has made me copies. I have seen in his window duplicates he has made of famous stones. In any case, I believe tourmalines are not the most expensive. Let us hope your father does not examine it too closely. As for the cheque, sign it over to me. I will give it to my accountant, and he will make enquiries. Maybe it can be turned into money for some percentage of its written value. That's all we can hope for. Do you have it with you?"

The baroness imagined that she understood Mlle. Corelli's frustration, because she also had money she was afraid to use. The bag of currency she had taken from Aegypta Schenck's armoire, she had not even counted it. Maybe it was enough to save her, pay her most pressing debts. But if the princess's money was marked or accounted for in some way, that would be the end.

No, she wasn't responsible for what the simulacrum had done. Claude Spitz was nothing to her. But at moments all morning she had been revisited by the sight of the princess's protruding eyes and tongue, the spirit bird fluttering on her lips. She would feel a sudden flash of heat within her body, which was the sign of her regret. There was no time to linger on those thoughts and feelings, with complications and difficulties piling upon her. The past was nothing, and she would find a way to conquer this.

Even so, she could not but remember the series of bad decisions that had brought her to this crisis—caught between two murders, and to protect herself against suspicion of one was to invite unanswerable questions about the other. It was her fault, it was all her fault. In the first place she had gone to visit the princess before she even had her hands on Miranda Popescu—why? Was it to gloat, to prove that she also was a powerful woman who could influence the fate of nations? And then the second time—was it to punish her? Ask for her forgiveness, her help? Not to kill her, but that's what she'd done, and at the same time she had let her simulacrum loose in the empress's palace. Did she think it wouldn't be affected by her own moods, her own violence?

This was the way she always did things, she reflected later, after Mlle. Corelli had gone away. She lay back on the horsehair settee, the folded cheque in her hands. She was an artist, that was it. An artist, not a criminal, and if she found herself involved now in murder and robbery, she had been driven to it, she was sure, by desperation and the cruelty of others. Once when she was sixteen years old, an Italian critic had called her one of the great artists of her generation, and the way to art was not to think too clearly, not to plan things out, but to follow where your heart and emotions led. Well, they had led her into a cesspool now, and it was time for thinking to take over.

The cheque was signed and countersigned. She unfolded it now and spread it out on the small table. It was for a half million francs, which was not as much as she had hoped. Hadn't she heard Spitz say he would pay two million?

Domnul Luckacz was a fool, and she had led him by the nose. She couldn't be sure all the others were as foolish. Mlle. Corelli had used the word "cabriolet" to describe Spitz's carriage, meaning, she supposed, a hired cab. If so, was there a driver? Or had Spitz driven the horse himself?

Jean-Baptiste had served Turkish coffee in small red cups. It had gone cold, but the baroness took a small, sweet sip. She imagined this was the last time she would sit on this sofa, the last time she would sit in this room, because now it was clear to her that she must go. She had the cheque, the tourmaline, and the princess's money, all of which were tainted and questionable, but they would have to do. She couldn't stay here—that was certain—waiting for the police to search the house. But she would take the train to Budapest, across the border into German-occupied Hungary. She would write Mlle. Corelli from there, saying the cheque had proved worthless after all. If her fears were groundless and no danger followed her, then maybe she'd return.

She wondered whether she would take her son.

At that moment there was a knock on the door, and Jean-Baptiste came in with the mail. Bills and invitations, invitations and bills, and one small, anonymous note, reminding her of an appointment at two o'clock. What was that? Oh, yes. Her simulacrum had promised Herr Greuben she would meet him at Cathedral Walk. In a way it was a stroke of luck. If she was to cross the border, then she would need a German visa.

Jean-Baptiste had not left her. He stood in the middle of the carpet, his hands behind his back. She glanced up at him, aware once again of the tremor in his Adam's apple. What did he know? There had been blood on her clothes, a strange and brilliant jewel. A policeman had come and gone. He must have his suspicions. No, but there was more, obviously.

"Ma'am," he said. "Please, ma'am." He was stuttering and afraid, which was unusual. "I-I-I wanted your permission to take your bedsheets and your clothes from last night. Burn them, ma'am. I wanted to burn them."

She said nothing, only stared at him. His bladelike face. His high, narrow shoulders which were hunched now, as if he were expecting some blow from behind. His eyes were too close together, so that they looked as if they were set into the sides of his sharp nose.

"I've been with you, ma'am," he stammered. "Last night I saw him push his way in—I would have helped. Don't think I'm judging you for what you did. I dragged him down the steps after you went upstairs. I swear he was still alive. His carriage was at the curb and the box was empty. I drove him to the Targu bridge and left him."

She stared at him, his high forehead and clipped, receding hair.

"Ma'am, you must know this won't stop here. I cleaned the stairs and the tile floor. I took the candlestick. But with that boy upstairs—please ma'am, I know you are in trouble. I know you have no money, and this morning I heard from the butcher as I went to buy your ham—the baron's pension was revoked. I-I-I have to tell you, I have a little saved. I bought the ham myself. I have a house in the mountains that my father left me, and I want you to know that you could always share it . . .

"As my w-w-w—," he added after a pause.

She stared at him. It took a moment for her to understand. "As my wife," he was attempting to say.

She tried to imagine what she must be feeling—her hands felt hot.

Doubtless she had a kind of affection for this loyal man, who would work for her forever without pay. His words were touching, but at the same time she was angry—how dare he? She was the Baroness Ceausescu. He was a servant, an ugly old man, almost as old, almost as ugly as her late husband.

The Baroness Ceausescu. But she was also a whore's daughter with no place to go, not a five-leu penny to her name. No one but a lunatic would take her in—how dare he insult her by reminding her of that? Now, as was her habit, her thoughts resolved themselves into two competing claims. Of all women she was the cleverest, strongest, best. But at the same time there was no one in God's universe as pitiful, as evil, as selfish, as contemptible as she.

"As my g-g-guest," he finished, finally.

He was too much of a coward even to ask her. She looked up at his frightened face. She felt disgusted and polluted now. At the same time she was convinced that very soon he would reject and spurn her as she deserved. It was true—he was a worthy man, son of a respected schoolteacher in Cluj.

"Thank you, Jean-Baptiste," she said. "Thank you for your wishes and for what you've done. What time is it?"

"Past noon, ma'am."

"Then I must go. I have an appointment at two. Put out my coat and some clothes into a bag. Here is the key to my closet. You are right about the boy upstairs."

"Don't worry, I will close up that room. This afternoon, will you buy me a train ticket to Budapest? I feel . . ."

"With what, ma'am? There is no money in the house."

"Then perhaps you can lend me a small sum."

He stood for a moment, expressionless. "And the house, ma'am?"

"The baron left it to my son. Not to me."

For a long time she had been aware of the small bell ringing on the fourth-floor landing. "I will bring some food to the boy. I will tell him to be on his way," she said.

He nodded, turned to go. As soon as she caught sight once more of his retreating back, as soon as he opened the door into the front-door hall, she closed her eyes. Now suddenly she was overcome with horror. There in the vestibule where the policeman had been standing, there at the bottom of the stairs, the simulacrum had—what? Murdered a man? Or no—he was still breathing, thank God. How had she done it—struck him with a candlestick? Had the jeweler tried to touch her? No, not her, but an unfeeling and murderous automaton—Jean-Baptiste had driven the carriage to the bridge into the Gypsy town. Had anyone seen him? One thing was for certain. It was all her fault.

One thing was for certain: She could not continue in this way. This morning she would mark a new beginning, leave this place behind. She could do a hundred things. She was still beautiful, or at least men still told her so. She was only thirty-four years old. Across Europe there were dozens of theater managers who would hire her. She would take back her old name.

Eyes closed, she listened to the distant ringing of the bell.

KEVIN MARKASEV—THAT was not his name—had no memories from childhood. But because the mind abhors a vacuum, in his hours of captivity in the baroness's house, he had invented a story for himself—a family in Odessa and Roumania. Trips to the Danube delta with his cousin. These were the stories he had borrowed from the woman with the crystal ball in Bucharest, and told to Miranda Popescu on the hill. In that place he had felt more alive than ever before, and almost by now those stories were his own. Without them, whole years were blank, effaced. But he imagined his family could not forgive a boy who was so sensitive. Who was consumed with nightmares and strange dreams.

Often in his dreams a man came to him and told him what to do, a small man with a big head and little, red-tinged eyes. He was a gentleman in elegant clothes, with a star around his neck. And Markasev obeyed him as he would have obeyed his own father.

Now as he sat thinking in the baroness's cage, nothing seemed real—not this life, these dreams, or any part of his past. Yet there was a part of him that coveted normality. Every morning since the night when he had stumbled into the baroness's house in Cluj, as he woke chained or caged in the half-light or the dark, he had lain still without understanding for a few moments, expecting to find himself safe in the whitewashed bedroom in his mother's house in Odessa, and his mother calling him.

When he rang the bell, always he imagined she might come for him, though he could scarcely remember what she looked like. Now the door opened, and in the light from the yellow room he saw the baroness standing on the threshold. She had a bowl of hot milk and toast. He could smell it.

He thought of her as the lady of comfort and tears. He didn't use her name. She had saved his life. Often she appeared to him, as she now did, dressed in soft, simple clothes, bringing food or water or a towel to wipe his face. Her hair, cut short around her face, was a soft color which combined black and brown and red, and when she bent down to wash him, as she often did, he could smell in it or on her skin a small odor of nutmeg or lemon oil, some rich and bitter fragrance. Her eyebrows were thick, and her eyes were very dark, very blue, almost purple in some lights. Her skin was pale without any red in it, but instead a kind of milky blue, the color of milk with the fat skimmed away. Her forehead was wide and smooth. There was no line on it, no wrinkle around her eyes or mouth, because when she was angry, as he'd sometimes seen her, she did not contort her face. And when she cried, as she often did, she did not wail or moan or change her breath. The tears brimmed on her lashes, flowed over her smooth cheeks. Now as she unlocked the cage and bent down over him, he could smell the butter and black pepper in the bowl she carried; the smell made him weak. She wore a man's white shirt, partly unbuttoned. She put the bowl down on the small table and touched his forehead. Her hand, as always, was very cold— such a comfort on his sweating brow.

He was dressed in a coarse woolen shirt such as prisoners wear. He lay on a straw pallet in the middle of his cage. He was not bound. Sometimes when he woke, he would find the chains around his wrists. The lady was afraid of the strength of his spirit animal, she said. A mountain lion from the northern forests, she said. But the chain had enough slack in it to let him reach the bell pull. It might take hours but she would come to release him, feed him, talk to him.

Now she touched his burning forehead, held his hands. "Where did you go?" she asked, and he told her about his journey into the forest where there was a great cave with a fire burning in its mouth.

"You will not go there again," she said. "I have come to tell you I've petitioned the judge and he's resolved to let you free. Wherever you wish. Only you can't stay here. Whatever you want, I will try to provide it. I know a farmer in a place far from Cluj. Maybe he will take you in to work with the animals."

"Praise God," he said. As she was talking, he imagined the high meadows and the sheep. He imagined himself on the mountain all the summer months.

"Rest now," she said. "Take these pills. I'm going out for the afternoon, for a little while. Then we'll take you from this room."

SHE DID NOT LIE. The baroness knew a family in the Bucovina region, a German farmer in her husband's debt. They were under some version of German law there, and they would not turn the boy over to the empress's magistrates. Regardless, he would not be able, she thought, to identify her house. Nor did he know her name, she hoped.

There was still danger, but the boy had suffered enough. She would find him clothes, pack him a suitcase with her own hands. She would give him a gift, something of value from her house, because whatever he had done, he was just a boy, some unknown woman's son. She herself was the mother of a child she rarely saw, and for the sake of that child she would release the boy. If there was a risk to her, she would accept that risk.

These were her thoughts as she left the house and turned up the street, which debouched into Elysian Fields. This was a quadruple row of linden trees, a public park that was pretty in the spring and summer, with flower beds and shaded benches. On that cold gray winter afternoon there was no color in it, except for the clothes of the people. Consumed by her own imagining, the Baroness Ceausescu didn't notice, as she stalked in her high boots over the cobblestones, that the park was more crowded than usual. But when she came into the open place around Vespasian's fountain and saw in front of her the blue-tiled dome of the Sulimanye Synagogue, then she realized she was on the outskirts of a crowd. And with her instinct for social hierarchy, she saw it was an unusual group, made up partly of rich men and women in fur coats, partly of black-robed Christian priests, partly of shopkeepers, partly of the poor—beggars even, dressed in rags on that chilly day. There were soldiers, as there were at every Christian procession.

The baroness watched while the priests unloaded a gilded coffin from the back of the hearse, drawn by six black geldings, restive in the cold. The patriarch, a bearded man in silver robes, blew on his hands. There were many signs of grief among the crowd. Old men blew their noses, wiped their red-rimmed eyes. Old women stood counting their rosaries. The baroness also felt some emotion, even before she realized she was standing in the middle of the funeral for Princess Aegypta Schenck von Schenck. She wore a gray cap on her head, which she now removed.

Beside the synagogue was a small Christian chapel built of dark, unpainted wood. The baroness could see it through the naked trees, see the people milling around. Here in the capital city, the empress had forbidden any public exhibition of the cross of Christ; there was a small square tower with a weather vane on top. For no reason at all, the baroness found herself staring up at it, staring up at the huge bird that perched on it. So she was able to see clearly when the bird spread its wings and fell into the air. It flew unsteadily over the crowd, a Gypsy eagle with many broken feathers. It looked exhausted, as if it had flown a long way. Now it pulled in its wings and fell onto the hearse, where it perched on the high ridge of carved woodwork behind the cab. Some of the men cried out, stamped their feet, bent down for stones to drive the bird off, until the patriarch raised his hands. He pointed. There on the bird's breast, tied to its stringy thigh, was an iron crucifix.

Some in the crowd recognized it. "It is her sister's cross," one said. The baroness also had seen it before, on Princess Clara's neck before she fled to Germany. Then once more in a photograph of Miranda Popescu.

Around her men and women had fallen to their knees. She herself felt suddenly conspicuous. Full of regret, she glared up at the bird's sharp, mindless head. Aegypta Schenck had been well loved. She had not deserved to die at the hands of a whore's daughter, who so often acted without thinking.

Blinded by tears, she pushed her way out of the crowd and across the street. She pushed past Domnul Luckacz, who raised his hat. What was he doing there? She couldn't think about it. She was too upset. Nor had she regained her composure by the time she had reached Cathedral Walk, a promenade along the river bank, lined with restaurants and shops. Herr Greuben was waiting for her under the lamppost.

The baroness had put on a small disguise. She was dressed in a green jacket such as a student might wear. A woolen scarf was knotted around her neck, and she wore gold-rimmed spectacles. She had expected that Herr Greuben would sit with her in a quiet corner of the promenade, looking out over the barges and houseboats.

In summer bourgeois families strolled up and down. The cafés and restaurants put tables on the street. In winter only the hardy stayed out-doors, and she imagined Herr Greuben would prefer the privacy. She was surprised, therefore, when he led her across the street to a German restau-rant in the center of the block, where the lamps were already lit inside the plate-glass windows. "Would you like some good German pastry?" he asked. And she followed him inside, and the first thing that happened was her spectacles fogged up suddenly; the place was oppressively hot. Oppres-sively loud, also, and full of happy people smoking cigarettes, drinking cof-fee and schnapps.

Herr Greuben indicated a small, circular table against the wall, and she sat down. She stripped off her gloves, wiped her spectacles with her pocket handkerchief, while he raised his hand for service. "Why are we here?" she asked in French.

"It doesn't matter. Talk between friends. There's someone I'd like you to meet." Then a fat-faced, moustachioed waiter was there, and Herr Greuben was whispering to him behind his hand. At a neighboring table an old woman cut into a small meat pie. The baroness felt light-headed, hun-gry, faint.

The waiter smoothed the palms of his hands down the front of his white apron. He looked attentively at the baroness, who turned away. "Monsieur," he said to her, "we have a table in the back. We are honored."

Her face felt greasy, hot. She scarcely knew what he was saying. "Mon-sieur," she thought, confused. But she allowed Greuben to take her by the elbow; hadn't he just asked her to sit down? Now he led her to the back of the café, down the hall toward the washroom. There was another little room with the walls painted red. No one was in it except for a man reading a newspaper at a small table. He stood up to greet her. "Madame la Baronne," he said, bending down over her naked hand. "I am very pleased."

She saw the bald patch in the middle of his head, his straight black hair combed back to hide it. When he straightened up she recognized him, a small man elegantly dressed in black, his face ugly enough to seem deformed. His skin was covered with small lumps and splotches.

"Your grace," she murmured.

He was the Elector of Ratisbon. "I was in town when my secretary informed me. Please, would you care for . . . ?" And then he was fussing around her, drawing her down into a cane-backed chair, talking about nothing while the waiter brought coffee and an assortment of sweet cakes. With a kind of wonder she studied his disgusting face, not listening until he drew his chair toward hers. "My secretary informed me there is something you might know concerning Miranda Popescu."

He blinked, opened his eyes, which had been hidden before. To her they seemed enormous, scarcely human: an animal's eyes, a cow's or a horse's. Vulnerable, she thought. She peered into them, timidly at first. Herr Greuben stood at the door, pretending not to listen.

There was nothing to listen to. Ratisbon turned away. "Please, you must try one of these small tortes. They are from Bavaria. . . ." Then he was off again, prattling about this and that as if he'd known her for years, when she could only remember having met him twice years before, at official functions in a crowd of people. But she had read in the newspaper that he'd been expected. He was staying at the Athenée Palace Hotel. She wondered why he hadn't been at the empress's reception.

"Yes, I would have liked to have gone," he said as if he'd read her mind. "It was part of the reason for my visit. Particularly since relations between our countries are so tiresomely low. But then came that news about the shopkeepers in Bucovina—did you hear? They had a small social club, open to anyone of German ancestry. Just some old men, did you hear? Two nights ago it burned. Hungarian emigrés, mostly, but local people, too; they burned some of the shops. So I thought it would be difficult for me to attend under the circumstances, and besides, I had a migraine. All week I have been meeting with the German Friendship Union, very boring, I must tell you, and a visit to the palace would have been a welcome respite. Especially since I hear I missed the opportunity to see you dance in public! The thought of that alone has made me miserable. I remember I saw you in Berlin at the Federal Opera House before your retirement. It must have been, dear me, more than fifteen years ago. I was still a young man!"

Throughout this speech the baroness had been watching his hands. They were expressive and beautiful, and he used them when he spoke. He made delicate gestures in the air, while at the same time his face remained quiet and dispassionate. It was as if he didn't want to bring attention to himself even by smiling. In the Roumanian press there was some speculation about what was wrong with him. Leprosy was one suggestion. Smallpox seemed more likely.

He paused, picked up his knife and fork, and she admired the way he now consumed a cream-filled éclair, cutting it into tiny pieces that he ate one by one. When he was finished, not a speck of cream or pastry remained on his plate. Even his knife looked clean and polished, while she had, through her nervousness, made a mess of her own torte. It would not do, she thought, to pick it up, so she had reduced it to crumbs under her fork without managing to trap a single bite.

Was he a buffoon? she thought. No, he was one of the most powerful men in Germany. His cuffs were white as cream, and his hands tinged with a rosy color. His nails were trimmed and manicured, and he wore no jewelry except for a gold signet ring, incised with a small pattern of interlocking circles. It was a pattern she remembered from her husband's notes in his laboratory, part of a page in his handwriting in a code she had never been able to decipher. And then that symbol of seven interlocking rings.

"You think I'm a buffoon?" he asked. She could have sworn he spoke, and that only his tone was different now, serious and grave. But she realized she was looking at his mouth as he devoured the last of his cream éclair. The ring was on his right hand, which was holding his fork. Now she heard his other voice start to prattle on again about this and that, while the question remained. Unnerved, she glanced up at his eyes again. They were huge and brown and vulnerable.

He was a conjurer. That much was clear. But why did he bother with this double way of talking, this empty chatter? Surely it wasn't for Herr Greuben's benefit. And the waiter had already left the room.

No, it was a demonstration of seriousness, of power. His eyes looked as big as caves. For a moment, stupidly, she imagined herself wandering across the ruined landscape of his cheeks, coming to his eye and then peering inside.

"I know Miranda Popescu is alive," he said, while with his other voice he started to chatter and complain about the bitter weather that was colder than he'd expected. "I have known it all these years. Her mother is my guest. But the daughter escaped. For years Aegypta Schenck von Schenck kept me out of this place, but now she's dead. She is dead, and Greuben tells me that you know about the girl. Is it a coincidence?"

The baroness mashed her torte under her fork. Then she threw it down and took a sip of coffee. What did he mean about Aegypta Schenck keeping him away? He had been to Bucharest many times on the night train. But perhaps only the prattling man had come, and the conjurer inside of him had stayed away.

"I was curious to see you," said the Elector of Ratisbon. "Not because of your idiotic performances. I take no interest in the fine arts," he said, even though the prattling man at the same moment was describing with many subtle gestures of his hands a concert he'd attended the week before. "Your husband's corner was empty for a long time. Now you have occupied it. And if you are fumbling and clumsy at first, it's natural. Because you are a woman. Tell me, where is Miranda Popescu?" he said, while at the same time the prattling man was asking her another question which she supposed could be answered with the same answer: "Tell me, I had heard that Franjo Bozic was working on another symphony. Is that possible?" he asked, referring to a Serbian composer who'd abandoned his career years before, the result of a mental break.

"I don't know. I had heard rumors. . . ." Uncertain, she let her voice trail away.

"You must not tell me you don't know. I have searched for years. Make no mistake. Roumania will yield whether I have that girl in my hands or not. The important thing is to avoid bloodshed. Aegypta Schenck von Schenck is dead, and this morning I woke up with a picture in my looking-glass, a little Roumanian cottage in the snow. Diamond-paned windows, a stream and a wooden bridge without a railing. A small lake and a crack in the ice. The pine trees are all broken and the door stands open. Is that where she has hidden all these years? No—yesterday Greuben tells me you know where the girl is. This morning Princess Schenck von Schenck is dead. Is that why you were making such a spectacle of yourself last night? So that no one would suspect you were not there at all?"

At the same time the prattling man had asked her a question at least partly in a foreign language—Russian, perhaps. It was as if he were anticipating in advance her stammering excuses. "I-I don't know what you mean," she said. She pretended to take a sip of coffee, although her demitasse was already empty.

"Please, how rude of me," said the prattling man. "The baroness's cup is empty. Greuben, please signal the waiter." And he went on and on about this and that until the waiter had come and gone, and the Elector of Ratisbon spoke again. His enormous, liquid eyes seemed full of tears.

"Let me tell you this is not a game we are playing. This is no place for a stupid woman, playing with forces she doesn't understand. I've had enough of ignorant women—let me tell you I'm prepared to be generous. I will grant you a safe-conduct to Vienna and an annuity of three quarters of a million francs."

The baroness stared at the hands of the prattling man. He also was offering terms, suggesting that for a large sum she could be coaxed out of retirement for a series of performances abroad.

"Why would I accept?" she found herself murmuring. "Everything I have is here."

Now for a moment she was horrified because she had been tricked into suggesting that at least she did know something. No, not horrified. She looked down at her own hands, motionless in her lap. They were not trembling. She was not afraid. For a moment she tried to imagine what she was feeling. After all, she had come here willing to beg for a safe-conduct, willing to leave Bucharest that day with nothing but a stolen jewel, a cheque from a murdered man, and a bag of stolen currency that she had not even counted. But perhaps she felt this secret she'd discovered—the fate of Miranda Popescu—was the only thing that still belonged to her, and without it she had nothing.

And yet if she had managed to capture the girl, would she not have gladly sold her to this man? Why was she so stubborn—why did she feel now she would rather die than give him anything? "I will send my people throughout Europe looking for that little cottage," said the elector. "I will find it. Only you will make the job easier, which is why I will pay you. If not . . ." He shrugged. At the same time the prattling man had coughed into his napkin and murmured something inaudible.

"What?"

The elector's tears seemed to tremble on his eyelids, but they never fell. "Greuben tells me you've been useful to us. But you must understand you have been useful to yourself, because a war is coming. So you and all those who have something to offer me, you must remember what is best for you. I would prefer not to mention what I know. Let me just say this. Since Greuben spoke to me, I've had you watched. And since Aegypta Schenck has died, I know what you are. I know what you've been playing at."

The baroness stared at him, stared into his liquid eyes. Now she was listening to the prattling man. "If I had known what I was missing, I would never have stayed away from the reception. The chance to see you dancing with that charming jeweler, Monsieur Spitz. You spoke to that charming young lady whose family stole one of my country's greatest treasures. You shared Spitz's carriage, did you not? Who later turned up dead of a gunshot wound? You saw the paper. You are not a woman who goes unnoticed, and that dress, my dear!"

The baroness tried to understand what she was feeling. Anger, certainly. Yet there was danger here. These German pigs—the prattling man continued: "No, but my migraines. I had to send my secretary for laudanum, to the institute on the Soseaua Kiseleff. That's where your son is staying, is it not?"

In that red room she felt a chill.

There was no reason to be stubborn, she reflected. The elector was right. It was important to remember what was in her interest. "New England," she almost said. The words trembled on her lips. But as she looked into his liquid eyes, she realized suddenly she didn't believe him. There was no possibility of trusting him, even in a bargain between murderers. Anyone who so blithely threatened her, threatened her son, would never waste three quarters of a million francs a year on her after she gave him what he wanted.

Too late. "New England," the elector said. And the prattling man paused in midsentence to stare at her. "Where—what do you mean?"

She would say nothing else. She felt as if the prattling man had reached into her with his silver fork, his elegant hand, and snatched something away. She wouldn't tell him any more, though doubtless it wouldn't take long to find out where the girl was hiding. "You think it will be easy," she said. "The Austrians gave up without a shot. The Hungarians surrendered in six weeks. Now it's our turn. We will fight you," she said, her cheeks burning with embarrassment, because she knew that he knew that she cared nothing for Roumania. She would have sold him the white tyger without compunction if the terms had been right.

Nevertheless, the words made her feel better. "You miserable potato-eater," she said. "You odious, disgusting man. You must know our men will crush you, as they did at Kaposvar . . . ," and then she stopped because the prattling man was laughing at her, and at the door, Herr Greuben was laughing, too.

"Dear lady," said the prattling man. "Dear lady, please. I would love to stay and chat with you, but alas! I am a busy man. You see it has given me so much pleasure—something to tell my friends, I can assure you, that I had coffee with the great Nicola Ceausescu! Now please, my government would like to offer you some further payment, though the annuity we spoke of is, alas, out of the question. But Greuben will write you a cheque. What do you say to fifty francs?"

Later, after she left the room, as she plunged through the overheated restaurant, she imagined all the conversation had stopped, and all the patrons and the staff were staring at her. Then she plunged into the cold afternoon. She turned away from the riverbank, crossed the Esplanade, and found the tangle of old streets that led uphill to the temple of Jupiter.

The streets were frozen mud laid with duckboards. The houses were wooden cottages joined together at the eaves. Ramshackle wooden fences divided the backyards, where there were washrooms and latrines.

The baroness had not been this way in years. She knew the streets. When she was a child, when she had just begun to find work as an artist's model, she had often slept in the porch of the temple looking down over the lights of the Plevnei bridge.

Now she climbed uphill. Because of the small streets, the temple wasn't even visible until you stood outside its gates. Nor was it obvious when you came into the peristyle that from the western porch there was a view over this whole section of the city and the towers of the bridge. The lamps were lit in the sanctuary, and through the screen she could see the ancient statue of Jupiter in his chair—she felt no urge to pray. The despair she had felt in the restaurant had gone away, and she was thinking.

She walked out onto the porch and sat down on the steps. The streetlights were coming on at the bottom of the hill. She sank her chin into her scarf. Around her there were several other indigents, people who had made the porch their home, and now sat waiting for the temple servants to bring them their evening meal. The Baroness Ceausescu rubbed her hands together, then took out a cigarette and smoked it. She was wondering why she had seen Domnul Luckacz at the princess's funeral, when he had made his opinion of her so plain. Was he there in some professional capacity, perhaps as a member of the Siguranta? Or was he spying on the baroness herself?

No, these questions were not what she was interested in. Now she remembered what the prattling man had said: ". . . charming young lady whose family stole one of my country's greatest treasures. . . ." The phrase was out of character for him, too harsh, too heartfelt. What interest did the elector have in Kepler's Eye?

Old men were sitting near her. She took her handkerchief out of her pocket to wipe her nose. The tourmaline was wrapped in the cloth. Now she slid it into her hand, looked down. Even in the half-darkness it seemed to shine, a source of faint, purple light. It was hard for her to imagine now that when she'd first seen it, strapped on Mlle. Corelli's forehead, she had scarcely noticed it.

What was it Monsieur Spitz had said, that it had been dug out of the brain of Johannes Kepler? She had heard that story before, heard it dismissed, also, as a fantastic lie. But the Elector of Ratisbon had called it one of his country's treasures and she possessed it. She was not like these beggars here smoking their cigarettes, waiting for their soup.

She had heard part of the story. During the previous century, during the forty years of war, the Roumanian army had occupied the city of Prague. They had burned the castle of the Austrian emperor, who had been interested in curiosities and miracles. Kepler's Eye had been part of his collection. Mlle. Corelli's ancestor had been an officer in the Roumanian army.

Snow drifted through the marble columns. It had started to snow. The dry flakes landed on the sleeves and shoulders of her jacket, just a few, then more.

Now what was she to do? There was no point now in asking for a German visa. Soon the police would come to her house. Too many people knew about Claude Spitz, and it was likely the elector would find a way to denounce her, if only for the names she had called him. In her pocket she had Kepler's Eye and Spitz's cheque.

But she had not brought the princess's money. And what about her son? No, no—she mustn't run away. She would clear out the laboratory. Explanations would be found. Gypsies had killed Spitz. He was still breathing when he left her house, unless Jean-Baptiste had finished him.

AS THE BARONESS Ceausescu went over these considerations in her mind, the Elector of Ratisbon exited the little restaurant on the Esplanade. He had stopped for a while inside the door, chatting with the manager and one or two of the patrons. Once outside, he also felt the need for solitude, and so he wrapped his white scarf around his neck, pulled down his silk-brimmed hat, and struck out on foot toward his hotel, the Athenée Palace on the Piata Enescu. Herr Greuben followed at a respectful distance.

An old woman's death, a girl's reappearance on the stage of the world—surely these things were related. Herr Greuben had sent a message the night before. He had seen Kepler's Eye strapped to the forehead of some Roumanian debutante. No, she was the daughter of Professor Corelli, whose house had been invaded unsuccessfully five times before. It was unfortunate that laws must be broken. On the other hand, the stone was German property, stolen long ago.

A philosophic man, the elector was nevertheless conscious of a certain frustration, because this time too, if he had not taken a painkiller and retired early, doubtless he'd already have Johannes Kepler's eye. But by the time he could be roused, the girl had already left the empress's reception. Not that it mattered. She didn't possess it anymore. Why else would she have gone to purchase an artificial tourmaline in the Strada Stavropoleos; why would she have done that, if not to fool her father? Herr Greuben had been right to follow the jeweler's cabriolet—it had stopped at the house off Elysian Fields, and Spitz had followed the baroness inside. An hour later a servant had bundled him out, had driven the cab himself down to the river. Herr Greuben found it with the horse cut loose. He'd thought the man was drunk. No, unconscious with his head broken in. And the stone was not there, though the setting was loose among the pillows, a strap of chased silver that Mlle. Corelli had worn around her head. The stone had been pried out of its socket.

Greuben had not notified the police, though it was obvious Herr Spitz had been assaulted. How difficult it was for the elector in this barbaric foreign capital to find himself constrained by diplomatic niceties! In Munich or Berlin he would have access to the chief of police.

That afternoon he had been careful not to mention the stone to the Baroness Ceausescu. He had talked about the girl, though the stone had been uppermost in his mind. Now as he walked across the square under the streetlights toward the massed pile of the hotel, he scanned the sidewalk for a trace of his Roumanian agent, or else some employee of the German embassy. But there was no one, and in an instant he was surrounded by a pack of beggars. Derelicts and orphans always waited around the double revolving door under the statue of the Goddess Minerva, which was carved in an irritatingly muscular fin-de-siècle style.

The elector, famed for his generosity, paused under the streetlight to allow the beggars to come close. The children, of course, needed no invitation. Already they surrounded him in a circle and pulled at his sleeves. But it took a while for the older men and women to shuffle out of the ornate doorways and come toward him with bleared, hopeful eyes. Who were they? Military veterans, perhaps—that one had a wooden leg. Unfortunate women, more sinned against than sinning. In Germany there was nothing like this. Especially not in such a place. As he searched his pocket for his roll of coins, he looked up at the hotel's overdecorated façade. Above him in the first-floor ballrooms, a party had spilled out onto the balconies.

It was his custom always to carry several rolls of five-franc pieces. Now he peeled back the paper and brought out the coins. He pressed one into the palm of each child, then reached out to find the hands of the adults, some of whom still hung back. One in particular, an unfortunate, drunken woman with no hat or shawl, whose cheeks were dark with broken blood vessels, but whose eyes still glittered with intelligence—he took her cold hands in his, murmuring some encouragement as she flinched away, appalled by his ugliness.

All this will change, he thought. Bored now, he pushed through the crowd into the revolving door. Inside the lobby he stood stripping off his gloves next to the elevator, under the crude, gold, faux-Byzantine mosaic of the vault. He looked again for his Roumanian agent and saw a man separate himself away from the people at the desk to approach not him but Greuben, who was close behind. The elector removed his topcoat and slung it over his arm, then rode up alone in the wheezing cage.

Later, in his suite on the fifth floor, listening to the hiss of the steampipes in the overheated room, the elector waited for Greuben's knock. He stood by the French windows, looking out over the lights of the city and the dark expanse of public gardens. When the man entered, he didn't turn around.

"Sir, they found nothing," said Hans Greuben, "though I admit they didn't have a chance to search the entire house. She was still gone when they left, but the servant only went out for an hour. They searched her bedroom and the obvious places."

Without turning, the elector sat down into an armchair, set so that he could continue to look out the window. He stretched his short legs out in front of him. He frowned as he examined his shoes. "Where does she do her work? Her husband's laboratory—did you find that?"

Greuben shrugged. He stood in the middle of the rose-colored carpet, a young, handsome, worried man, dressed in a black overcoat which he did not take off. "Do you think," said the elector, "that she had the jewel with her at the restaurant?"

"I wasn't aware of its effects."

"Were you not? Were you not, indeed? Tell me, Hans. Is she an attractive woman?"

Again Hans Greuben shrugged. "No more so than yesterday. In any case, those stories are just superstitions."

The elector pressed his palms together in front of his face. In the past, he imagined, the baroness might have had the capacity to inspire many emotions—lust, envy, admiration, perhaps. But loyalty and selfless love were not among them. The jewel had the power to change that, for her and for him also.

"A superstition, is it? An old wives' tale. Hans—no doubt you think you are a modern man."

"Your grace?"

"I tell you, the properties of the stone are a matter of scientific fact. Science, you understand. I asked you whether you had found Ceausescu's laboratory—yes, it is true. There is a lot of superstition connected with those primitive alchemical experiments, and so it is a good policy to ban them by law. But you mustn't forget, even the great Isaac Newton was an alchemist, and it was to form an alchemical laboratory that he was invited to Berlin after the destruction of the British Islands. You see even that is an example of what I mean. To the vulgar mind, a moral and spiritual catastrophe, a proud nation destroyed by vengeful gods. As scientific men we know the cause: an earthquake along the Great Grampian Fault, a natural occurrence, and yet the effect was the same, a tidal surge that destroyed London. Now here we are in a primitive country, and we see women like Aegypta Schenck with her charms and prayers and potions—that is the oldest and least effective way of organizing these phenomena. Then we see Baron Ceausescu and his experiments—more efficient, certainly, because he was a man. So we can place his thinking at an intermediate point, and even admit he might have been capable of great things, if he'd had a German education. But you and I, Hans, have the benefit of much research, and if we are able to do more, it is because the scientific foundation has already been laid. The experimental stage, you might say, has already been concluded, leaving us as its beneficiaries, leaving us free to summon its conclusions and refine them into scientific principles, and then manipulate them at a distance, like Plato's philosopher kings."

Behind him, the elector could sense Greuben's skepticism, hear his disapproving sniff. So perhaps he'd been overoptimistic to include him in a category with himself. Perhaps he was just a servant after all.

And perhaps, the elector reflected, there was no one in such a category, which left him with a lonely duty. "I should like a whiskey-soda," he sighed. Confused with melancholy, he sat back, then allowed himself to press his fingers first against his lips, then against the hot, broken surface of his cheeks, ravaged by smallpox when he was just a boy.

"These anti-conjuring laws," he went on, "are against superstition only, a way of discouraging false principles, false explanations. You must see the distinction. On one side it is all hocus-pocus and darkness, though admittedly certain tricks have been discovered—no, not discovered, but stumbled on by chance. And they've been passed along in secrecy, not subject to public scrutiny or experimentation, because the thinking behind them is all wrong—that's what the enemy is. And on the other side we have the modern science of conjuring, and there is nothing about science that should be hidden or concealed—when I am in the government, you will see these are the first laws I will repeal, because they have outlived their usefulness."

Even as he said this, he felt a twinge of doubt. Darkness and hocus-pocus, but for twenty years Aegypta Schenck had managed to confound him. Superstitious nonsense, irrational and female, and yet if she'd not died, doubtless she'd still be thwarting him—"Aegypta Schenck kept me from this place," he murmured as he listened to Greuben at the cabinet, the reassuring clink of the bottles, the rattle of the ice. "Or rather when I came here I was not myself. Now here I am, and I can't think what to do. Miranda Popescu is in America—do you think so? Or is that another trick? It occurs to me we have no confirmation of any of this, but just our beautiful friend's word, which is not, I fear, to be trusted. . . ."

Herr Greuben stood behind him, holding the glass. "But your grace—"

"Yes, this is sad and exhausting work. Clara Brancoveanu's daughter. She is just a girl, you understand. Just a girl. And is there no one on God's earth who can protect her from me? No one. No."

There was a small table beside the elector's armchair. Herr Greuben laid the glass down on it and stepped back. Impassive, the elector sat with his fingers pressed together as the ice gradually melted and he fell asleep.

HIS HEAD FELL BACK, and his mouth fell open slightly, revealing his small, clean teeth. His eyelids trembled from the movement of his eyes. His hands were clamped together now, folded on his flat belly. From time to time his feet, stretched out on the hassock, twitched and shook.

Hans Greuben stood behind him. Bored, he examined the painted wallpaper beside the door, a motif of Egyptian landscapes: palm trees, crocodiles, and the dome of Kufu's great synagogue. He examined the portrait on the opposite wall, a beautiful woman dressed à la paysanne, as if for a country ball. She wore a peasant's embroidered vest, and her skirt was carefully torn. She had a hungry, wild expression on her face—Hans Greuben stared at her for many minutes, waiting for instructions.

If the elector had dozed off, what should he say, what should he do? Should he cough discreetly into his hand? Impatient, he approached the side table. The woman in the portrait was called Inez de Rougemont, he learned from a label on the gilded frame. A debutante from the previous generation, dead from a cancer in middle age; he thought he remembered reading her obituary. Now he leafed through the evening papers on the table, looking for news of Claude Spitz's murder. But the stories were painful to read, and so he stood for several more minutes examining the medallion on the carpet. It was intolerable to have to wait like this, and so finally he approached the elector's chair, intending to wake him and announce he would be going. When he got close, he heard some muttered words, and when he looked down he saw to his horror that the elector's eyes were open, that his pupils were trembling—the sign of a waking trance, as all the world knew and every child was taught. At that moment it was clear to him that the elector, despite his money and connections, was a criminal, was at that moment committing a crime, and all his lofty talk of science was a fraud, or self-delusion. And if Greuben stayed, then he'd be implicated—is this why he had killed a man, to suck up favor with a conjurer?

As he rode down in the elevator cage, he felt claustrophobic and afraid, desperate to be outside in the cold night. And once he reached the square, he couldn't imagine shutting himself up again inside a cab. So he walked home along the Soseaua Kiseleff, past the Institute for Mental Deviation, a large brick mansion set back from the street. He walked a long way to his small apartment in the north part of the city. And even when he reached it, he preferred to sit outside smoking cigarette after cigarette rather than go in.

He didn't understand the elector's preoccupation with Miranda Popescu. Cut off and alone, what did she matter in the clash of nations, the courses of destiny? Just one girl. The entire Brancoveanu family was finished, gone, destroyed. The elector, he thought, was a superstitious man. More than that—a conjurer, a criminal, not to be trusted. And Greuben, by accepting money, had made himself a criminal's accomplice; there was no chance now that he'd be able to break away. The elector was too powerful, and he knew about Herr Spitz.

Above Hans Greuben the stars glittered, clearly visible in that area of large lawns and dim or broken streetlights. When he was too cold to sit, he walked stiffly back and forth. When he was too cold to walk, he went inside and lay down sleepless in his overcoat, his heart full of thuggish misgivings and regrets. He was not a murderer, he told himself. He refused to imagine that he was. Herr Spitz would have died anyway from the wound on his head. If he could have brought him back to life again, he would have. It had been merciful to end his suffering. Still he was afraid that night the Jew would come to him while he was sleeping.

AT THE INSTITUTE FOR MENTAL Deviation, a lamp burned on the second floor. There, a boy sat in his dormer window, which he had opened through the bars. He was small, fair-haired, the only child of Baron and Baroness Ceausescu. He was named Felix, after the baron's father.

Often in that room he would sit without speaking, almost without moving for hour after hour, staring at the lantern flame. That night he could scarcely sit still.

His hands were stroking the windowsill, scratching at the bars. He understood there was a change in the atmosphere. He didn't know where it had come from, that it had gathered above the towers of the Athenée Palace Hotel and now was spreading over the city. But he thought he could feel in the steel bars of his room the tingle of an electric spark. He could feel a new sharpness to the air, a new thinness to the membranes that keep us from each other and the world, keep this world from the realm of spirits, devils, gods.

THAT NIGHT THERE was no space between the living and the dead. In the wooden church on Elysian Fields, in the small, subterranean chapel of St. Simon the Fisherman, two men sat waiting. They had broken open the coffin of Aegypta Schenck von Schenck, had taken out the body, wrapped in its shroud, and laid it on the stone table in front of the altar. They had put into her hands the Brancoveanu crucifix, made out of the nails of the true cross. They had pulled away a corner of the cloth.

One man got up now. Holding up the brass candlestick, the long white candle, he studied for the nineteenth time the part of her face he could see: the coarse gray hair, the big nose, the sunken eyelid. Was it moving? Was it moving now? He could not but imagine the eye underneath, trembling and motile. Was that a tremor of the cloth over her lips? For the nineteenth time he took the brass hand mirror and slid it under the shroud, drew it back, examined it. Surely soon there'd be some mist upon it. Or else they would wake up to find the shroud was empty, the body gone. Surely this was all still part of the princess's design, the instructions she had left for him.

NEARBY, IN THE HOUSE on Saltpetre Street, Kevin Markasev lay still. Hourly he had expected the lady of comfort and tears. Now she had come, and he pretended sleep so as to watch her. She had lit the lamp. She sat in the leather armchair next to a dusty table. Markasev watched her through the bars of his cage. Nor was it possible to tell by any movement of her shoulders or contortion of her face, any sound or quickness of breath, that she was weeping. Only once she turned toward him, and he could see the tears on her face.

That night he too was aware of a new beginning. Often at intervals during the past few months, he had felt the presence of the ghost in that house, tasted in his mouth the strange sulphuric taste that ghosts bring with them. But that night with the skin between the worlds nearly effaced, he was aware first of a snuffling creature. He imagined it nosing in the shadows, the red pig of Cluj.

And as if conjured out of the baroness's tears, there he was now, her attentive husband, brought back out of the land of the dead to comfort her. His eyes closed down to slits, still Markasev could see him as he moved around the room. Markasev could see him before the baroness felt his presence: a bald man with the greasy skin of the dead. Big sagging features, little pig's eyes—it was a face Markasev recognized from dreams. The man was dressed in a military uniform, the star of Roumania around his neck.

In his dreams the man had been a devil to him, a cruel father and a master. But now Markasev could almost imagine he had been redeemed by wretchedness, by his love for the lady of comfort and tears. She sat in her armchair, biting her fingernails while he moved around the room. He was studying her face, reaching out to her and then pulling back.

Only when he came close to her did he seem spectral or ephemeral, when he reached as if to touch her with his knotted, long fingers. Then the boy could see his flesh was weaker than her flesh. He reached out as if to touch her hair; she flinched away, brushed her hand against her ear as if a fly had lighted on it. Then she turned, staring at him, though she couldn't see him.

"Who's there?" she said, no tears now in her voice. Markasev could see she had a green stone in her hand. It glittered softly in the light.

On one of the side tables stood a ouijah board. The baroness had laid it out and consulted it many times, though not for several days. Now by itself the planchette started to move. It trembled and chattered across the board. But when the baroness got up to look, it skated rapidly from letter to letter. Markasev couldn't see, couldn't read, nor did he have to. For at the same time the old baron opened his leathery mouth, whispering words too softly for his wife to hear. "My love," he said. "Dear one."

"Who's there?" cried the baroness. She could not smell the odors of the red pig of Cluj, thought Markasev. She had no taste of sulphur in her mouth. She couldn't see her husband as he held out his weak, arthritic hands. But she was reading the words as he whispered them, and in a moment she relaxed. "Oh, it's you," she said. "What do you want?"

"My dear, I saw you weeping—"

There was no trace of tears now on her cheeks. As if impatient with the slow letters, she cut him off. "Someone in my house. Someone went through my clothes, my boxes. Jean-Baptiste—"

"It wasn't Jean-Baptiste," whispered the old man.

"How do you know? The door was locked. Oh, I have many troubles," and her eyes brimmed up again.

Markasev watched the old man acting out a pantomime of sympathy. He wrung his hands, held them out in supplication, though his wife couldn't see. Finally he spoke. The planchette started to move. "What's in your hand?"

"A jewel I planned to sell. Tonight I must be gone. The police will come—"

"You will not sell it. It is Kepler's Eye."

She was talking and not reading. Now she stopped, looked down at the board, the planchette skittering from letter to letter. "Those men came for Kepler's Eye."

Markasev listened to the old man whispering. "There is a man in the first circle now. He told me how a man shot him as he lay in his carriage with a broken head. That man was looking for Kepler's Eye. You must keep it. Do you know what it is?"

IN HIS CAGE, Markasev gave up his pretense of being asleep. He raised himself up on his elbow. He rearranged the blanket over his cold feet. But the baroness was bending over the ouijah board. She had the green stone in her hand: WHEN JOH KEPLER DIED IN TUBINGEN HE HANG IN PUB MARKET & ALL WEPT HE WAS THIEF & MURDER & THEY WEPT FOR HIM MEN & WOMEN IN CROWD FIGHT SOLDIERS BECAUSE OF LOVE

"What are you telling me?"

LOVE IN THE STONE KEEP IT

"What do you mean?"

LOVE WILL PROTECT U C

There was a story that Johannes Kepler had maintained a thousand lovers, which didn't seem to be what the baron was talking about now. "What do you mean?" Nicola Ceausescu said again.

KEEP IT U WILL C

Then, after a pause: LOVE WILL PROTECT & STONE WILL BRING 2 GREATNESS IT IS CHANCE 4 U & NOT MY GIFT BUT CHANCE SO HOLD IT 2 YOUR SKIN & TRUST & DO NOT B AFRAID 2 LEAVE ALL THIS MY LOVE

This wasn't helping. She had come home to find her bedroom broken into, her boxes and drawers rifled. Even the secret compartment under the pipes had been opened, the money spread across the bathroom floor. The thieves hadn't cared about it. She had come home thinking she would empty out her laboratory that night, send Markasev away, but it was late, too late, she knew.

DO NOT B AFRAID TO GRAB THE TYGERS TALE

He was delusional. Death had made him crazy. With her right hand, she batted the planchette across the floor. She had the tourmaline clasped in her other hand. Of the heart's emotions, love was one she understood the least. How could love protect her from the danger she was in?

Then there was a knocking at the quilted, outside door, and Jean-Baptiste saying, "Please, they're here."

No reason to ask who. As she hurried through her yellow room, past the clothes strewn across the floor, she looked out through the windows onto the street and saw the black police carriage with four horses. Jean-Baptiste was talking: "Don't be afraid. I spoke to them as they came in."

There was something unusual in his voice, a thrill of nervousness and triumph. When they came to the stairway he took hold of her elbow. On the way down he touched her back. He was a spry old man, and she felt a trembling in his fingers. "Please, Nicola," he murmured, the first time he had ever used her given name. "Don't be afraid," he coaxed, placing his hand on her back as they reached the landing. "You'll see."

In fact she was allowing him to bring her down the stairs. Her thoughts were dark and sluggish. She had the tourmaline in her left hand. She felt it slide between her fingers when she squeezed it. Surely they would not put her in prison, either for one crime or the other.

"Be quiet when you meet them," murmured the old man. "I've burned your clothes, all trace. I've left you a letter and some money. Please let me tell you, I could not let them search the house."

She turned to face him on the last landing. The light in the vestibule had not been lit, and the whole stairwell was in shadow. Down below stood a policeman by the door onto the street, and light streamed from the blue sitting room.

Jean-Baptiste stood close to her. She could smell his breath, a little brandy. In contrast to his threadbare coat, his slovenly, unshaven look of the morning, he now appeared carefully and meticulously groomed, dressed in a dark suit she had not seen before. He seemed agitated, and he licked his lips. His eyes were full of urgent pleading.

"What have you done?" she whispered. And she reached out with her left hand and almost placed it on the front of his shirt over his breast. Almost she touched his necktie, which was askew. Now she felt some sympathy with his excitement. Some sympathy, also, for him.

"Ma'am, are you there?" The voice was one she recognized: harsh, fussy, and with a Hungarian accent. It came from the blue sitting room, and now she looked down and saw Domnul Luckacz on the threshold, a black shadow with the light behind him.

Animated now, full of anxiety, she came down the remaining steps. Luckacz stood aside and she crossed into the room, which was quite warm. There was a fire hissing in the stove. On a small side table stood a silver candlestick.

"Ma'am, your servant was telling us how it was," said Domnul Luckacz. "I understand your feelings. I wish you had told me when I was here this morning."

Was it only this morning? She was staring at the candlestick, which Jean-Baptiste must have brought from somewhere. Immediately she felt a kind of separation, as if a part of her had stepped onto a stage. "He's been with me a long time," she murmured.

"Of course. You felt a loyalty, I understand. You understand also—"

"You have a job," she breathed. Still she hadn't turned to face him, to face Jean-Baptiste.

"We have a job to do," agreed Luckacz. "Let me say at once there are some favorable circumstances. This man was protecting you. We would like you to make a formal statement—"

"I am exhausted," she said.

"I understand. Tomorrow I will bring the notary. I do not wish to inconvenience you or add to your discomfort. Nevertheless I must assure you. There will be a public statement."

She was staring at the candlestick. "Is your investigation finished?"

"By no means."

"May I ask who your informant was?"

"Ma'am, I'm not able—"

He was quiet when she turned around. He was dressed in a green over-coat, but as before, his hat was in his hands. The light fell on his gray hair, his dyed moustache, and illuminated also the same odd, stricken look that she had noticed for the first time in her bedroom that morning.

Like an actress on the stage, she brought her left hand to her forehead in a long, languorous gesture, then let it fall. She looked at the carpet at her feet, then glanced up at the carefully shined shoes of Jean-Baptiste, who stood in profile behind Domnul Luckacz. He wouldn't look at her, but stared instead at the policeman, invisible in the shadow of the hallway. The baroness watched his Adam's apple knot and subside, knot and subside.

And when he turned to face her, she felt tears come. He seemed lost, his eyes bright and rheumy, rimmed with pink. A helpless old man. "I'm asking for a reason, for your informant's name," she told Luckacz. "Monsieur Spitz died of a gunshot wound, is that not right?"

"How do you know that?"

Ratisbon had told her. "I am acquainted with Herr Greuben from the German embassy. If that is the source of your information, then you should ask yourself . . ."

She let her voice trail away. As on a stage, every movement and inflection seemed false to her, though always, then and now, her audience was taken in. "I understand that you are trying to help us," Luckacz said. "But—"

"He is a poor old man. We have no firearms in the house."

Luckacz held up his hand. "All this can be part of your statement. Please remember it is in your interest to be discreet."

"Yes, of course," she said, tears in her eyes. "And of that other matter in the Mogosoaia forest, have you heard something about that?"

"Not yet."

She swallowed back a sob. "Please don't let him suffer for the crimes of others. Herr Greuben—remember. You might find you cannot trust these Germans. You above all should understand that."

She couldn't look at Jean-Baptiste. Instead she spoke to Luckacz: "Leave me now. Only if you would, please let me keep a policeman outside the door. Tonight I am afraid to be alone."

Which was the truth. Already once that evening, Ratisbon had sent his men to find the tourmaline. When he came for her again, she would be gone. "Leave now," she said. She held out her left hand, and allowed Luckacz to kiss it. She felt the tickle of his moustache on the back of her hand, which she kept clamped in a fist around the stone.

Later that night, much later, she took it out as she sat at the table in her kitchen. She rubbed it between her fingers, the green eye of Johannes Kepler. She put it carefully beside her plate.

She had sat down with a bottle of beer and a ham sandwich: the first time in years she had tasted this substance, which she had asked Jean-Baptiste to buy for her that morning. But since the previous night, when Aegypta Schenck von Schenck had laid out under her nose the slices of meat and bread, she'd thought about it: the smell of the grease, the way the fat and muscle yielded between her teeth. Then she had forced herself to eat, because of the part that she was playing. But in the morning she had woken with a hankering, and now she ate sandwich after sandwich until the packages in the zinc icebox were gone.

There was a letter in the middle of the enamel table top. It was Jean-Baptiste's letter, and as he'd said, there was money in the envelope. She hoped he had not sold his house in the woods.

10 *Tara Mortilor*

IN THE GERMAN CITY of Ratisbon, in her third-floor room in the elector's house, a woman sat at her casement looking up at the night sky. She was not aware of the conjuring in Bucharest, nine hundred kilometers away. She was not aware of the elector in his trance and the wind that rose from it. She had risen from her bed, unable to sleep—there were no bars in her window, but the drop onto the tiles was perilous, impossible. In the town, where would she go? No one knew her name after these years. She had grown old in this upholstered room. In the mornings the hair in her brush was streaked with gray.

Books were brought to her whenever she wished. Sometimes musicians came to play for her. She was allowed ink, brushes, paints, paper, and for two decades she had used them with great skill, drawing from memory the faces of the great men and women she had known, painting from memory the landscapes she had seen. Especially she had amused herself with a series of sketches of someone she had never known, but who had grown up from babyhood under her imagination's eye. Her daughter was a woman now. Clara Brancoveanu had not seen her since the first day of her life. But, in pencil or pen-and-ink, she drew her portrait several times a week. Where was her daughter now in the wide world? Inevitably, inaccurately, her drawings could not but suggest a memory of her own face when she was young, or else a memory of her dead husband's well-loved face.

That morning she had drawn, in pen-and-ink under a gray wash, a portrait of a young woman reading a letter. She was beautifully dressed, elegant, graceful, as Clara Brancoveanu once had been.

THE PRINCESS WAS WRONG about many things. But she had gotten some things right—the position of the body, the attitude of weariness and lassitude. Across the ocean, in her shelter in the hunters' camp, Miranda sat with her back hunched, overcome with exhaustion but unable to sleep. Andromeda lay on a sleeping bag, staring at her with pale eyes.

Andromeda lifted her muzzle from her paws. She lay in the shelter one of the hunters had vacated for Miranda, a round canvas tent over a wooden frame. Bearskins covered the floor, which was of frozen dirt. Even so, the shelter was warm inside. There was a small woodstove, vented by a pipe through the roof.

Andromeda thought about the smells from the bearskin. Miranda sat on her cot. She was reading and rereading the letter Splaa had given her at last. She held it up next to the candle. "Listen," she said.

Her voice was awkward and unsure. Andromeda thought it couldn't be natural for her to read to a dog.

"My dear,

I find it hard to express myself in this language I speak only badly to someone with no memory of me. O if you only knew how many letters I have torn and thrown away or kept only for myself. A friend has smuggled this out for me in his violin and I have sent it to my cousin, my husband's sister, so that she will send it on to you—so *tentatif*, as the French say. Did you take French in school? Aegypta tells me you may never receive this message. But if you are reading it now you have received it, *n'est-ce pas*? At least I can pretend.

So let me tell you how much I am thinking of you for all this terrible time. Do not think it was my choice to give you up. After your father was killed, I came here to Ratisbon because I was afraid of your father's enemies—a terrible decision! You have heard of the battle of Kaposvar? These Germans will not forgive me for what I did for my country. By an accident I discovered the elector's plan after he had made of me some kind of prisoner in his house. He allowed only Aegypta to visit me, because I was with child (you, my darling!)— two harmless women, he supposes. Aegypta stole the battle plan from under his nostrils! He was with the army when I was delivered. Aegypta gave me something to make you come early and it was a good idea because the elector was furious when he came back and you are gone. Do not trust him for any reason. He is a bad man in this terrible world. Aegypta crossed the border with his papers in your nappy! O but why am I telling you all this? Only to say I would have given anything to go with you but could not. Aegypta told the nurse I miscarried so I had to stay there to pretend. Besides I was a species of prisoner as I said. My dear they knew I was ill because I cried day after day. It was the discomfort of losing you. Since then every day I must weep sometimes when I think of you growing up alone without your mother or your father among strangers as Aegypta tried to tell me. She says you are safe in some English language country. Please, what country is that? Now I am in my room here in this house and my only hope is that you grow up strong in freedom. Always remember who you are from the great families of von Schenck and Brancoveanu especially. I know you will have the great heart from your father whom they murdered. From me maybe some kind of a 'style personnel', and the constant nature to wake up every day hoping to see your face as I have seen it in my dreams. What kind of girl are you become? Each day I am asking myself, supposing something different, some new story. But one day you will tell me from your mouth and I will know for myself, because one day I will embrace you for the second time.

Your affectionate mother,
Clara (Brancoveanu)"

Andromeda had closed her eyes. "Wait, there's more," Miranda said. "There's another whole letter:

"My dear niece,

Here you are among us once more again, which means that a great hazard will begin today, which will lead to our freedom from black tyranny, and our deliverance from foreign powers. Do not worry if you do not feel prepared, because no preparation is possible for what you must undertake. If you are alone and without friends, it is because help is hidden and will come from the strange places. This is as it must be when the weak fight against the strong. With God's help, we shall prevail. Now I give you the first instruction to seek me out. You must put your trust to my dear Rodica and faithful Splaa, and they will lead you. In Albany, I have left another letter in the hands of Ion Dreyfoos, who will bring you home. Then in Mogosoaia we will find our weapons in the land of our ancestors. Do not shirk from this and do not linger, because we wait in slavery. You are the white tyger that was prophesied. Many will attempt to stop you or prevent you, so have a care.

Aegypta Schenck"

Miranda refolded the first letter, slipped it back into the envelope with its big wax seal. Andromeda could hear her small escaping breath. "You know, just somehow I was expecting something more. Especially the second one."

She read it again, folded it up. "Aegypta Schenck—what kind of name is that? 'Mogosoaia'—are you kidding me?" Shivering, she wrapped a blanket around her shoulders, then turned around to look at the little stove.

The dog, by contrast, was overheated. She lay on a bearskin, panting and yawning with her tongue out.

There was movement at the entrance to the shelter, which was covered by a blanket. Peter Gross pushed through the hole, then stood up straight. "Talking to yourself?"

Miranda shrugged, turned, smiled. "I guess."

Peter squatted down. He was dressed in a new woolen jacket. He reached out his left hand toward Andromeda, but stopped when he heard her small, throaty growl. "She doesn't like you," Miranda said. "She's not going to hide it now."

"Well, sure." He sat down against a pile of blankets midway between Andromeda and the cot. "Bad news?"

Miranda shook her head. "Unbelievable."

Then in a moment, "You can read it if you want."

He stretched out his left hand for the envelope. "You know," he said, "before all this I'd never even really heard of Roumania, except in that poem my Mom taught me. Now I wake up and it's the most important country in the world."

"Is that what you've done—woken up?"

Now he was reading the first letter. But he was talking to her, which made Andromeda think he was saying something he'd rehearsed. "I thought this was a dream because I didn't feel anything at first. Now I think it was because I was afraid. My father used to say it's why cowards are so dangerous. When I saw them put you in that boat, that felt really bad. And when I think about my father . . ." He raised his eyes from the letter to look at her. "So maybe I've come out of it a little bit.

"That felt bad for me, too. When I saw you on that sandbar."

Her expression when she said this was a little odd, Andromeda thought. But then Miranda smiled. "I've been thinking about it, too. I've been thinking about it all day. You know when I was a kid, I used to love those books where the girl feels she doesn't belong, and she's having some kind of problems and she wakes up in a different country—just like this. And she fits into that place like a key into a lock, and everything that made no sense now suddenly makes sense. There are the good guys and the bad guys, the wise king and the shining prince. But I get the feeling we won't find any of that here."

"There's me," Peter said. Andromeda pricked up her ears.

Miranda smiled. With her left hand she drew her hair out of her face, perched it behind her ear.

She said, "This isn't that kind of story because it's not a book—the book was before. And everything is different, but I'm not any different. I'm not smarter or prettier or stronger. I don't feel I've come home. It doesn't all make sense to me. It's just another place, another bunch of adults and their problems. These women," she said, indicating the letters in Peter's hand, "—my mother and the woman from my dream—I've wanted to meet them my whole life. I've wondered about my mother my whole life—what kind of woman she is, whether I'd ever meet her. And now I have this photograph and this letter, and you know what? She's a stranger."

"I think you've changed," said Peter, but she interrupted him:

"In books you always know the rules. Or at least that there were rules if you could learn them. That's the difference between stories and real life, I thought. But maybe nothing real ever makes sense, ever feels like home. Understanding it won't help. That's what I mean."

She had shrugged the blanket from her shoulders. Now she sat forward on the cot. Maybe she also had rehearsed something to say. "When I was tied up in that boat, and I saw you disappear behind those trees, I thought at first I felt so sick because I was afraid. But I've been thinking about it lying here, and it's because of you—we can't risk losing each other. It's because we're the only people who know each other from before. When you say you feel bad about your father, I know what that means. And I know you're the only person here who knows anything about me—this," she said, indicating the letter in his hand, "it's just a fantasy. I mean, what am I supposed to do about this? Go live in some palace on some throne?"

"I gather you're supposed to go home and help out. I gather they're in some trouble over there."

"And what am I supposed to do about it?"

"I don't know. But it sounds as if your aunt has some ideas. She's sort of been leading you step by step."

"You noticed that? But who is she? I have one memory of her, and then a face in a couple of dreams—it's not like you. It's not like Stanley or Andromeda or you. And it doesn't mean we have to pretend our lives didn't exist. We were starting to be friends before, and maybe that was the way the story was going to end up making sense. Maybe it'll be harder now. But we can try."

He didn't say anything, so she went on. "So I'm sorry about getting you into this mess. I know it's my fault that you're here. And I wanted to say I'm sorry because of how I treated you after school started and Andromeda came home. I know it sounds stupid, because it seems like a long time ago. Do you forgive me?"

He shrugged. "It was a long time ago."

"We can't lose each other anymore," she said.

"Okay."

"So I have to ask you—are you coming with me?"

Peter hesitated. "As opposed to what?"

"Oh, I don't know. It seems like everything's been pushed back a couple of hundred years. Maybe you could go west with the gold rush. Or go to New York City and play the harmonica on the street. Or hang around here trying to get home. There's got to be some way of getting home."

Peter shook his head. "I've always wanted to go to Europe. I was always jealous of kids who got to go."

Miranda smiled. "So it's a deal? You'll come with me, and then maybe I can do something to help. Whatever else, my aunt has got to have some powers. Magic powers, whatever—it sounds stupid to say. But there's got to be some way to send us home."

Peter smiled, showed his crooked teeth. "I wasn't about to leave you," he said. And then Miranda put out her hand out for him. When he started to reach toward her with his left hand, she said, "No. The other one."

Which was enough for Andromeda. More than enough. In a moment she had nosed her way out through the slit in the shelter's skin, out past the blanket and into the clear night. The snow was dry under her paws.

The camp consisted of three round shelters and a central space of trampled snow. Coming south from the Hoosick River, she and Miranda had climbed mostly uphill for almost seven miles. They had left behind the great woods and the great trees, and climbed into an area of birches and aspens and thorn bushes. From time to time the trees gave out completely. The hunters' camp was in one of these clearings, at the bottom of a shallow bowl surrounded by outcroppings of rocks. Above these on the south side there were some sheer rock walls, and a small stream dribbled under a layer of ice.

In the middle of the circle burned a small, smoky bonfire, and the men sat around it on tree stumps and logs, drinking coffee in the dark cold. Splaa was there, and the three others whose winter camp this was—hard, sun-blackened men who looked as if they'd lived outside for years. They were frightened, apprehensive, and Splaa was trying to reassure them. They spoke English, though it wasn't their first language. They wore wool-lined leather coats, leather pants, rubber boots. In those woods, with the help of traps and lines, retrievers and hounds, they hunted beavers, otters, foxes, and larger animals.

As the yellow dog made a circle around the fire, another dog rose to growl at her. He was a yellow-eyed, brindled mastiff named Jack. "Good boy," said his master, a thick, squat, bearded man. He caught hold of his collar.

The thing that sucked about being a dog, the fly in the ointment, thought Andromeda, was other dogs. Some were dangerous and mean from the beginning. Others, friendly at first, turned nasty when you didn't let them smell your butt.

Among the seven dogs at the camp, Andromeda had imagined first a hierarchy of physical power with Jack at the top, and she thought he might be vicious because he felt threatened. She was a larger dog than all but two or three. But some of the nastiest were among the smallest, and Jack himself seemed to defer to one hound about half his size. So that wasn't it. There was some more complicated arrangement that might involve breed, age, sex, family relationship, and temperament; whatever it was, it seemed to work pretty well. Harmony pretty much reigned. She herself was the only irritant. Though she'd been in several skirmishes and near-fights, and though she'd always managed to chase her attackers away, that never seemed to bring the others closer to accepting her. Yet it was clearly possible, even easy, she suspected, for a newcomer to gain acceptance. So that evening she dug a place in the snow and sat apart outside of the circle of firelight, watching the others. Certainly there was a language of gesture and smell. Certainly also there was another more conventional language, not of barking so much. Once she was sensitive to it, she was able to hear a whole vocabulary of grunts and moans. The dogs spoke to each other in short, terse conversations, rarely more than a few words. How was she to learn?

And why did she care? What could these dim-witted brutes offer her, that she wasted time thinking about it? It was more interesting to listen to the hunters talk about the wendigo—the ghost Miranda saw the night before. It comes to you in the shape of someone you love. Then it leaves you heartbroken in the snow, and brings bad luck to everyone around you—which was such bullshit; she knew what Miranda had seen. Sasha Prochenko had come to her.

Most interesting was to leave the firelight altogether. Near ten o'clock she got up, shook off the melted snow along her underside. That day there had been a wind, and the temperature had dropped. Drifts had formed. But now the wind was gone and the stars burned. And though part of her longed for the acceptance of the other dogs, for the contentment of sitting without thinking any thoughts, there was another part that came alive as soon as she had left the circle of firelight. Because of the warm temperatures of the last few days and then the sudden freeze, there was a layer of crusted snow that allowed her to move quickly. In many places the wind had blown it clean. In the clearings it gleamed like a clean white piece of paper.

Away from the firelight her senses came alive, and her nose was no longer stuffed with the overpowering smells of camp: smoke, charred meat, and the urine of the seven dogs. As she left the clearing and moved away through the thin woods, she felt she was pushing through a net, each cord of which was the circle of urine marks that each dog had drawn around the fire. Her instinct was to stop often, restrained by the net, but she pushed through. On the far side she filled her lungs with cleaner air, which was nevertheless scented with a myriad small traces of animals and men. They seemed to draw glowing lines in front of her on the snow. There was the trail the men used, trampled with their boots, over the lip of the bowl and downhill toward a small pond.

At the top of the rise she scratched among the exposed rocks and at the roots of some small bushes. Then she ran parallel to the man's trail that seemed to glow beside her in the small trees. From time to time she was interrupted by the holes and scratches that animals had made across the snow, field mice and rabbits, foxes and raccoons—so many, she had never guessed how many—each with its distinctive shade of burning colors—lime green, pink, purple, and amber, which nevertheless started to fade the instant the animal had passed.

These visual patterns did not replace her sense of smell. Instead they were the way her brain made meaning out of what was otherwise a chaos of small odors. Beside the fire, the stew of powerful, familiar scents made it possible to relax, possible to sleep. Out here in the night, her brain was kept alert and agitated not just by these impressions, but by the other senses that they overlaid. Her eyes were sharper than those of the girl she had been, seeing mixtures of movement that had been unknown to her before. Her ears, also, could hear new sounds. And since even for Miranda and Peter every sensation in this world seemed stronger, richer, clearer, then it was no wonder that the dog felt overburdened by delight.

She danced down the hill and through the hummocks of the frozen swamp that filled the north end of the beaver pond. She danced onto the ice, blown clean by the wind. She was sliding and jumping there in a little circle when she heard a sound that made her stop.

It was at the limit of her hearing, a howl that reached a quick high note, and then sank slowly down. Another voice interrupted, then another. Andromeda knew what she was listening to. It was a family of wolves, away and to the west, where she now saw the outline of a range of mountains, black against a darker black.

At the same time she was aware of something else, a gleam of red on the west side of the pond. Moving stiffly, hesitantly now, distracted often by the sound of the wolves, she walked over to investigate. Another man had come to the pond in the last few hours, someone who was not one of the hunters and was not like them either. Some member, she now recognized, of the family of wild men who had attacked Miranda along the river.

She saw the red line of the trail through the frozen grass. The color was still hot, but fading now. It was easy enough to follow and she took off, avoiding as before the heavy print of the boots that broke through the crust. Instead she followed alongside.

At first she had been hindered by the sound of the wolves. Each time she heard it she had stopped and lowered her muzzle to the snow. The fur had bristled along the ridge of her back, and her ears and tail had sunk down. But after the first few miles the sound grew more sporadic, and besides, she no longer responded to it in the same way. Instead she bounded forward, her ears straining to hear, and this was partly because already she was used to the sound. Partly also because she had identified only two voices, and not an entire pack. And partly because another instinct was leading her now, a sensation of hunger that increased mile after mile.

Of all her senses, the dullest by far was her sense of taste. Nothing tasted like anything as soon as it was in her mouth. So it was odd that hunger could possess her in this way and drive her forward.

Surely the smartest thing would be to return to camp. Often the hunters would throw her bones. If Miranda was awake, then she would find her something. But Andromeda felt she must go forward, and the sound of the wolves now, when it came, seemed to promise a big supper.

After the third mile there was something else, a smell she didn't know. Dirt and meat, blood and hair, and she was aware of it for a long time before she burst out through a ring of broken trees into a wide, round clearing where the snow was trampled flat. In the middle was the source of the smell, a circle of snowy mounds.

The dog stopped at the edge of the wood, one paw held poised above the snow.

It was a family of mammoths, a bull and three cows in the middle of the field. They were arranged in a circle, their heads facing outward and some little ones between them. They were asleep or resting, their heavy bodies lying in the snow. From time to time one or another of the adults would raise its head and make a heavy, snuffling noise. Now as the dog watched, the bull raised his head to look at her, and he lifted his curved tusks above the snow.

After a few minutes the dog moved into the woods again. She made a circle through the fringe of the trees, laying her line at intervals as she squatted to piss. So impressed was she by the power of the mammoths that she acted without thinking, without realizing that she was overmarking the line laid by another animal. This one she heard rather than saw, a low growl that made her tremble. Unable to move, she sank down with her ears low, her tail under her. Nor did she object when the wolf came to smell her, smell her legs and stomach before lifting his own leg over a broken tree just inches from her nose.

He was a beautiful creature. Nor, after he had smelled her all over, did he continue to notice her. He also was preoccupied with the mammoths, she imagined. He stood in the wreck of fallen trees, his nose held high. Then without glancing back at her, he retraced his steps. He had been coming along the man-trail from the west, and now she followed him, stiffly and shyly at first. But she found herself imitating his fast, straight-legged walk, and she followed him along the man-trail which was gleaming brighter now, and which led along the bottom of a wooded ridge.

Mile after mile, and she could see the light through the trees. The bonfire at the hunters' camp had been little and discreet. Here, it seemed, whole trees had been set alight. She followed the wolf through an open space of saplings and bushes until she had a better view.

The fire had melted back the snow in a muddy circle. Wild men and women stood around it, warming not their hands but their whole bodies, for most of them were naked, or practically so. They had stripped down to their leather underpants, looking ridiculous, Andromeda decided. Once she had gone with her mother to see a production of Stravinsky's *Rite of Spring* at the New York City Ballet. It had featured a lot of nudity, and people with expensive haircuts pretending to be cavemen, accompanied by shrieks and crashes from the orchestra.

Andromeda thought there was something self-conscious and unreal about these people, too, though mercifully there was no dancing. There was, however, a lot of body paint. Occasionally people staggered out of the circle away from the fire. They stood in the snow, their bodies steaming in the sudden cold.

They had no dogs. And their eyes were so blinded by firelight, Andromeda imagined she could come to the edge of the circle without being seen. Behind her the wolf had continued on. He had not stopped.

Two men stood away from the fire but facing it. They smelled like many kinds of garbage and meat, and they seemed to be talking to each other. Andromeda stepped close and paused behind them, sniffing the air, curious as to what their language might sound like. "Ooga booga," she imagined. So she was surprised to hear one talking in an English accent. "It will be snow," he said, shuffling his feet.

If dogs could laugh, Andromeda would have laughed. She stood on three feet, one foreleg poised above the snow. But the red-bearded man was aware of her. He turned, and she scampered back into the dark. For a few minutes she crouched behind a bush, chewing the ice out of her feet, watching the shadows until she got bored. Then she was aware again of the wolf's trail, gleaming behind her like a ribbon of yellow light.

She followed it to a big tree, two hundred yards or so from the bonfire. It was an oak, with heavy branches that grew straight out from the trunk. It was the only big tree in what was almost a meadow of bushes and scrub. And there were other wolves there, circling the trunk or else standing on two legs against it, scratching at the bark, peering into the branches. Something was up there. Andromeda saw a rope around the bottom of the trunk and stretched up taut into the darkness to a big, huddled shadow on a low branch.

One of the wolves jumped up halfheartedly, then dropped down. They paid no attention to the yellow dog who lay down in the snow at a safe distance, chewing and licking at her paws. When the shadow moved, she looked up. In any case she had already caught a scent she recognized. It was Captain Raevsky up there, and now he moved and she saw the glimmer of his eyes as he looked toward the fire. Many smells came off of him, borne to her on the cold, dry air above the marking of the wolves. Dirt and sweat and fear. She saw him stretch his leg out on the branch. In the small reflected firelight she saw his face, and it was bleached and broken like the moon.

IN BUCHAREST IT WAS ALMOST morning. In the Athenée Palace Hotel, the Elector of Ratisbon still sat in his chair. He had not stirred in more than a day. His first conjuring was finished, and he lay back as if asleep, his feet up on the ottoman, his face painted with sweat.

He had thought Miranda Popescu would be easy to find, that she would glimmer like a candle in the black wastes of America. But for hours he had let his mind range far and wide and had seen nothing. Had the baroness lied to him? No, because he could feel something there past Codfish Bay, a presence that was thwarting him, turning away his eyes. It was as if he were peering into a gray fog. When he came to himself, he was angry and frustrated and a little frightened, too. He recognized the power that was keeping him away. But Aegypta Schenck was dead, he knew. Surely she was dead. If he hadn't known she was dead, he could have sworn . . .

Even so, his conjuring had roiled the air, had brought with it a storm that was taking shape over the North Atlantic. There was no power anywhere that could hinder the sinking pressure, the gathering circle of the winds. But in Bucharest the elector was resting, drained and tired, and as often happened when his strength was low, he was pursued by waking nightmares.

In his own mind he was a man of destiny, of modern science, born to greatness. Many of his political and social programs, introduced first to his own peasants and factory workers, were now spreading across Germany and across Europe. For years he had wasted the resources of Ratisbon on the delegates of the German Republic. He had spared no effort to ingratiate himself. He had no doubt that when the new elections were held, there would be a high place for him in the new government.

Or rather, yes, he did have doubts, and sometimes his doubts threatened to overwhelm him. Because of his compelling ugliness, he told himself, it was impossible to seize and hold the trust and loyalty of other men. For this reason, for years he had attempted to possess Johannes Kepler's tourmaline. Kepler, also, had been an ugly man.

Now he had promised himself that he would find a way to free the German citizens of Roumania, without bloodshed if possible. In this way he hoped to earn the thanks of his grateful nation. Yet he must be careful. Even at the apex of their superstitious decadence, these Roumanians had beaten him before. Aegypta Schenck and Clara Brancoveanu had betrayed him, and General Antonescu had ambushed him in the woods of Kaposvar. His small force had been destroyed before it reached the frontier. He had been six kilometers from the crossing when he was stopped, six kilometers from the station where the munitions train was to have met him. On the far side of the border German partisans had waited, an army of malcontents ready to march on Bucharest with him at their head. But Antonescu had blown the tracks up and the guns couldn't get through. Six kilometers, for the love of God!

Of those people who had humiliated him, Schenck was dead, Brancoveanu was in prison. Antonescu commanded the Roumanian armies; did he understand, when he saw the elector across the room at some official reception, how terribly and completely he would be crushed when the time came? Twenty years was a long time in politics, but even so it was amazing to Ratisbon that he could travel freely in Roumania, stay indefinitely at this hotel after what he had done, what he planned to do. Because the empress was so desperate for German money and investment. . . .

These were the thoughts that, never far from his conscious mind, the conjurer's trance had rendered into a kind of dreaming code. He found himself back in the woods of Kaposvar, riding in the dark night toward the station and the border crossing. From time to time he would attempt to consult his watch. He was late for the train to Berlin, and was afraid that it would leave without him. As the horse galloped along a dark forest path, he would let go of the reins to search for his watch in the bizarre, pocketless clothes in which he found himself, and which he now recognized to be the prime minister's robe of state, a kind of straitjacket of ermine and gold braid. And yes, his worst fears were justified, for as he came out of the woods beside the railroad track, he saw the train coming to meet him, passing him by, leaving him helpless in the dark. And as the train passed he was able to peer into a luxurious, candlelit, private car, with horsehair furniture on which reclined the grotesque, gigantic frame of General Antonescu. Near him Clara Brancoveanu and her sister-in-law held up between them a smiling baby, whose diapers were stuffed with documents and money.

The train rattled by, and he watched the blue lights of the baggage car until they disappeared. He was left alone. And his horse was gone. Also his absurd attire, and he was standing in ordinary gentleman's clothes. Now the train tracks were gone as well, and he found himself in the woods again with the white tyger above him, crouching on the branches, or else stalking him behind the bushes. He started to run, slipping often in his patent-leather boots until his suit was torn and wet with mud.

IN HIS ARMCHAIR in the Athenée Palace Hotel, beneath the portrait of Inez de Rougemont, the Elector of Ratisbon grumbled and cried out. In that comfortable, safe room, his thoughts were full of panic and despair. In the north Atlantic, the storm of his anxiety was gathering force, but it had not reached the dark woods of New England. In her shelter in the hunter's camp, Miranda Popescu spoke to Gregor Splaa.

Past midnight he had seen her light still burning. He had come in to apologize again, and then to ask permission to go with the hunters in the morning. A family of hairy mammoths had been discovered on the other side of the lake, the great elephants of these woods. One pair of tusks could make you rich.

He had Rodica's purse of silver nuggets, but it wasn't a lot. Prices had quadrupled just in the last couple of years. He was having to pour out money just to these hunters so they could stay, especially since Miss Popescu had seen the spirit by the river.

So he thought if he could make the kill, then it would be something he could do to help, to redeem himself, and they wouldn't have to beg their way from Bremerhaven to the Roumanian frontier. He had always been better with animals than men. Never in his life had he killed a man. That whole time in Rodica's house with the soldiers camped outside, he had been trembling with fear. And in the morning he was not in his right mind, or else he would not have . . . He could not have . . . Rodica had been a mother to him, though she was a Gypsy.

When he'd entered her tent, Miss Popescu was still reading the letters he had given her. She sat cross-legged on her cot, holding her mother's letter to the candle flame. At the same time she was inspecting the bracelet on her wrist, the tyger bracelet of her mother's family. She turned her wrist back and forth, examining one by one the golden beads. Her leather pack was open on the floor.

"Miss, you should not wear that," he said.

She looked up, a dark-haired young woman with pale skin and small, slightly protruding ears. His heart went out to her, alone in the wide world.

Watching her play with the most precious relic in all Roumania, he had spoken without thinking. But now he reminded himself: It was not his place to question her. She put the letter down, slid the beads between her fingers. "I thought it was mine."

He bit his lips, which were already chapped and bleeding. "It belongs to the Roumanian people."

"I thought it belonged to the whatchamacallit. The white tyger."

"So they say."

"No one else has worn it?"

"That's the trouble, miss. Too many have worn it. You are not the first since Miranda Brancoveanu. In the bad times . . ."

"What?"

He shrugged. "People pretend. The white tyger."

"And?"

He shrugged again. "It ends badly."

She was staring up at him. When he had first seen her in the house he'd shared with old Rodica, he had been shocked by how insignificant she looked, how thin and frail—her wrists and shoulders, her long fingers and neck. Now in just four days she seemed stronger and heavier, more womanly as far as he could see under her woolen shirt. And there was something in her face that recalled her father. And perhaps, he thought, the melancholy that now came over him was unconnected to her frailness, no longer so apparent. Perhaps it had a different source, which was in the memory of Blind Rodica, who was dead, who had sacrificed herself for this woman, and whose name he'd just touched over in his mind. And he'd been aware of her all along, he supposed, because the girl was wearing some of her clothes, the red woolen shirt he recognized. It was still too big for her.

He had been with Rodica when she bought it new, at a trading post on the Hudson River. But after all that and a minute of stupidity, she was dead.

"I'm sorry," he said. "I told your aunt I would protect you, and I did not. I am ashamed. Please," he continued, but she interrupted him with a gesture of her hand.

"Tell me about the white tyger," she said. She had not taken off the bracelet, which she was fingering one bead at a time. She had not asked him to sit down. He was more comfortable standing, though the roof of the round tent was low.

"Miranda Brancoveanu came out of the mountains," said Gregor Splaa. "People told stories. First she was alone, and everywhere she went the people . . . No, there was a king, a Turk named Kara Suliman, and he sent soldiers. He burned the villages where she'd been hiding. Living in caves. She had the strength of the goddess Minerva . . ."

As he was speaking, he could hear the change in his voice, the softness and the sadness enter in as he remembered Blind Rodica who'd believed all this. Even the part about the goddess, though she was a Christian. It didn't matter to her. He found himself staring not at Miranda, but into the candle flame that burned from a small stub of wax on a camp stool next to the cot. Rodica's hairbrush, too. The tent seemed hot inside.

He put his hands to his cheeks, touched his beard, which itched. "You don't believe these stories," said Miranda.

"No."

"What do you believe?"

He shrugged. Then after a pause, "A debt to your family who took me in. Your mother is alive after these years. The empress is greedy and cruel, and Antonescu is a tyrant, and a war is coming. If the white tyger can protect us, then that too."

But was it possible to think this young woman could change any of that? He'd scarcely heard a shred of news from his own country—just a few rumors in the past twelve years. Just a few old copies of the Roumanian newspapers, which he'd seen on his infrequent trips to Albany. Just a few terse letters from Aegypta Schenck, which Rodica had read to him—this was his country now, he thought, where Blind Rodica's house had burned. He didn't know anyone in Bucharest. Could anyone blame him if he wanted to arrive there with some money in his pocket? Rodica had talked of wages, but he wondered if Aegypta Schenck had any money to pay? She was living by herself in Mogosoaia.

The girl sat cross-legged on her cot, squinting up at him. "What did she look like?"

"No one knows. Blind Rodica had a vision. Black hair, she said. Dark eyes."

The girl fingered the beads one by one, as if she herself were blind. "I could refuse this."

But she couldn't, of course, Splaa thought.

Suddenly he felt close to tears. "I must tell you again how much I am ashamed. I didn't pretend I was a soldier. Once Rodica told me I would know what kind of man I was, and if that's true, then I'm ashamed. I could do nothing. You'll see I will not be that man again. I will bring you to Ion Dreyfoos and your aunt Aegypta. I will protect you from those men who would sell you to Ceausescu's widow or the empress. In Roumania you will find friends . . ."

All this had burst out of him, and he felt he could go on for a long time in this way. But Miranda Popescu put her hand up, and he paused. How sad she looked!

"You have other friends to help you," he continued. "You don't have to rely on me. These hunters—"

But she interrupted him. "They won't say a word to me. The white tyger! They saw me screaming in the snow because of a bad dream."

Splaa said nothing. Then: "They don't judge you. You were right to be afraid. They think you saw the wendigo."

He had explained this before. The wendigo was an evil spirit in these north woods, a superstition. "It brings death, these people say. You see it in a shape you recognize—a person known to you. It was the wendigo that led you from the river."

But if that was so, he thought, would Blind Rodica come for him? What would he tell her, if he saw her by the water, or in the snowy woods?

"No," Miranda said. Then in a moment she went on. "Tell me, who is the Chevalier de Graz? Who is Sasha Prochenko?"

This was easier. "I never knew them. They were friends of your father's. Pieter de Graz was a great champion. He beat all the Turkish wrestlers at Adrianople during the war. Afterward, the sultan signed the armistice."

"And?"

"Why do you ask? When the generals put the empress on the throne, your father spoke against them. He gave a speech in the old Senate, and they all listened—it was in the newspapers. Your father was a hero in Roumania, a hero in the army. So they paid his friend Ceausescu to denounce him. But there were riots in the Field of Mars and Brasov and Timisoara. And so they murdered him while he lay in prison. So—a great man and a patriot—this was long ago, twenty years. Those men were your father's aides-de-camp. Prochencko was a cavalry officer, very blond, I remember. Very popular with ladies. De Graz was a great champion, as I said."

"And . . . ?"

"Miss?"

"Was he—I don't know—a nice guy?"

"He was a famous soldier, decorated in the wars. Your aunt sent them with you to protect you. Don't you remember? What became of them? They lived in Constanta when you were just a child."

IN THE NORTH ATLANTIC and over Greenland, a storm was gathering. But it was still far away at dawn. That night Miranda dreamt that she'd awaked to a gray light in her little tent. And when she raised herself onto her elbow, she saw her aunt, Aegypta, sitting on the floor, dressed not as Miranda first remembered her, in a fur coat and leather boots at the railway station in Roumania, nor as subsequently she had seen her in her dreams. This time she appeared to be naked under a gray sheet, which she had arranged around her body to conceal everything but her head and hands. The material seemed to glow in a subtle way, the color of gray clouds with the sun behind them. Rather than the light of morning, that was the radiance which had filled the room.

She had been sitting with her legs crossed, her back bent, her chin sunk on her breast. But as Miranda came awake she raised her head. And without any kind of greeting or acknowledgment, she started to speak. "The coins I have given you are for a purpose, and you must bring them when you come to meet me in the land of the dead. I did not think that it would come to this, but now I'm glad I was prepared, for I could do little where I was. Now I have taken a risk, but I have confidence in you. The gold is for the boatman and the sphinxes. The silver coin is for the king of the dead. Death can be defeated. Take Sasha Prochenko and follow the cave to the end under the yawning wall. Free me and I will bring you safe at last. Without me your hope is small."

There was more, but this was the part Miranda remembered when she woke up. She lay on her back and wondered whether it made sense to think of her aunt as a living, breathing person, who was living right now in Mogosoaia or Constanta. What would she say to her, when she saw her face to face?

Her aunt had given her a few specific directions—find Ion Dreyfoos. Give the gold coins to the sphinx. And some general ones—save Roumania from slavery. Between them was a big gray area—what was she supposed to do? Wear a crown and yell at people? It was impossible to visualize, and so to distract herself she thought about Peter when he'd visited her in the tent. All the previous day she had felt awkward about it when she saw him.

Boys had always been interested in Andromeda. That summer when school started, she had come back and told Miranda about meeting some random Italian on a beach. And if they hadn't had intercourse exactly, they had gotten close—Andromeda had given her the blow-by-blow, as she described it. To Miranda it had seemed like fascinating messages from outer space. She had always been shy about that kind of thing, because of her period. But now she had to wash out her underpants twice a day and walk around with what felt like a roll of toilet paper between her legs—how long was that supposed to last? No wonder she was thinking about sex. With Peter in the tent, there'd been a moment, as Andromeda called them.

How she wished Andromeda was there to talk to! It'd be just too weird to talk about it with a dog.

Part of her felt, if not happy, at least a little bit excited. Not that there weren't problems, and certainly she didn't know what to do; she knew he was interested. She'd give anything to discuss it with Andromeda—it was so stupid and confusing. Before—and it must have been because she was a shallow person—she just couldn't imagine him touching her with the stump of his arm. Now that problem was taken care of, but not in a way that comforted her. De Graz's hand was almost worse.

Before, Peter had seemed too old. Now he seemed too young, except for moments like that moment on the riverbank, when his roaring mouth had terrified her. Most of the time, of course, he was his sweet old self. And there had been something between them in the tent.

So she was all mixed up, needless to say. She lay listening to the sounds of the camp coming to life. At the entrance to the tent, the yellow dog lay curled up asleep.

Oh, she would have loved to talk to Andromeda just for five minutes! Not to a dog, and not to Sasha Prochenko—it was the name from Miranda's dream. Shivering among her blankets, she remembered the ghost's face, the man sitting on the log smelling of tobacco and cologne.

After a cold night, a cold morning. It was hard to get up and stagger out of bed. Splaa brought her a pot of steaming water. He had a knife at his belt.

"Did you ever meet my aunt?" she asked him as she washed her face.

He stood at the entrance to the tent. "Your mother and father had a house north of Constanta on the sea," he said. "I was just a boy when your aunt came to visit. Once she spoke to me as I was brushing down her horse. A black gelding. She came with some professors and philosophers, a great lady with an estate in Mogosoaia. Later she lost that."

As usual, it seemed as if Gregor Splaa was telling her everything except what she wanted to know. The more of his information she had, the less it helped her. "What was she like?" she asked.

He shook his head. "You'll see. Very kind."

He was peering out the doorway as if anxious to be gone.

"May I come with you?"

"These are dangerous creatures, miss."

"But I'd like to see them."

"Miss, they're as big as houses. Snap a tree like nothing."

"But I'd like to." It was more than that. She thought she'd experiment with telling people what to do. So far, relying on other people hadn't worked so well.

Splaa's hair was tied back, his beard was tucked into his shirt. He stood scratching his nose while Miranda washed her face and hands.

He went away and came back to report. The hunters would not let her, because she'd seen the wendigo. They were afraid of the bad luck. Miranda persisted, and he went away and came back again. This time he'd been able to effect a compromise.

One of the men in the camp was injured. He had hurt his arm, and Splaa was to take his place. So the hurt man stayed back with them after Splaa and the others had left, a tall man with a name that sounded like Kempf—that was as close as Miranda could make out. He had a big chest and no neck, and wore no coat over his leather shirt. Peter and Miranda ate a breakfast of meat porridge in the empty camp, while Kempf fussed one-handed with his shotgun, a heavy weapon about five feet long. His other arm was in a sling.

Miranda sat on a crate in a trampled circle of mud and ice. She drank hot coffee, her mittened hands clasped around a tin cup. It was a cold morning, but not bitter, and there was an odd stillness to the air. The clink of the spoon in the iron pot, the occasional snorting of the mules in their pen, made an odd, flat reverberation. The sun was a white disk among the fast, white clouds.

"Bad weather coming," Peter said. "Woolly mammoths! Wait till I tell my dad."

Across the fire, he smiled at her. He'd slept well, he'd said. No dreams. He smiled and showed his teeth.

His forehead was hidden by his brown curls, pushed down low by a wool cap. He had stripped off his gloves, was holding his palms toward the fire. When he held them side by side, the difference between his hands was especially strange. Now he stretched out his right hand, flexing the hairy fingers. "Look at this."

His own tin cup was empty. He picked it up by the rim, and with his forefinger and thumb he bent it closed, until its mouth was a sealed line. Then he reversed it in his hand, and with his finger on one point, his thumb on the other, he bent it back into shape.

She looked at the birthmark in the joint of his thumb. "Do you know anything about wrestling?" she asked him.

He smiled again, confused, and she was happy to see him smile. Suddenly she didn't want him to be anything except the boy she first had met, chewing grass, lying above the ice house weir. He seemed happier over the last day, since they had talked, since they had had their moment. His cheeks had some color in them. "Let's go catch a heffalump," he said as she stood up. She slipped her pack over her shoulders.

This time in the hunters' camp had been a welcome break. And even if it had been hard to fall asleep at night, she had lain snug in her sleeping bag, the yellow dog—Andromeda—curled on a felt mat.

She imagined they were dependent now upon the hunters' schedule, and they'd be staying where they were for a few days. It didn't help to worry about the future. First things first, and the first thing was to get to Albany, which was only about forty-five minutes' drive. It didn't help to think about Raevsky, and wonder whether she'd poisoned him with the black pills—whatever she'd done could not be changed. What helped was to sit on a wooden crate, drinking hot coffee from a cup that warmed her mittened hands. What helped was to let herself feel part of this landscape where the tiny snowflakes seemed to glitter as they fell.

Later they walked through the woods and past the beaver pond. Andromeda ran on ahead, following the trail of men and dogs. But then Kempf took them away from the trail, around to the left, up through the rocks. They climbed to a bald place above the trees, and they could see the meadow below them, the broken saplings and uprooted bushes.

Here they could watch the hunt from a safe distance. Under the lowering clouds they could hear men shouting and dogs barking. "They want a big one. Ivory," Kempf said. "Not calf or cow. They want to . . . ," and he made a gesture with his gloved hand.

"Separate," Miranda guessed.

"Yes, separate. You see."

He wouldn't look at her as he was talking. When she turned to him, he stared resolutely away. His big, bearded face looked doubtful and unsure. But he was interested in the bracelet, and Miranda could see him take some furtive glances when she moved her arm.

She and Peter sat listening to the barking and shouting and, in time, the gunshots. Colder and colder, they sat on the rocks. Then suddenly Andromeda was barking, too, and they saw an animal in the tall trees below them, closer than they had expected. Trees swayed and cracked around him as he stepped into the near side of the meadow. And it was true—he was as big as a small house, like an elephant only much larger, and covered with hair, and without the floppy ears, and with a long, sloped skull that rose almost to a point. He shook his head from side to side, showing his enormous, curved tusks, and now suddenly they could hear him bellowing as he raised his trunk.

"Why don't they just shoot it?" said Miranda, holding her ears. "It's stupid to torture it."

"Many guns not kill." Kempf had gotten to his feet, and now they could see the men and dogs coming into the meadow. One shot off his long gun, then stepped back to reload. One was carrying a torch, and Miranda saw it was Gregor Splaa, running in front of the animal as if to force it back into the open. Because now it was turning into the trees below them, a stand of young evergreens, and it was smashing the trees down with great sweeps of its trunk and with its body as it turned.

They were all on their feet now, and Kempf was leading them behind some rocks where they wouldn't get hit by any stray bullets. It didn't seem likely, and soon they climbed up where they could see better. The dogs were leaping through the trees, jumping and biting at the animal's enormous legs, which were nevertheless hidden in a kind of skirt of hair. Now it was closer, just below them at the bottom of the rise, where it turned to face its enemies.

Miranda could smell the smoke. She stopped, but Peter kept going, climbing down a little way below her where she couldn't see. Andromeda stood on the topmost spire of rock, showing no inclination to run down and join the other dogs. After a few short barks she was quiet now, poised on three legs, sniffing the air. Miranda was watching her, but looked down soon enough to see the cornered beast charge. Bellowing, wagging its head from side to side, it knocked the first man down with its great tusks, then trundled forward and seized the second in its trunk. It lifted him above the trees. He was Gregor Splaa.

Again Miranda looked away, up at the dog perched above her. She found herself holding her ears again. Kempf was standing forward with his gun tucked in the sling of his wounded arm, but all the firing had stopped and all the barking, too. The animal had curled its trunk around Splaa's body and was waving him like a flag. Miranda could see the other man scramble back.

Then there was someone else, someone who had grabbed Splaa's torch out of the snow. He was holding the torch in his right hand, pushing it between the beast's raised tusks. She could see the great mouth sag open, see the tiny, staring eyes, see Splaa's body twist as he was shaken back and forth: every detail, she thought. But for several moments as she watched the man prodding his torch in the beast's face, watched him force it back against the rocks—she didn't recognize him. She saw the mass of brown curls. She saw his lips pulled back. But it wasn't until she glanced around her that she realized who it was. It was Peter, who had climbed down through the rocks.

She was too shocked to feel anything at first, or anything but fear. He leapt from the scything tusks and then forward again, forcing the torch against the beast's mouth. Miranda could smell something else now, an odor of singed hair. The animal was turning. It was swatting at Peter with the body of Gregor Splaa as it turned below her through the trees. Miranda could see its head come up, its tiny, enraged eyes, but there was nothing in its trunk now. Then it crashed away into some bigger trees, then around the corner of the rise and it was gone, then even the noise of it was gone.

Two men stood in a space of broken trees. One was Peter, and the other was a hunter with a gun. Miranda came down through the rocks with the yellow dog at her heels. Kempf came with her. Gregor Splaa lay twisted on his back. No one had moved him.

Peter stood with the extinguished stick in his hand. "You stupid jerk," Miranda said. "What are you doing?" She knelt over Splaa's head.

But the yellow dog went up to Peter and licked his hand. He squatted over her and for several seconds she allowed him to rub the yellow fur where it was thick behind her ears. Now everything was quiet. The other dogs sat with their tongues hanging out, and then the man with the gun called out to them, and took off limping in the mammoth's track. When Miranda called out to them, Kempf turned around. His expression was so angry and so fierce, it took away her words. He strode off in the direction the animal had come until he also disappeared among the trees.

But they must have been going to get help. Peter squatted in the snow, and Miranda sat down next to the head of Gregor Splaa. After a moment, he opened his eyes.

He lay on his back, his pelvis twisted. She examined his hooked nose, soft beard, and scabbed lips.

"Let me tell you what you want to know," he said.

Miranda's throat seized up with tears. "Can I bring you something?" she said. "Can I bring some water?"

"It doesn't hurt," he said. "But I am thirsty." And he actually smiled.

She fumbled at her belt for the water bottle she had brought from camp. "You see your aunt would have been better served by a great warrior, not an old cow like Rodica or a stableboy like me. Please forgive me."

He spoke with a softness and fluidity that was very different from when she'd first seen him in the house by the pond. He must have been frightened then. But not now, maybe—she held the bottle to his lips. "Thanks for your tears, miss," he said. "And you'll remember us, won't you, old Rodica and me, when you come through Vulcan's Gate with the crowd cheering? You'll say a word in the temple for two stupid fools? Listen, it doesn't matter. These are honest men—they'll take you to New York. My bag is in my pocket. Give them a grain of silver every day. Go to the fish market where they salt the sturgeon fish. Look for Ion Dreyfoos. He will help you. He's a servant of your aunt's. I hope there'll be money for the steamship, only take care. Dreyfoos will make you documents for the trip through Germany. He'll do the work for free."

Miranda reached out for Splaa's hand and took it in her own. It was warm. And the air around them was warm also. Miranda could no longer see her breath. And it had started to snow, just a light, quiet dusting, a scattering of small flakes, and then more.

This is how the storm started. The snow sifted through the trees, and they barely noticed. Gregor Splaa was talking, and she held his hand. He was telling her the history of Roumania, softly and unhurriedly—"Miranda Brancoveanu fought against the Turks, and her son was Constantin Brancoveanu, the golden king. He was the one who first established all our rights under the common law. He freed the serfs and took away Constanta from the Turks. You understand this is your family, and his daughter was Queen Sophia . . ."—on and on, but Miranda wasn't listening. Instead she squeezed his hand and watched the snow filtering down in larger flakes now. Where were Kempf and the others?

Gregor Splaa talked. Miranda held his hand, and from time to time she would force herself to concentrate, because he was trying to tell her things that might prove useful or essential. So she would try to listen to his recitation of old names and deeds, until she was distracted again by anxiety. Where were the three hunters? Had they stolen Splaa's money and abandoned them? It was snowing harder now, and there was a wind. The sky was a white shield. It looked scarcely out of reach above the trees.

After twenty minutes the tracks of their boots were filling up with snow. The hunters had not come back.

"Where are they?" Miranda said. Then she understood. It was because of the wendigo. She had seen the wendigo, and this accident was the bad luck she had brought.

So if no one was going to help her, she had to decide what to do. "We can't keep him here," she said, standing up. The snow was accumulating on Splaa's legs. She stooped to brush it away with her bare hands as Peter came to her. Out of the shreds of broken pine trees that surrounded them, he had found several long, pliant boughs. Now he was stripping away the needles and weaving the poles together into a crude litter. It didn't take long.

The dog was running up and down the trail to the camp, which was disappearing.

"My father would say we shouldn't move him," said Peter. "Any kind of spinal injury, you risk doing permanent damage." At the same time he was weaving together his litter of boughs, as if his brain and hands thought different things. "It's probably three miles to the camp. We can't expect them yet. It will be too hard to move him, just ourselves."

He spoke as if it might be possible to get him to a hospital. "This is what we're going to do," Miranda said. "I'm not impressed by this. The longer we wait, the harder it will be. We'll just retrace our steps. They'll find us on the trail if they come back. We can't let him freeze to death." As she bent over Splaa's body, she could still hear him murmuring his lists of ministers and kings, although his eyes were closed.

She took the bag from his pocket. She fingered for a moment the heavy silver grains, which she could feel through the canvas cloth. Then she put the purse inside her shirt. The wind was cold now, and it blew the snow in their faces. "Help me," Miranda said, and then Peter and she were lifting Splaa onto the web of branches. It was easy, because he was so stiff. And she was right. He didn't feel anything. The low murmur of his voice went on. He didn't open his eyes. "Does it hurt?" she asked. She took off Rodica's coat so that she could arrange it around Splaa's legs. This was getting easier, she decided. And maybe that's what a princess was, someone who didn't care whether people lived or died.

Splaa was reaching for her hand, but she didn't give it to him. Instead she put on her mittens and went to stand at the top of the litter, while Peter stood at the bottom. "This isn't going to work," she said. And it didn't, really; she could tell how flimsy the litter was as soon as she squatted to pick it up. The boughs were woven into a lattice, which slipped and gave way at every step. The wood was springy and sagged down. Her mittens were clumsy. Still, she put her back to Gregor Splaa and picked him up and headed up the trail, following the yellow dog. And they could only go a little way before she had to rest and adjust her grip—the track had almost disappeared in the driving snow. For a while they were in the shelter of the rocks and the big pines, but by the time they came across the main trail from the camp to the pond, the storm had begun to punish them, and it was hard to find their way. The sky had gone from white to yellow, and the wind was picking up. The snow stung their faces.

Gregor Splaa was oddly light, as if some part of him was gone already. When she stopped to catch her breath or to adjust the slipping lattice of boughs, Miranda put her ear to his lips. She could still hear the soft, relentless flow of information that was no doubt vital, that no doubt could help her make sense out of all this.

They turned uphill toward the ridge. The camp was on the other side, she thought. Though it wasn't yet noon, Miranda guessed, you could scarcely see five yards ahead. In some places the snow was around her shins.

The dog was out in front of them, and they followed her through the small trees. They climbed the slope, unable to talk, unable to do anything except keep some kind of rhythm with the stretcher as they stumbled forward into the driving snow; it was impossible. As time went on, Miranda found her elbows and fingers getting stiff and weak, found herself slipping and falling forward sometimes, while at the same time the stretcher of pine boughs was coming apart. Pieces were falling off of it, and now the bottom opened up, and Gregor Splaa fell into the snow. She sat down heavily beside him, and listened to the thump of her heartbeat. "This was a stupid idea," she said.

Andromeda had come back for them, and was sniffing at Splaa's face. "We can't stay here," Miranda went on.

"No." Peter's shoulders and wool cap were white.

"Is he . . . ?" he said, and paused while she bent down over Gregor Splaa. With the wind howling around her, and her ear an inch from his lips, she could still hear him whispering. "There's a gun that you must get, and your aunt knows about it, which belonged to your father and his father. It's a bone-handled revolver, and . . ."—on and on. She turned away.

"He's still alive," she said.

Peter stepped onto the discarded lattice and kicked it apart with his heavy boots. He kicked it away off the side of the path. Then he bent down and grabbed Splaa by his armpits and lifted him up. Made burly by his snow-covered coat, he looked like a man lifting a child. He took Splaa over his shoulder in a fireman's carry, then turned up the path again, where the yellow dog waited with her foreleg poised above the snow.

And Miranda stumbled after him. Her sweatshirt was covered with snow, even though she'd tried to brush it off when she put on her coat again. Immediately she felt the snow begin to melt inside her coat. That frightened her, though she felt obscurely angry, too—frustrated by Peter's new strength and competence, though the stretcher, she thought, had been a bust. She tried to console herself with that, because the rest—Peter going down and chasing the mammoth away, Peter carrying a grown man over his shoulder, for all the world as if he he'd beaten the Turks at Adrianopole— was scaring her. In her mind she caught a glimpse of his distorted face as he stood on the sandbar. After one day, and she was afraid she was going to lose him again. So instead she concentrated on Splaa's head swinging back and forth upside down against the middle of Peter's back. It bobbed as if his neck were made of rubber, and his eyes were closed. "He is dying now," she thought. "Right now," and as her mind formed those words she saw his mouth was hanging open and some object was coming out. If it hadn't been for the cold, the snow, the numbness of her cheeks, she might have been horrified. But now she watched in frozen fascination as a creature re- vealed itself, a long and disgusting snake or slug, whose black, oiled body was too hot for the snow, which melted immediately as it fell on it. The creature was shaken out in increments, a little at a time as Splaa's head bobbed and swung—first the long tail. But now it was obvious, as two legs pulled loose, that the beast was not a snake at all, but rather some kind of lizard. A fat, soft body was shaken out, then stunted forelegs which were scratching at the man's lips as the lizard struggled to free its head out of Splaa's mouth. Splaa no longer seemed a man or even a child, so much as a puppet or a doll.

Frozen, out of breath, Miranda looked down at the tops of Peter's boots, where the snow was going in. She didn't see the lizard drop. When she raised her eyes, they stood on the ridge looking down, and there was no camp at the bottom of the bowl. An outcropping of rock was unfamiliar. They had lost their way. The storm had covered up their tracks.

———

THAT NIGHT, THOUGH, the weather was clear in Bucharest, where the elector sat again in his armchair in the Athenée Palace Hotel. During the day he had received a message from Hans Greuben. The baroness's house was empty. There was a secret passageway under the street, it had turned out.

The elector had eaten some crackers, drunk some soda water. Then he had prepared for Greuben a detailed package of instructions. Among other things he was to forward (by diplomatic courier to the steamship *Carpathia,* now docked at Bremerhaven) a letter for the German agent in New York, who was to make enquiries concerning the whereabouts of Miranda Popescu, etc., etc.

There was also a letter to the director of the Institute for Mental Deviation in the Soseaua Kiseleff.

Now he was looking for two women, the elector thought, a strange preoccupation for a grown man. Or rather, not the baroness so much as the jewel she had stolen. And not the girl so much as what she represented, a fantasy of failure.

The elector's hands trembled on the arms of his chair. And when he sank into his trance, he was again troubled by a dream of the white tyger. Again he was running through the woods, slipping in his patent-leather shoes. Again he fell into the mud, his fingers locked around a glowing jewel. Lying on his back, his suit spattered and ruined, he felt something new overtake him, a new conjuring that uttered from his body through the casement window into the night air.

At that moment, from Codfish Bay to the Hudson River, almost a meter of new snow had fallen, and the tallest trees had been blown down. But that was not enough. That was just an utterance of the elector's frustration. Again he was frustrated by the ghost of Aegypta Schenck, an old woman who had spread her gray cloak, it seemed to him, over the entire breadth of New England. For this reason he had been obliged to send a message to the German agent. And for this reason he was now obliged to fall back on unsubtle and unspecific means.

For a moment in the darkness of America he had seen a flicker of light, and he struck at it. All of this was an offense to his conception of the scientific process, but that old bungler, that superstitious fraud Aegypta Schenck had made it necessary with her idiotic prayers and supplications—she was able to frustrate him from beyond the grave! She forced him to choose a weapon that did not require perfect aim. That night the inhabitants of the spirit world, hovering in the air above the great hotel, might have seen a small disturbance in the form of a colored flare, the tail of a penny rocket as it rose from the fifth-floor balcony. But even they would not have guessed at its cargo, a single microbe conjured from the mud, now speeding on its silent way.

IT WAS A SMALLPOX VIRUS, recently isolated by a Viennese professor. The elector was immune to it, having suffered in his youth. He sent it now into New England as a gift, and it arrived when the storm was at its worst. Peter and Miranda stood together in the snow after hours of wandering. They had long since abandoned the body of Gregor Splaa. Andromeda, the yellow dog—she had to think of her as Andromeda—was at her heels.

"We need to find someplace to wait it out," said Peter, his mouth close to Miranda's ear.

"Let's keep going," she said. They'd retraced their footprints many times, each time silted up with snow.

"You're no help," she said to the yellow dog. Not for the first time she wondered if the beast could really understand her. Andromeda had not left them for a moment, and as far as Miranda could tell, she had not even attempted to find the camp.

Now she got up and shook the snow out of her coat. For a moment she stood on three legs, her nose pointing into the wind. Now the afternoon was closing in, and it was getting dark. And yes, there did seem to be some kind of glimmer of light over there, against the side of the unfamiliar cliff, which now bulged over them.

"Can you see that?" Miranda cried.

"No."

Anyway, they would be better in the shelter of the cliff. There were some taller trees there and the wind was less. Her face felt scorched and burned, her hands numb. "Come on," she said and then they staggered forward. And maybe it was just a trick of the light, because she no longer saw what she'd imagined, a bright place in the trees as they came over the rise.

Her hair was stiff with ice. It wasn't until half an hour later that she saw the fire burning up ahead.

The sky was getting dark. And now in front of her she could see a fire at the entrance to a cave, some shapes moving around it. "There they are," she said, too relieved and exhausted to consider that the hunters' camp had not been pitched below these looming rocks, among these trees.

It was the wild men. The fire burned so brightly as they approached, Miranda almost found she didn't care. She was not afraid. "They're not my enemies," she thought. She was being stupid and she knew it, but she couldn't stop her thoughts. "In the boat they saw I was a prisoner. Maybe they were trying to rescue me."

There was an overhanging ledge, and then a deeper cave, and the fire burned among some boulders. Miranda cried out, and the wild men came to help her and Peter into the shelter of the rocks out of the wind. They brought rags of cloth to wipe their faces. "No one's a cannibal," Miranda thought. "I read it in a magazine—that's nonsense." She took off her mittens, then pushed her frozen hair out of her eyes. Andromeda had disappeared.

"You," someone said. The word was recognizable. And she recognized the man, also, though now he wore a bearskin shirt. He was a big man with yellow hair. Now he did not have his club with its quartz head. But he was angry. He came toward her, and she raised her hands.

An old man now shuffled forward out of the mouth of the cave. He stepped between the big man and Miranda. Reaching out his hand, he pulled the ice-clumped sweatshirt from her wrist, revealing the golden bracelet of Miranda Brancoveanu.

"Tyger," he mumbled toothlessly. He had a shock of white hair, and his face was thin.

But that was all it took. Later in the cave, Miranda found herself encouraged. The wild men brought food, roasted pieces of meat in wooden bowls, and a mush of pounded corn. They had built a small fire for her in a protected place. The cave was long and high, with a roof that disappeared into a blackened cleft. Somewhere there was open air, because the smoke flowed upward into the crack. Grimy snowflakes sifted down.

The wild men left her and Peter more or less alone. They clustered around the larger fire at the cave's mouth, ten yards or so away. Miranda sat in a litter of rocks the size of heads, cross-legged with her backpack in her lap.

She put down her bowl of corn mush. Near her, rising up into the darkness, there was a flat rock wall. By the light of the fire she could see painted pictures on its surface.

"What now?" Peter said.

She shrugged.

"I mean, what do we do now?"

She rubbed her nose. "I guess we go to Albany. We've got a name, Ion Dreyfoos in the fish market. We've got some money now—that's good. Maybe we can buy food from these people."

She stood up to examine the pictographs. Directly above her the roof was low and she had to stoop. But when she came to the wall, there she could straighten up. In the crackling firelight she could see the shapes of animals in black and ochre and red, painted on the uneven surface. Also human beings, simple and stylized, and she could see immediately there was a story to the pictures, though she couldn't make it out in the uncertain light. "Look," she said. She returned to the fire to select a burning stick.

"No, don't touch it," said a voice, and she saw the old man hobbling toward her from the mouth of the cave. His back was bent from osteoporosis, and he carried a cane. It was a twisted stick, which he used to negotiate the uncertain ground, but now he raised it up and brandished it, striking the bulge of the roof. "Drop it now."

"Have you seen the dog?" she asked him.

"Keep your dog away."

While everyone else she had met here, apart from Gregor Splaa, knew English, if at all, as a second or third language, these people were native speakers. They had no other tongue. And perhaps their way of talking had devolved here in the woods, or perhaps it always had been harsh and simple, and difficult to understand. The old man brandished his stick, but his face wasn't angry. He seemed to smile out of a toothless mouth. His cheeks were fleshless, his eyes gleamed. And though he hadn't wanted her to profane the wall of pictographs with her stick, he had no compunction against hammering at it with his own cane, pointing at the masses of figures.

"There, look," he said, and at the end of the stick she could see what now was unmistakable, the low beach and the city overwhelmed by waves as big as mountain ranges, and the people crushed and drowning. The land was split apart, and the sea entered in. Then on the surface of the waves, a few small boats.

"What's that place?" she asked, though she had guessed.

The old man seemed angry now. He brandished his stick. "You were there," he said. "Brancoveanu!" His blue eyes glittered. He made a few sounds more, and she realized he was singing or trying to sing, and realized also that she recognized the tune out of some movie or something, and the words:

"And did those feet in ancient times,
  Walk upon England's mountains green?
  And was the holy lamb of God . . ."

The old man was dressed in sheepskins. "People of the lamb," he said. "That is why we fight against the dog men." In fact he cleared up a couple of things as he stumbled back through the cave, rapping on the painted wall. One of them was what had happened to Captain Raevsky, whom Miranda discovered just a few dozen yards in back of where she'd been sitting with Peter. His hands were tied together, and his ankles, too.

He was wedged among some boulders in the dark. When he raised his head and saw her, an expression of hope and hopelessness moved over his face. His right eye was swelled up and was almost closed. His cheek was bruised.

Seeing him, she felt a mixture of apprehension and relief. He didn't speak to her. He stared at her for a minute or so, then looked down at his hands again, his face in shadow. There were shouts from the mouth of the cave, and the old man left her. Miranda returned to her little fire.

"Raevsky is back there."

"Who?"

And she found she had to describe to Peter who he was, the man who had attacked her on the ice, killed Blind Rodica, kidnapped her, all that. "What's wrong with you?"

Peter shrugged. "I'm not feeling well." Miranda thought he looked a little pasty, wrapped in a blanket and his wool cap pulled down.

Her description of Raevsky had allowed her to remember all the bad things he had done. Even so, it was hard for her to sit unconcerned beside the fire, now that she knew he was tied up behind her like an animal. It was hard for her to eat her food, drink her water. Peter wasn't talking to her except in grunts or monosyllables, and Miranda found herself looking behind her all the time, trying to see some movement in the back of the cave, where Raevsky lay hidden in a dark recess.

"Gregor Splaa was wrong about a lot of things," she said. "He told me not to wear my bracelet, which was wrong."

"Sure, you're a celebrity," Peter said inconsequentially. "And Splaa was obviously a moron." Miranda stared at him, trying to decipher his tone of voice, which was sarcastic, she now decided. He must have come down with a cold or something, because his nose was wet and red.

"How are you feeling?"

"I think I'm going to lie down."

All this trouble, she thought, was because of her. Thinking about Gregor Splaa's inadequacies, she felt a stab of regret. She knew why he had challenged the mammoth with his torch—it was because of her. Apart from the money for the ivory, he'd been trying to show that he was not a coward.

It was because of her that Raevsky was tied up behind her, that Rodica was gone. "I'm so sorry," she said.

"About what?"

"I'm sorry I brought us here. I'm sorry about the storm."

"I think I'm going to lie down. If you think the weather is your fault, this princess thing is going to your head."

Then in a moment: " 'Oh, life is a wonderful cycle of song.' "

She smiled. He had made a nest of blankets between the boulders. He drank some water from his bowl and lay down on the blankets. Miranda sat beside him, looking at the fire, thinking about Raevsky, thinking also about Kempf and the others—where was Andromeda? How could Andromeda have left them? No, she hadn't left, but she couldn't have come into the cave. She'd led them to the cave, and then gone off to find some refuge from the storm. Miranda pictured a fallen tree with a bank of snow beneath it, a shelter she could excavate and lie in, and watch the light from the cave's mouth.

The wind whistled in the opening, a giant with a stone flute. The wind stirred the smoke, shredded the flames of her small fire.

Andromeda—what had her aunt called her? Sasha Prochenko. And that was disconcerting, as it was worse than disconcerting now to see Peter's big, hairy hand playing with the edge of his blanket, and to think that hand had once belonged to someone else, someone she'd known. But the name de Graz brought her nothing but a half memory of a figure up above her on the terrace, telling her to come up off the beach.

Her hair was dry, finally, and she was warm. But every few minutes she looked over her shoulder to see if she could detect some movement from Captain Raevsky. When the white-haired old man clambered back from the cave's mouth over the rocks, she asked about him.

"He killed a man," he said, looking carefully into her face. He squatted down and poked at the fire with his stick. His beard grew high over his cheeks, which were hollow and without meat.

He must have meant the man who was wading across the stream. That death had been for her sake also, and Raevsky had rescued her.

Now the old man produced from inside his rags a bowl of liquid and held it out. It was quite pleasant, a watery honey beer. "Thank you," she said, and he smiled. His gums were pink. He was mumbling that song again. "And did those feet in ancient times . . . ?"

" 'Jerusalem.' William Blake," whispered Peter from where he lay.

"Bring me my bow of burning gold," mumbled the old man. "Bring me my arrows of desire. . . ." Then he broke off, interrupted himself. "Let me see it."

"What?"

"The bracelet. What you have."

She held up her wrist, and he poked at the bracelet with his forefinger, never touching it. "What does it mean to you?" she asked.

The old man's eyes opened wide. "The tyger fought the dragon at the beginning of the world," he said. "The dragon was the god of the dead, and the tyger chased him. When the flood came to London, she built her castle on the high ground. She took her boat over the water and saved the people who were drowning. She put her veil over the sun."

"You asked for it," whispered Peter from where he lay among the rocks.

Nothing was more depressing than to listen to the accomplishments of Miranda Brancoveanu. But these stories were so exaggerated, they made Miranda want to laugh. Instead she pressed her lips together, nodded sagely as the recitation of miracles went on.

After a while the old man got up and tottered away. When he was gone, Miranda heaped some more wood on the fire. Peter hadn't eaten much of his supper, and there was meat left in his bowl. She picked it up, and then she clambered back over the rocks to where Captain Raevsky sat by himself.

She had taken a knife from the hunters' camp, and now she pulled it from its sheath. Raevsky held up his wrists. Miranda watched the tears run down his cheeks, from under the swollen lid of his right eye. He rocked back and forth. *"Multumesc,"* he said—thank you. She knew that much at least.

Miranda bit her lips and said nothing. She would not talk to this man. She put the bowl down on the rocks.

"Multumesc," he said again, though she'd done nothing.

He tried to wiggle his fingers. She stood above him with the knife, watching him fall over onto his side and crawl painfully to the bowl that she'd set down. She watched him grovel with his face in the bowl. Then finally he rolled away, rolled onto his back.

"So," he murmured, "never have I failed so much."

She didn't want him to talk. She stood above him with the knife in her hand. "Always I am thinking of the Baroness Ceausescu," he said.

Miranda didn't want to hear about that. She clambered back over the rocks. She imagined she might bring a blanket for Captain Raevsky, perhaps one of the blankets that Peter had cast off.

He was lying on his side, and there was sweat on his face. Miranda put the back of her hand against his forehead. "How are you feeling? Can I get you something?"

In just a few minutes he looked worse. He grabbed at her with his right hand, and she sat with him, examining the strong fingers, the black hair on the back of his palm and wrist. "What's happening to me?" he murmured. "Is it my hand? My dad once told me how a body can resist a transplant. Is that what's happening? And why is Andromeda a dog?"

It was as if this question was liberated by his fever—they had never spoken about it, because it was too large a subject, and because it led directly to his hand. "I think my aunt made a mistake," Miranda said.

Peter murmured, "Sure. No one could have asked for this."

Just because she hadn't spoken about it, didn't mean she hadn't given it some thought. "Do you remember that first day, when Blind Rodica brought that little animal out of the soldier's mouth? And then when Gregor Splaa was on your back . . ."

She hadn't told him this but now she did, how she'd seen that lizard drop from the man's mouth. "I think Andromeda had a dog inside of her. Don't you think that's appropriate?"

When she came into the hunter's camp, she'd told them all about Andromeda, how she had seen Andromeda. That was how the talk had gotten started about the wendigo, or whatever it was. But she hadn't told Peter about the man with the tobacco smell and the cologne. She didn't want to think about some strange man growing inside Peter like a tumor, making him foreign among all these other foreigners, making him sick—no, he was the one who had said that. Anyone could have caught a cold in this cold storm.

Now she stopped talking, because he wasn't paying attention. She took off her sweatshirt and rolled it up into a pillow for him—it was warm beside the fire. Then she lay down beside him and listened to the wind roaring outside, and watched the dirty snowflakes falling from the roof.

Peter tossed and turned all night. Miranda lay beside him, but in the morning when the gray light crept over the boulders from the entrance of the cave, she felt she had scarcely slept at all. Her thoughts had been so disordered, though, in retrospect she understood they must have been dreams.

For a moment she lay wondering about Andromeda. Again she pictured in her mind the shelter that Andromeda had found under some fallen branches. Then she opened her eyes to the sound of someone calling her name. Peter sat wiping his face. "I have a fever."

His eyes were ringed with red. His cheeks were pale. Miranda gave him water from the bowl, then wet one of Rodica's handkerchiefs and washed his face. She couldn't think of what else to do, and so she sat holding his hand, talking to him about this and that, listening while he talked. "Three summers ago my dad rented a cabin in North Carolina in the woods near Hot Springs. It was when my mom was still going to be okay. She was in remission, so my dad was teaching me how to shoot. He always said he was going to wait until I was strong enough to aim with one hand. He bought me a twenty-two, and then he set up Coke cans on the fence. He had a brother in Greeneville, so we used to go swimming in the river, the French Broad. I started to do all those things sort of late. I couldn't even swim until that year. The good thing about my cousins was you don't have to prove anything. My dad had lots of relatives in Greeneville."

Miranda didn't know what to do. She sat holding his hand, his big new hand, with its heavy knuckles and black hair. She examined the birthmark in the shape of a bull's head. She was waiting for the old man to come, and finally he did, carrying a bucket of hot water and a burning stick, with which he built another fire. "Is it still snowing?" Miranda asked him, though she could tell the wind was less.

He didn't answer, because he was looking at Peter's face. "He has a fever," Miranda said. The old man glanced at her. Then he turned to Peter and was poking him with his stiff fingers, taking his pulse, then bending over him to smell his skin and his breath. "Open," he said, and when Peter opened his mouth he peered inside, peered at his tongue and at the whites of his eyes, which were now pink. Then he tottered away without a word, leaving Miranda to wash Peter's face and hold his hands; he was lying down now, and Miranda had made as comfortable a bed for him as she could.

"I met a girl that year," he said, "and she wrote me a letter when we got back home. Then the next summer we drove down that way . . ."

Miserable and sad, Miranda listened to him without listening. She was cold without her sweatshirt, but Peter didn't feel it, and at times he would throw off all his blankets. Parched, he would call for water, his face streaked with sweat. At other times he would complain of the cold and his teeth would chatter. Then she would wrap him in blankets and put her arms around him until he stopped shaking and could talk again. He told her about the time he'd been chosen for the soccer team. Later, though, he'd had to quit because his grades were poor. He told her one night he had broken into the college chapel and slept on the altar. At the same time he was reciting scraps of poetry, most of which she didn't recognize. " 'But since I am a dog beware my fangs'—I knew it all by heart, every line. Then I went in and failed the test, though I knew it better than they did. Were they stupid, that they couldn't tell? It was my secret. I knew the entire play line by line. That was my diamond cost me two thousand ducats in Frankfort. I worked on it all week. I had it in a box without a key."

She couldn't stand listening to him. She got up and left him, and walked back into the cave. She took the knife and threw it underhand into the shadows. She imagined Raevsky inching toward it over the rocks, groveling and struggling with his face in the dirt. She said nothing to him, but went back and sat near Peter with her arms around her knees.

Later the old man brought soup. But Peter pushed the bowl away and spilled it. Some others of the wild men stood around, including the big man who seemed to be their leader.

He watched, but didn't come close. The old man had some kind of medicine, some bark or powder that he'd mixed in hot water in a tin cup, but Peter wouldn't drink it. He didn't seem to recognize where he was. His face was flushed and red, his eyes ringed with red. Patiently, the old man poked at him with his stiff fingers; Peter's shirt had come undone, and the old man pulled it back to reveal some sores on his side, a rash of hard red bumps. He grunted when he saw it, pursed his lips. After a while he got up and tottered away.

But Peter let Miranda hold his hands. He let her wash his face. The light in the cave grew stronger, and Miranda realized the storm was less. No more snowflakes came down. The wind no longer whispered in the rocks. Miranda lay down beside him with her arm around his neck, his head against her chest. After a while he was still and seemed to sleep. Rocks dug into Miranda's back and side, but whenever she tried to shift her position, he stirred. She imagined if he could get some rest, then he would wake up and his fever would have broken, and so she lay without moving for as long as she could. She also must have dozed off for a little bit, for she imagined her aunt standing over her in the cave, dressed in her gray clothes and saying, "It is time now. Come to meet me. Death can be defeated. Do not fear." But Miranda was sick of her damned aunt, and in her dream paid no attention, and her aunt bent down to poke her or shake her, and she woke up and saw a shadow was blocking the light, and it was Raevsky.

Startled, she raised her hands. "They are gone," he said.

She didn't know what he meant, but then she struggled up and saw the cave was empty. The fire was out. Sunlight came in through the rocks. She moved, and Peter stirred, but he wasn't better. There was blood in his face, and his skin was burning. Sunlight came in from the mouth of the cave, and she and Raevsky carried Peter forward into the light that shone over a landscape transformed by snow.

They set Peter up in the entrance to the cave, lying against some rocks that had been put there for the purpose. This was where the wild men had stayed, and the sticks of their fire still glowed. Miranda held Peter's burning hand. He was talking again, but she didn't understand him. "It is Roumanian," Raevsky said.

Miranda didn't want to hear anything about that. She stood up in the entrance to the cave and called for Andromeda over and over. And then Andromeda came picking her way through the snow, along the track the wild men had left. She came to lick Miranda's hands. "Your father had two friends," Raevsky said. "And so, they disappeared. People said were murdered."

Miranda shook her head.

"No, but is true. This is some kind of spell. At first I think this is de Graz's son—but is not so. I recognize this face. Is like a child now." He pointed to the mark on Peter's hand. "I recognize de Graz's mark. But that is twenty years before, the year your father died."

Miranda dug her hands into the thickest fur of the dog's neck. "Fifteen years," she murmured. Then she stood up, tears in her eyes. Raevsky was still talking, but she interrupted him. "Do you know where we are?"

"I can find the river. When they took me I was sleep like a fool."

His right eye was blackened, swollen shut. He sat rubbing and chafing the welts on his ankles and his wrists. "We'll stay here today," she said. "If Peter is no better, then we'll go down. You'll take us to Albany—will you take me there? You won't make any trouble?"

Raevsky bowed his head. "No boat."

So she told him about the boat she had hidden among the balsam trees. "There," she said. "Now you must promise."

"The Baroness Ceausescu will not hurt you," Raevsky grumbled. "She will be your friend. The *Carpathia* will wait. Also, this boy—de Graz—it is the variola. *La petite vérole*—what you say. The small spots. Me, it will not hurt. But you have an immunity?"

"I don't think so."

He jumped up, astonished. "But you must not touch!"

Later he built a fire and went out to find food. He staggered out from the cliff face and in places the snow was around his shins. Peter sat with his eyes closed and fell asleep again. Miranda and Andromeda sat with him, watching the sun sink through the thin trees.

"Don't leave me again," Miranda said.

She had been cheered to see the sun, the shadows on the snow. Peter was resting, and she was happy about that, too. Andromeda sat with her, whimpering sometimes. She herself felt very tired. She sat cross-legged, and fed the fire with chunks of birchwood, a quantity of which was stacked against the wall.

She had a name and a place: Ion Dreyfoos, in Albany. But it was something to strive for. What had her aunt said? Death could be defeated? And then something else. Follow the cave to the end under the yawning wall.

Raevsky didn't return at sunset. They had no food. Light-headed, exhausted, hungry, she made up a bed for Peter and then laid him down. She had melted some snow in a broken bucket, and she gave him water to drink. He didn't speak to her; his skin was flushed and burning. His eyes couldn't focus, and he couldn't speak.

"It'll be all right," she said to him, an assurance she did not feel. It had been stupid to tell Raevsky about the boat. He'd never give up on his obsession, but she would force him to take Peter with them, that was all. And if he didn't come back, then in the morning they would follow his tracks. Why was she so stupid all the time?

She lay back against a boulder by the fire, where she didn't have to look at Peter anymore. As darkness filled the world outside the circle of the fire, she closed her eyes.

Immediately it was as if she had fallen into the middle of a dream. But it was a dream that was like the waking world in every specific part. In the dream she lay against the boulder with her eyes open, watching the yellow dog who had run back deep into the cave and now returned. The darkness was complete, and the fire had burned down, and the dog started to whimper more insistently. She took the cuff of Miranda's coat between her teeth and pulled. She let go and whimpered again, and took a few steps into the cave. With one foot poised over the ground, she looked back over her shoulder.

Outside the dream, Miranda hoped Raevsky was mistaken, that the wild men were mistaken, and that Peter had a fever that would break. But in the dream she saw him gasping for breath, his face a mass of discolored spots, and she knew that he might die. "What is it?" she asked. She didn't want to leave him alone, but with part of her mind she imagined for a moment that the yellow dog had found something, some new cache of food, perhaps. She got up and allowed herself to be led into the back of the cave. The dog stopped there to scratch at her leather backpack where it lay.

With the other part of her mind, Miranda was remembering her aunt's words, as clear now as if the old woman was whispering in her ear. Follow the cave under the yawning wall. The gold is for the boatman and the sphinx. Meet me in tara mortilor.

Miranda slung the pack over her shoulder. The dog led her on past where she had seen Raevsky, where the cave was narrow and black. The dog was barking softly, scratching at something in the dark, and Miranda reached into her bag to find the cigarette lighter with her father's initials on it, and which Stanley had put into good working order years before. She saw the sparks, and then it lit, and she could see a cleft in the rock where it was just possible to squeeze through.

In the pack she also found the coins, which had been shaken from the box into the bottom seam. She pulled them out, examined them, slipped them into her pocket, where she felt also the rings from Andromeda's ears. "You've got to be kidding," she murmured. But Peter was sick, and the dog had already entered in. The flame from the cigarette lighter burned straight and blue. And perhaps there was a glint of some other light on the other side of the cleft, and perhaps the cleft was wider when she started to push through. In fact none of this was real. She stood with her hand on the rock and it was warm under her hand. The dog had disappeared up ahead, and she could hear it barking.

IN BUCHAREST, PAST midnight, the Baroness Ceausescu walked along the esplanade. A fog had drifted in along the river. In it the streetlights seemed to glow at many times their size. The baroness walked beside the iron railing, which she touched at intervals with her gloved hand.

In Bucharest, also, there was a warmth in the air, a wetness to the mist. The baroness's hair was wet with beads of condensation. One hand was on the railing, and the other grasped the tourmaline inside her glove. That was where she kept it now, in the nest of her palm.

Kevin Markasev followed at her heel. She walked through the warm mist, and around her the city seemed deserted.

BUT IN NEW ENGLAND, as she came out of the cleft into the country of the dead, Miranda sensed immediately that she was not alone. There was the dog in front of her, barking at something. In her left hand she held her father's cigarette lighter, engraved with his initials and his family's coat of arms. In the mist the small flame made a glow many times its size. Her wool cap was wet with condensation and she pulled it off, stuffed it with her mittens in the top of her pack. She stood peering into the darkness, then stepped forward into the open air beyond the cave. She raised the lighter, and by its flame she saw she was in a forest of birch trees. At her feet she recognized a round stone in the shape of a skull, and farther on there was the body of a woodchuck nailed to a tree trunk, stuffed with money and photographs. Around her, here and there she saw the gleaming eyes of animals, but she wasn't frightened. She knew they couldn't hurt her. She knew they were curious about the light, and as she stepped forward now they moved around her legs, the spirits of the dead in their animal shapes. There were otters and rabbits and wolves and snakes, all together, because in this land there was no hunter and hunted, no predator and prey. Some of them blundered against her ankles but then pulled back shyly, aware she was a stranger. Some whispered in sibilant voices to each other, and some spoke to her. One, a fat black lizard in the crux of a tree, recited to her the kings of Roumania. It was Gregor Splaa. "Miss," he said, and his tongue flickered out. "Miss, what are you doing here?"

"Peter's going to die," she said. "My aunt . . ." She could hear the dog barking up ahead. She turned away, repulsed by the lizard's ugliness, but then a few steps farther into the wood she saw it again in the same place. "I will go with you," it said. "Let me go with you." Without waiting for a response it climbed onto her shoulder as she walked past, and climbed inside her open coat. It worked its claws into her sweater, and she could feel it in her armpit, whispering to her whenever she turned her ear. "You are in the white wood. Go this way to the water. Sasha Prochenko knows the way."

When the trees gave out, Miranda found herself at the top of a rise, and the ground under her boots was dry and sandy. The yellow dog came back, and Miranda could see her in the mist, prancing with happiness, tongue hanging out. "He was your father's man," whispered Gregor Splaa. "There were two of them, and they were not friends. De Graz was the hero of the army. Prochenko was cautious in that way. A coward, people said, not to his face—it was not true. Not a coward like me. Your father loved him."

"He's a girl," Miranda said.

"A bitch, now," agreed Gregor Splaa. "You will depend on him because de Graz is dying."

Miranda felt the lizard's claws digging into the wool above her chest. This dream had begun to frighten her. She had to remind herself that that was all it was.

The dog's tongue was hanging out. "Andromeda, her name is," said Miranda.

"Call her."

Miranda walked down through the tough, high grass onto the strand. A warm wind came off the water in front of her. A stork flew overhead. "Sasha," she whispered, and to her surprise the yellow dog came back to lick her hand, grab her by the cuff, drag her down the beach.

She listened to the lizard's soft, insistent voice. "Once at the siege of Varna, Sasha Prochenko convinced the Turkish officers that the peace had already been signed, and the prince had decided to surrender the city for a million dinars and the crown of Constantin Brancoveanu, which the Turks had stolen many years before. The truth was the peace really had been signed, and Prince Frederick really had surrendered the city but without compensation, because the defenders couldn't have held out another day. They settled for half a million and the crown, which was considered a victory. . . ."

Miranda slipped her cigarette lighter into her pocket. There was a greater light shining on the water, and Miranda could see the boat now coming toward her over the small waves. She could see the wide deck. The light was at the masthead, burning like St. Elmo's fire, a white path over the water that lapped at Miranda's boots. She stood in a scum of foam left by the waves, smelling the sweet water, and watching the birds fly around the light as the flat boat came in. It grunted ashore on the coarse sand. The deck was empty. But then the animals were struggling through the water from the beach and climbing up the lines until the boat was full of them. And the dog led Miranda through the shallow water.

She had heard nothing as the boat came in. But once she climbed the ladder and stood upon the deck, she could feel the shudder of some kind of engine. The door to the wheelhouse opened and a woman came out. Impatiently she kicked through the beasts which crowded around her legs. All of them, it seemed, were small and meek. There were rabbits, badgers, mice. They scuttled away from the woman's feet, clearing a space on the steel deck that rang under their claws, under the old woman's feet as she approached.

Her face was thin and sharp. She was not tall. She peered up at Miranda through a single eye. The other one was squinted closed. "What do you want?" she said, then relented when Miranda proffered one of her gold coins. "Make sure you have another for the trip back."

"How many do you have?" asked Gregor Splaa under her coat.

"Four. Three now. And the silver one."

"That's not many. Listen to what she says."

But Miranda couldn't hear anything above the thrum of the motors. The steel plates of the deck vibrated under her feet. The old woman had already moved away from her, back to the wheelhouse. As soon as she disappeared through the door, the boat reversed its engines and pulled back.

A wind stirred in Miranda's hair as she moved to the front of the boat. As it turned, she watched the fish leaping from the churned-up water. This lake was full of living things. The clouds were full of birds. And the boat behind her was full of small animals moving softly and without fear. Now the wind blew the hair from her face as she stood in the bow, leaning on the rail. The boat had turned, and they were heading back the way it had come, into a mist that hid the sky and shore. At intervals she was aware of a soft sound above the trembling of the motors, a high, hooting whistle up ahead, which grew louder and louder until she saw a blue light glowing in the fog.

It was a buoy at the entrance to a long breakwater. The boat came into a empty harbor. Miranda could see a dock on wooden pilings, and a row of blue lights on the shore. The engines stopped, the boat drifted forward, and the old woman was moving back and forth with great alacrity and spryness, setting the lines and the automatic winch, which pulled the boat up to the dock. "Help me," she called out. Miranda went to her and together they pulled down the gangway and set it in its slot. The dock was three feet or more above them, and the gangway sloped down at an angle. As soon as it was set, the animals streamed across it and up into the town. Miranda could see houses now, a row of shop fronts.

"You'll be last," said the old woman. So Miranda waited until all the beasts had gone, and then she climbed up with her lizard and her yellow dog, and stood in the parking lot behind the dock. A slope of broken asphalt and gravel led to the front street of a dark and empty town. There were no people, no lights in any of the windows. The shop windows were empty.

"Where are the sphinxes?" she thought, remembering now what her aunt Aegypta had told her. Then as if conjured from these thoughts, she saw two women cross the street into the parking lot. Each carried one end of a leash, the other end of which was bound to the collar of an enormous beast. It snarled and slavered when it saw them. It pulled its lips back to reveal teeth that were grotesquely large, and it was scratching at the ground, straining at the double leash. The yellow dog whimpered and put her tail between her legs.

The women, however, did not seem concerned. They laughed and chatted as they ambled down the street, not exerting any effort to keep their animal restrained. Now that they were closer, Miranda saw they weren't women at all, but rather girls. They looked to be twins about ten years old. And they were innocently dressed in white patterned frocks. One wore a ponytail. The other had her hair cut short.

As they sauntered toward her, Miranda could hear their high, trilling laughter, see their plump, bare arms. Their animal was full of urgency, which they didn't seem to feel. Her own yellow dog had yelped once and then disappeared among the piles of wooden boxes and pallets that covered one side of the lot. "No help there," Miranda thought.

"Welcome, welcome," laughed the girls, speaking in uneven unison, and in voices older than they had a right to. "Don't worry about him. He's all right."

And in fact their dog seemed a little more friendly now that the yellow dog was gone. He had stopped snarling. He sniffed insistently and obnoxiously at Miranda's crotch, which the twins found amusing. "He likes you," they said. "He's called Cerberus."

Miranda reached down to push his head away. Her fingers sank into the coarse, silver hair around his neck, and she wondered if it was possible that the creature was a wolf. She'd never seen a wolf. But she recognized from TV specials or as if from dreams the ferocious yellow eyes, the texture of its thick, coarse fur.

She was wearing Blind Rodica's coat, though she'd unbuttoned it. Even so, in the mist she'd been too warm. But now she looked up at the sky and saw that it was gray and clear. The mist had disappeared, and the air was colder. She looked up and saw there was a mountain behind the town, a snowcapped mountain that rose up many thousands of feet, and whose topmost spires of ice were touched with pink from the rising sun.

The air was colder, and she could see gooseflesh on the twins' bare arms. The sea behind her was gray and silver. Cerberus yawned and looked up toward the mountains. "Tell me," Miranda said, "what I must do."

The twins laughed. "You've been to school. It's like a test. You're good at tests. Aren't you good at tests?"

The wolf, if that's what it was, had settled by her feet and was staring up at her. Now it opened its mouth to yawn, and the smell of its hot breath was so disgusting, Miranda felt a small door had been opened into hell. None of this was real, yet even so, she was close to tears.

"Aren't you good at tests? You are familiar with the theory of Pythagoras? You know the date of the 1848 Rebellion?"

"I think so."

"You know who wrote 'Jerusalem,' by William Blake?"

She found she couldn't swallow the lump in her throat. She stood looking at the wolf, breathing its breath, while the twins chuckled. "That's excellent. So answer me: What are you doing here?"

Miranda looked up at their smiling, relentless faces. In the new light she could see color in their cheeks, stripes of yellow in their tawny hair. At first she'd thought they were identical. But one had a wider face and lighter eyes. She was the one with her hair cut short, and now she continued independently of her sister: "You've been led around from place to place, and what's to show? Your friend is dying! You could have gone with Raevsky from the beginning. That's why I'm asking you. What are you going to do now?"

"I'm on my way to Albany," said Miranda, and at that moment the other girl, the one with the ponytail and the narrow face, opened her mouth to show a gold coin balanced on her tongue. Then she closed her mouth again, and Miranda knew that if she put her fingers into her pocket now, she would find two coins left beside the silver one—not three.

"If you had a chance to save de Graz's life, how would you do it?"

"I'm here to meet my aunt," Miranda said, and again the girl with the ponytail opened her mouth to show a gold coin.

One more question, Miranda thought, and she wouldn't have enough money for the boat. She took a step backward, and immediately the wolf started to growl. She could smell its breath.

"You've heard of Einstein's special theory of relativity?" asked the girl with the ponytail.

Miranda nodded.

"And the Counter-Reformation?" And then immediately: "If you could make one choice that would change history, what would it be?"

When Miranda didn't answer, the wide-faced girl smiled. "Ten seconds," she said. Miranda wondered if at that moment, in the cave in the Hoosick valley, the virus that had infected Peter was gathering itself to enter her. Or perhaps she was already delirious. Ignoring the beast at her feet, she turned toward the water, took a step back toward the boat.

A man was walking toward her from the freight shed and the piles of boxes, a tall man smartly dressed in a tight, cream-colored jacket. "Sasha Prochenko," whispered the lizard inside her coat, and she recognized him. Andromeda turned into a man, his yellow hair, pale eyes, beautiful face.

He was not as hairy as he'd been in the dark woods outside the hunters' camp. But Miranda remembered the smell: tobacco and cologne. His hands were in his pants pockets. His collar was turned up. He strolled toward them over the broken asphalt, a smile on his face, an unlit cigarette in his mouth.

"Ai un chibrit?"—Got a match? he said.

Miranda imagined even the girls were struck by his good looks. They giggled a bit, and did not object when he hiked up his trousers to squat next to the wolf. *"Ai un chibrit?"* he said again, and Miranda gave him her father's lighter. He flicked it to produce the flame, and lit his cigarette while at the same time as he was stroking the wolf's fur around its ears.

"Nice animal," he said in an accent so thick that Miranda scarcely understood him. He squinted at her through the smoke. The cigarette was in the corner of his mouth. He kept her father's lighter in his left hand, while with his right he dug his fingers into the thick fur. He smiled up at the two girls. The wolf was yawning happily. Sasha Prochenko's hands were quiet and slow. Holding the wolf's head with his right hand, he slid the lighter into its mouth. Blue flame erupted from the silver box, and the wolf leapt up and pulled itself loose. The wide-faced girl let go of her leash at once, but the other was pulled down onto the asphalt as the wolf turned tail. Miranda caught a scent of burning hair.

"Go," said Sasha Prochenko. He had not gotten up, not stopped smiling, even though the wide-faced girl had jumped onto his back and was scratching at his cheek. He took the cigarette from his mouth, blew on the tip, and pushed it into the back of her hand. "Go," he said again, and Miranda went.

And as she ran up the slope into the front street of the town, she saw someone coming toward her whom she recognized. It was the woman who had pushed the book into her hands at the train station, the woman who had warned her about Kevin Markasev, the woman who'd appeared to her the night before the hunt and predicted some of this. It was her aunt Aegypta, dressed in a fur coat with a collar of foxes, and their heads hung down. She wore a lamb's wool hat, with her gray hair pulled back under it. She wore long gloves, and lipstick, and powder on her big nose, and when she put her arms around Miranda's neck she smelled of cinnamon and dust.

Miranda was conscious of an enormous feeling of relief. She clung to her aunt's coat and wouldn't let go. She rubbed her face in the stiff fur, hiding her face from what was happening behind her.

She was surprised to find the woman did not tower over her. Her aunt's face was level with her own. They stood embracing, while Miranda breathed in her aunt's smell and felt the fur prickle on her face. Aegypta Schenck was rocking her in her strong arms.

"My darling," she said. "You must not think that I would give you up. Oh, it has been so long."

She brought Miranda up into the street. They stood in a row of shop fronts and quaint Victorian buildings, a deserted tourist town in winter, and above them hung the slopes of the white mountain. "Come," said Aegypta Schenck, and she brought Miranda to a shop where there were lights inside. It was a restaurant or a café, and the old woman led her in and sat her down at a round, marble-topped table where there were coffee and cakes. "Let me look at you," she said, and she took Miranda's leather pack, then pushed back her coat and stripped it off.

The lizard was gone. "Let me look at you," repeated the woman, and she pushed Miranda's hair from her forehead. "Oh my darling, we have been successful. You still have the silver coin?"

Miranda slid it from her pocket and put it on the table, the coin stamped with the head of Alexander the Great. "Then we are free," the old woman said. "Roumania will be free. All my plans . . ." Tears glistened in her dark eyes. Above them, Miranda noticed, her eyebrows had been penciled on.

They were the only people in the restaurant. There was no one at the counter behind them where the register was. Behind that there was a red velvet curtain that covered the back wall.

"You planned this?" Miranda said, looking down at her croissant. It was made of papier-maché.

"Yes of course. You do not think that I should let that fool, Nicola Ceausescu, get the better of me? It was Rodica's mother who had the pawnshop in the Old Court. Rodica's mother who led her to the book. Perhaps I even misled you a little bit—oh, I am sorry. Please forgive me. I must make others do these things, even if there should be risks. Do you understand?"

"No."

"Oh, I will have time to tell you! And your mother will be glad! Because you have grown into a wise girl, to do what is right. This was a risk, but I must take it, because I was a prisoner in Roumania. Everywhere I was constrained and watched. There was the *Siguranta*—the police—and also our great enemy in Ratisbon. I could do nothing to go with you, only these small warnings. I could do nothing where I was. An old woman in a hut in the woods, an old bird in a cage! But Jesus Christ came out of death. In Roumania they will put an empty coffin in the ground."

Miranda didn't understand any of this. She was focussed on one thing. "What about Peter?" she asked.

When her aunt did not reply, Miranda told her the story of the past few days. She told her about Peter and Andromeda, and Blind Rodica's death and Gregor Splaa's. She told her about Captain Raevsky, and the wild men, and Peter's sickness. Her aunt made little sympathetic clucks. But then at moments she would smile, as if none of this dire information could change her mood.

"We are in battle with an enemy," she said finally. "It is the one who holds your mother prisoner. And even he is just a servant of something worse. Oh, I am sorry about Splaa and Rodica! They were my loyal friends. I am sorry you are all alone! This smallpox sickness is a coward's weapon, but our enemy would like the world to suffer as he suffered."

Miranda stared at the old woman. "I am sorry," Princess Aegypta said again. "De Graz is a soldier, and this is not a soldier's death."

Miranda stared at her, searching for an answer in her proud, ugly face. "My child, I can help you now. Use the coin to bring me from this place, and I will help you. Oh, but I am sorry for de Graz. His mother is still alive, an old woman in Bucharest. There will be an empty place for him in the mausoleum of his ancestors. . . ."

"His mother died of cancer," Miranda said. "She was a secretary in the English Department. She used to teach him poems. . . ."

She watched a flicker of impatience pass over her aunt's face. "Yes, of course. That is the story you were told. And it is hard to give it up, I know—these stories of your childhood. Now we wake up, and we must not be frightened. There are sacrifices that must be made. These matters are more important than his life or my life, or yours."

Miranda lifted her coffee cup and brought it to her lips. But though the cup appeared full, she smelled and tasted nothing.

Aegypta Schenck put her hand out, and put it over Miranda's hand, where it lay on the surface of the table. "Girl, you must not think I would have given you up. You lived with me until the empress destroyed me. Do you remember those days by the sea, or in the woods at Mogosoaia? No—I took them away from you. I thought I'd spare you pain and confusion— now it occurs to me that I've miscalculated. God forgive me, I have made mistakes. I've been working toward these things since before you were born. And I keep telling myself that this white tyger is more than what you want and what I want."

She smiled again—a false, constrained expression, it occurred to Miranda now. "I know it is hard, and you are still a child. But I could not have given you more time inside the book. Our enemies are strong and getting stronger."

"I am not a child."

"Indeed not. When was it—the last time we saw each other?"

"I don't know. Stanley told me I was three."

"Stanley? Yes. Of course. So do you think that you were three years old when I stood on the platform of the Mogosoaia station and put the book into your hands? I tell you, you were not yet nine."

Miranda shook her head. "Twelve years ago," her aunt went on, relentless. "Did I not say that something would be pulled away? Can you forgive me—can you believe that this was for the best?"

Miranda took her hand from her aunt's big hand. She couldn't think about this now. She had to think about Peter. "I'm not going to let him die," she said. "Don't make me choose between the two of you. You brought us out, and you can send us home. I'll take him to the hospital in Pittsfield. Or maybe he won't even be sick. Give me some days at home, and I can say good-bye, and then I promise we'll come back, or I'll come back at least . . ."

Her aunt stared at her, and Miranda felt a chill.

The old woman clucked her tongue sympathetically—"My poor child. It is true you do not understand. That book is gone. That is all finished, done."

At that moment, Miranda thought she might raise up her hand, put her hand over her aunt's mouth to keep the words from coming out. Except she'd known it all along—"We can't go home?"

"To what, child? This is your home. There is nothing there."

Miranda felt her eyes well up, and then some tears were on her face. "Well, then you can cure him here—can't you? Can't you do that, if I do everything you say?"

Aegypta Schenck looked at her. "Ah well," she said at last. "Perhaps it's for the best as it is. You must be brave and think of that. I seem to have made terrible mistakes with him and with Prochenko too from what you say. First a female, and now his own spirit creature—these were proud men. And the calculations were so difficult."

After a moment she went on. "They swore an oath to your father. I had not thought they'd be so loyal, especially Prochenko, but they grew to love you when you were a child. They were not my first choices, I should tell you. But when the empress turned against me, there was no one else. De Graz had a reputation, and they didn't like each other."

"What are you saying?" Miranda thought. And then aloud: "You're saying it is best to let him die?"

The old woman shrugged. "The damage is already done."

She said nothing else about it, and when Miranda spoke again, she asked a question that was not quite to the point. "Tell me, if you love me. If all this was for the best, then why was it so cruel?"

Her aunt's dark eyes had a yellowish cast. "Child, I know it's difficult. All that is gone. You must not dwell on it."

"Please," Miranda said. "I want to know. This year in school we read about the First World War."

Aegypta Schenck wiped her red nose on the back of her hand, a coarse, unladylike gesture. "If you want to know, then you have already guessed."

Then in a moment, "It was because of you."

Miranda shook her head. Her aunt went on. "Let me see. The First

World War—we made historical projections. A European war was necessary, then and later, if there was to be no war in Massachusetts. That was all. These events made you secure. In the end that was all I cared about."

Then she continued after a moment. "Please put it from your mind. When I first started work, I would have made that place into a paradise. It was in my mind to write the book of paradise, and we would all be characters and not just you. When the empress turned against me, it was still half-finished. After that, all I cared about was your protection. And don't you think," she continued, hurrying now, stumbling over her words, "if that place had been like heaven, then you'd have been happy to come here?"

It was cold in the restaurant. All this time her aunt had not taken off her coat. Now she slid it from her shoulders to reveal an evening dress, a diamond choker around her wrinkled neck. She took the lamb's wool hat from her head and laid it on the table. Her hair was carefully pinned back with tortoiseshell combs.

Happy to come here, Miranda thought. Then she spoke. "His father was Dan Gross. He lived on White Oak Road."

Again there was that flicker of impatience. "Don't dwell on it. It is finished now."

But it wasn't finished. "That place," Miranda said, "is what I am. Rachel and Stanley. Christmas Hill. Andromeda and Peter. That is what I am."

"Of course. And you will be something else—the white tyger. All of us, we leave our childhood behind. I also, I am becoming something else. Do you think that I'm not terrified?"

Then in a little while: "Come, child," she said.

They had been sitting near the window. The sun had risen over a shoulder of the mountain, and the morning light had reached into the street. In the plate glass of the window was a fiery glow.

"You're not listening to me," Miranda said. "You told me I had two friends, and I must have faith. One of them, you said, would show me a sign. He would show me something from my own country. Or was that just trying to trick me? Mislead me, like you said?"

The old woman rubbed her eyes with the back of her hand. "I do what I must do. These friends—you have no duty to them now," she murmured. "You are the white tyger."

They sat in silence for a few moments, and then her aunt went on. "You lived with me for seven years in Mamaia castle on the sea. Your mother was not there. But I made a promise to her in Ratisbon that I would keep you safe. Oh, and it made me happy to keep that promise, when I saw you playing with Juliana on the tiles and playing in the water. I would have kept you near my heart, except the empress and Antonescu defeated me when you were just a child. Do not blame me for that. I cannot bear it. All the choices that I made, they were for you."

Miranda sat watching the sun come in the window. "You're not listening to me," she said again.

The old woman looked down into her empty cup. She pushed her chair suddenly backwards, and clapped her hands. "Then you will explain it to me when we are safe. You are the white tyger. You must do what you think best. Now we must meet the timekeeper."

She stood up, and Miranda stood up, and she led Miranda deeper into the restaurant until she found the side door. Opened, it revealed a dark alley between the wooden buildings, and the old woman led Miranda down it, away from the front street and into a neighborhood of dilapidated sheds and greenhouses, long galleries hung with small cracked panes that were just now catching the sun's light.

Above them Miranda could see the white mountain, and for a moment she could glimpse a picture in her mind. It was both clear and evanescent, as if it had been momentarily inserted, then removed. She saw a building high up on the mountainside, a pavilion at the top of the glacier where the light was touching now. She imagined several old men and women, thin and stiff and pale, peering down from the parapet. Names for them came to her—Venus, Apollo, Artemis.

Down below, she and her aunt walked through a courtyard of neglected grass and trampled earth. They walked beside a clapboard wall, its white paint peeling. Now Miranda could see in front of them an old man beckoning them on. He was dressed in spattered overalls, and when he reached the door of one of the glass galleries, he pushed it open.

His face was thin and narrow, mottled black and pink. His hair was white and thick. He held the door for them, and they stepped into an enormous and untidy space, a greenhouse that went on forever, and whose glass roof was shining now in the sun's rays. And the greenhouse was packed with cages in long, double rows: wood-and-wire cages in stacks four and five feet high.

"Here you go," said the old man. "You have your money? Come with me." He led them over the duckboards, then down a cramped and narrow passage between two rows of piled cages, in each of which, as Miranda could make out, there was a small and silent animal.

"Here you go. Here you go," muttered the old man. He led them past gerbils and rats, foxes, turtles, snakes, rabbits, birds, insects—all kinds, and some Miranda didn't recognize. In most of the cages there was a bed of cedar chips or straw. The animals watched her calmly through the netting or the bars. There was no movement or display.

"Here you go, here you go," and they were peering into a cage at eye level, where a small bird sat on a wire swing. It was a little bird, whose iridescent feathers were tinged with dirty sunshine through the windows. A battered brass plaque was affixed to the bars of the cage. On it was engraved A. S. V. SCHENCK.

Miranda turned, and in the cramped space behind her she could see her aunt stare hungrily at the bird. The old man paid no attention to her. "You have your money?" he said. "Take what you like. She's a beauty."

Miranda hesitated. "And . . . is everybody here?"

"Most of them. Most of them. Here we have . . . ah, many, many. You are rich?"

"No." She pulled the silver coin from her pants' pocket and held it up.

"I thought so," muttered the old man. "I thought so. Yes, just the one. Any one you like, maybe."

"What about Pieter de Graz?"

"Yes, yes, well, he should be just coming in." And the old man took off down the duckboards. He pulled some spectacles from the breast pocket of his overalls and slipped them on. Then he was fingering the brass plaques on the cages, until he found one at the bottom of a pile. "Here."

Miranda got down on her knees, then on her hands and knees. She could see the plaque, but it was dark inside the cage. "Here you go," said the old man, slipping a brass flashlight from another pocket and then twisting the top. A small light came out of it.

"I don't see anything."

But then she did—a red beetle no larger than a dime, standing in a corner of the cage. "Aren't there any larger animals?"

The old man squatted down. "A few. A few. They're in a different place. This size here, it's more convenient. There're an awful lot of bugs."

She peered in at the beetle. "How would I carry it?"

"Well, I suppose we can give you a little box. I don't see why not."

Aegypta Schenck had followed them down the passage. She stood behind them, shivering in her fur coat. "Please," she said.

The old man didn't hear her. He didn't turn around. "Maybe I can't do this," Miranda said. "You've been planning my whole life."

"Child, this is not the time for infantile rebelliousness." The princess spoke sharply, but her face was empty and fearful. "It was not my choice to give you up. Do not punish me, Miranda Popescu! Don't you see this is a terrible place?"

Miranda felt her eyes fill with tears. "Do you have a little container?" she asked.

"Well, yes. Yes, I think so. Let me see." And the old man was going through his pockets until he found a small wooden box, painted with a Chinese street scene. It was of a kind Miranda remembered from her childhood. Her fingers easily found the secret panel, the lever that held the spring.

"If not me, then what about your father?" said Aegypta Schenck. "He is here. Prince Frederick is here—"

"Well, no," muttered the old man, as if it had been Miranda who had spoken. "Butterfly, isn't he? Gone a long time. You'd need more money . . ."

"I am sorry," said Miranda. "Don't you see—I can't. You've made it too difficult, and he's my friend." She touched the lever and the drawer to the box jumped out.

She thought, "This is not real." None of this was real. In the real world she was lying with Peter in a cave in the woods, and this was all a dream.

But in the dream the old man reached to pat her hand. "It's a good choice, young lady. A good choice. Tell you the truth, that old bird's about done. This one's got some tread on it. Years of wear."

He slid open the wire door and reached in his hand. The beetle hopped onto his thumbnail.

"That's the way of it. You see he's happy to get out. Even a few minutes, that's too long."

He held out his hand, and for the first time she noticed how pretty the bug was, its shining red carapace.

She studied it for a moment, the subtle geometric pattern on its wings. Then she forced herself to look up at Aegypta Schenck. She braced herself for an expression of anger, but didn't see it. Her aunt's face, which had been sullen, now was calm.

"So it is nothing, the future of Roumania," she said, rubbing her nose on the back of her hand. "Is it nothing against Pieter de Graz's life? But if you ask me, he will not thank you for saving him from his duty as a soldier. Nor will he love you for forgetting your own future. Perhaps you are a child after all."

Miranda couldn't look at her. She held out the silver coin and the man took it. Then with great care he laid the beetle into the box, along with some strands of grass. "Should be all right for an hour or so," he said.

"Okay."

But she made no motion to get up. Now the decision was made, she felt she could not bear to see the old woman's face again, or listen to her voice: "Believe me," said Aegypta Schenck. "I have suffered for this. Suffered and prayed. Please, Miranda, do not steal it from me."

"You'd better get back," said the timekeeper.

"Okay."

Miranda bit her lips, forced herself to look up. "How can you say good-bye to someone you've never met?" she thought. "Please don't hate me," she murmured, prepared for an expression of anger and contempt on her aunt's face. Instead, and maybe it was just a trick of the dirty light, but she was surprised to see a softer look, less pinched, less worried.

"God bless Roumania," muttered Aegypta Schenck.

What did she mean? "Please," Miranda whispered. "We all do what we can."

"I know! By Jesus Christ I know. You will forgive me?"

What did she mean? "There is nothing to forgive."

"Oh, but there is. God bless Roumania and you."

Then she went on. "I told you the white tyger had a choice. Now the hard way is best, and perhaps I was too proud when I thought that I could tell you this, and this. So now I am made humble by the white tyger. Oh, but don't forget. I have left a message for you at the shrine of Venus."

Miranda shook her head, and her aunt continued. "So—not even that. Forgive me. A hard lesson—an old habit, and you cannot now imagine how I planned. That was my book, too. Now it's gone. Now I must trust you, which is hard. And I must only hope that you could not have helped us if you'd followed every plan of mine. So—what will come now?"

Miranda shook her head. Thank God this was all a dream.

"Oh, my dear," said the old woman. "Then is this good-bye? I hoped we'd have years in front of us, and then your mother, too. Oh, but it was worth the risk! But for God's sake," she continued, "do not leave me in that cage. For God's sake you can get me out."

Miranda looked down. She slid the box into her leather backpack, empty now of all her Roumanian things. Only the last gold coin in her pocket. Only the locket on her neck. Only the tiger's-head bracelet that still glittered on her wrist. The sun was shining, and the air in the greenhouse was full of shining motes of dust. When she glanced up again, her aunt had disappeared among the narrow rows.

On the way out of the greenhouse, Miranda and the old man passed the cage where the little bird swung back and forth. A brandywine bird. Miranda found she knew the name.

She paused. "Can you open her up?" she said. "Can I see her?"

The old man frowned and mumbled. "She was my aunt," Miranda said.

The old man's eyebrows were heavy and dark, although his hair was white. He peered at her for a moment, and then undid the latch on the bird's cage. He reached in his big, battered hand. "Come," he said, "come on. Just for a minute, now." But as soon as the cage was open, the bird flew at him and pecked him on the knuckle. Then she was out the wire door. Cursing, he grabbed at her with his bleeding hand, and managed to pull out one of the iridescent tail feathers. But then the bird was gone, beating at the glass roof until she found a broken pane.

The old man danced a little angry dance. He raised his stiff hands to the ceiling, mumbling a string of curses and vulgarity. No longer interested in Miranda, he hurried to the door. When she followed him, she found he had grabbed up a battered, paint-stained ladder from a patch of weeds, and was raising it against the greenhouse wall. Above him on the ridge pole, the little bird sat in the sun, and above her rose the white mountain.

When Miranda came to the harbor again, the boat was waiting. And when she came to the far shore, it was easy to retrace her steps. And when she woke up in the morning, bundled against the cold in the entrance to the cave, she found she was holding Peter's hand.

And later, in the chapel of St. Simon the Fisherman, in the wooden church off of Elysian Fields, the priest and the sacristan gave up hope. They had been sitting with the body of Aegypta Schenck von Schenck until the body, quite suddenly, began to decompose. Toward noon they rubbed her gray old flesh with perfume, and put her on a bed of flowers, and nailed her coffin shut.

III

The Invasion

11 Transformations

"MADAM," SAID GENERAL ANTONESCU. "UNDERSTAND: The German army invaded Hungary after such a disturbance. They are looking for a pretext. They claim to be protecting lives and property. Now there are five regiments at the frontier."

For Antonescu this was a long and complicated explanation. Enormous, gruff, he stood with his hands clasped behind his back, staring out into the piata from the third floor of the Winter Keep, in Bucharest. Dressed in a uniform of midnight blue, a star on each shoulder and on his throat, he looked out of place in the jewel box of the empress's study. Out of scale also, his shaved skull in uncomfortable proximity to the ceiling. Though the empress's secretary had poured tea for him, he had not picked up his cup. Nor, since he entered the room, had he sat down, and the empress imagined he was afraid he might break one of the delicate chairs, shatter the cup between his fingers.

He was watching a procession of priests. Their hands were painted red, and they carried branches ripped from pine trees, along with trumpets and bells. It was the feast of Lupercalia. "That is why," he continued without turning around, "this is important. I have been informed the Siguranta has questioned this man, Hans Greuben, a German national and an embassy employee, about the jeweler's death. The Siguranta and the metropolitan police. I have a letter of protest from the German ambassador. It must not be allowed in this current atmosphere. You know there have been riots against the German minorities in Transylvania, doubtless instigated by provocateurs."

Again, this was a long speech for him. The empress turned her body in her chair and examined the back of his head, the folds of skin where his head joined his neck. A fragrant breeze came from the open window. "Do not bully me," she said. "Someone else—the servant has confessed to the crime. I believe if you are interested, in one month you will see the sentence carried out."

"Why so long?"

"Because there are people who think he is innocent. I myself—it is absurd. Why should he murder this man? It is clear he is protecting his mistress, who has disappeared."

"You suspect her?"

"All the world suspects her. I have spoken to the chief of police. She killed this man Spitz without a doubt. Shot him—knocked him with a candlestick."

The baron clasped his hands behind his back. "Why should she do such a thing?" he asked without turning around.

"Because she is an evil woman," said the empress. Her teacup shook between her pudgy fingers. It clattered on the saucer as she replaced it on the table. "You don't know her. She used to dance in the music halls before the newspapers discovered she was an artist. She seduced Ceausescu when he was deputy prime minister, though he was old enough to be her grandfather. God knows who was the father of her son who never learned to speak. She was a cruel mother, I have no doubt, and because of her he was put into an institution where she never visits him. It is only the Elector of Ratisbon who has taken an interest. He tells me he will bring the boy to Germany, to a surgical clinic there."

The empress was agitated. She patted her red cheeks with a handkerchief. She was horrified by any cruelty to children.

THE GENERAL STARED out into the piata where the priests were leading forward a white goat with ribbons in its horns. He was looking south over the rooftops of the old town. At the limit of his vision, scarcely a kilometer away, rose the boxy headquarters of the metropolitan police. There in his prison cell, Jean-Baptiste sat playing chess. If at that moment he had been able to hear the empress profess his innocence, he would have been more worried than consoled. Perhaps he would have made a careless blunder with his pawns, which in this endgame might have been fatal. He had made his decision. He had no desire to revisit it, nor hear it questioned by others. His dirty, peeling cell in the Curtea Veche was comfortable to him.

Partly this was due to his state of mind, and partly to the efforts of his new friend Radu Luckacz, who had taken an interest in his comfort. The policeman had brought him books, extra blankets, tobacco, newspapers. He kept the rooms well heated. Often he shared some of the pastries and meat pies that his wife packed for him. Or sometimes, when he was able, he sat down to a game of chess, as he had now. It was a good occupation for the two men, as it allowed them to be friendly without requiring them to speak.

About Jean-Baptiste's situation there was nothing to discuss. He was an old man with no living relatives. His small property he had already disposed of. His legal affairs had been resolved out of his hands.

They hadn't much in common, the Hungarian émigré and the old man from Cluj. The one crucial area where their tastes and interests overlapped could not easily be mentioned, or admitted even to themselves. From time to time Jean-Baptiste would break the comfortable silence with an anecdote about his former employer, the Baroness Ceausescu—these stories were not connected to each other, or apropos of anything. Nevertheless the policeman listened avidly, sucking on his pipe as he perused the pieces on the chessboard.

"I was the baron's man for many years, and his first wife. After her death we had a certain routine, and I remember when he told me he was to marry again. He told me the name—I was suspicious. I had seen the billboards at the Ambassadors. She was a personality, and there were rumors of scandal. So on my night off I bought a ticket in the upper circle—just myself. Every seat was full. It was a performance of *Ariadne at Naxos*—you see I didn't think much of it at the time. I thought the baron was making a mistake. She was just a child. But now I find that I remember every movement she made on the stage. That's what real art is, I suppose. You can't get it out of your mind. I didn't know much about it, but I could tell she had a spirit. And it was quite a shock, I tell you, in the third act, to see her in her torn clothes, her hands dripping with blood. I remember wondering what kind of employer she would make. To tell the truth, it was difficult at first. She had a great deal to learn about being a lady."

Or, "I can tell you she found it difficult to entertain. The baron lost most of his personal associates after Prince Frederick's death. But the house was full of people from the government, and sometimes I'd find her crying in a rage when she was asked to plan a menu for a dinner party. That was when we became closer, I think, because I was able to help her with the silver and so on."

Now the baron's house on Saltpetre Street was empty, and the baroness had disappeared. Unspoken also between the old servant and the policeman were any thoughts about where she might have gone. Domnul Luckacz, though he had made enquiries, had not seen her since the night he had taken Jean-Baptiste into custody.

THAT HAD BEEN THREE DAYS ago, in wintertime. Now, suddenly, it was spring. The air was fragrant, soft. Luckacz sniffed at it appreciatively as he was walking home along the Strada Iuliu, his hands in the pockets of his green wool overcoat.

He was eager to get home while there was still so much light in the streets. He was happy at the prospect of seeing his wife and daughter, but in front of him a young man hurried along the sidewalk. There was nothing about him to attract Luckacz's attention, not his dirty boots or baggy clothes. Not his cap or ripped umbrella, or anything except the thrill that went through Luckacz's body and his teeth. It was a sensation he recognized, and so he turned aside at the corner of the road.

Up ahead he saw a crowd, which was scattering and parting to allow two boys to come through. They were from the countryside, dressed as wolves and carrying, as the traditions of Lupercalia demanded, whips made of goatskin leather. They were hacking at the people as they passed. Seeking to avoid them, the young man in the baggy overcoat crept into one of the stone doorways of the houses that lined the street, and Luckacz caught a glimpse of his face. When the boys had passed, he followed him into the grounds of the temple. Its stone façade was decorated with pine branches, splashed with red water to symbolize blood.

Radu Luckacz was not religious. For him as for most citizens, these celebrations had a civil function only. He was surprised, therefore, to see the young man in front of him pause in the temple vestibule, strip off his glove, and put his fingers into the bowl of holy water. In the church itself, which was full of incense smoke and soft music from the organ, he was surprised to see him slip into a pew, then go down on his knees in prayer.

The church was dark and full of shadows. Domnul Luckacz sat immediately behind the praying figure. To distract himself, for a few minutes he studied the gold statue of the goddess on the altar, the snake feeding at her breast. Then he turned again to the young man in front of him. He had removed his cap, revealing a quantity of chestnut hair.

On that first day of the springtime festival, most of the activity was in the streets. The church itself was quite empty. Presently the young man rose from his knees and sat back in the pew. Domnul Luckacz slid forward. Breathing deeply, he tried to catch some scent from the glossy hair, but could not.

"Ma'am," he whispered, and the baroness stiffened, did not turn around. The policeman licked his moustache and his upper lip. He was aware suddenly of the sound of his own voice, of the officiousness and fussiness that he could not prevent. "Ma'am, I came to your house with the notary to take your statement, at twelve o'clock, as we had agreed. I was disappointed . . ."

Above the music of the organ, Luckacz thought he could hear a soft, deflating hiss. "Ma'am, it was impossible . . ." Dissatisfied, again he let his voice trail away.

"Have you come to arrest me?" whispered the Baroness Ceausescu.

"By no means. The statement was not necessary, because the man confessed. Only I would have supposed . . ."

Again the soft hiss of air escaping. "Is he well?"

"Ma'am, you must have read about it in the newspapers. He is in good spirits, considering the circumstance. There is one month left. I confess I don't understand. I would have thought your statement might have prevented—"

This time she interrupted. "What about Herr Greuben? Did you question him?"

"I did, under limitations. There was a question of diplomatic immunity."

Now the baroness turned around. No trace of the young man remained. "This was a murder charge!"

"Indeed it was, ma'am. Indeed it was. And it is my opinion that a statement from you would have prevented . . . Would have saved . . . There were extenuating circumstances that were never brought forward."

"You don't need extenuating circumstances. The man is innocent. Didn't you tell me Domnul Spitz died of a gunshot wound?"

"I didn't tell you. But it is true."

Her eyes, as she glared at him, were almost purple in the half-light. He imagined his heart might swell and break. But he persevered. "Ma'am, nevertheless, there was the matter of the candlestick. And as you know, he has confessed."

"That was to protect me," she murmured fiercely.

Domnul Luckacz took out his pocket handkerchief to wipe his lips and wipe his cheek. He couldn't look her in the face. "As you say. As for the German, we were not allowed to search his rooms. There was no evidence . . ."

"What do you need?"

"Please, ma'am. There is no point. It is too late. My superiors . . ."

"What do you need?" she asked again.

He shrugged. "Please, it is useless. He has an alibi, which is supplied by the Elector of Ratisbon. There is no weapon. Nor were we allowed to take his fingerprints, which might have been useful. As you may know, there was a chain made up of flattened silver links . . ."

All this time they had been whispering in the back of the empty church. Smoke from the candles in the side chapels, smoke from the incense braziers hurt his eyes. He dabbed at them with his pocket handkerchief. The baroness was clutching the back of her pew between her naked hands, and Luckacz recognized her signet ring—the pig of Cluj. Why did she continue to wear it? Altogether she was full of mystery. Now he glanced up at her face that seemed to hang disembodied in front of him: her high cheekbones, small nose, flawless skin.

"In any case," he murmured, "it is too late."

Candlelight gleamed in her hair. The light touched and made golden every hair of her brows and lashes. "What is important now . . . ," he murmured, then broke off, cleared his throat. "I believe he might appreciate a conversation with you. An interview. He is attached to you."

These words were difficult for him to say. Again he felt a distance from himself. He listened to the sound of his harsh, ugly voice. "He is very . . . attached to you."

Fierce as that of any goddess, her face drifted before him. He saw her clench her fists on the back of the pew, and he imagined she might strike him. "What good is that?" she said after a moment. She spoke out loud for the first time, and a young priest, hurrying down the aisle, paused to look at them.

"The Germans pushed you out of your own country," she said, "and you did nothing. Now they shoot us in the street and you do nothing. What do you need—finger marks? Weapons? I can get you these things. The elector's alibi means nothing, as you know.

"These men," she said, "watch for me everywhere. You ask me why I left my house—I was afraid of them. Hans Greuben, I have seen him and his men watching for me in the streets. Everywhere I have seen them in their long coats—you must know this. Why do you allow these murderers to torment us?"

Luckacz kept his hat in his lap. He found he was kneading the brim between his fingers. "He would ask for a visit from you, if it is possible. I also . . ."

"Yes. But if I come, maybe Herr Greuben will find me there. Maybe you yourselves would find a reason to arrest me."

"Ma'am, I swear—"

HOW COULD SHE DOUBT HIM? How could he earn her trust? But there was nothing to be done, because she was not afraid of being arrested. No, it was her guiltiness that prevented her from visiting the old man, her faithful servant, Jean-Baptiste.

No matter how she twisted and turned, the jeweler was dead because of her. And if she could not remember killing him, still she could not forget the feel of the soft white cord in her hands, when she had pulled it tight around the neck of that old lady in Mogosoaia—sweet God, it was intolerable. Sitting backwards in her pew, grasping the dark wood, she stared up at the stained glass window above the door. It took a moment for the pattern to come clear: a cat licking her paws, the spirit emblem of the church.

She looked again at the policeman, his thick gray hair and black moustache. He seemed nervous, the way he looked around. Why was that? What was this to him? But for all she knew, there were others outside the church. For all she knew, others would meet him here; she jumped up, seized her umbrella and her cap. Then she was outside, squinting up into a sky that contained both sun and rain.

No one was waiting. She put the cap on her head. Breathing deeply, she forced herself to walk slowly down the steps, out the iron gate into the street. She put her left hand into the pocket of her overcoat and swung her umbrella like a cane. Then at the corner of the street, she forced herself to read the printed notice on the wall, announcing that the murderer of Claude Spitz the jeweler had already been arrested, thanks to the deft and ever-watchful metropolitan police.

Swinging her umbrella, the baroness turned the corner and strolled eastward away from the river, until she found the poorer streets behind the university. This quarter, previously unknown to her, was where she had stayed since the night Jean-Baptiste was arrested. It was full of rooming houses and cheap hotels.

She had taken a room on the fifth floor of an ancient and dilapidated building. Her landlady, also ancient and dilapidated, seldom budged from the parlor on the first floor. Fat and weak-legged, she sat in the window soaking her feet all afternoon, peering anxiously at passersby. It was intolerable. The baroness would have to move. She had come here in search of anonymity, because the place was full of students who came and went at all hours. She had not expected to be studied and judged every time she came to the front door. Still she put her finger to her cap and smiled, even waggled her umbrella familiarly while she squinted at the sky as if concerned that it might rain. An elaborate pantomime: She shrugged, even put her hand out—palm up, fingers splayed—before she reached for the doorknob. All the time the fat old woman glowered at her from under her gorillalike eye ridges; what was the theory that Aegypta Schenck had packed inside her book? That men and women were descended out of apes? An absurd notion. Though one could see how it had occurred to her.

Absurd because we still have animals inside of us, as Cleopatra kept her cat. We are not the end of some process. That was Aegypta Schenck trying to make sense out of the world. Instead we all have animals scratching to get out, which is why sometimes it is so hard to stay in our own skin. Why our skin seethes and prickles and we wake up desperate—the baroness scuffed and banged her way upstairs. She kicked at the splintered banisters, the steps ground down. Each passage was lined with four or five doors. Each room contained some nameless striver. It was intolerable.

Now finally she stood at the door of her miserable room under the roof. She knocked and Markasev opened it, stepped aside.

He had not gone out that day. He had spent his time cleaning and re-cleaning the one small room, waiting for her to return. He had washed the windows, which had been opaque with grime.

She closed the door, hung up her overcoat and cap. She slid their supper from inside the breast of her jacket—a packet of cigarettes, a rasher of sliced ham. She put them on the table, which was covered with oilcloth. Marka-sev had already laid out two chipped, scrubbed plates, a loaf of bread, a pot of mustard.

From her pockets the baroness produced two bottles of beer. Markasev found teacups and they drank from them, sitting on either side of the oil-cloth table while Markasev made sandwiches. The meat parted between the baroness's teeth.

All this was bought with Aegypta Schenck's money, which the baroness had stolen from the shrine of Venus.

"Once when I was small," said Markasev, "I watched a calf being born. The cow was crying out and crying out, and my father held the lantern. Dionysus was there and some other of my father's men, and they were wor-ried, because the calf was turned and wasn't coming out. In the lantern light, I could see the wet hooves. I was just to go out for a moment to see before I went to bed. But my father was afraid for the cow, and he forgot about me. So I was there for hours until my mother came and got me. Dionysus had his arms inside the cow. There was some blood. Then from my window, all night I heard the cow crying out, until I fell asleep. But in the morning I went out, and both were resting in the straw."

Lately Markasev had surprised her with these small recitations. They were more numerous as the days went by. But it was hard to imagine any of them were true. She knew this one was not. He'd learned this scene from a book she'd read to him. She'd bought him some books in the market stalls.

"What was your father's name?"

"He was a red pig," said Markasev, which made her laugh. The boy had regained some kind of a sense of humor! Whatever had happened at Cluj was now behind him. He never spoke of it.

When she had first moved from the house on Saltpetre Street, she had imagined she would send him away. She had packed some clothes for him. She had pressed some of Jean-Baptiste's money into his hand, had taken him on two occasions to the Gara de Nord. Both times he had cried and begged until she had relented. She had not wanted to cause a scene in the crowded station.

Now he was thriving in these new circumstances, though their diet was meager and unvaried. He had a new habit of cleanliness, and washed himself every day in cold water from the tap. He was too tall for the baron's clothes, so she had bought some trousers and secondhand dress shirts from the thieves' market; she had always had a gift for clothes. The blue-green and apricot and plum colors helped his pallor and his lustrous black hair. She had bought him a razor, though he scarcely needed it.

She got a certain pleasure from seeing him in the light of day. It had been cruel, she decided, to keep him shut up for so long. Now she sat drinking her beer while he peered at her from under his single thick brow, his head cocked like a dog's. And as so often happened in his presence, she found herself thinking about her son Felix, shut up away from his mother in the Institute for Mental Deviation, and no one to fix him sandwiches in the middle of the afternoon.

At the end of his life, because of his guilt, the Baron Ceausescu had become concerned with purity. In his laboratory he had labored over the most difficult of alchemical tasks, to find a way of separating out the pure ingredients of matter. In his governmental work he was responsible for a body of laws intended to purify and renew the country itself.

Citizens with mental imperfections were resettled into government facilities. The baron's only child was one of these. And though elsewhere the new laws were ignored, he'd felt it necessary to set an example. He himself had delivered the boy to the stone building on the Soseaua Kiseleff.

The fees there were enormous, and sometimes the baroness tormented herself with wondering what might happen to her son, now that she could no longer pay.

As if he'd read her mind, the boy said, "Let us see it."

She slid the jewel from her pocket now and opened her hand. She laid her hand on the tabletop with the jewel in her palm, and they stared at it for a few minutes.

Her house, the life she had left, had been full of beautiful things, of which only this remained. Since she'd possessed it she imagined it had changed color, and become more purple than green. Now it tingled in her palm, picking up light from the window and reflecting it back, glowing as if it itself were a source of light.

She felt comforted by it and Markasev, glad to keep them with her. But when she looked at him, thoughts of her son clouded her mind. Now as they finished their beer and cigarettes, she decided to go out again, to walk north along the Soseaua Kiseleff and stand outside the wrought-iron gates of the Institute for Mental Deviation.

Always she had taken pleasure in walking the streets. The sun had now decided to stay out, so she discarded her umbrella. And she brought Markasev with her as one might take a dog on a walk; he was happy to be included. He rushed down the stairs ahead of her. But he stopped when he got to the hall on the ground floor.

The door to their landlady's apartment was open, and the woman herself stood on the threshold, glowering suspiciously, the baroness imagined, but no. She smiled. "Domnul Enescu," she said. It was the name the baroness had given herself.

A savory steam came from the room behind her. "I tried to get your attention just now as you came in. Please, you must know we are a family here. I have been making supper this afternoon, sarmale and creier pane cu sunca—have you eaten? We don't stand on ceremony. No, but I see you and your . . ." Her eyes, small in her fat face, moved uncertainly to Markasev and stayed there.

"Unfortunately—" the baroness began.

"No matter, no matter. I can see you are busy. But this evening, all right? We don't stand on ceremony. Two young men such as yourselves, I know you have an appetite!"

"How strange," thought the baroness. The woman seemed eager to continue speaking. The baroness, again, found herself making a pantomime as she slid out the door, this one of friendly dismissal and heartfelt regret. They had been here two days and already they had attracted attention, she thought. Soon they must move.

They walked north past the hill of Venus and the racetrack, and in among the grand houses. As they approached Floreasca Park they discovered many familiar addresses, which she had visited with her husband when she was rich.

Set back from the road, surrounded by walls, these mansions seemed as impregnable as fortresses now. Walking with Markasev, as she had instructed, five paces behind, she was reminded how isolated she'd become in these past years. When she reached the corner of the Calea Dorobantilor, she saw Helena Lupescu walking her borzois—a woman she had once counted among her intimate friends. Now she scarcely glanced at the baroness as she stalked past, dressed in a wolfskin coat.

The baroness felt her spirits rise. Herr Greuben and the rest, they would not recognize her, though they were setting traps all over town. Doubtless she would see him that same afternoon, watching outside the Institute for Mental Deviation.

How was it possible to extract her son? Or would they simply discharge him now that she no longer paid the bills? Or would they—terrible thought—remove him to some charity ward, maybe in some other building? Her mind, ordinarily so full of schemes, was helpless when she thought about it. In this context only, she felt she was a poor, weak woman, with all the world against her.

How much easier to fall into a rage. These Germans who plagued and constrained her, she would find some method to defeat them. Herr Greuben—she would find some method; what had Luckacz said? He had found the silver band that had held Kepler's Eye. He wanted a sample of Greuben's fingerprints—that was no good. For all she knew, it had been the simulacrum that had pried the stone out of its setting.

Fingerprints, weapons—Luckacz thought like a policeman. That was not her way.

She walked rapidly past a row of foreign embassies, and it was only when she saw the wrought-iron walls surrounding the institute that she slowed her steps. She crossed the boulevard to stand under the linden trees opposite the gate. She imagined she blended in with the crowd. Markasev, as he'd been instructed, stayed five paces away.

She stood for twenty minutes, looking for Greuben or one of his associates. The red-haired man, the dark man with spectacles—she had come to recognize several in his company as they waited at various addresses and houses.

The morning she had left Saltpetre Street, she had crossed in her secret tunnel under the street, in order to avoid the policeman Luckacz had left at her door. That had been the first time she was aware of Greuben waiting for her. He was reading a newspaper at the corner, not bothering to hide. That morning she had seen him from an upstairs window and again from the shelter of the wall. And since then she had noticed him several times, walking along the esplanade or in the student neighborhoods. She hated and feared the sight of his dark mackintosh and fedora, his yellow hair and moustache. It was hard for her to remember she had ever found him charming or handsome. Whenever she saw him now, it was his animal nature she was most aware of, the prowling beast inside of him, which she imagined left a stench that she could smell. Often she could sense his presence before she saw him. That afternoon she could not. There seemed to be no one at the gate.

She crossed the boulevard, forcing herself not to think, not to make a plan, and it was just as well. Because it was a trap after all, as she imagined when she had walked through the gates and down the gravel path toward the larch tree that obscured her son's window on the second floor—it was full of sparrows. There was no one at the window, she saw. It was barred, and the sash was open. She felt light-headed, and a choking sensation made it hard to breathe. But then in front of her she saw Greuben coming down the wide steps, and with him were both the red-haired man and the dark man with spectacles.

A black carriage stood in the drive, marked with the colors of the German Republic. The horses were restive. The coachman sat on the box. Bare-headed, dressed in their mackintoshes, Greuben and the others opened the doors, and now she saw a boy coming down the steps behind them. He was led by a nurse, a fair-haired boy just approaching his tenth birthday; she stopped and stood still. The men took no notice of her, she thought. They looked through her as if she were a pane of glass, she thought, gripping the tourmaline in her pants' pocket. But the boy could not be fooled by any of her disguises or by any space or separation. He looked toward her, smiled and waved. "Mother," he said, perfectly clearly, the first word she had ever heard from his lips, and when they heard it, the Germans turned to look. Greuben pointed.

But they could do nothing to her, the baroness decided, in this public place. She was a Roumanian citizen, after all. "What are you doing?" she said, coming forward now, holding out her hands. "Felix—please, where are you taking him?"

Greuben smiled. "The elector has found a place for him in the new clinic in Ratisbon. You will see it is a lucky chance. Madam, I am pleased to see you. We have something to discuss."

There was an animal inside of him, a small, feral beast that peered out through his eyes. "But don't you see, there's nothing wrong with him. Felix—please—what have they done?" She held out her hands, and the boy would have come to her, she was certain. There was a happy innocence in his face, in which she now saw traces of her own mother's good looks, and traces of herself as well—he was so tall! These people had robbed her.

"Madam," Greuben said, "the papers have been signed."

"Oh, you are monsters!" she told him. "Please, for the love of God." Still she tried to keep a pleasant voice and smile through her tears, because she didn't want to frighten the boy, whose small face was clouded now with doubt. They were pulling him to the door of the carriage, but he turned to look at her.

Greuben said, "The elector did not expect us to be able to negotiate so soon. It is a simple transaction. You have something—"

Beyond him, suddenly, she was aware of an officer of the metropolitan police in his midnight blue uniform and crimson cap. His glossy moustache and brass buttons made him look like someone playing a part, a policeman out of musical comedy. His face was stern and grave, and he actually had a silver whistle in his mouth, out of which now came a little peep.

Greuben held out his hand, but she had taken a step backward. Who was this man with his ridiculous whistle? Had Greuben summoned him? Obviously not. His face showed both displeasure and surprise. The jewel belonged to the Corelli family, after all. No, this was the empress's idea, thought Nicola Ceausescu as she stepped back and looked around. This was not the way to deliver her son, who was now shut up inside the black carriage.

No, the Germans would take her jewel and leave her with nothing. She held it in her hand. She would not give it up.

"You there—stop!" shouted the policeman. She turned and strolled back toward the wrought-iron gate, pretending not to hear. She imagined Greuben with his arm on the policeman's sleeve, trying to restrain him while the baroness looked for other uniforms in the crowd. There were a lot of people now around the gate.

"You there!" shouted the policeman. "Are you deaf?" She could hear his boots on the gravel.

Two other policemen, one in uniform and one in plainclothes, were coming toward her from the street. As she approached them, she said a prayer to Venus, goddess of love. And something else, a small charm that she'd learned from her mother's mother long before. She had never been a powerful conjurer like Ratisbon or Aegypta Schenck. She had learned a few things from her husband's books, and remembered a few things also from her childhood in the mountains. This charm of misdirection was one of them, which she had learned with her uncle's goats in the mountain pastures, used again and again on the audiences in the theater, and now here. Murmuring a charm, she stepped into the crowd of people around the gate and disappeared, one of a dozen strolling young men or women who now looked momentarily alike in their baggy, cheap clothes.

On the stage of the Ambassadors Theatre, the baroness had often seemed to appear and disappear out of knot of lesser performers. Now at the gate, the policemen lost sight of her for an instant. And it was only after their chief had blown his whistle, had seized hold of the elbow of a startled French tourist, that one of the others observed a young man in a linen jacket, his hat pulled down over his chestnut hair. He had already crossed the busy street, was already walking purposefully away, when the man in plainclothes raised the alarm and stepped off the curb. He waited for a gap in the flow of carriages and carts, all the while shouting and gesticulating until a boy ran up behind him, thrust his hand between his shoulder blades, pushed him into the path of a man riding a bicycle, who knocked him flat.

THE TWO MEN IN UNIFORM chased after Markasev, but he lost them in the park. Then he returned to the route he had followed with the baroness—he didn't know this city. But as darkness fell he found himself once more in front of their student lodgings, and she was in the alcove, waiting.

She was the lady of comfort and tears, but that night she was angry. This was in spite of the kindness that she showed him. As soon as he appeared under the street lamp, she stepped down and put her arms around him—"I was worried. Are you hurt?" And she said many more small things like this, while at the same time pushing his hair back from his forehead. It was a gesture he imagined from his childhood, and his mother had sat with him when he had a fever. But when the baroness embraced him and crushed his face against her neck, her skin felt cold compared to his, which surprised him. Mixed in with the smell of bitter herbs that always clung to her, that night he was aware of a more rancid smell.

"Greuben," she said. "Greuben." Her eyes were red because she had been weeping. But they were dry now, as if her tears had all burned up. She grabbed him by the elbow and drew him inside the vestibule, which again was full of delicious smells. Their landlady's door was ajar, but the aroma no longer came from there. Instead it seemed to lead them upstairs, where they found, next to their door, arranged in grease-stained paper bags, their dinner laid out for them, together with a note—*Dear Domnul Enescu. Young men such as yourself,* etc., etc.. The baroness unlocked the door, and after she had lit the lamp they unwrapped a container of dumpling soup and another of sarmales—stuffed cabbage leaves, which were a favorite of Markasev's. The baroness was too angry to eat, but he sat down at the table and watched her pace the floor. He was breathing in the smell of the spiced meat, and after a while he served himself with trembling hands; she didn't notice. He ate and ate.

The baroness stood at the garret window, looking down into the street. Then she turned, and he could tell she had come to a decision. Her beautiful face was smooth as always, free from grimaces or smiles, and because of this her expression was unreadable. Rather it was in the language of the body, as always, that she was preternaturally articulate; he watched her strip off her jacket and roll up her sleeves. He watched her rub her wrists and forearms as if washing them. He watched her rub and worry each finger in turn, until she came to the middle finger of her left hand, which carried with the band reversed her husband's signet—the red pig of Cluj. This she drew off, slipped into her pocket, and then pulled out the tourmaline, which she held in her naked hand. "Please, ma'am," he said, "there's food for you," but she shook her head.

Then she smiled not with her lips but with her shoulders and arms. "No," she said. "But we'll invite one more."

Carelessly she threw the stone onto the oilcloth surface of the table, where it lay next to the paper carton of creier *pane cu sunca*—breaded brains with ham. Then she raised her fists to her face and stood without moving for a long time. Markasev chewed quietly and slowly so as not to disturb her. He knew enough about conjuring to recognize it.

He sat stiffly in the chair, his mouth full of food. Then the spell was over, and he swallowed and took a drink of warm beer, left over from the afternoon. He watched her shoulders relax, watched a new lightness come into her step as she moved over to the door and opened it, peered outside. "How lovely of that fat old woman!" she said as she shut the door, stood for a moment with her back against it; she seemed almost giddy. "How kind—I like this place!" she said. Then she was on her knees, pulling her old suitcase from underneath the bed, opening it, laying some shirts inside. "That smells so good," she said.

"Yes, it is good."

"Well . . . good!" she said, clapping her hands. She seemed like a girl, almost, full of shy levity as she rolled up her pajamas. "You know, there's really no reason to stay here anymore. I think it's time to take a trip!"

"Where?"

"Oh, I don't know. The countryside. The mountains. Or we could go abroad, to Germany!"

She told him stories of her travels for half an hour or more. When the street door opened, four flights below, they both heard it. They heard the footsteps coming up the splintered stairs. Or rather, she heard them and he watched her, watched a brittleness and artificiality overtake her gestures, though she was still gay. "Once I was visiting Germany on the train. So many beautiful little houses and villages; I think even the country people are rich. It was in wintertime, and in every little station people waited for me in the snow, and some child would pass me flowers, and I would wave from the coach door. There, you see it is a lovely country, full of lovely people . . ."

Crack, crack, crack. Markasev watched her listening as she talked. He heard the steps on the landing, on another flight of stairs. Then there was a pause, and he imagined someone looking for the door, choosing theirs among the three on the top landing.

"Open it," said the baroness. But when Markasev didn't move, "Come in," she said. The room was warm and full of good smells. The door swung inward, revealing the outline of a man.

"Come in, come in," she repeated, her voice bright and hysterical. "Ah, Monsieur Spitz."

This name was unfamiliar to Markasev. She said something more in a language he recognized to be French. But because of the eloquence of her hands and gestures, he had no difficulty understanding she was welcoming the man in, offering a place to sit.

"Please," he imagined her saying. "You are welcome here."

The stranger now took a few faltering steps inside the door. Markasev sat at the table with his greasy plate in front of him; he was astonished. Not since they left Saltpetre Street had he seen the baroness speak to another person in this way, as if they had a prior acquaintance. He had gotten used to thinking she was friendless in the world. How had this man found them? Why was he out of bed, out of the hospital, when he was so obviously sick? His face was livid, and at every step he grimaced in pain. A bandage covered most of his head under his hat, which he labored to take off; he was beautifully dressed in old-fashioned, formal clothes. Velvet trousers, silk stockings to the knee, a woolen cape that now fell open, and Markasev could see the stranger's bloody hand, pressed against his side. His waistcoat and jacket were stained with blood.

But if the baroness knew him, he gave no sign of recognizing her. He peered stupidly around the room. The baroness said something else, and he looked at her, his face bewildered. Markasev turned also, because her voice had changed again. It was coarse and guttural and foreign as she pronounced the foreign words. She was standing in the shadow of the lamp, her face half obscured. Looking at her, Markasev saw no trace of the lady of comfort and tears, no trace of the young man in student clothes, no trace even of the artificial girl she had seemed just moments before. He knew she'd been an actress because she had told him, but he had never seen in her a transformation like this, of the kind that had delighted audiences across Europe. She stood with her hands on her hips, a menacing shadow. It was not possible to think of her as a woman.

The stranger—Monsieur Spitz—choked out some painful words. "Who are you?" he said. No doubt speaking in French was too much effort, and the baroness, too, switched to Roumanian.

"Let me help you," she said in a coarse, country accent. "Let me—" Still keeping to the shadow, she came forward, made a gesture with her hands.

The stranger grimaced, touched his head. "Don't touch! Don't touch. Where am I?—tell me that. Who are you?"

"You're with friends. People who know what those men did to you."

"What man? It was a woman, let me tell you—beautiful—heartless bitch! God in heaven, let me find her. I went to her house but she was gone. I will follow her—"

"No—"

"Let me tell you. She had such shoulders, like the goddess. How could she have done this? Ah, it hurts. It was a silver candlestick, which she took from the mantel, and I did nothing, nothing at all! Nothing to—"

Why was this man not in bed? He staggered forward and seized hold of the back of a chair, which he used to support his weight. He bent his body around the wound in his side, while he worked to recover his breathing.

"That woman has already been punished," said the baroness. "Would you believe it when you saw her so proud? Chased from her house. In the streets without a penny, and the police—you'll never find her. She has sunk too low."

For a moment no one spoke. Then, "Oh, I'm tired," confessed Monsieur Spitz. "This bullet in my ribs. If you know something, tell me. I woke in my carriage with a man robbing me. In my pockets as I lay helpless. I cried out, put my hand up—he shot me in the side. Robbed me."

Markasev wondered if the man was blind, or mostly blind. One eye was half covered by his bandage, and the other was dark with blood. He thrust his nose out, sniffing at the smells of cabbage and grease. His head lolled from side to side. "The thief—I barely saw him in the dark. Sweating face. Yellow hair. Who are you? Do you know him?"

"Yes."

"Then tell me," and the baroness told him. She gave him an address in the northern reaches of the city. "Oh, I will find him. Cruel, thieving bastard—Greuben, that's a German name!"

He would not sit or be comforted. Now he seemed eager to be gone. He pulled himself upright and staggered back toward the door.

"And when you speak to him," pursued the baroness, "tell him to look for Radu Luckacz at the headquarters of the metropolitan police. And tell him you were sent to him by a third party, by the Elector of Ratisbon. Will you say that for me? Will you do me that one favor?"

Monsieur Spitz glared at her out of his bloody eye. Then his face softened somewhat, and he wagged his big head. Where was he going? How was it possible for him to imagine he could get back down the stairs without collapsing? Surely a doctor was what he needed, and a place to rest. Yet they heard the crack, crack, crack of his feet kicking the stairs, and he was gone.

Afterward, Markasev sat quiet in his chair. He listened to the sound of the baroness's breathing, which was broken and forced. In a moment he decided she was weeping. She turned toward the window, then sat down on the bed and put her arms around her knees. Her face was turned away.

"Are you hungry?" he asked after a little while. When he said nothing, he got up to clear the table. He wiped their dishes with a greasy rag, and wrapped up the food she hadn't eaten. When he was finished, he saw her lying back against the pillows, and he imagined she had fallen asleep. He stood drinking his warm beer, then made a nest for himself on the round carpet and blew out the light.

BUT THE BARONESS was not asleep. Nor was she thinking about Spitz or Hans Greuben. But in her mind's eye she was looking at her son's small, handsome face, his smile when he said her name—the first word she had ever heard him speak. Now it seemed obvious to her that there was nothing wrong with him, that nothing ever had been wrong—a slow learner, as she had said when she was pleading with her husband. She herself had scarcely spoken until she was four years old.

Or had she pleaded, really? She'd been twenty-four when he was born. Her husband had brought in doctor after doctor, and maybe she'd been cowed by the unanimous insistence of those old men. But now she had to admit she'd been relieved at first and even glad to be rid of the whole sniveling, puking mess—the evidence that her husband had once lain with her. And more than once. No doubt it had been easy for her to believe the child was damaged in some way.

Now she couldn't sleep. She put the jewel on her bedside table. She lay on her back, chewing her nails, listening to Markasev's even breath. And at first light she imagined she and Markasev would have to leave, perhaps even leave the city.

But in the morning she woke after a strange dream, and found she was feeling none of the same urgency. She lay in bed, which was not her habit. She sent Markasev out to buy cigarettes and the newspapers, and then sat smoking and reading by the window. The story didn't appear until the afternoon, in a small box on the second page. It retold the story of the murder of Claude Spitz the jeweler, how a servant of the Baroness Ceausescu (since absconded) had confessed to the crime. Then it added this new complication: Someone else had come forward to claim responsibility. A German national, he had begged to be locked up, had refused the protection of the German embassy. He had provided the police with evidence from the scene of the crime, as well as details never reported in the press.

That day the German ambassador protested, claiming that the man had been tortured by the Siguranta. Antonescu made a public apology, promised to intervene. But the ambassador took the night train to Berlin. And shortly before dawn, five regiments of German cavalry crossed the border near the town of Kaposvar.

12 The Wendigo

AND IN NORTH AMERICA, Peter and Miranda sat together at the entrance to the cave. They were hungry. Peter squatted among the boulders, rubbing his unequal hands together.

"If he took the boat," said Miranda, "then he's already gone. Even so we've got to follow him, because there's nothing to eat. Andromeda has hurt her leg. How do you feel?"

"Better." Peter scratched at the hair on the back of his big right hand. "I feel better."

The previous morning, when he had first woken on his sweaty tangle of blankets in the entrance to the cave, he had lain quietly for many minutes, too exhausted to move. Miranda was there, and she had hugged him and kissed him on the forehead and the cheeks. He was surprised by this, by the way she touched him; at times she was in tears.

His fever had broken during the night. The spots on his chest and face were gone. But he was too weak to move—all day he was too weak. Miranda sat with him talking, and she held his hand and washed his face. Sometimes she got up to call for Andromeda or Raevsky.

Later the yellow dog came in, mauled and bitten on her neck and paws, because she'd met some larger animal that night. She limped over to put her head in Miranda's lap. Miranda had dug her hands in the thick fur, hugged the dog's head until she whimpered.

Later, toward evening, when Peter had struggled to his feet and gone outside, he found Miranda standing among the rocks. And when she saw him, new tears came to her eyes. "What's wrong?" he asked her, and she shook her head. "What's wrong?" he said again, and she relented, smiled.

"I dreamt I was twenty years old," she told him.

She said she wanted to find Raevsky's footprints, and after fifteen minutes he followed her a little way into the trees. Weak and exhausted, he stood next to a birch tree. He was surprised to see her at the bottom of an odd, small dell, taking her clothes off in the snow. She was only fifty feet away, but she didn't see him. He stood breathless, without moving, and watched her peering into a circle of ice between two trees as if it were a mirror; the sun had not yet set. Then she took off the old Gypsy's bulky coat, and lifted her shirt up so her skin was bare. She was touching and pressing at her breasts. Her back was partly toward him, and he couldn't see. She was looking at her hands, and she undid the front of her pants and turned away from him completely, and he could see the arch of her back as she leaned to examine herself, as he imagined.

Because her coat was off and he could see her body, he felt a new embarrassment. He looked down, and there was the yellow dog beside him.

She had limped up through the snow to stand beside him on the edge of the small dell. The hair rose from her back, and Peter had listened to her low, soft growl. She'd turned her heavy head, pulled back her lips to reveal their pink underside. Peter had known that if he moved or spoke, the dog would have bitten him.

Afterward, Miranda had built a fire, had lain down beside him in the cold. In the morning he had woken up alone. Now, squatting by the fire, he told the truth. "I feel better," he said, though he was hungry, of course. "I had such nightmares."

Miranda's face took on a stricken look. "I dreamt I was twenty years old," she said again, as she had the day before. She stared at him for a long moment—the hugs and kisses were all gone.

She stood up and rubbed her palms on her dirty black jeans. "We'll stay tonight," she said. "You rest up—we couldn't reach the river before nightfall, anyway. If there's a storm, I don't want to get caught out in the open. The thing is, though, we've nothing to eat."

"Which way is the river?" Peter asked.

She shrugged. "The jerk left a trail."

But in the afternoon the jerk came back, lugging a canvas bag. When Miranda hid his boat, she'd kept some supplies in it, which the wild men hadn't found. These included some biscuits and a long gun for hunting—Raevsky had shot an animal on the way. He'd hung the body in a tree a few miles from the camp, and while Miranda put up the canvas tent, he and Peter went to look for it.

The previous morning, Miranda had had to lift a bowl of melted snow for Peter to drink. But now he felt his strength returning and, unwarrantably, his good spirits. For the whole time since he'd arrived in these woods, he'd been sick to his stomach. But maybe the fever had burned that sickness out of him. Now he felt stronger, purified by hunger as he slogged behind Raevsky in the afternoon light, through the small birches. His heart thudded in his chest, and the snow dragged at his boots. He stopped for a moment and breathed deep.

Suddenly he felt like laughing, throwing snowballs at Raevsky's retreating back, and there was no reason for it. They were still lost. Splaa and Rodica and the others were still dead. But he wasn't afraid of Raevsky any more. He wasn't afraid of hunger or the future. He found himself mumbling part of a poem that his mother had taught him:

"Away to the hills, to the caves, to the rocks—
  Ere I own a usurper, I'll couch with the fox;
  And tremble, false Whigs, in the midst of your glee,
  You have not seen the last of my bonnet and me!"

As he chanted these words, he found his feet had picked up the rhythm, and he caught up to Raevsky in the wet snow. He was gratified to see the captain turn his head and pause—was that a frightened expression on his swollen face? It was! The old man put up his hand to make a sign against the evil eye. How did Peter recognize the gesture, which he'd never seen? Raevsky stood panting, out of breath in the long light.

"No closer," he said, putting out his hand. "So, you are what I cannot understand. Two times, you are a dead man."

He swallowed his breathing down. Peter and he stood face to face. "I thought she was alone," Raevsky said. "I thought I will find your corpse. She was sick, that was my fear. What will I tell my lady?"

His left eye was surrounded by a black ring. The eye itself was covered with a red, sticky film. Again Peter found himself smiling. In his mind he caught a glimpse of Miranda with her shirt hiked up, examining her slender waist and mottled rib cage, her skin covered with goose bumps, he imagined.

The captain had shot some kind of big monkey, and had hung it from a leather strap up in a tree. It was a shame—there was another smaller monkey that had climbed into the branches and was chattering at them as they slogged up. When Raevsky pulled out his long revolver, the little monkey started to scream, and scurried down the far side of the tree. Peter saw it watching from a distance as they unstrapped the big, hairy body and let it fall.

"So," Raevsky said. "I know what this is. This is the wendigo. Ishu told me the story. So, my men are gone. Now I am cursed and damned."

He seemed to share in Peter's giddiness. He clapped his hands together, and in the snow he made a capering little dance.

Peter was the one who dragged the stiff body. In some places it glided over the snow. At other places where the undergrowth was thick, Peter had to hoist it up and carry it. Still he felt happy to use his muscles. The old man went in front.

They made good time, and in an hour they were back. The air was warmer, and Miranda had built a fire away from the rock face, with a big pile of new wood that she had gathered in their absence. She had pitched Raevsky's tent. The yellow dog was snarling at the body of the ape, which Peter flung down in a bare place on the stones away from the fire. The old man was rummaging in the canvas bag, and now as darkness gathered he came forward with a bottle and a knife. He took a drink of what smelled to Peter like good Turkish ouzo, but he didn't offer it around. Instead he squatted down over the corpse and expertly, immediately, began to butcher it. He skinned away the heavy pelt and cut big chunks of gray, greasy meat out of the chest and thighs. The black blood stained the snow.

Peter went back to the fire. He didn't want to look. But the high spirits that had sustained him were flagging now, and he felt weak from hunger. He sat with Miranda, and they ate biscuits and stared at each other until Raevsky came back. He'd cut sticks of green wood to serve as skewers, and Peter and he roasted the meat and ate it, and Peter had never tasted anything so good. He burned his fingers, burned his mouth on the tough, sinewy, disgusting lumps of flesh.

The dog wouldn't touch it, and neither would Miranda, so there was more for them. Andromeda curled up ostentatiously in the entrance to the cave. Peter could see her eyes shining in the darkness when he turned around. Miranda and the old man were arguing about Albany, but Peter found he didn't care much about that. It seemed a tired, stale old argument. After a while he wiped his fingers in the snow and on his pants, and drew from his pocket his harmonica, which his uncle had given him in Greeneville.

He could smell the ouzo across the fire, but he wasn't going to ask for it. Instead he cooled his mouth with snow, then spat it out and began to play— whisper music at first, but then a tune. And the tune suggested an old song that he'd learned so long ago he couldn't remember. His mother had been born in Quebec, and had taught him some French nursery songs by rote. He didn't speak any French. But after a few moments he lifted his mouth from the harmonica.

"I don't want to discuss it." Miranda said. "I want you to get us to Albany. Will you do that one thing, finally, after all the harm you've caused? Don't you owe me that?"

Raevsky said, "I have lost five men and my sister's son. I was beaten by those savages and did not tell the dark from light." He shrugged and muttered, "Do not talk to me."

Miranda had cut a strip of birch bark and made a map, drawing on the white surface with a piece of charred wood. "That's right, isn't it?" she said after a moment, pointing toward the west where the sun had set.

"There is nothing you must fear," protested the old man. "She means not to harm you, I swear on my parole. She is . . ." He looked up, his eyes bleary with drink.

He looked across the fire at Peter. And then he started to clap his right hand against the bottle in his left, in rhythm to Peter's song. He knew the words, too, and he started to sing. In a moment he grinned, and Peter could see where he was missing some of his back teeth. His face gleamed red in the firelight, and there was juice or liquor in his beard.

"So," he said. "Gypsy singing from Baia Mare. So, I am eating meat from the wendigo, and drinking with a dead man. Truly my life is over. At first I thought you were too young, but now I see it in your face. I am drinking with the Chevalier de Graz."

He raised the bottle. Peter felt a shudder in his chest. He bent again to the harmonica. The steel was cold against his teeth. But the instrument was more responsive now that he was playing it for the first time with his new hand. He could do a lot more things with it.

Later, when the fire had burned down, he lay down in the tent with Miranda and couldn't sleep. She had gone to bed early, but he had walked into the darkness a short way, and climbed up by the rocks onto the ridge to see if he could catch a glimpse of the new moon.

When he came slipping down again, the old man had already passed out. He was curled in his feather bag, huddled among the rocks beside the fire. The bottle lay beside him, carefully corked, and Peter paused to open it and savor the well-remembered scent. He cleaned out his mouth with a big, burning swallow, then stoppered the bottle again and laid it down.

The tent was an ordinary pup-tent—rectangular, with a peaked roof supported by two poles. The flaps were untied. Peter crawled into the tent, then sat down to undo his boots. In the almost complete darkness, he was aware of Miranda's smell. In his mind he pictured her as he had seen her the previous morning. Then he groped among the blankets so he could feel where she lay. She was asleep, he decided.

He lay down without undressing, and put his hands behind his head. He listened to the thumping of his heart. But he must have dozed off, because in the middle of the night he woke, disoriented, to find some more light in the small tent. He raised himself on one elbow, imagining the old man had built the fire up again. There was a glow outside that he could see through the canvas wall. And there were shadows of movement, too. He saw the shadow of the dog as it passed between the fire and the tent.

Miranda was in a sleeping bag, her face uncovered in a nest of tangled hair. He examined her in the fire's filtered glow, her straight, narrow nose, her delicate black eyebrows, her small, protruding ears. A lock of hair lay across her lips, trembling when she breathed. The shadow of the dog passed quickly over the canvas wall.

THE BARONESS CEAUSESCU spent that day in the rooming house behind the university. In the evening she sent Kevin Markasev into the streets to purchase groceries. He stood in the shadows when he returned, a paper bag in his hands. "You know there's a crowd of people in the Strada Inocentei," he said. "There were students giving speeches in the park. These things were hard to find."

The baroness wore a sleeveless cashmere vest over a white shirt. Around her neck there was a tiny golden chain, just visible in the lamplight. She wore black trousers and leather boots, which left a mark on the bedsheets. She wasn't listening to Markasev. Instead she was reading the agony column in the *Roumania Libera*: "Stay away. The numbers are seven and seventeen. M."

And another: "Don't you see how you have broken my heart? I will always remember. Meet me at the clock tower at five. All is not lost. Carlos."

And a third: "Madame La Baronne. The boy is already in Germany, where he is cared for. I make no bargains with thieves, and in the current crisis you will find it impossible to hide. Give me what I want. The stations and the gates are watched. Every day I expect to hear of your surrender." Then there was a small coronet printed above the initials T.G.R.

That morning the baroness had sent a letter to the Elector of Ratisbon, at his suite in the Athenée Palace Hotel. In it she'd proposed a simple swap, and indicated how to reach her. This was his response.

She threw the paper aside and leaned back against the iron bars of the bed. There was a package of cigarettes on the side table, and a paper-covered book of one-act plays. In the ashtray was her husband's signet ring, the pig of Cluj. Beside it, on the stained wood, lay the tourmaline, shining softly in the glow of the lamp.

She laid her head back on the pillows and lit a cigarette. Holding it between her lips, she undid her gold cufflinks and rolled up her cuffs, exposing her small forearms and bony wrists. She was a beautiful woman, but her hands were not beautiful. She had big, raw knuckles, and nails that were bitten till they bled.

"The university has closed," said Markasev. Every day his speech was clearer and more complicated: "The miners are on strike. Trifa and the others are all free. People are drinking and playing music. They've let your servant go. You know, that man who used to bring me food."

THE BARONESS SAID nothing to this. She took another swallow of smoke, and let it out in a slow stream. Abruptly she turned to him, and he could hear her soft, harsh voice. "Did you get what I wanted?"

"Yes, but it was hard to find."

"Give it to me."

He came to her bedside, and she moved her legs so he could sit. From the paper bag he drew a bottle of Egyptian whiskey. She put the cigarette into the metal ashtray, and took the bottle from his hand.

She uncorked it, and he could smell it. There was a wineglass on the table, and she poured some whiskey into it and put the bottle down. She did not drink. The whiskey in the glass was amber-colored and the smell was sweet.

"What else?" she said.

He took out a box of twelve brass cartridges. The baroness drew up her knee to show a revolver in a leather case under a fold of the quilt.

"Pick it up," she said.

There was still a bottle of milk in the paper bag, and some soft old apples. He put the bag down onto the floor beside the bed, but did not reach his hand out for the gun. He knew nothing about guns. This one was strapped into its leather case. He could see the drum was empty.

The baroness pushed it toward him with her boot. "It was my husband's," she said.

Still he didn't pick it up. She had lifted her body from the pillows until her face was near his. He inhaled, and under the smell of whiskey and tobacco he could smell her bitter smell.

"We have enemies," she said.

He couldn't think of any. Their landlady was kind to them. People in the building and on the street—they smiled and waved.

"One enemy," she said.

In her husband's laboratory, sometimes she had sat this close. That was good, and he remembered. She was the lady of comfort and tears, and she had brought him things to eat, and fed him with her own beautiful hands. Sometimes he had put his head onto her lap.

Now abruptly she got up, pushed him away. She walked back and forth across the narrow floor, and then threw open the door onto the landing. Her coat hung from a hook; she seized it and her small student's cap. "Come," she said, and led him down the stairs into the crowded street. And it was true—there were no enemies that he could see. It was a cold night, but people laughed and talked as if it were midsummer. They sat on the steps of their houses. The baroness walked with her hands in her pockets, and she led him through the streets around the university, and then north through the Field of Mars into the Piata Revolutiei. They saw soldiers of the metropolitan police, and also German staff officers in uniform, particularly as they approached the Athenée Palace Hotel. All the lamps were lit, and in the portico of the restaurant stood five men smoking cigarettes, dressed in the black boots and the black raincoats of the German diplomatic corps.

"There," said the baroness, pointing. "Potato eaters. They laugh at us in our own city." Then on the tramway platform, she pointed out the undercover policeman slouching in the corner, a newspaper stuffed into the pocket of his coat. "They are everywhere," she said. "I can do nothing. You know they will arrest me if they find me."

That was the end of it, and they went home. As usual, he walked behind her, and he could see the people turn aside to watch her as she passed. When he was back in their snug room, he watched her drink a glass of whiskey on the bed. It seemed to make her body hot, and she stripped off her cashmere vest, unbuttoned the buttons of her man's shirt, so that sometimes when she moved he caught a glimpse of her small breasts. She held the tourmaline in her hand, and once she pressed it against her forehead as if to cool herself. She scarcely spoke, but left him standing in the middle of the room on the dirty rug, a small coiled circle of rags. While he stood there she turned out the light, and he could hear her taking off her shirt in the dark. By the time his eyes became accustomed to the dim, reflected light, she had drawn up the sheet and turned away from him.

The next day she took him to the Gara de Nord, and together they watched the first trainloads of German troops come in. They looked more like policemen than soldiers of the regular army. Their only weapons were the pistols underneath their long coats. They were bareheaded, or wore soft, billed caps. Only the officers wore the ridiculous spiked helmets of the propaganda posters, which had lined the wooden fences of the railway yard until the week before.

"If he knew who I was, then he would have me locked away," murmured the baroness, indicating an old officer on crutches. She took Markasev by the arm as they walked. "These places are for Germans now and not for us. If they weren't watching, we could leave the city. As it is, they have us trapped."

These were dark words, but Kevin Markasev felt nothing but happiness. All around him he could feel an energy and gaiety, as if the political crisis had resolved all private quarrels. Lovers embraced shamelessly on street corners, and old married couples walked hand in hand. The shops were open late, and they were crowded, as if everyone had money to spend. The coffee shops, especially, were packed and brightly lit, the billiard rooms and public houses overflowed. There was a curfew that was universally ignored. The streets were full of children, though it was past their bedtime. Provocatively dressed young women wandered through the crowd, offering smiles and kisses to strangers.

That night the baroness allowed him to walk beside her, and it was only when they turned into the Strada Iuliu that she let go his arm. Later, in their attic room, she again permitted him to sit beside her on the bed, as she showed him how to load the revolver, how to hold it in his hand.

"There is a man who has stolen my heart," she told him. "Kidnapped my son. Stolen him from his bed. Oh, there is such cruelty in this world!"

Tears glittered in her eyes. Swallowing his fears, he put down the gun. Her white shirt was unbuttoned, and she smelled of sweat. Her shoulders and her neck were damp with bitter sweat. She turned her mouth away. "Hush, child, hush," she whispered. She had seized his wrist in her left hand, but her right fist against his chest pushed him away. He could see that she was weeping, and the quiet tears ran down her face, and she could not be comforted, at least by him.

The tourmaline lay in the rumpled bedsheets, glinting like a glass eye. The baroness released him and he stood up. Wordlessly, she indicated the small nest of pillows and bolsters where he slept at the foot of her bed. Then she took her boots off. Then as she had the night before, she extinguished the lamp and stood up suddenly to undress. He heard the shirt fall, the buttons of her trousers give way, and while he blinked in the darkness he was sure that she was standing naked, or else in her underclothes. And as before, by the time his eyes adjusted, she had slipped into the bed and turned away from him.

He stood for several minutes, and then lay down on his pillows with his head under the blanket. In time he wondered if she was asleep. But she was not. He uncovered his face and listened to her quiet, harsh voice: "Theodore von Geiss und Ratisbon. You will know him by his face. He had the smallpox. Every morning after breakfast he stands in the entrance of the hotel, distributing five-franc pieces to the prostitutes—it is a ritual. An event, like the ringing of the bells in the temple of Mars."

ON THE NIGHT of the German ambassador's ultimatum, the Elector of Ratisbon had gone to Targu Mures, to meet with influential members of the German minority in Transylvania. But he was able to catch a train back to Bucharest, and in the German-language newspaper he had read the story of the crowds turning out to welcome the advancing troops, pelting them with pine cones and pieces of bread. At second hand he was able to witness the collapse of the Roumanian army. Entire divisions surrendered to inferior forces or else refused to fight.

He read about the demonstrations in the Piata Revolutiei. Like everyone, he was thrilled to hear of the destruction of the Siguranta headquarters and the release of Zelea Codreanu, Valerian Trifa, and other political prisoners. The rapidity of these events astounded Europe. A truce was declared in a few days, though in the mountains there were places of resistance. Trifa and the others were negotiating with the German government.

They had promised to arrange the abdication of Valeria Dragonesti, which the elector thought was a foolish idea.

From his hotel balcony he could see into the square. All night the area around the Winter Keep was packed with people, and the atmosphere seemed oddly celebratory. There were no fights, no counterdemonstrations, for which the elector was grateful. Since Kaposvar, he had detested violence.

Yet in his happiness, as always, there was a grain of discontent. These men negotiating with Trifa—he was not among them. Always his position in Roumania had been unofficial, dependent on a network of relationships, and now he found himself excluded. The new ambassador was not his friend, nor were any of the people newly arrived from Berlin. As for the military officers—he had grown accustomed to their polite contempt. They had not forgiven him for his failure years before.

Along with his message to the baroness in the *Libera*, the elector had written a letter of protest to the German foreign secretary, offering his continued service to his country. He expected a reply in a few days, but in the meantime he found himself with nothing to do. Muffled in a sheepskin coat, he stood before dawn on his hotel balcony with a schnapps and soda in his gloved hand, and let his thoughts return into the darkness past Codfish Bay. It was an idle reflex at first, a trick of the mind, until he saw the fog had dissipated to the west. Whatever protection Schenck von Schenck had managed to provide her niece, now it was gone. The whole expanse of the dark forest lay before him, west to the Henry Hudson River.

Eagerly he scanned it and saw nothing. His eye roamed back and forth, searching for a sign. The mist hung in clumps in the valleys until the wind blew it away, revealing the fold of the Hoosick River. South of the stream, below a rocky ridge, a single campfire burned.

BUT IT WAS ASHES in the morning when Peter woke up. He crawled out through the tent flap and saw her standing by the ashes of the fire. The dog was with her. "He's not here," she said.

She meant the old man, Raevsky. His sleeping bag was empty, and the bottle lay broken on the stones. "I've been waiting for an hour and he hasn't come back."

Miranda had brushed her hair and braided it. She stood with her boots on, but without her sweater or her coat, wearing instead a baggy, short-sleeved shirt he hadn't seen before. She must have pilfered it from Raevsky's supplies. It was a cold morning, but her arms were wet, as if she had been washing in the snow.

"Did he go hunting?" Peter asked.

She pointed to the long gun leaning up among the boulders. Then she knelt down over the cinders of the fire, blowing them alive and feeding them with slivers of wood.

Peter watched her for a moment. He rubbed his dirty teeth with his right forefinger, then turned aside to spit. The monkey meat, so delicious the night before, now felt queasy in his stomach. He looked up to where the corpse had lain—it too was gone.

They made a breakfast of dry biscuits and hot water, boiled in Raevsky's old tin pot. The dog's foot was better, and she had gone away into the trees. In time she appeared again among the birches, and barked softly in her bizarre, quasi-human way—a sound like a man clearing his throat. They got up to follow her. Miranda took the gun.

The dog led them through the woods until they found an open patch of snow below the rocks. The snow had a crust, because it had hardened and softened several times. Peter could see where the old man's heavy boots had punctured it, making a series of dark holes. But there were other marks as well.

Above the crust there was a layer of light, dry, powdered snow. Perhaps a quarter of an inch had fallen during the night. In it Peter could see the footprints of another creature, an animal not heavy enough to punch through the crust.

The little, handlike marks were plain—it was another monkey. Peter bent down to examine the print of the small, naked pads, the long toes and nails, which decorated the snow between Raevsky's boot marks. The trail was clear across a stretch of open ground. But in the conifers on the far side, under the tall trees where the snow was thinner, it vanished.

In silence Peter and Miranda spread out among the trees, while Andromeda ran around them in a circle, nose to the snow. They came together again, still without speaking, and trooped back to the fire.

"Well," Miranda said, staring down into the low flames. "Now it's just us."

During these days, Peter had been drained of his capacity to feel astonished, and he imagined it was the same for Miranda. She stood with her hands in her pockets. The air was cold, and she had put on Blind Rodica's coat.

"It's time to move," she said. "We've got some freedom now."

"What do you mean?"

She turned up the collar around her face, and tucked her hair inside the coat. "I don't know," she said. "It feels weird. Maybe they're leaving us alone."

Her hands, when she took them out of her coat pockets, were raw and chapped. She rubbed them together, then knelt down and warmed them at the fire. "I mean we have to find a way to save ourselves. We can make choices for ourselves. We don't have to go to Albany. We don't have to show up in Roumania at all. I'm not even sure they'll be so glad to see me anymore."

"Doesn't your aunt live there?"

"I don't think so. I don't know. Germany would make more sense—Ratisbon, maybe. Where would you like to go?"

"Florida," he said, and she smiled.

"My grandparents have a condo in Palm Beach," she said. "What the heck."

They spoke with a mixture of lightness and seriousness, then and later as they made their plans. They would wait one day for Raevsky, and in the morning they would leave. They wouldn't try to find the hunters or the wild men. There was no reason to expect a good reception in either place. And with the number of biscuits they had, they couldn't waste time looking and risk getting lost. Raevsky's map was a simple one, and maybe he had left more food by the river. In the morning they would go and find the boat.

"What do you know about the wendigo?" Peter asked, but Miranda shook her head. These days when she didn't want to talk about something, she just ignored him.

"It's a ghost, isn't it—is that what you saw? That night above the camp . . ."

"We'll go someplace warm," she said. "I guess New York is a real town. Rachel used to take me to New York about once a year, when Dad was busy with his grading. We'd stay with her sister. We'd go to movies and musicals on Broadway."

They sat side by side among the rocks. Whole subjects seemed erased, blacked out, like the dark places on an ancient map.

"When I was sick," he said, "I must have been a little crazy. There's a moment I thought I was going to die."

She shrugged.

He was venturing into a dark place on the map. "I remember how you were," he said. "When I was sick."

She had given him water, washed his face, lain down with him. She had slept beside him and never left him. Still there was a barrier between them, which maybe they had brought to this world from the other one. "If I had died," he said, "do you think I would have ended up at home?"

She didn't answer. He let some time go by before he spoke. "I used to think if I were normal, if I just had two hands like other people, then there'd be nothing I couldn't do," he said. "Anything I wanted, I could have. It doesn't matter. I don't think you're telling me the truth."

"About what?"

He stopped, then started again: "Choices for ourselves. Is that what you think, that you're free from all this crap all of a sudden?"

Miranda didn't look up. Finally she spoke. "It's just I'm not sure they're going to welcome me now. Even if my aunt is still alive. Before, it was like playing a game of chess. But no, you're right. Part of me still thinks I've got to go to Albany and find this man Ion Dreyfoos. And if I don't, then terrible things are going to happen."

Peter stretched his right hand to the fire. "And what about me?"

She looked at him now. "I'm hoping you'll come. I always hope you'll come."

Why was she so stingy? She made him angry. Always from the beginning she had thought she was too good to be even his friend, let alone anything more. Or else he was the one who was convinced of that.

He flexed his fingers, examined the dark hair on the back of his hand. He had a birthmark in the lap of muscle near his thumb, a shape like a rabbit with its long ears. "I think you're fooling yourself," he said at last. "And anyway this princess thing has gotten out of hand."

Miranda stared at him pugnaciously. Her jaw was set, her lips were closed. But in a moment she was smiling. She brushed a strand of hair back from her wide forehead, then rubbed her nose. "Whatever happens," she said, "I want you to be with me. You and Andromeda. Will you promise?"

He didn't promise. He didn't have to. Instead he stared into the flame. "That old man Raevsky called me something more than once. Degrats, or something. Do you know anything about that?"

"I don't know anything about that," she said, too carefully.

Then she went on: "I know who you are. That's who I want you to be, because that's who I am, too. This place has its hook in all of us. That doesn't mean we can forget what's most important."

Above them on the rocks, Andromeda started to whimper. She stood facing into the line of trees. Peter glanced that way and realized he was looking at Raevsky, who was standing between two birches perhaps a hundred feet away. He was swaying on his feet. Then slowly he came forward. And Peter could see there was a small animal beside him that was holding his hand, pulling him into a crouch while it slid forward on its ass. Peter looked, and looked again, and realized what he saw. It was the creature that had crossed in front of him and Miranda and Andromeda that night as they came down toward the fire on Christmas Hill.

Yes, there it was, the same naked belly, round head, and lidless eyes. It led the old man for a few steps, then paused as he stumbled forward by himself.

Peter got to his feet. Miranda got up. Andromeda stood above them on three legs. And none of them moved as they watched the old man shuffle through the broken crusts of snow—barefoot, they could see that now.

Behind him, the animal had climbed back into the shelter of the birches. It stood watching for a moment and then disappeared. The sun was down behind the trees.

Miranda put her hand out. The old man hobbled toward them step by step. He was mumbling and muttering. Peter could hear the words.

The dog whimpered and snarled. It was the end of the afternoon, and the light was fading. Miranda took a step forward.

"Blestematele de picioare"—my damned feet, whispered the old man.

His feet looked burned—blackened and filthy, and covered with some kind of grease. His hands, too, were split and raw. His cheeks were bloody, and his face was chapped and wind-burned.

"*Picioarele mele arzande,*" he said.

They sat him down on his own sleeping bag. He seemed scarcely to recognize them. But when they came close, he tried to seize hold of them with his still-powerful hands, as if through touch and proximity he could remind himself. "*Imi pare rau,*" he said. I'm so sorry for it.

They wrapped his feet in blankets and gave him water to drink. He sat huddled by the fire, his hands clasped around a tin cup. Peter sat with him while Miranda took the gun and went out with Andromeda into the woods. Peter didn't want to leave her alone with Raevsky. They were gone about half an hour. But they discovered nothing except Raevsky's boots, which Miranda laid out on the warm stones. In the meantime, the old man's head nodded. Peter helped him to the tent and laid him down. But he could not be left alone. He seized hold of Peter's hand and wouldn't let go until he fell asleep.

IN THE MORNING he had made a strange recovery. He shook Peter awake and whispered in his ear. "We must leave," he said—he had recovered his English. "Come, we must leave this place."

Peter smelled his stinking breath. "So, I will survive like you," said the old man. "Nothing kills me. I can live beyond my time."

He climbed out of the tent into the dawn light, and when Peter followed he was sitting by the ashes of the fire with his pant legs pulled up to his knees. He picked and rubbed at his feet, which were covered with scabs. With great care, he dabbed them with liquid from a small glass bottle. Then he drew on two pairs of socks, one cotton and one wool, and eased his feet into his stubborn boots. "So, you see," he grunted, and then labored to stand up.

Once on his feet, he moved with a combination of stiffness and spryness that was painful to watch. But he was anxious to be gone. "So, I take you to Albany. Albany first. Then we will talk about the rest. Today. Tonight. Tomorrow. In Albany we eat with human food."

Miranda's hair was tangled and she was yawning, and rubbing at her face. She had spent a cold night in the cave. She was moving slowly, and it was strange to see her standing in a patch of sunlight as the sun broke through the clouds, yawning stupidly while Raevsky struck camp. He hopped and capered as if every step hurt him, as if by arching his back and raising his shoulders he could put less weight on his sore feet. He ripped apart the tent and stowed it in the boat bag, along with the bedding and the tarpaulin, and everything he had brought up from the river.

They were ready before Miranda had properly woken up. Peter hoisted the bag onto his back. It made a clumsy burden—a canvas duffel bag, and Peter put his arms through the loop handles as if they were the straps on a backpack. Miranda and Raevsky had an argument about the gun, but finally he allowed her to carry it. He went in front, and led them with crazy swiftness through the woods. When they reached the place where he had shot the ape, he led them in a wide half circle, Peter noticed, and down a rocky ravine on the far side. They passed between two bald hillsides. Then there was a long slog to the valley.

In the afternoon they reached the bend in the river where Miranda and Raevsky had camped. The flat-bottomed boat was waiting for them, drawn up on a black layer of pine needles under the tall trees. Miranda was tired, and so they sat down for a meal of biscuits and water while the old man unlaced his boots. He drew his feet out, and rewrapped them in cloth strips soaked from his little bottle, all the time crooning and mumbling in Roumanian. His battered fingers trembled not so much from fatigue as from suppressed excitement, and his voice was gasping and high. Altogether the change in him was astonishing, when Peter remembered the grim soldier who had surprised them at the ice house with his men. Now he was like a madman—his face and hands were never still, and he picked at his lips and beard. Nor could he rest until he'd loaded up the boat again and loaded them aboard, and stepped gingerly from the overhanging bank into the stern, and pushed them away.

The pirogue was heavily loaded with the three of them and the dog. The current was swift, and divided often between low sandbanks lined with the trunks of broken trees.

They went on for an hour or so. "Stop," said Miranda as the light grew dim. "There's a place." She was in the bow, and she paddled them to shore beside a beach of sand and stones, ignoring the entreaties of the old man to go faster, farther. "We'll camp here," she said. "It'll be too dark to see."

The decision was the only sensible one, as in places the water was shallow enough to rip the bottom from their boat. In other places there were hidden snags. Abruptly the old man finished arguing, and as the boat came to the bank he leapt ashore, and started to build camp with the same frantic and unhealthy energy. They had stopped on a wide, curving strand of pebbles and small stones, and immediately he started to clear a place in the bare sand, flinging the stones into the water. Then he and Peter pitched the tent while Miranda gathered wood and lit a fire.

Andromeda had a rabbit to eat, but the rest of them had biscuits for supper— biscuits Raevsky had bought for his men in Bremerhaven. They were flat, hard, and indestructible, each baked with the image of the German lion. Peter and Miranda soaked them in hot water. But for their hunger, they would not have been able to swallow them down, and even so, Peter's gorge and stomach seemed to resist every mouthful. But Raevsky sat crosslegged on the sand, cracking the hard strips between his teeth.

Later he heated water in a biscuit tin to wash his face and neck and beard. He laid out a bar of soap on a flat rock. He rubbed his hair with a ragged towel. All the time he was humming a song, the same song Peter had played on his harmonica two nights before. Peter's mother had taught it to him:

Radu Mamii nu mai bea
Uite potera colea
Insa Radu n-asculta
Potera-I-conjura . . .

After the old man had scoured his face red, he sat down on the rocks with them and rubbed his hands together. "So," he said. "I must not go to sleep."

When Peter asked him why, he shook his head. "The wendigo! I saw the wendigo! I shot the big one, but there was the small one, and I saw it run away. But I was hunting with a dead man, drinking with a dead man. De Graz, tell me what you see? I saw a fire shining and a wind blowing, and my lady. No, I did not see her, but I heard her voice. Is strange I came awake to follow? Is strange so I am waiting for this night? Why did she run from me in the cold snow? I did not see. My lady has bright hair that is red and brown. Eyes are blue and dark. Skin so clean, body so clean, thin like a boy. Now I see her so, as she was when I said good-bye at the Gara de Nord. I kissed her hand! She wore no gloves. I could smell something on her wrist. She wore no coat, but a small coat and trousers like a boy. I would die for her, I think, but so I am the last who did not die. All they died for her except for me. So I was like a ghost who can feel nothing, and I was walking in the snow without my shoes. I thought I heard her voice. Maybe she will come again tonight."

He talked like this for quite a long time. Miranda rolled her eyes. She had put up a second tent not far away, and she stood beside it brushing her hair while the old man talked. Then she was making a small pantomime of tiredness. She yawned, tilted her head, closed her eyes, and put her folded hands together next to her cheek. She mimicked a snoring noise, then waved and crawled inside her tent.

Two nights before, with Raevsky passed out by the fire, it had seemed natural for her and Peter to sleep in the one tent. The next night, Raevsky had been injured. It was just as natural to put him under shelter, and he hadn't let go of Peter's hand. Trudging to the river, Peter had been hoping they could go back to the first arrangement. But when they reached the boat, among the supplies they had found there, Miranda had picked out a second tent.

Now he found himself wondering if he should try to follow her inside, or even if her snoring noise and little wave had been an invitation. How could you know these things for sure? He sat up for a while longer, listening to the old man sing:

> "'Stop drinking, my dear son.
> I fear the soldiers will come for you.'
> But Radu wasn't listening . . ."

13   *Dr. Theodore*

LATER THAT NIGHT THE BARONESS Ceausescu sat on her bed, looking out the window into the dark street. Beside her on the coverlet lay two of the afternoon newspapers, *Roumania Libera* and the *Evenimentul Zilei*. Both presented on their second page a description of the same event. According to one, an unknown anarchist had made a reckless and murderous attack on a German officer. According to the other, a nameless patriot had struck a blow for freedom.

Yet the details were the same. At first light a young man had approached a group of soldiers near the Athenée Palace Hotel. Without provocation he had shot and killed Herr Sergeant-Colonel Boris Blum, liaison to the Second Army. The *Zilei* gave some biographical information: He was a native of Danzig, two years from retirement, and the father of eight boys, four from each of his two wives. He was well loved and admired by subordinates and superiors.

The baroness put her thumb over the sketch of a fat-faced officer with a handlebar moustache. The paper trembled in her hands as she reread the description of the young man's arrest. He was being held in one of the station houses of the metropolitan police. He had not revealed the names of his accomplices. There was no letter in his pocket, no identity card, nothing to suggest who he was or why he did what he had done.

That day, waiting for Markasev to return, the baroness had spent her time in bed, chewing her fingers and smoking cigarettes. She had not dared to go into the street. In the evening she had borrowed the newspapers from her landlady, who had knocked upon her door. Now she lay back against the pillows, holding the *Roumania Libera* folded into thirds in her left hand, while with her right she fumbled for the tourmaline inside the dirty bed-sheets.

She was conscious of a sudden feeling of relief. If the papers had lied, if the boy had given her up, surely the police would have found her by now. All evening she had waited for the sound of their footsteps on the stairs.

Now she grasped the jewel and touched it to her forehead and her eyes. As if the power of the stone had opened some inner gate, she felt a current of emotion. Her eyes itched, though she did not weep. Her skin was hot. A shudder of dry sobs passed through her. Fear and rage no longer could protect her from herself. In disgust, she threw the paper to the floor.

Everything she loved, everything she valued in the world was gone. Her clothes, her name, her son, her reputation, her position in society—all was gone. The Elector of Ratisbon had chased her from her house, chased her out into the streets, chased her into anonymous and disgusting lodgings where she lived hidden from the world, ashamed and afraid to show herself. The Elector of Ratisbon had threatened her with arrest, exposure, death, and sent his hired thugs to search for her.

And now the one thing she had found and kept, the boy whose life she'd saved, who had loved her and followed her and kept her from loneliness, and whom she too had loved in her own way—the elector had destroyed him as well. There was no limit to his malice or his efforts to humiliate her.

And there was no limit, finally, to her unhappiness. She, whose talents had been praised by connoisseurs all over Europe, whose palm had been kissed by the Turkish Sultan of Byzantium, was reduced now to poverty in a single, squalid room. Yes, it was true she'd made mistakes. Yes, it was true she'd been improvident and rash. Oh, she had many regrets, for which she punished herself daily. Surely that was enough, more than enough, and there was no reason to accept more punishment at the small, sexless hands of this monstrous and potato-eating man.

Sobbing, she leaned forward over her knees, holding the tourmaline in the pit of her stomach. Still she had no tears. But that was because she was not like these other women who would weep and cry and beg for mercy. No, she had resources of her own. Perhaps she could not match the skills of her great enemy. Perhaps she could not match his cold and devious mind. The symbol of his house was a banded serpent, and that was how she imagined him—crushing, relentless, slippery, and cold. But she herself had powers no one could match, an artist's passion and an artist's soul. What was it the French newspapers had said? "There is a conflagration burning on the stage of the Rivoli, fed out of a beautiful young woman's heart."

She had not lit the lamps, and the room was dark, illuminated only by reflections from the street. She held the tourmaline to her stomach. Slowly, all day and night she had been making up her mind—it was a risk, but she would take it. She would not live here like an animal in a hole, until her money ran out and she went begging in the streets. No, she would return to her husband's laboratory. She would find a way to break the serpent's grip.

She rose to her feet. She would take nothing, she decided; if she didn't come back, her landlady could accept her clothes and Markasev's in place of rent. She threw open the hall door, and in the slanting gaslight she saw his shirt hung on a hook. It was a red shirt that she had bought for him in the Lipscani market, and it hurt her to see it hanging there empty—where was the boy now? If he were to die during his interrogation, no one would claim his body, unless she did. Oh, but it would hurt her to see his body mauled and strangled (if that was what was going to happen) by the metropolitan police, in that greasy station in the third ward. Once she herself had spent a day there, arrested for soliciting when she was twelve years old.

She left the door unlocked. Quietly, carefully, in the hours before dawn, she tiptoed down the splintered stairs into the street.

IN THE MIDDLE OF THE night, Peter started awake inside his tent. Raevsky was beside him, curled up in his sleeping bag. Peter had laid down blankets over the cold sand, and at first he thought it was the cold that had woken him, along with the light from the campfire. Or was it the moon that cast a soft gray light through the canvas walls? No, the moon was still new.

Peter lay on his back. Finally, he had not dared to try Miranda's tent. Not after Andromeda had gone in. But now someone was standing next to the fire. Peter saw the shadow on the wall. Who could it be besides Miranda? Maybe she'd expected him after all.

He slipped his boots on, then got up to his knees and pushed open the tent flaps. Miranda had gathered together some big pine cones. Once Peter had gone car-camping in California with his mother and father in the old truck, and they had built fires with pine cones like this, six or eight inches long.

Miranda had thrown a pile of them onto the embers, where they burned up suddenly and spat. They cast a short-lived, garish brightness that was like a flare, and by its light Peter could see her standing with her hands behind her back.

She was across the fire from him, and the outline of her body was distorted by a wavering curtain of heat. But he wondered if she'd left her hair loose around her head, or braided it, or tied it back. He wondered if she wore a coat, or just a shirt, like him. The temperature had dropped during the night. On the rocky strand, crusts of ice glittered like jewels.

Then she stepped forward, and Peter saw he was mistaken.

What had Raevsky said? Hair both red and brown—Peter couldn't see. Skinny as a boy—he supposed so. She was an older woman, though not old. Her face was still unlined. What had Raevsky said? Skin so clean . . .

The wendigo had led Raevsky out into the snow in his bare feet. But Peter had his boots on, though they were unlaced. Now he stood up, stepped out of the tent. The woman's arms were bare.

Was she a ghost, who would fade and disappear? No, she had built the fire up with pine cones. And now she spoke: *"Am vazut focul tau printre copaci"*—I saw your fire through the trees. You've about reached our house.

So he must be dreaming. And this was not Raevsky's wendigo. There was nothing boyish about this woman. She wore a sleeveless, embroidered vest, a long skirt, boots. Her hair was long and braided. Her skin was a greenish color in the light from the pine cones, which was fading now.

"You must be freezing," Peter said.

"Yes, I am cold."

She continued in a language that wasn't English, but he understood. "It's all right," she said. "We're just around the bend."

The fire was leaving them in darkness. The woman gave a helpless little smile. She was looking right at him, not flinching away. He didn't know much about these things because of his arm, but at that moment he understood he could step forward and embrace her, and whatever he wanted he could ask, and she'd submit to it, to anything at all. But he didn't move, and in a few seconds he knew something had changed, and that if he stepped forward now then she would laugh and resist, push him away without any conviction, and end up by submitting just the same. Still he did nothing, only stood there as the fire died, and in a few more seconds he knew that she had changed again, and she would laugh and smile and pull away, and disappear and leave him. "I will expect you," she said. "I will see you tomorrow. There'll be Belgian waffles."

She clasped her hands over her naked arms and started to move away. "It's the temple of Aesculapius," she said. Then she was gone. The air was dry and still. Beside him, the water sucked at the icy stones.

WHEN MIRANDA WOKE, SHE LAY for a few minutes in her sleeping bag, looking into the peaked roof of the tent. She felt thin-skinned and brittle-boned. She lay on her back with her hands crossed behind her head. She listened to a shuddering in her stomach, a sensation that had passed beyond hunger, while at the same time she was thanking God that they had found the river and the boat. Soon at least they'd be out of these woods. They'd be away from this landscape of snow and trees and dead men—they would find a way. They had money—the purse of silver grains that she had taken from Gregor Splaa. They had the rings from Andromeda's ears—maybe they were worth something. Or if worst came to worst, she could sell her bracelet.

She imagined sitting down with Peter for a talk. What would she say? What did she feel? How did it affect your feelings, to have given something up for someone, if that's really what she'd done—did it make you resentful? Or did you hold onto someone, because you felt you had nothing else? The previous night she had lain awake, wondering if he'd try to come into her tent, wondering what she'd feel if he did try.

It was too hard to think about, and she wondered if her hunger was a distraction or a relief. She imagined in detail the food she was going to eat. There were numerous courses, especially if you counted candy bars, which probably wouldn't be available. Then she was interrupted by the sound of Peter drumming on the taut canvas above her head. "Come out! Come out! Waffles this morning!"

He was already up, already dressed. He was in a good mood, and while they pulled down her tent and broke camp, he told her about a dream he'd had about his mother. "She was always a crappy cook," he said grinning, rubbing his chapped lips. "But she had roast turkey and pie and Belgian waffles—it was like Thanksgiving."

"Belgian waffles?"

"I'm telling you. You'll see."

Rousing Captain Raevsky proved more difficult. He had slept in his boots, and now he couldn't take them off. He cursed and muttered in Roumanian. He couldn't walk. He crawled out of the tent on his hands and knees.

"Shall we cut the laces?" Miranda asked him.

"No. Not so yet."

He was useless when they were packing up, stowing their bags aboard the pirogue. He put his arms around their shoulders, and they almost had to carry him down to the water. They laid him in the middle of the boat and took their places at the bow and stern. Andromeda curled up under Miranda's feet. There were crusts of ice along the shore. "Are there rapids lower down?" Miranda asked. "Or is it flat like this?" They couldn't carry the boat, and the bags, and Raevsky, too.

Miranda also was astonished at the change in him. He lay curled up in the bottom of the boat. Nor was it possible to think he was still a threat, that he could do anything but entreat her to go with him to Roumania, to his lady's house.

It wasn't until an hour or so later that they came around a long, slow curve. On the left side the gorge fell to the river in a wrack of broken trees. On the right the land opened out, and the trees gave way to scrubby undergrowth. There was a sandbar, and shallow water on the right hand side. A man was on the shore.

"Stop," Miranda said. She was in the stern. She turned the boat out of the current. There among the pines about a hundred feet from the water, she saw a house. Just a moment before, when she had glanced that way, there had been nothing.

"What?" Raevsky said. He propped himself upon the canvas bags, and raised his hand as if to push away a blow.

The man on the shore also lifted his arm, a slow, awkward gesture. Miranda said nothing, because she was looking at the house. It was a small, bark-covered cottage with black, rough sides and protruding eaves.

"What's wrong?" Peter said. "Why are we stopping?" Miranda took her paddle from the water and let the boat drift. Couldn't he see? The cottage had a metal roof that caught the sun. Chopped wood was piled under the eaves. Then it was all hidden for a moment as the bank rose beside them. They came to the shallow water. The man stood above them on the bank.

"Welcome," he called out, "to Aesculapius's house."

Miranda had three memories from Roumania. One was the train station at Mogosoaia. One was the castle on the beach. And one was this cottage in the pine trees with the metal roof.

"Oh," she said. Raevsky reached for her paddle, but she held it up.

Again, as she brought the boat in, the man raised his hand. She looked up into his face as the boat slid along the bank. His hair was yellow. He was dressed in a baggy canvas overcoat.

"What's wrong with him?" Peter said. "Is he sick?" He was talking about Raevsky, and had turned around in the bow and put his paddle down. Raevsky was muttering in Roumanian. He lifted up his hands.

Now he was shifting his weight, rocking in the boat as if he meant to upset it. They were so low in the water, it wouldn't take much. Andromeda was curled up with her tail between her legs. "Hey, stop that," said Peter, and when Raevsky struggled to stand up, Peter pulled him down. When Miranda looked again, the man on the shore was gone.

"Did you see that house?" she said. "Stay here."

The beach was easy and gradual where she had brought the boat in. "I'll be back," she said, and stepped into the cold water, which seeped through her boots. She ran up the beach away from the pirogue, then up the river-bank.

Where was the cottage now? Where was the man? The forest had closed in. She walked upstream along what seemed to be a path. Where it turned into the woods, she hesitated.

"I'll be right back," she shouted. She put her hands in her pockets and stepped under the trees. Up ahead she saw the outline of a building.

In a minute or so she stood at the edge of a clearing. Smoke rose from the chimney of the bark-covered cottage, and she stood looking at it, rubbing her arms and waiting for Peter. Now she wanted and expected him to follow her—should she go back? Where was the man she had seen?

While she asked herself these questions, she was moving forward over the crusts of snow until she came onto the porch among the piles of chopped wood. The door was ajar, and she stepped through it, remembering as she did so the way the heavy, blackened wood felt against her hand, remembering also the wrought-iron latch, the dark, wood-and-plaster interior: a single room, heated with a big, blue ceramic stove. Along one wall there was a battered wooden table, battered wooden chairs.

The man stood next to the stove. When she crossed to him, he held out his hand. But he didn't touch her. He bent over her fingers and brushed them with his lips, which was ridiculous. His hair was yellow and thick. He had taken off his canvas coat. Under it he wore creased, formal trousers and a white, formal shirt.

"Princess," he said. "We are honored."

She didn't look at him. Instead she looked around the room. There was the burned place on the floor where a coal had leapt out of the fire. There was the iron candelabrum, smaller and shrunken now. Once it had been twice her size. There was the yellow bowl on the table. It was filled with bread. But Juliana had used it for potatoes sprinkled with salt.

There was the place on the table leg the borzoi puppies used to chew. "My name is Theodore," said the man. "I have a clinic here. There are some smallpox patients now who tell me they have seen a great sight in the mountains. But I did not expect you'd be so beautiful—"

Miranda interrupted him: "I used to live here."

Dr. Theodore scratched his chin. "Often when we are in danger," he said, "there is a feeling of remembrance. In fact, these buildings are quite new . . ."

DR. THEODORE SMILED. And in his hotel suite on the fifth floor of the Athenée Palace Hotel, the Elector of Ratisbon also smiled. He was the one who had produced this great illusion, and who now sustained it by an exercise of will. Only in his mind could it continue to exist, this cottage on the banks of the Hoosick River in the empty wilderness. He had known Miranda Popescu would recognize it. Her father's gardener had lived there.

The elector had thought the sight of the cottage would lure her from the river. He had thought to make an image that would welcome her and call her home. The white tyger—she was easy to fool! After everything, she was a stupid girl.

He lay on the sofa in his suite, propped up on cushions, a glass of water on the floor beside him. It required stupendous energy and precision to hold all those objects in his mind, to give them density and substance on the banks of that wild river, thousands of kilometers away. His brain was stuffed and full. His temples throbbed. There was the food he had provided on the long peasant's table: luncheon rolls, a bowl of apples, a pitcher of cold water, a rasher of ham—all quite tasteless, he was sure.

Years before, after Aegypta Schenck's disgrace, he had journeyed to Constanta as a tourist. He'd been looking for some trace of this same girl. He had wanted to see the laboratory of Aegypta Schenck, and had been disappointed to find nothing; he had walked through Prince Frederick's abandoned castle on the beach. He had walked through the gardener's abandoned cottage.

And perhaps it was not necessary to recreate it so perfectly. But a skilled craftsman does not easily disown his skill. He was confident that out of all the conjurers and scientists in the history of the world, only he was capable of this mnemonic display. Out of nothing he'd made hundreds of inanimate objects that you could pick up and hold in your hand. And more than that, he had been able to send someone who could carry on an actual conversation with the girl. Others—the miserable Nicola Ceausescu, for example—could dispatch a lifeless version of themselves over a limited range. But he had sent an incubus and succubus across half the world.

The incubus was Dr. Theodore, an idealized image of himself. But the succubus he had created from a painting on the wall of his hotel suite—he could see it from where he lay. It was a full-length portrait of the Countess Inez de Rougemont, painted, according to the style of a previous generation, *à la campagne*. She was dressed as a Roumanian peasant, in a long skirt and an embroidered vest that left her arms naked. Her thick hair was twisted behind her head in a peasant's braid. And in the portrait, her face was frozen at the moment of vulnerability, of sexual consent.

Not considering himself a connoisseur of female beauty, he had chosen her image more or less at random—on the walls of his suite hung several paintings of society women from twenty years before. But the countess had been famous for her sultry and exotic looks, and the elector thought that he could use them to ensnare the boy. Already he had sent her—the dead countess, the succubus—into the camp, to lead the boy away into the woods. That had failed, and so the elector had added a refinement. Like the mythical wendigo of the North American woods, the countess at moments would show glimpses of another face, another person that the boy had loved. At least that was the elector's plan, and for that purpose he had left a soft, blank region in the countess's face, on which could be superimposed another image of the boy's own choosing.

All that was intended to disarm him, draw him away, and the dog, and the broken old soldier—the elector had seen them all around the fire, now that Aegypta Schenck's protective cloak had been withdrawn. He desired to be alone with the girl, who was meant for him, or else for Dr. Theodore. Lying on his sofa, with a movement of his hand he made Dr. Theodore move. How beautiful he was—his second self, who appeared to him sometimes in dreams. If in his youth he had not been afflicted with disease, perhaps he would have grown into this man who now rubbed his smooth cheek with his forefinger. Who now opened his red lips and said, "Will you join me? Please, sit."

The elector could be clever and charming, and he was aware now of the doctor's clumsiness. No doubt it would be prudent to end this quickly. But the elector had searched and wondered for so long! Miranda Popescu was a helpless girl.

He was distracted by a knock on the door, and in America the doctor's mouth sagged open. The knocking would not stop. "Come in," said the elector, sitting upright on the cushions—oh, his head was aching! His heart pounded, his blood throbbed. But with the pride and arrogance of a great athlete in the middle of a race, he pulled himself erect, slid his feet off the sofa onto the floor.

It was his new agent at the embassy since Herr Greuben's arrest. He had a ridiculous name—what was it? Ganz, Franz Ganz—was that possible? The elector's head was reeling. Half the world away, Dr. Theodore stood with his hand in his pocket where he kept his knife.

"Excuse me, your grace," said Franz Ganz. "I would not have disturbed you. But you instructed me to tell you under any circumstances—you know we have been watching the Saltpetre house. I am here to tell you that the subject has returned."

What was the man talking about? Momentarily, the elector closed his eyes.

"The subject Nicola Ceausescu," Ganz continued. "She has returned home. Before dawn we saw a light and we investigated. I believe there is a secret entrance under the street."

So that was it. The elector brought his fist to his forehead, which was burning. "We are not involved in this," he said. "The metropolitan police have an outstanding warrant. They should be notified. I'm asking for a piece of German property, which I'm sure . . ."

"Yes, your grace. I spoke to a Herr Luckacz at the precinct. I had the impression there would be no action taken. With the change in government, you understand . . ."

The elector stared down at his small black shoes, which seemed abnormally far away. On the toe of the right shoe there was a cut in the shiny leather; he would have to search for another pair. What an intolerable waste of effort that would be. "She stole something that belongs to Germany," he said.

"Yes, your grace."

"She is a criminal, complicit in the murder of a Jew. Please tell the ambassador. Tell him to provide a detachment of four soldiers. It is important to clear Greuben's name."

"Yes, your grace."

"The ambassador has taken residence in this hotel. On the first floor."

Franz Ganz was a bald man, dressed in a black overcoat and a fedora, which he now placed on his head. "I know where the ambassador lives," he said, obviously aggrieved. What did it matter? Only the tiniest fragment of the elector's cerebrum was available for conversation. It was remarkable that he made sense at all, that he didn't babble like a monkey. If Ganz had been aware of what the elector was doing, he would have been amazed.

But he wouldn't leave. He stood in his hat and overcoat, shuffling his big feet. "Your grace," he said. "It is possible the ambassador will be occupied. He is inquiring into the death of Sergeant-Colonel Blum, you understand. . . ."

"He will allow himself to be interrupted, if you say you come from me."

The elector turned his head, and in a moment he heard the door close. But this bald man had already hurt him, wounded him, distracted him, and not more so than by mentioning that name—Boris Blum.

The previous morning he'd been standing in the portico of the hotel under the Minerva statue, looking at the ugly, pitted face of Colonel Blum as he stumbled drunkenly to the revolving door. As always the square was full of beggars, and the elector saw a woman grab the colonel's arm. He saw the man smile, saw him pulling at the end of his absurd moustache, digging into the pocket of his military cloak. Then in a moment someone had appeared out of the crowd, had pushed a revolver into the colonel's fat stomach.

But that was not the end of it. That was not what had disturbed him. He had stood in the portico while men rushed to overpower the boy. As they were leading him away, they passed quite close.

Under his heavy, single brow, the boy's eyes were clouded. Idly curious, the elector had searched for the five signs of hypnotic suggestion. Idly appreciative, he had admired the boy's pale, handsome face, preternaturally still in the middle of the uproar. But when he saw the elector, it was as if he suddenly awoke. And an expression of such violence had come into his eyes that the elector was astonished. He understood the bullet had been meant for him.

"YOU MUST GO. Go now to help her." Captain Raevsky lay in the bottom of the boat. Peter thought he had gone crazy. Miranda and Peter had pulled him down before he capsized the boat and ruined everything, but where was Miranda now? Peter had seen neither the man nor the house.

They were in shallow water, and Andromeda was whimpering. Peter sat back on his knees in the flat bottom of the pirogue, and looked away from Raevsky for a moment—where had Miranda gone? Why had she left him with this lunatic, who when he looked back had actually drawn his revolver, and Andromeda was barking now. The old man had a wild expression on his face, and he gestured with the gun—"Go now, help her!"—what was he talking about? But Peter couldn't see Miranda on the shore. And now the old man heaved himself over the side into the freezing, shallow water. He splashed up the beach, then stumbled, and continued on his hands and knees. He had a revolver in his right hand, and from time to time he raised it up. "Oh, God—don't you smell? Do not eat the food," he said. "Oh, it is poison."

Whining, the dog jumped over Peter's legs and scrambled up the bank. Peter brought the boat in about twenty yards downstream, then stepped onto the stones and pulled it up onto the sand. Then he followed as quickly as he could, although he didn't understand why. What was the danger? And if there was danger, why had they left the boat?

When he got to the top of the bank, there was a woman walking toward him from the line of trees. It was the woman from the night before, and now he could see her more clearly. Her dark hair was pinned back from her face, which was expressionless. As before, she was underdressed, and her arms were bare. She wore a long black skirt over heavy boots, and she was walking toward him over the crusts of snow, and through the stubble of frozen grass. In one hand she held a long, heavy bone. Gobbets of meat hung from its smooth, white ball—it looked like the leg bone of a deer, or even a cow.

In her other hand she carried a waffle on a plate.

"Nu, opreste-te," shouted Captain Raevsky from the edge of the woods, and he brought his gun up to fire. But he must have gotten it wet. Nothing happened. The woman didn't pause, and there was nothing in her face to suggest she saw him or the dog that now ran barking and snarling toward her through the tough, golden grass. No, she was for him alone, and maybe it was the waffles, and maybe it was some other bitter and unwelcome illusion, but she seemed older now, more maternal, and in her beautiful face he now saw a resemblance to his own mother, though the cow bone, of course, was all wrong. Nevertheless, he paused as she came toward him, and for a moment he forgot about Miranda. Raevsky was shouting like a crazy man, and the dog was barking, and he scarcely heard them. He felt nothing but anger at what he knew was a trick.

"I WANT TO SHOW MY friends," Miranda said. She turned her back on the doctor and walked to the door. There were long, diamond-paned windows on either side of it. On her way she stepped over the place on the floorboards where the burning piece of charcoal had left a mark; it was gone now. But she had seen it just a moment ago, and seeing it had made her remember—what? Yes, Juliana had snatched her up when she was playing on the floor with the wooden wagon. Miranda had sat staring at the red coal as it sank into the floor, until Juliana had brought a cup of water. Where was Juliana now? Where was the puppy, Rex? Where were Andromeda and Peter? The sun must have sunk behind a cloud, because it was darker in the cottage.

She felt the presence of Dr. Theodore behind her, and she turned. The long table was gone. The bowl had broken on the floor, the dish of ham, the plate of croissants, though she had not heard a noise. One of the apples was still rolling toward her. Dr. Theodore was smiling and his red lips were moving, but no sound came out. And the far end of the room was shrouded in darkness as if night had fallen, though she imagined it was scarcely nine o'clock. Behind her as she turned again, she saw the iron latch of the door had gone, but there was still the hole where it had been. She thrust her fingers into it and pulled the door open. The river was out of sight behind the trees. But she heard shouting down there, and the dog barking.

IN BUCHAREST IT was the end of the afternoon. In Saltpetre Street, in her husband's laboratory, Nicola Ceausescu stood at her husband's table. There in the small glass, the baroness could see the battle as it first emerged. Yes, that was it. Under the pyramid's dark surface, she could see the serpent coiled to strike. The glass was clouded, but she was not wrong. She saw the serpent curling back on itself, pale as a fish's belly—it was the Elector of Ratisbon. And in the darkness at the bottom of the pyramid, now as she decided to challenge him, she saw her own spirit animal take shape. And it was a cat as she'd predicted, a stinking, baggy-kneed old alley cat, or no. Maybe not. She could see more clearly now. In her right hand she held the tourmaline, and she brought it to the surface of the glass.

All day she had been reading in her husband's books, preparing for this confrontation. Now she was ready. She was willing to take a desperate chance against a strong opponent. She was in her own familiar house again, in the cold, hidden, quilted room under the eaves. In front of her stood the ironwood table, the tall, crystal pyramid. The tourmaline seemed to light a flame inside of it.

Through Markasev she'd struck at the elector and she'd failed. But in the baron's papers she had found other ways to fight. Every human being has a spirit creature, and sometimes those animals will bite each other, scratch each other, overwhelm each other, even when the people they inhabit are far apart—in this case, she thought, on opposite sides of the same city. A trained alchemist can manipulate that fight, though there is always an element of chance.

Until the sport had been banned by her husband in the year before his death, bear-baiting had been popular in the lower wards of the city. Often when she was young she had picked pockets and solicited among the crowds—one place she remembered especially, an abandoned warehouse in the Nerva Road. Inside was the arena with the cloud of tobacco smoke, and the smell of liquor and vomit, and the rows of shouting men and the money changing hands. Dogs, wolves, and bears all fought, and in the intervals, smaller animals fought in cages or aquariums—the baroness's crystal pyramid was like one of those small cages. Once she had seen a snake and a rat. The furry, enraged creature was dropped in, the snake was taken by surprise, though it was stronger and faster, and the rat was its natural prey.

Surprise was essential, which was why, as the darkness inside the crystal dissipated, the baroness was horrified to see the fight already joined, as if instead of choosing her moment, she had broken into an ongoing struggle. Nevertheless, the little cat seemed to be holding her own. Always the baroness underestimated herself.

She could see the small, peering head of the reptile, the outline of the cat. It seemed for a moment to exist in two dimensions only, drawn on the inside of the pyramid's black base. Drawn in white ink, for a moment. And then it took shape as if from its own image—not a seedy, scratched-up creature, as she had anticipated. But it was something more elegant. Its long, striped tail curved back and forth, back and forth.

For a moment the baroness stood astonished as the little creature struck out with its paw, then jumped back out of range. In its corner, the serpent coiled and writhed. Yes, she would attack him. She would attack him as he sat in his hotel room in the Athenée, or as he walked the streets. She would crush him with her paw, and he would die of an aneurism or a heart attack. Or she would seize him behind his thin, white neck.

All night she had pored over her husband's *Life of Zosimus*, searching for a charm. She had sent a message to her husband on the ansible, but he had not responded—that was good. She was relieved. She had no need of him. This was her fight now. Always she had simultaneously imagined herself as something greater and more miserable than she was. With the split parts of her mind she was now watching the white cat and the snake. And in one part she was doubtful and astonished. But in the other part she felt a growing sense of triumph: It was true. She recognized this little beast from paintings and embroidered images—the delicate head, the unimaginably rich fur. So rare it was, not seen in generations, feared extinct. But now she knew, and she'd been a fool not to suspect before. In all the legends, the white tyger had first appeared in the Carpathian mountains near the town of Pietrosul, where she, Nicola Ceausescu, had been born.

She could not be mistaken—she was staring down at her own spirit animal, fighting her own enemy. Still, how could it be possible, a criminal like her? Had Kepler's Eye transformed her, changed a ragged-eared old cat into this perfect, small, and vicious beast, who now pulled back her paw? Her husband had suggested something of the kind. But if so, what about the Popescu girl? Everyone had made such a fuss over her, the baroness included—that was all wasted labor now, and wasted money. Nothing mattered but the outcome of this fight. Oh, she had taken a chance, but if the baroness prevailed here, as the white tyger had prevailed against the Turks long before, then tomorrow and the next day, what else could be attained?

THE BARONESS CEAUSESCU was mistaken about all this. One thing was true: The Elector of Ratisbon was poised to strike. But the battle was not yet in Bucharest, but on an empty stretch of river far away. "Stop, what are you doing?" Miranda said. She stood in the doorway of the little cottage, and she could no longer see the path she had followed from the water. It had disappeared. The trees blocked out the light. Andromeda was barking, and Dr. Theodore had come up suddenly behind her, and when she turned from the door, she had the impression that the room had gotten smaller, had closed in. The details were lost in new shadows, out of which loomed the doctor's handsome and immobile face. One hand was in his pocket, while the other reached out toward her. And without any expression or intonation, he was saying, "I have a smallpox clinic. I was able to import the vaccine from Europe to save lives. I had not thought you were so beautiful. Will you join me for an apple?"

Frightened, she fell back toward the open door, but it had disappeared. In its place there was a dark, rough, plastered wall.

"Now you see you are my guest," murmured Dr. Theodore, though in Bucharest the elector found himself gasping for breath. His hand trembled on the coverlet. Prostrate on his sofa, he felt the weight of these massed illusions, and it was too much of a burden.

But if he was worthy of the position he had coveted for so long, then there was nothing he must not attempt. The more difficult the challenge, the sweeter the triumph. Who else but he was capable of carrying out these separate struggles across half the world? In one part of his mind the succubus flung down her bone and dish. And in another part the clear-eyed Theodore flattered and scraped, while at the same time he was gripping in his trousers pocket the knife that would end this crushing headache once for all. Was it time yet? Was it time?

On the Hoosick riverbank, the doctor pulled out his hooked blade. But in Bucharest the elector found himself staring once again at the fat face of Herr Ganz the attaché. How had the man come in? What was he doing here? The elector sat up on the sofa, his hand shaking.

"Forgive me, your grace. I wouldn't have disturbed you, except for a matter of urgency. The ambassador requires your presence."

"What?"

"Immediately, sir. He has a matter to discuss. General Stoessel is there."

The elector had not expected such a quick response to his letter to the foreign minister. Now he slid his legs from the sofa and stood up.

Perhaps out of a premonition, that morning he had dressed in formal clothes. It required only the addition of his dinner jacket to make himself complete. But what should he do with this pain in his temples? The succubus had grabbed hold of the boy, while at the same time the incubus held out his knife. Was it possible for the elector to break away and allow everything to disappear? No, the trap for Miranda Popescu had been too laborious for him to end it now. And surely it would be a mark of greatness to achieve these triumphs simultaneously—the thanks and plaudits of his country, and the death of the white tyger. He would put in the hooked knife just at the moment he was shaking the general's hand. With modesty and humility, he would receive the appointment or commendation or whatever it was, and no one would be aware of anything at all.

Like all great men, he had secrets he could never reveal. Now with a new and frantic energy, he put on his dinner jacket, which was hanging from the back of a chair. He made fists out of his hands. Staring straight ahead, he followed Herr Ganz out of the door and down the hall toward the elevator. He didn't glance at the long patterns on the carpet, which threatened to nauseate him.

As he rode down in the cage, he found himself suppressing a little smile. He had heard Stoessel was an old-fashioned fellow, the kind of man who had no understanding of the complicated world. Like most of the military officers, he had no appreciation of the enemies that must be conquered on all fronts, no conception of the dangers that threatened Germany. No doubt he was galled and irritated by the prime minister's new appointment, if that was what it was. No doubt for him and the other generals it suggested a change of power, a new ascendancy of modern, younger, scientific men, no longer hampered by old prejudices and laws. No doubt that was why he had given the elector so peremptory a summons—out of a lingering sense of spite, which in the future he would not be able to indulge.

The elector sifted gradually and slowly through these thoughts with one one-hundredth of his consciousness. Elsewhere, on the riverbank, he had managed to divide the succubus into three parts. One was a cloud of darkness that had settled on the man with the gun, blinding him as he knelt crippled in the frozen grass. The other was a white-headed eagle that was stooping from the clouds onto the back of the dog. And one was the woman—Inez de Rougemont—struggling with the boy.

The elector found, as he came out of the elevator cage on the first floor above the lobby, that he had lost most of his peripheral vision. Up ahead, Herr Ganz was holding open the door to the drawing room, which had been taken over by the German general staff. It was a small room, overdecorated and overheated. The elector stood on the threshold. Another man sat in an armchair next to the stove. The ambassador was at the windows, looking out over the square.

"Come in," said General Stoessel. He was standing at the doorway of an inner cloakroom. He was in full uniform, with epaulets and black boots.

Once again the elector suppressed a smile. Stoessel was grotesquely small. The top of his head, as he came forward, was at the level of the elector's cravat. And the elector himself was not a tall man.

The general's voice was high and thin. "I want to thank you for your information about the presence of the Baroness Ceausescu in her home, and to tell you that I have sent a detachment of military police. It is important to keep the rule of law in this country, and to resolve once and for all this matter of the Herr Spitz's murder. Now. Here is your train ticket to Berlin, at seven o'clock this evening. I must ask you to surrender your passport."

In the cottage on the riverbank, where there were no longer any doors, for many minutes now the incubus had shifted back and forth and up and down inside the little room, trying to trap Miranda Popescu against the walls or behind the furniture, while at the same time he engaged her in conversation—"Please, have one of these rolls." The symbol of his family was the banded serpent, and it occurred now to the elector that Dr. Theodore was like a serpent in a cage, weaving back and forth, threatening a helpless creature until . . . Where had she gone? The corner where he'd trapped her was now empty.

"Excuse me?" he said. With the small part of consciousness at his disposal, he went over what Stoessel had said. Why did they need his passport? But then he thought he understood. If the foreign minister was going to offer him a new appointment, doubtless he would need new diplomatic papers.

"Because of our position as guests in this country," said General Stoessel in his absurd, high voice, "I do not feel I have the authority to order your arrest. I have conferred with the ambassador on this subject. Nevertheless it is my duty to request you to return to Germany to answer charges there. Herr Greuben will travel with you under guard."

The elector found this difficult to follow. His head was aching. The evening sun shone through the long windows, and many of the details of the room were now lost to him, swallowed up in shadow. The new ambassador, a white-haired man with a white goatee, had turned toward him. He was wearing a boiled shirt with gold studs. He walked over to the desk and sat down.

The general was speaking. "You are acquainted with Ambassador Behrens, are you not?"

Ratisbon had taken a few steps into the room. "What . . . ?" he murmured. "What . . . ?"

"Charges, that is all," said Stoessel. Was that actually a monocle hanging from his buttonhole? How was it possible that there were men like him still living? When the elector was welcomed into government, all these fossils would be put in a museum.

On the riverbank, the boy had slipped out of the succubus's grasp. Using the four-kings defense, he had turned her wrist around.

"Charges," the general repeated. "We have been listening to Herr Grueben's story. We are glad we have been able to save his life. Trifa has been quite cooperative. But I must say I am disheartened by your role in this, because I knew your father. He was a fine man, an officer and a statesman from a great and noble family. In his name I now ask you—is it true what this man says? Are you guilty of these crimes?"

"What . . . ?" said the Elector of Ratisbon. In the cottage on the Hoosick riverbank, the incubus struck and missed, struck and missed. All pretense was abandoned now. The knife was in his hand. Outside, the succubus roared and threatened in the cold grass, but the boy had seized her in his hands. How could he be so strong? Was there a man alive who could accomplish what the elector was trying to accomplish? No, not one.

"Do not pretend you are a fool," said Stoessel. "Whatever you are, I know you are not that. And don't imagine I'm so old and stupid that I could not recognize what is obvious—that you have engaged in witchcraft here under our noses, perhaps even in this hotel. Herr Grueben has sworn to it and signed the paper. Let me say this is a sad day for Germany, when the Elector of Ratisbon is revealed as a common conjurer."

The elector turned toward the third man, slouched in his armchair by the stove. And now for the first time he recognized Hans Greuben, his face covered with half-healed bruises, and his expression open, vacant, terrified. "He sent a corpse into my room," he murmured now.

What was the fellow talking about? He felt he should explain, and yet all explanations were beneath him. These old troglodytes—Ratisbon turned and stumbled out the door. His head was throbbing, and he needed air. He ran his hand along the marble balustrade. He stood above the lobby at the top of the marble staircase, then stepped insecurely down. At the midway point he tripped and almost fell. His heart staggered, and he grabbed hold of the banister to catch his breath. Injustice and ingratitude had wounded him, that much was sure. It could not be, for example, that the girl had hurt him. Below him on the tile floor, soldiers and civilians walked back and forth. Gathering his strength, he closed his eyes.

"PLEASE DON'T BE ALARMED," said Dr. Theodore. He stood blinking in the middle of the imaginary room, in the cottage on the riverbank, a smile on his face. In his hand was a small pruning knife with a hooked blade. "I had not thought you were so beautiful," he said. "I am grateful for the opportunity. Let me say it is an honor to meet a princess of the old blood, a princess of Roumania."

He stumbled toward Miranda with his arm outstretched. He made a few weak gestures with the blade. He was easy to avoid. But the room had no doors or windows. As Miranda backed into a corner, the objects and contours of the room seemed simultaneously to fade and darken. Moment by moment the light dimmed; it had no source. Now Dr. Theodore appeared as a dark silhouette, and now she couldn't see him, and it was dark.

But she could hear his voice, which changed. The murmured platitudes were gone, replaced in a moment by new language in a tone that was louder and more resonant. "Now it is time for what your family has done."

All at once, the light came surging back from the tall windows. Miranda stood again in Juliana's cottage, and every detail was in place. There were the scuff marks on the banister to the upper room, and the place where the rail had been broken and repaired. There were the scratches on the newel post where Juliana had measured her as she grew.

And in the middle of the room, Dr. Theodore had been replaced someone else. Dressed in a black suit, the new man was smaller and more delicate. His hair was dark and glossy over a bald spot. He was looking at the floor, his chin sunk on his cravat, his face partly obscured by his high, winged collar. But when he raised his head, Miranda was astonished by his ugliness, his ruined, cratered face, out of which peered two lustrous brown eyes. His hands were clasped behind his back.

There were some medals and ribbons pinned to his lapel. Now he removed his hands from beneath the tails of his coat and showed them to Miranda. They were small and manicured and empty.

"Help," Miranda murmured. The man smiled. His teeth were small and white.

"It is time to pay a bill," he said. "After twenty years I will be able to tell your mother of your death."

All this time he had been moving closer. "You are just a girl. But our future does not add up to the sum of our abilities, as I learn every day. Perhaps one day you might bring help to your country. In this way I can compare you to a pawn that has struggled down its track. In one more move it will become a queen and dominate the board. But at the moment of transition, you are vulnerable. Yes, you did me harm long ago. But I am fighting for my country. At the moment I am most despised, then I must fight the hardest. And because I have a deeper knowledge than the imbeciles who run my government, I can see what they don't see—you are a threat to us."

He had been moving closer, but Miranda had not moved. She found it hard to listen, because of the man's pitted cheeks and twisted nose. She watched his red lips open and close over his teeth, while at the same time she looked past him and around the room. Everywhere she touched and grasped at objects in her mind. Even in this moment of danger, she could not prevent herself from noticing the one starred windowpane, or the place where the cat—Alphonse—had clawed the upholstery, or the painted photograph of the Santa Sophia that Umar had brought back from Constantinople. Every detail brought with it a small story that she now remembered. And she imagined if she searched these stories she might find something to help her as the ugly man came toward her step by step.

Yes, there was something, a brass ring set into the floor. One day when no one was home, Juliana's niece had showed her how you could lift up the edge of the Turkish carpet, which was no longer there. And you could twist the ring just so and pull it up, and there was a compartment where Umar kept a gun in an oiled cloth, a pistoleta left over from the Spanish campaign. Yes, and she remembered crouching on the stairs to the upper room, listening to Umar as the lamps were lit, as in his harsh voice he was saying that the empress had turned against the Brancoveanus, but they would find some secrets if they came for the little girl. The next day her aunt took her to Bucharest in the carriage.

"Now you see," said the ugly man. "There was a chance for Great Roumania, but it has passed. Your father and your aunt are among the martyred dead. Your mother is my guest in Ratisbon. You are the last, and after you there will be none. Please, I see the bracelet on your wrist. Bring it to me. Put it in my hand."

The door was behind him, and now she found herself maneuvered into a corner of the room, as he came toward her on his little feet. Beside her was a window made of diamond-shaped panes, and she turned toward it now and hammered at it with her forearms until some of the glass broke. She was protected by Rodica's quilted coat. And even though the glass fell down around her, she couldn't push out through the leads, supported (as she now remembered) on the outside by a layer of black chicken wire. She could never get out that way. And so she turned just as the ugly man came up behind her. As he reached for her she ducked under his arms and scrambled over the litter of glass shards. On her hands and knees she searched for the little ring. But she couldn't find it.

The ugly man grabbed hold of her and pulled her up. When he put his hands under her coat, she could feel their coldness. He clutched her firmly in his small hands, and she was shuddering and twisting, and she couldn't pull away. So then she pushed against him suddenly with all her strength, and thrust the heel of her left palm against his chin, while with her right fist she was thumping on his chest. And all the time she was shouting and crying, "You shit, you shit, you shit. You piece of shit . . ."—the kind of language she'd picked up from Andromeda and used only self-consciously; it had never seemed completely appropriate until now. And she must have caught the man by surprise, because he swayed on his feet and then tumbled to the floor with her on top of him. One of her hands was around his wrist, holding the knife away. And the other was thumping on his chest. And in her heart she felt a surge of triumph as she felt his body subside into helplessness, and she beat on his chest as if by striking him she could be rid of all the accumulated suffering of the past week, all the angers and frustrations—she didn't need Umar's gun, or any directions from her aunt. She didn't even need Raevsky, or Andromeda, or Peter. But with her own hands she could defeat this creature, who now writhed and slipped away from her. And under her hands he seemed diminished, smaller every second as the light dimmed and the room flickered around her, and the objects in it lost their solidity. Before the darkness was complete she staggered up; the door was open, and she could see the trees outside.

AND AT THAT MOMENT IN Saltpetre Street, in her husband's laboratory, the Baroness Ceausescu looked into her crystal pyramid. In the district police headquarters, six German soldiers received their orders. But even if she'd known of their approach, she would not have been able to break away from what she saw.

The pyramid was oriented to the points of the compass. If she looked into the south and north sides, she saw the fight, as she imagined falsely, between herself and the Elector of Ratisbon, the serpent and the tyger. But in the east and west sides she saw a simpler and clearer image, the elector on the stone staircase of the Athenée Palace Hotel. He was standing by himself, one hand on the banister, one hand pressed against his heart. It was difficult to read the emotions on his damaged face, but the baroness imagined a turmoil of distress. She placed her bitten, bleeding, tobacco-stained fingers on the crystal surface, while at the same time she looked down at the pages of one of her husband's manuscripts, held open by the tourmaline.

Frightened, she had watched the snake command the center of the pyramid and push the tyger back. She'd watched it strike and miss, strike and miss. What would happen to her if those fangs struck home? But she could not watch and do nothing while the destiny of the white tyger, her own destiny, the destiny of Great Roumania was decided. She thought if she could force the elector to relax his grip on consciousness, just for a moment, then the tyger would have a chance. She had seen the little beast pushed and harried against the walls of the pyramid. But the snake was losing strength, and she could see that, too.

So intent she was, in her moment of anxiety and triumph, that she could not feel the presence of her husband's ghost behind her. She could not feel the proximity of his cold hands, which he held out as if to touch her on the shoulders. Nor could she hear the whisper of his voice, as he spoke with her the old spell, copied in his handwriting years before. It was a witch's curse, a fainting spell, uncertain in its efficiency, especially now as his wife mispronounced the words. But the baron wished it speed, and saw it taking momentary shape above the point of the pyramid—just a trick of the light, really, or an evanescent shadow of the red pig of Cluj.

The baroness didn't see it. She was peering at the tiny figure of her enemy, standing by himself on the marble staircase. One hand was pressed against his heart. And as she watched, she saw him pitch suddenly downstairs. With his arms over his face he rolled and slid. Then he lay crumpled at the bottom of the stairs, and her view was obscured by the men who rushed to help him.

ON THE HOOSICK RIVERBANK, the woman gave a screeching yell. Peter had his arms around her. Now there was no longer any hint in her of Miranda or his mother, or any frailty or helplessness. The braid had come loose, and her coarse hair was wild around her head. Her lips were pulled back to reveal her teeth, and she was trying to bite him, trying to scratch him with her long nails as the yellow dog barked, and Raevsky stumbled and staggered blind, waving his saturated gun. On the top of the bank, he lost his balance and then slid down suddenly onto the strand, where he sprawled by the water's edge.

The yellow dog was in the high, frozen grass at the edge of the pines. Again, the bird that had tormented her came stooping from the sun, and sank its talons into her back. But the dog jumped away into the undergrowth, and the eagle couldn't follow her among the brambles. In a moment it rose up to the sky, disappeared among the clouds—Peter saw it rise, saw the light catch its feathers. He had the woman's head in the crook of his right arm, and he sank the fingers of his left hand into her scalp, and pulled her head around, until he was staring at her violent and distorted face. And once again he caught a glimpse of something familiar, the black eyes and flashing teeth of a proud lady he'd seen several times when he was young, but once especially, dancing with an old man in uniform in a high-ceilinged, high-windowed room—she'd thrown her head back, laughed aloud from the pleasure of dancing, or else some whispered joke. And in this fantasy or memory, he himself was in a sky-blue cadet's uniform, standing shyly by the wall. Even a name came back to him—La Condesa de Rougemont, and then the name was gone, and the memory was gone, disappearing like a fragrance or a wisp of music.

CAPTAIN RAEVSKY STUMBLED to his knees beside the river. As the blindness cleared out of his eyes, he saw Pieter de Graz above him on the bank, with his right hand around a woman's neck. All around there was the sweet stench of witchcraft. De Graz was behind her with his right arm locked around her neck, his left arm against her stomach. He was trying to crush the breath out of her, though she was not a breathing creature as Raevsky knew. Then suddenly he released her and fell back, but at the same time the yellow dog came jumping and snarling out of the undergrowth, and grabbed hold of the woman's long skirt, and shook the tattered cloth from side to side. The dog was searching for something to bite, but there was nothing inside the skirt now, no flesh or bone. Just a few rags in the dog's teeth.

Raevsky let his gun fall to the stones. Sore and crippled, he staggered to his feet and staggered up the bank. But de Graz and the dog hadn't waited.

The dog was barking, running upstream along the top of the bank, where there had been a path. De Graz ran after her, and then Raevsky followed as best he could, limping and swearing; they hadn't far to go. The dog was barking, and de Graz was calling out Miranda's name; the river made a turn, and now they plunged into a belt of pine trees. Raevsky was behind them, and as always if you could just get your feet moving, then they wouldn't betray you, and he was running now. He kicked through the frozen stubble and then through the trees, and was in time to see Miranda Popescu on the far side of an empty clearing. She turned around toward them and he saw her face; she didn't see them, couldn't hear the barking and the shouts. Then she stepped into the trees and she was lost.

IN ROUMANIA, THE ELECTOR HAD suffered a small heart attack. For a single second he lost consciousness when the back of his head struck one of the long marble steps. And in that one dazed moment, all of his stupendous mental work was lost. Unsupported by his power of concentration, the incubus, the succubus, the cottage itself and everything in it—all of it collapsed and disappeared, leaving only the pine trees and the empty riverbank. And of course the boy, the dog, the man, but not the girl—where had she gone? As he lay waiting for the doctors, he watched them search among the tall trees without results.

He looked again when he was on the train to Germany. He saw the boy and his dog and the soldier. They had built a fire on the bank above the boat, and they huddled around it in the dark. They had found Miranda Popescu's quilted coat, but the girl herself was not with them.

At the moment of collapse, she'd been in the cottage itself, just another object out of hundreds there. Perhaps with the other objects she'd been transported back. It was only later that he thought to turn his gaze eastward, after it was too late to find her. Too late and too early.

FRIGHTENED NOW, MIRANDA ran down through the trees. She must have gone the wrong way. She must have gotten turned around; how was it possible she couldn't find the river? Even the trees were wrong—the tall pines had disappeared, and she found herself in a forest of oak saplings. And the dirt was sandy and smelled of salt.

"Peter!" she called out. "Andromeda!"—where were they? Almost she felt angry that they couldn't find her. She wanted to share what had happened with the ugly man. And though she couldn't understand it, she knew it was significant. She knew something had changed. The victory had left her flushed and burning—it took her several minutes to realize she was hot. The light that spilled in through the trees was hot and yellow. She could smell dirt and green grass. She could hear the chattering of birds.

She paused to catch her breath. "Peter!" she called. Where could he be? She'd climbed up through here from the boat, but now the path had disappeared. And she must have come around in a circle, because in front of her she saw the roof of Umar's house again.

She saw it again, and yet as if for the first time, because everything was different. The dark eaves and shining roof were different now, more solid and more real, and in their proper place among these little trees. And how hot she was! She was conscious of the smells of her own body and her clotted, tangled hair, which itched.

After a moment she stepped forward. She broke through a clump of juniper bushes, and then stopped again. In front of her was Umar's formal garden, much overgrown. Paths of soft grass made their way among the brambles that had covered Umar's roses and poppies. A thicket had grown up around the statue of Athena, and the stone bench was invisible. Briars grew over the Magdalena fountain. Irises were in bloom.

Time had gone by since she'd last been here, ruinous time. Maybe the false house along the Hoosick River had been closer to her memory—insubstantial, insufficient, changeable. But this was the real thing. And even if some small details were unfamiliar, still it all stank of home, every rock and tree and bush.

Home, and it was she who had brought them there—Peter and Andromeda, wherever they were now. She'd find them soon enough. Right now she preferred to be alone, at least for a few minutes more. She wanted to savor these small feelings, as well as something else that maybe she'd find awkward or impossible to explain: Again, it was because of her own strength that she was here. Her aunt had not helped her, nor Raevsky, nor Peter.

She took off her sweatshirt, then bent to unlace her heavy boots. She stripped off her wool socks, and rubbed the dirt out of her toes. She pulled up the sleeve of Blind Rodica's shirt—there was the golden bracelet on her forearm. And for the first time since she'd put it on, she didn't feel entirely like a fraud, like someone half pretending to be herself. And maybe this white tyger thing was going to work out after all.

Through the long-needled trees she could just see the corner of her father's house. Barefoot, she followed the path toward it over the big slate slabs, almost hidden in the soft grass. She was conscious now of the sea air, the murmuring of the water. Near her a brandywine bird perched on a strand of briar. It cocked its head and sang its cheap little song, then fluttered off down the path.

She followed it until she came to the high bank. There were the steps that led up to the terrace, guarded by the stone lion. Beyond, there would be octagonal red tiles, French windows, and the stone tower above her head—part of her wanted to climb up that way at once. But part of her resisted—there'd be time to explore the castle room by room. There'd be time to find her own turret window. Maybe it would be more fun with Peter anyway.

In the meantime, Miranda followed the path away from the stone building. The wind was off the water, which she could glimpse now through the hillocks of tough grass—the rocky shore, the flat, murmuring water of the Black Sea.